r the bridge in spite of Matilda's rattle trap-
roney's Bistro glances up from sweeping his
Street. He shakes his head, shouting some-
I smile and wave, doing my part to enhance

a.m., downtown Beaufort wakes up with a
ay, the streets will flow with tourists and
buy a slice of lowcountry life. If only people
wn to Jones McDermott's—may he rest in
é on the corner of Bay and Harrington.

Beaufort Gazette called the Café in a story
is funeral. More like *forgotten* treasure. If it
ost of them senior citizens over sixty—the
ure.

urch Street, I swerve into the Café's gravel-
ot. Stopping in the shade of a thick, ancient
or chokes and, at last, dies. "Ho, boy." When
refuses to fire.

hat way."

with a few soap-worthy words, I fish my cell
f my backpack and autodial Dad. While it
he back of the Café. The paint is faded and
ternoons of baking in the hot South Carolina
leans and slopes.

ath from a heart attack a few weeks ago, I've
vith the rest of the crew—Andy, Mercy Bea,
ke a go of things. Business is slow. Money is
rtunately, the heyday of the Frogmore Café
ne alongside beehive hairdos and eight-track

r the third time. *Come on, pick up.*

Sweet Caroline

A Novel

Rachel Hauck

THOMAS NELSON
Since 1798

NASHVILLE   DALLAS   MEXICO CITY   RIO DE JANEIRO

To my siblings—Danny Hayes, Joel Hayes,
Peter-John Hayes, Rebekah Gunter—
who show up on these pages one way or another.
Growing up with you was fun.

© 2007 Rachel Hayes Hauck

Published in Nashville, Tennessee, by Thomas Nelson. Thomas Nelson is a registered trademark of
Thomas Nelson, Inc.

Thomas Nelson, Inc. titles may be purchased in bulk for educational, business, fund-raising, or
sales promotional use. For information, please e-mail SpecialMarkets@ThomasNelson.com.

Publisher's Note: This novel is a work of fiction. Names, characters, places, and incidents are
either products of the author's imagination or used fictitiously. All characters are fictional, and
any similarity to people living or dead is purely coincidental.

Scriptures taken from the NEW AMERICAN STANDARD BIBLE®, © 1960, 1962, 1963,
1968, 1971, 1972, 1973, 1975, 1977, 1995 by The Lockman Foundation. Used by permission.

ISBN 978-1-59554-896-2 (repack)

Library of Congress Cataloging in Publication Data

Hauck, Rachel, 1960-
  Sweet Caroline: a novel / Rachel Hauck.
     p. cm.
  ISBN 978-1-59554-337-0
  1. Restaurateurs—Fiction. 2. Country musicians—Fiction. 3. South Carolina—Fiction. 4. Chick
lit. I. Title.
PS3608.A866S84 2008
813'.6—dc22
                                                                    2007050414

Printed in the United States of America

10 11 12 13 RRD 6 5 4 3 2 1

But today I make it ov
ping. Paul Mulroney of M
walk as I rumble down Ba
thing I can't quite make ou
community relations.

At seven thirty in the
slow, sleepy feel. By mid
tanned retirees looking to
would make their way do
peace—little Frogmore Ca

"A town treasure," the
about Jones the day after
wasn't for the regulars—r
Café would be *sunken* trea

Making the light at C
and-crushed-shell parking
live oak, the Mustang's mo
I try to restart, the engine

"Fine, swell, great. Be
Anointing the momen
phone from the bottom
rings on his end, I study
peeling from a thousand a
sun. One side of the porc

Since Jones's sudden d
been managing the place
and Russell—trying to m
almost nonexistent. Unfo
echoes in the Valley of T
cassettes.

Daddy's phone rings

Mercy Bea Hart, the Café's senior waitress, steps through the kitchen door, lighting a cigarette, indicating to me with a jab at her watchless wrist that I'm late.

Thirty-some years ago, Mercy Bea had her fifteen minutes of fame when she won a Jayne Mansfield look-alike contest. Got her picture in a Hollywood magazine and appeared on *The Mike Douglas Show*. Ever since, she's maintained her once-won image—dyed-blonde bombshell hair, curvy figure with just the right amount of cleavage, red lips, and long, lacquered fingernails.

"Yeah, Caroline, what's up?" Dad's crisp question is accompanied by the grind of heavy equipment.

"Matilda."

"Again? Caroline, it may just be time to get rid of that thing."

We've had this conversation. "Can you tow it to CARS? Please?" I glance at my watch. Seven thirty-five. While I take care of the Café books, I also wait tables, and my regulars arrive at 8:02.

"Where are you?" Dad asks.

"The Café parking lot." Hitching my backpack higher on my shoulder, I lean against the car door. The morning is muggy but breezy, fragrant with the sour scent of the dark, soft pluff mud of the river marsh.

"At least you made it to work this time." A chuckle softens his tone. *Kudos for Matilda.* "See, she isn't all bad."

"Keep telling yourself that, Caroline. I'll be along after this job. I'm down in Bluffton, and we're having trouble with the equipment."

"Thank you a thousand times over, Daddy."

"You're welcome a thousand times over."

Pressing End, I stuff my phone into the front pocket of my backpack and head for the Café's kitchen door. Mercy Bea snuffs out her cigarette in a stained-glass ashtray. "You're late."

"What are you, the time-clock gestapo? I was caught in bridge traffic."

"Can't be running in here late, Caroline." She settles the ashtray on the windowsill and follows me inside. "And you best get rid of that broken-down heap. Half the town's push-started you. Growing tired of it."

"How lucky I am to live in such a warm, friendly place. How's business this morning?" In the office, just off the kitchen, I flip on the light and unzip my backpack.

"Slow. I cleaned the bathrooms for you." Mercy Bea leans her shoulder against the doorjamb and picks at her brilliant-red fingernails. "Land sakes, I've got to get my nails done."

"You cleaned the bathrooms? For me." Tying on my apron, I gaze over at her.

"Don't act all surprised." She pops and cracks her gum. "You covered for me a few times when my young-sons got into trouble." Mercy Bea is a single mom of two teen boys she affectionately refers to as "young-sons."

"So . . . anything new from Jones's lawyer?"

Aha. This is why she cleaned the bathrooms—to butter me up for information. Not that I'm keeping secrets. "Not since he called last Wednesday. He's still tied up with an estate case in Charleston. Said he'd be down as soon as he was free."

"Well, you let me know if you hear from him, now."

"Don't I always?"

Even though I'm not the senior Café employee, Jones's lawyer, Kirk Harris, deals directly with me. My guess is because I've been handling the business side of the Café for two years. It's the reason Jones hired me.

"I could use your help around here, Caroline. Someone to teach the Café ropes," Jones said to me one afternoon when I stopped by for some Frogmore Stew.

Learning the Café ropes wasn't high on my list of life goals, but between Jones's aged puppy-dog eyes and a mental picture of my Granddaddy Sweeney looking down from heaven, whispering, "Be sweet, Caroline; help out my old friend," I couldn't say no.

Jones started me out waiting tables, then added on bookkeeping and ordering. Turns out everyone at the Frogmore Café wears multiple hats. Though I'm not allowed to cook. All on account of almost burning down Beaufort High when I took home ec. But that's another story.

Exchanging my flip-flops for my black work clogs, I glance at Mercy Bea. "So, how'd your date with Ralph Carter go last night?"

Mercy Bea responds with a Cruella Devill cackle. "Oh, dear girl. He was a loser with a capital L-O-O-S-E-R."

"You mean L-O-S-E-R."

"That's what I said."

"You added an extra *O*."

"Caroline, I can spell *loser*." Her exhale is edgy. "I've certainly acquainted myself with enough of them."

Whatever. "So, all your great hair dye and makeup went to waste?" I retrieve my pen and order pad from the desk, then stuff my backpack into the bottom drawer.

"On him, yes. Though I looked pretty darn hot, if I say so myself."

"Miss Mansfield would be proud."

"I had a little bit of a flirt with a Marine pilot when L-O-S-E-R went to the toilet. Turns out he was married. But"—she jabs the air with her finger—"in my defense, he wasn't wearing a ring, and the wife was outside on her phone."

I snap my fingers. "Those darn non-wedding-ring-wearing pilots."

Mercy Bea whirls away from me with a huff, stopping long enough to point at the clock. "Hurry on out. The breakfast-club boys will be along soon."

I return to the kitchen. "Morning, Andy." The exhaust fans over the oven compete with the soulful sounds coming from the mini boom box on top of the reach-in. All I can hear is the bass line. "What's today's special?" The Emmitt Smith–sized cook looks up from pulling a couple of green peppers from the lowboy. "Barbeque chicken with choice of three vegetable sides—greens, corn, fried okra, corn on the cob, fried tomatoes, peas, or mashed potatoes. Bubba's Buttery Biscuits, of course, and a drink. Choice of dessert. Pluff Mud Pie or vanilla layer cake."

"I ordered more produce and shrimp Friday. Should come today."

"What'd they say over at Fresh Earth Produce?" Andy chops peppers for one of the breakfast-club boys' country omelet. "Rice Dooley is wanting money, I bet."

"Well, he doesn't consider us a charity." I snatch a hot, fresh biscuit from a baking sheet. Steam rises from the fluffy white middle when I pull it apart.

Rice: *"We need some sort of payment, Caroline. Look, I know Jones didn't leave y'all in good shape, but can we see something?"*

Me: *"I understand, Mr. Dooley. I'll get a payment to you this week. But we need corn and shrimp or the Frogmore Café is without Frogmore Stew."*

"I know you're doing all you can to juggle things, Caroline." Andy whacks an onion in two.

The soft bite of my biscuit melts in my mouth. "Unfortunately, there's more debt to juggle than credit."

In the aftermath of kind and compassionate Jones McDermott's death, I discovered a hard truth: he was a horrible businessman. As a result, I've learned how to tap dance around due dates, how to stretch imaginary dollars.

"Any word from the lawyer?" Andy asks, turning to the stove, pouring eggs into a hot skillet.

I'm going to write "Nope" across my forehead and point to it when people ask, "Any word from the lawyer?"

"Nothing new."

"Are you thinking what I'm thinking?" Andy leans over the prep table toward me. "Mercy Bea is hoping Jones left the place to her?" He grabs a handful of diced veggies and sprinkles them on the cooking eggs.

"Why would she want this place?" I gesture to the dingy white kitchen walls and cheap linoleum floor. "It's a money pit, in need of some serious loving. The old girl needs an owner with deep, generous pockets."

"Mercy Bea or the Café?"

Brushing biscuit crumbs from the corner of my lips, I laugh softly and head for the dining room. "You're bad, Andy."

A guttural *um-um-um* vibrates from the cook's immense chest. "This money pit is putting food on my table, paying the bills. Gloria's been out of work for over a month now on account of her back. I need this job. I'm believing God has a plan."

The cook's confidence makes me pause at the kitchen door. "If there is such a thing as an all-knowing, all-seeing All Mighty, He *might* have a plan for the Café. But Jones? I'm not so sure."

Andy's large shoulders roll as he laughs. "Guess you're right about Jones. Yes sirree. But the wife and I are praying, Caroline."

"You do that. I'll wish upon a star."

Daily Special

Barbeque Chicken

Choice of Three Sides: Greens, Corn,
   Fried Okra, Corn on the Cob, Fried Tomatoes,
   Green Beans, or Mashed Potatoes

Bubba's Buttery Biscuits

Pluff Mud Pie or Vanilla Layer Cake.

Tea, Soda, Coffee

$6.99

2

The Christmas bells dangling down the glass-front door
ring out as three retired Marines—Dupree Cornwallis, Luke Gold, and
Pastor Winnie Smith—file in wearing their *Semper Fi* caps over their
graying, receding hairlines.

Always faithful.

"Morning, fellas," I say, bringing around their orders. Five mornings
a week, when the bells chime at eight-oh-two, Andy sets their food in
the window.

"'Sweet Car-o-line,'" Pastor Winnie sings, clapping his long-fingered,
dark hands together as he slides into a booth along the front wall by the
windows. "'Good times never seemed so good.'"

Luke and Dupree supply the trailing *bump, bump, bumps.*

"You boys are feeling good this morning."

"God done made a beautiful day." Pastor Winnie always testifies.

"I was up all night, peeing." Dupree grunts as he slides into his side of the booth. He starts every morning with a bathroom story.

"No coffee for you, then? Caffeine, makes you . . . you know . . . go."

Luke chuckles. "She's got your number, Dupe."

"Worse than trekking to the head a hundred times in the night is facing the morning without coffee." Dupree drops his cap, embroidered with the Third Marine Division emblem, on the far side of the table. "Make mine extra black."

"Have it your way. Do you want to move to the booth by the restrooms?"

"Listen, Wet-Behind-the-Ears, I was drinking mud water in the Korean forest before you were a glint in your granddaddy's eye. Caffeine don't scare me."

The breakfast-club boys are the silver lining in my Café career. If I'd turned Jones down, I would've never met Dupree, Luke, or Pastor Winnie.

"Ignore him, Caroline." Mild-mannered and recently widowed Luke unrolls his silverware as I fill their coffee cups. "He's complained about the mud water for fifty years." He looks up at me. "Any news on the Café?"

Nope. I point to my forehead.

Luke wrinkles his.

I sigh. "No news."

"Don't know what I'd do without this Café." Pastor Winnie says, mixing his eggs with his grits. "Jones was one of the first in town to defy the old Jim Crow laws. Let the black man and the white man eat together."

Dupree nods. Luke *um-hums*. In that moment, their affection for the Café sweeps over me. When they lost Jones, they lost a friend. The Café is all they have left of him—a symbol of their friendship and youth.

Along with hundreds of other combat veterans, their names are on the Vet Wall.

When Jones bought this place in '57, it was a run-down 1850s home. In the process of fixing it up, he discovered two soldiers' signatures under a tacky layer of '30s wallpaper. So he created a memorial to the hundreds of veterans who have fought for our freedoms over the years. Since then, vets from World War I to the Iraqi conflict have signed the Wall. Their sacrifice is not forgotten.

Mercy Bea bumps up next to me with a pot of coffee. "Morning, boys." She checks to see if their cups need refilling. Which they don't. I'm on top of it here.

"Morning, Mercy Bea."

"How're you doing, Luke?"

He clears his throat, scratching his thumbnail across his brow. "Getting by. Never imagined I'd live life without Melba."

"It's hard on the man when the wife goes first." Mercy Bea flicks her free hand with an air of authority. "See it all the time when I take a shift at the nursing home. Men need women. Can't live without us." She checks the coffee level at table 4. "Women, see, are really the stronger of the sexes. We live long and healthy lives after our men go on."

"Ha!" Dupree slaps the table, calling after Mercy Bea. "A man can live long and fine without a woman. Especially a nagging one."

"Dupe," I say, "she's not insulting men. Just making an observation."

"Well, she best to hold on to some of her observations." He raises his voice, turning his chin over his shoulder so she can hear him loud and clear. "She might be able to trick a smart man into taking her to dinner."

Holding my laugh in, I point to his plate. "Your eggs are getting cold."

Dupree jerks his napkin from under the silverware. "Has my wife been by here? Giving you nagging tips?"

The Christmas bells clang again as two men enter the Café and take a seat at the counter. "I'll be around with more coffee."

The Café routine goes on as morning sunlight gleams through the windows. Jones would've wanted it this way.

After the breakfast rush—and I use the term loosely—the dining room is bright but quiet. Mercy Bea leans against the counter, reading the *Gazette*, sipping iced tea from a mason jar. In the kitchen, Andy ups the music as he preps casseroles for lunch. Russell, the Café's dishwasher and part-time cook, punches in and powers up the old dishwasher.

Snatching up another warm biscuit, I tuck away in the office to face the bills, sitting in the dilapidated desk chair and launching QuickBooks while I gaze around the long, narrow quarters. Jones was a pack rat. He saved old cookbooks, menus, place mats, and the odd broken oven knob. Once the Café is sold or handed over to the new owner, I'll volunteer to help decipher this mess for cleanup.

Bending under the desk, I open the tiny safe and pull out last night's deposit. If I didn't know better, I'd swear the bag was empty. Business is such that I only trek down to the bank once or twice a week. Every time I do, the bank manager, Mr. Mueller, gives me a look like, "Don't be asking for a loan, Caroline."

Don't you worry, Mr. Mueller. When Kirk finally gets around to reading Jones's will, I'll be free . . .

My thoughts jump to my friend Hazel Palmer's latest brief and cryptic e-mail: *"I went way out on a limb this time for you, Caroline. Risking my rep. So, do you want the job or not? Yes or no."*

My friend, the sarcastic CFO. Did I ask her to climb out on a limb for me and dangle her reputation? No. It's all about ego when one becomes senior management for a major European development corporation.

"Caroline?" A light knock echoes outside the office door.

"Hey, Mrs. Atwater." I motion for my former math teacher turned domestic engineer to enter. It's nice to see her. Even better, she's not asking me for geometry solutions.

No, I do not know what percent of a rectangle's area is increased if the length and width are doubled. How will this improve my life?

"Morning, Caroline." She hands me a set of keys. "Jones's carriage house is cleaned out, ready for new residents." With a glint in her hazel eye, she settles in the chair on the other side of the desk. "I see Jones was a hoarder in the Café as much as his house."

"He hated to throw stuff out." I drop the keys in the top desk drawer, next to another odd key I found taped to the side of the file cabinet a week ago. "I'd clean out the office, but I'm waiting to see what the new owners will do. So, what's the decluttered carriage house look like?"

"Walk across the parking lot and check it out. It's quite lovely. Polished hardwood floors, open-beam ceiling, fresh paint. The kitchen is from the sixties, but, hey, avocado green is coming back."

"If you're a hippie."

"Exactly." Sitting back, she props her hands on her slightly round middle. A seventies-style red bandanna shoves her brown curls away from her forehead. "Any word from the lawyer?"

"Nothing new." I tap the deposit amount into QuickBooks. If only I could add one more zero. "Just that he's still busy with a big estate case. Do I pay you for cleaning or . . ."

"We're square. The lawyer paid me when he hired me." Mrs. Atwater hunches forward. "I've known you a long time, Caroline . . ."

She's going to give me the *speech*. The one she gave her class every semester. I rock back in my chair, catching my foot around the desk leg as the seat lists to starboard. I'm determined to pay attention to her this time. For real. And believe her. A little.

"You're one of the brightest, kindest women I've ever met. Even though you hated geometry."

"Hated? No, Mrs. Atwater, really, I like—"

She laughs. "You're not in tenth grade, Caroline. You can confess: you hated it."

I wrinkle my face. "It's just there were so many triangles, rectangles, and circles . . ."

"As I recall, you earned an A."

"I cheated."

"Ha. You didn't. Which brings me to my point."

How'd she work that one around?

"Look at you, Caroline, hanging around, making sure Jones's old place stays afloat. You're selfless. Even in high school, you carried a serious personal responsibility about you that your friends and classmates didn't."

"Being abandoned by a parent does that to a girl." Reaching for a thin wire that was once a paper clip, I wish she'd focus her intense gaze elsewhere. "I always felt Daddy needed me, you know? If I left, what would he do?"

And what would I do so far from home? Morph into her*?*

"I understand. But your daddy is doing fine now. Isn't he engaged? Your brother's married." My old teacher leans forward, placing her fingers on the edge of the desk, her expression almost a yearning. "Caroline, you have so much untapped potential. Don't let your mama's weirdness hold you back. I'll tell you right now, I was disappointed when you turned down the Clemson scholarship."

"Look, Mrs. Atwater—"

"How long you been working here?"

"Two years."

"And before here?"

My back stiffens. "Mrs. Farnsworth's Landscaping & Nursery. Bookkeeping, mostly. Spread more manure-laced fertilizer than I liked, but she's a nice lady."

Mrs. Atwater wrinkles her nose. "Of course she is. So are you. Too nice. Before Mrs. Farnsworth, you worked for your brother when he took over Sweeney Construction after your granddaddy passed. Before that, you managed the office for your dad's well-drilling business."

I jam the wire in one of the wormholes that pepper the wooden desktop. "I know my own job history, Mrs. Atwater. It's hard to say no to people in need."

"What about your need? You think God only put you on this earth to do other folks' chores?"

"First of all, I don't believe God put me here for anything. Second, what's wrong with doing other people's chores? If more people would help out—"

"Sure, but there's something just for you. A field you're supposed to plow and plant—" Mrs. Atwater pinches her lips. "You know what, I'll shut up. Who am I to judge? I've overstepped my bounds. Forgive me." She rises. "What the world needs is more people like you. One who puts others above herself."

"Don't make me out to be a saint, Mrs. Atwater. I'm not." The wire's tip is stuck in one of the worm holes. I jerk it free.

"I gave up teaching to save my sanity. If I had to grade one more test . . ." She pauses at the office door, shaking her head. "But I'll never stop encouraging my students, no matter how old they are. Just take care of yourself, Caroline. Don't waste your potential."

The words bounce around the crowded office, hurting my ears. *"Don't waste your potential."*

As I hear her car fire up and pull away, I glance out the small office window—the panes need washing—and muse about my unrealized potential. A creeping sensation runs over my torso and down my arms. *I'm already twenty-eight. What am I going to do with my life?*

Worse than dying is never having lived at all.

Early afternoon Daddy comes around and hitches my broken-down car to the back of his truck. "I'll pick you up when I'm done with my last job." He rests his elbow out the window of his battered blue work truck. "Henry and Cherry are coming over for dinner."

"Yeah, Cherry said she thought they'd make it." My brother and his wife of eight years join Dad and me for dinner once a week or so. But we're sloppy with family traditions and lately we've been more on the "or so" side of things than the "once a week."

"Posey's cooking up something good." Dad clicks his tongue against his teeth and fidgets. "I want to run something by you kids."

"Yeah, like what?" Bending left, I try to see his eyes, which are focused straight ahead, out the windshield. "Don't tell me Posey gave back your ring."

"Here I am towing your broken-down heap to the shop and you're poking fun at me." He shifts the truck into gear.

"Dad, I'm teasing. You know Posey loves you."

The truck inches forward as he eases off the clutch. "I'll talk to you later. See you around five or half past."

As he drives off, I catch a smile on the corners of his lips.

What are you up to, Dad?

He's delivered a lot of news to Henry and me over the years. Most of it bad. *"Mama left for good this time . . . Got a call from California. Your Mama says Merry Christmas, but she's not coming . . . Your mama's passed on. They're doing an autopsy, but it looks like she was drinking and driving."*

But today, there was a different light in his eyes, a different tone in his voice.

Back inside the Café, I grab a plate of Frogmore Stew—shrimp, corn on the cob, potatoes, sausage, and onions—and head to the office to tally the day's tips.

Meanwhile, Andy's showing Russell how to make Jones's signature Bubba's Buttery Biscuits.

"Now, careful, boy. Treat the dough nice. Like you're handling a woman."

I pinch my brow and glance over my shoulder. Andy gives me a jolly wink.

A soft red burns across Russell's smooth cheeks. Andy hit close to home, I reckon. The twenty-something dishwasher-slash-cook is a student at University of South Carolina's Beaufort campus and more than likely has handled a woman. Or two. At least spent a good bit of time trying. Nevertheless, Andy's reference has him flustered and embarrassed.

Okay, on to counting tips. Hmm . . . clearly I didn't think this through. How can I eat corn on the cob and count money?

Since Mercy Bea leaves in a few minutes, I set my food aside and divvy up the money.

For some mysterious reason, the Frogmore Café customers don't get the concept of 15 percent. Well, except the breakfast-club boys. They leave a hundred-dollar tip every year for my birthday and Christmas Eve.

I make two piles of money. One for Mercy Bea, one for me. Pretty meager. And she's the mother of teen boys, and I . . . live at Dad's. What the heck. I shove my dollars in with hers and slip the money into her envelope.

At that precise moment, the senior waitress peeks through the office door, breathless.

"Are you all right?" My leg muscles tighten, ready to spring.

"He's out there." She fluffs the ends of her overly sprayed hair.

"Who? Ralph Carter?" I grin.

Mercy Bea twists her red lips into a grimace. "No, Ralph is not here. *Your* man is here. J. D. Rand. Dang, Caroline, he's handsome. Got arms the size of a tree trunk. Shoulders like rocks."

"He's not my man."

"What do you mean he's not your man?" She crouches close as if she's about to tell me a huge secret. "He's been in here every day for the past three weeks."

Yeah, I know. "We've gone out a few times."

"Are you two . . . well, you know." Her eyebrows wiggle.

"Mercy Bea, no." Embarrassment explodes in my torso and rings in my ears. "What is wrong with you?"

The nosy waitress angles toward me. "Miss Goody Two-Shoes, he's one fine, *fine* deputy. Not my type, mind you—too pretty for me. But I appreciate his qualities. I can see why the ladies fall all over him."

I point to Mercy Bea's tip envelope. "First of all, there's your tip money. Second of all, if I was, well, *you know*, I wouldn't tell you."

I busy myself with my plate of Frogmore Stew. Not that it's Mercy's business, but I've never . . . *you know*-ed . . . in my life. When I was sixteen, Daddy sat me down for a "little chat" when his office manager's daughter, Janie, turned up pregnant. He started out with, "The backseat of a car is no place to become a woman." Then his voice cracked, and his foot started tapping. Fast. "Sex should be between two people in a committed relationship."

I never looked him in the eye. Never asked one question. No sirree, Bob.

"Do you understand, Caroline?"

I nodded. *Please, can I go now? Is that Henry outside with his buddies?*

"Caroline." Dad bent forward to see into my eyes. "Here it is. You gals got it. The boys want it. Talk about woman power, all this nonsense about wanting to be like men. Shoot, you ladies got it made. Look, baby, as long as you don't give in, you're in control." He stood and wagged his finger. "You're not the blue-light special at K-Mart. Don't act like you're for sale, cheap."

To this day, I can't shop at K-Mart.

Mercy Bea shakes her tip envelope under my nose. "Hey, where'd you go? J. D.-land?"

I glance up, corncob between my teeth. She wrinkles her face. "Wipe your face, girl. He's asking for you."

3

Hey, beautiful." Beaufort County deputy J. D. Rand smiles at me from the other side of the counter, tucking his Foster Grants inside the top of his uniform. His greeting is like a warm splash. But I play it cool.

"Hey yourself." I fill a glass with ice and Diet Coke. "Want some lunch?"

"Is the special still any good?"

Lowering my chin, I peer at him from under my brow. "You want me to ask Andy if his special is fresh?"

"On second thought . . . bring me the special." J. D. grins with a pound of his palm against the counter.

"What sides do you want?" I jot "Spcl" on my order pad.

J. D. glances at the Daily Special chalkboard. "Green beans and salad. That'll do me. Got to fit into my uniform tomorrow." He winks.

My skin flushes hot. "B-be right back." *How does he do that to me?*

When I return with his plate, J. D. cups his hands over mine. "Are you free tomorrow night?"

"W-what'd you have in mind?"

"We could go fishing. Or down to the beach?" His long-lashed, chocolate gaze lands on my face while his thumb traces the fleshy part of my hand.

I gulp a deep breath. "F-fishing sounds fun."

"It's a date then." His smile is intoxicating, his invitation flattering, and I find my reserve melting. In the past, J. D. was known as a ladies' man, but in recent years, his rep has actually chilled. The word among our friends is he's settling down, growing up.

"I'll pick you up around six?" J. D. pats the massive bicep choking his uniform sleeve. "After my date with the gym." He nods with another teasing grin and wink.

"Six o'clock, tomorrow."

His bravado is endearing. Handsome as all get-out, confident in an I-wear-a-badge kind of way, J. D. grew up with a drinking daddy who cared more about José Cuervo than his own children. J. D.'s worked hard to cover the hole his daddy dug in his heart.

For me? Okay, I admit it's nice to have male attention that isn't wrapped around, "Hey, Caroline, warm up my coffee, will you?"

By five p.m., the Café is closed, empty, and silent. Andy and Russell cleaned the kitchen and punched out. Finished with my side work, I launch e-mail while waiting for Dad to pick me up.

> To: CSweeney
> From: Hazel Palmer
> Subject: Are you ready this time?
> Caroline,

An amazing opportunity has opened up here at SRG International in Barcelona. And I do mean amazing. Not like the other two jobs I offered you before. Ten times better. Do you want it? I went way out on a limb this time for you, Caroline. Risking my rep.

Yes or no?

 Hazel

 CFO, SRG International, Barcelona

Resting my chin in my palm, I fiddle with the paper-clip wire. Hazel's e-mail is full of hidden meaning. Let's see . . .

Job with SRG International, Barcelona. Better than the previous two jobs she wanted me to take (one as a receptionist, the other as a clerk in accounting).

If I say yes, she'll kill me if I back out like before. But, hey, Mrs. Farnsworth pleaded.

Hazel wants me to say yes before telling me about the job. She cannot be serious. Does she really think this conniving tactic will work?

I click Reply and wiggle my fingers over the keys. Mrs. Atwater's admonishment drops from the high places of my mind. And my own yearning to see life outside of Beaufort flutters its clipped wings. Who cares what the job is? I can trust Hazel. Right? She's never steered me wrong. Well, once, when she convinced me to try out for cheerleading. That was an embarrassment waiting to happen.

The memory of my botched split makes me shudder. I exit out of e-mail. No, I'm not taking Hazel up on her job.

However . . . the cheerleading debacle was a long time ago. Hazel's matured since then. She has my well-being in mind. I could go to Barcelona. Jones is gone. Daddy's not alone anymore. Henry's married. My friends are moving on . . .

I launch e-mail again. Then ex out. I sit there, pondering.

When have I ever done anything remotely spontaneous? Half-wild or a quarter crazy?

Never.

Back to e-mail.

To: Hazel Palmer
From: CSweeney
Subject: Re: Are you ready this time?
Hazel,
Yes, I'm ready. No. Wait, what is it? Will I like it? Can I do the job?
I'll do it. Mrs. Atwater stopped by today. Yeah, I got the speech. So,
I'm seriously considering "yes." Tell me more.
Love, Caroline

When Dad and I walk through the kitchen door, his petite, fifty-something (she won't confess her true age, other than, "I'm between fifty and a hundred") fiancée, Posey Martin, stands at the stove, muttering.

"What's wrong, sugar?" Dad turns her so he can kiss her smack on the lips.

Dad! My gaze shoots down to my feet.

I confess: the kiss gives me the heebie-jeebies. It's weird to watch my father behave like, well, a *man*. He and Mama were never affectionate in front of Henry and me because she got weird on him just when we would've started curling our lip with an, "Ah, gross."

"Chicken ain't frying up right," Posey says when Dad releases her. "Hey, Caroline, the Mustang giving you fits again? Hank, why don't you mix up your famous corn bread?"

Dad claps his hands together. "Sounds like a plan."

Some—mostly Dad—say his corn bread is the best in the county.

But instead of digging out the mixing bowl, my father grabs Posey from behind with a growl. She squeals. He snarls against her neck.

Oh, my eyes . . .

Head: Eyes, why didn't you warn me?

Heart: Grow up. Have you ever seen him so happy?

Eyes: Hey, don't blame me. I just look where you tell me, head.

Head: Eyes, look away. He's almost touching her . . . you know, chest area.

Heart: For crying out loud, he's hugging her. Again, have you ever seen him so happy?

Never, actually.

The kitchen door bumps me in the rump. "You're in the way, Caroline."

Ah, there it is . . . snarkiness. That is more like my family. Henry opens the cupboard for the tea glasses. "What's with your car now?"

Dad answers for me, retrieving a mixing bowl from the bottom shelf. "Carburetor. Wayne's going to flush it out again. Be ready in the morning."

"Why don't you get rid of the thing, Caroline?" Henry props himself against the counter, elbows sticking out. "People are starting to talk, calling you Breakdown Sally."

"Who is *they*, Henry? Hmm?" He's making it up, surely. Getting a rep is one thing, but a nickname?

"Everyone in Beaufort." He laughs—not in a ha-ha-isn't-this-funny kind of way, but in a you-are-so-naive kind of way.

Cherry pushes through the door. Another bump in my rump. "Oh, hey, Caroline, sorry. Baby, I thought you were getting glasses."

Henry holds them up.

"Say, Cherry, have you heard people call me Breakdown Sally?"

Studiously avoiding my gaze, my sleek-haired, china-doll-faced sister-in-law steps around me. "Posey, what can I do to help?"

It's true. I'm Breakdown Sally.

"Wayne's ready to take the Mustang off your hands, anytime," Dad offers gently, pouring corn bread mix into a pan. "Bet you could get eight thousand out of him, Caroline. Buy yourself a nice, dependable car."

Translation: snoring.

"Good to know." *Still . . . not selling.*

"Why do you insist on holding on to that piece of junk? Don't you see? It's a metaphor of how Mom felt about you, Caroline." Henry's bitterness stands under the spotlight of his words and takes a bow. "She missed Christmases, birthdays, and graduations. Marriages."

His birthdays, *his* graduations, *his* wedding. Cherry never even met her.

"Henry." Dad's tone sends a caution: *tread carefully, son.*

"Come on, Dad, even you think she should dump *that* old car."

Dad stirs the corn bread mix with vigorous strokes. "Because it's a lemon. Not because your mother gave it to her."

"How much are you making down at the Café, Caroline? Enough to keep that thing running?" Henry holds up his hands. "Don't answer. I already know."

I stare down my big brother. "Drop. It."

"No, Caroline. You know what that stupid car is? A picture of your life. Hanging on to something old and broken, afraid to try something new, still living with our father 'cause you can't afford a life of your own."

"Stop it, Henry." If his tone wasn't so brutal, I'd see his point. I bat away the sting of tears.

"Am I wrong?" He holds out his hands, each gripping a glass. "Am I?"

"Henry. Move on. New topic." Dad's command leaves no room for argument.

My brother holds his next thought, but the dark light behind his eyes reminds me his bitterness will reappear. He wears it like a badge of honor.

"Well," Dad says in a Mr. Rogers voice, "since you're all in here . . . Cherry, want to wait on those glasses?" Dad takes Posey's hand. "We've set a wedding date," he says without preamble.

"Dad, that's wonderful."

"How marvelous." Cherry slips her arm through Henry's.

Dad clears his throat. "We're leaving Saturday for the Bahamas."

After a moment in which we all stare with mouths open, Cherry giggles. "You're eloping?"

Dad cuts a glance at Posey. "We got to looking at schedules and finances—"

"Dad, you and Posey do what you want. We're not children. We understand." This from Henry in his CEO-of-Sweeney-Construction voice.

"Yes, Dad, please do whatever you and Posey want," I chime in. "A wedding in the Bahamas sounds very romantic."

Posey presses her fingers under her expressive green eyes and sniffs. "We didn't want to leave you kids out, but I had my big wedding the first time around. When Eric died, I never thought I'd marry again. Then I met your dad . . ."

"Met me? Rammed your Miata into the back of my truck." Dad raises her hand to his lips, gives it a grinning kiss.

Head: Look away, eyes.

"Well, how did I know there was a stoplight in the middle of a bridge?"

Posey is what the Gullah call a *comeya*—a lowcountry newbie.

Henry strides forward and shakes Dad's hand in a manly-man way. "May you have a long, happy marriage. If anyone deserves it, Dad, it's you."

I stifle the oncoming tears. "Hear, hear."

4

Hazel cannot keep the "amazing, incredible" job opportunity confined to cyberspace. She has to call.

"Isn't it like three in the morning there?" I ask, though I love hearing her voice.

"Three thirty, actually." Her rushed tone is high-pitched, excited. "I get up at four thirty on Tuesday, Wednesday, and Thursday so I can be in the office by six. So I'm only losing an hour of sleep."

"Have you been consuming caffeine?" I stretch out on the sofa as Dad, Posey, Henry, and Cherry play hearts at the dining room table. Jim Croce croons from Dad's old turntable.

"Only a cup. Listen, about this job—"

In my mind, I envision Hazel pacing a Spanish-style living room in baggy, silk pajamas and slappy slippers with little heels. "Do I have to get up at four thirty for this incredible job?"

"No, you don't have to get up at four thirty. I like to get into the office before the meetings and phone calls start."

"So, this job . . ."

"You know about my boss, Carlos Longoria, right? Sure you do; we've talked about him. As a matter of fact, he's on the cover of this month's *Forbes*."

"Sure, Carlos." I've seen him on many magazine covers, read about him via Hazel's e-mails. "The European Donald Trump. Runs a large development and property company. Y'all build and buy apartments, condos, villas."

"Right. If you can live in it, we own it."

"A grass hut?"

"Sri Lanka."

"Mud hut?"

"Okay, no mud huts. Even Carlos draws the line somewhere."

"And he considers himself a Donald Trump?" I tug the scrunchy from my hair and shake it free.

"He does. With great pride. And he's a big fan of *The Apprentice*."

I bolt upright. "I'm not going on TV."

"No, no, he's not talking TV . . . yet. For now, all he wants is a hard-working individual with a bright mind he can mold into a Mini Me, rather a Mini Him."

"And you offered up me?"

From the dining room, Cherry and Posey slap high fives as they win another round of cards. A frustrated Henry jerks away from the table with an, "I need more tea."

"I've convinced Carlos *you* are perfect to be his first apprentice. You have no preconceived ideas or agenda or college professor telling you it should be like *this* instead of *that*."

"Hazel, I'm a waitress. A bookkeeper. Hometown girl with only a high-school diploma."

"Actually, he loves that about you. When I told him about how you helped your dad and Henry rebuild their businesses, his eyes glowed."

Running my hand through my hair—it feels dry against my fingers—I correct her. "Hazel, I didn't help Dad rebuild his business. I filled in when his office manager quit."

"You organized an entire network and computer installation. Did the same thing for Henry. Brought all the accounting and inventory online."

"Right, but I didn't help them *rebuild* anything." My thoughts form a pleasant thanks-but-no-thanks reply to my overeager, overachieving friend.

"Well, look what you did for Jones and the Café." Her enthusiasm is undaunted.

I laugh. "Okay, you got me. I introduced computers to Jones and learned to run a very small café. Woo-wee. The business world just tilted."

"Caroline, you're a team player, a problem solver. You work well under pressure and have phenomenal people skills."

"I do?" I ease against the back of the sofa.

"Never mind your amazing ability to see good in people. Your compassion toward your mom always blew me away."

"Now you're just talking crazy."

"C, wouldn't we have so much fun? Living in Europe together? But, if you agree to this, you can't change your mind because of some family or hometown emergency."

Her summation of my skills does little to bring clarity. Me? In Spain? "Hazel, you really think I can do the job?"

"One hundred percent. You are ready for this kind of challenge, girl. And, you're exactly what Carlos is looking for—raw material."

Well, in that case . . . But, I catch my "yes" on the tip of my tongue before Hazel hears it. Never, ever have I done anything like this. Daytona Beach for spring break my senior year is my biggest brouhaha so far.

Well, except for the time Mama got a wild hair and decided to rearrange holidays, celebrate Christmas on Halloween, New Year's on Thanksgiving. For my fourth-grade Halloween party, she sent me to school wearing a red-velvet dress and black patent-leather shoes, carrying a free gift bottle of Clinique's "Happy" wrapped in Santa paper.

Yeah, this Barcelona thing requires some thought. "Can I call you in an hour?"

Hazel's slow sigh billows in my ear. "Call me at the office. I'll e-mail you the number. Caroline, just say yes."

As I hang up from Hazel, a shout rises from the dining room. Dad and Henry finally won a hand.

I grab the kitchen flashlight and steal out the back door, heading around front to my sanctuary—the ancient live oak. Parting the Spanish moss that dangles from gnarly limbs like hippie beads, I hike my skirt to my knees and climb to my pew about ten feet up, wondering if the God of Andy might be available to talk.

Daily Special

Tuesday, June 5

Country Ham

Butternut Squash, Green Beans, Cheese Coins

Bubba's Buttery Biscuits

Upside-Down Apple Cake

Tea, Soda, Coffee

$6.99

5

To: CSweeney
From: Hazel Palmer
Subject: Carlos's call

Caroline,

Carlos is extremely pleased you said yes. He buzzed into my office first thing this morning asking for your number. He's calling you at four your time—TODAY. Be ready.

Questions you might want to ask him are his expectations, job description and duties, your role on the team and with other projects. Think outside the box when you talk to him.

He'll probably ask you questions like your strength and weaknesses, expectations, give you a salary range. BTW, he realizes this is all new to you.

This is muy *fab, Caroline. Muy. Figure your arrival date for a*

week on the Mediterranean, in a villa, my treat, so we can have
some fun together before work consumes your life.
    Love, Hazel
    CFO, SRG International, Barcelona

Late in the afternoon, the Café is bathed in warm, sleepy sunlight that falls in speckled patterns across the thin threads of a weary carpet. The old walls and ceiling beams creak and moan, sounding every bit like an old man stretching as he rises from his favorite chair. Funny, I've been hearing the sounds for two years, but today I listen and am comforted.

The old girl's going to be all right. Get some new owners—by inheritance or sale—who have the wherewithal for an extreme makeover.

Across the counter from me, Mercy Bea leans against Joel Creager's table, telling him about her youngest young-son's basketball shoes.

"Two hundred dollars. Can you believe it? And he ain't done growing."

Joel sips his coffee while shaking his head. "Glad I never had no kids. Who can afford them?"

Smiling, I wipe down the ketchup bottles. I'll miss afternoons like this once I'm in Barcelona.

An electric flutter runs down my torso, causing me to draw a long breath.

While sitting in the tree last night, talking to the stars, or perhaps God if He wasn't otherwise involved—solving crime or formulating an eighth world wonder—this strange peace blanketed me. I'd felt something like it once before—the night Mama died.

When it persisted, I figured it to be my answer, climbed down from the tree, ripping my favorite skirt in the process, and called Hazel.

The Café door's Christmas bells jingle. Kirk Harris, Jones's lawyer, walks in.

"Kirk, hello." What perfect timing. He'll give me the terms of the will; I'll give him my resignation. When Carlos calls—TODAY—I'll be ready to talk start date.

Mercy Bea abandons Joel and shoots over to Kirk. "Darlin', we've been watching for you."

In his early thirties, the genteel lowcountry lawyer looks like a disheveled Ross Geller from *Friends*. Unruly dark hair, quirky, uneven manner. Today he looks as though he might have slept in his suit.

"Caroline, you ready to see the will?" He starts for the large booth in the back with a quick step, shrugging to shed Mercy Bea.

"Mercy, why don't you get Kirk some coffee. Looks like he could use some. Bring a plate of biscuits." I trail after Kirk, ignoring Mercy's scowl. "How'd the inheritance case turn out?"

Kirk drops his briefcase to the tabletop as if he's just used up his last ounce of energy. "We settled it last night. Then celebrated . . ."

"Party too much?" I ask, sliding into the booth across from him as he pops open his case.

"I forgot I'm not in college anymore."

He passes a document to me. Jones's will.

This is it, Jones. Our final good-bye. For a moment, I entertain sadness.

"Unless you love reading a bunch of legalese, just flip to the red sticky flags."

"Kirk, before we do this will thing, I want to give you my resignation. Of course, I'll stay long enough to—"

Kirk snaps his eyes to my face. "Resigning? Oh, no, no, no, Caroline." He chuckles.

"'No'? What do you mean 'no'? I have a job. In Spain." I spit out "Spain" in case the drank-too-much fog has hampered his hearing. "In Barcelona."

"Here we are . . ." Trailed by Andy, Mercy Bea sets down a whole pot of fresh-brewed coffee, an oversized hand-painted mug I'm pretty sure was made by one of her young-sons—the handle is crooked—and a heaping plate of biscuits. "Move on over, Caroline." She shoves against my shoulder. "Slide in next to Kirk there, Andy."

"Don't look like we're needed, Mercy Bea."

The Charleston lawyer pours his own coffee and downs a big swig without waiting for it to cool. I wince.

"I'd like to talk to Miss Sweeney. Alone," he says.

"We share information around here. No secrets." Mercy Bea keeps shoving me around until she's sitting square in front of Kirk.

Andy doesn't bother to sit. "If you don't need me, I got work to do. Look, all I want is to keep my job and pay."

"I'm sure you'll find things satisfactory, Andy," Kirk says, bestowing a long, hard gaze on Mercy Bea, who pinches her face into a stubborn expression. But she's met her match in Kirk. He sits back, gulps more coffee, and stares her square in the eye.

She can't last long . . . *Three, two, one . . .*

"Oh, all right." Mercy Bea exhales a blue word while sliding out of the booth. "You'd think a loyal employee would get some special consideration. But, no . . . it's too much to ask. Caroline, I'm clocking out."

"Wait fifteen minutes, Mercy Bea, please. Miss Jeanne will be along for supper soon."

"Russell is here." She tosses her head. "Apparently, I'm not needed."

Ho, boy. "Fine." I glance at Kirk. "Miss Jeanne is one of our loyal customers, a born-and-raised Beaufortonian."

"Interesting." His tone betrays him. And he's looking a little green. The boy needs two aspirin and a long sleep. "Turn to the red sticky flags, please. By the way, that's your copy of the will."

"My copy? O-okay." I flip to the page marked by the flag and read.

*WILL OF **Jones Q. McDermott**, a resident of Beaufort, South Carolina. I hereby make this Will and revoke all prior Wills and Codicils.*

BENEFICIARIES: I give the Frogmore Café and carriage house to the following persons: **Caroline Jane Sweeney.**

Caroline Jane Swee— "Me?" I fire my gaze toward Kirk. "That's my name. Kirk, what? Jones left the Frogmore Café to me?" My middle tightens with an eerie shiver.

Kirk shoves his glasses up the bridge of his nose. "This is why you can't go to Barcelona. Congratulations, you're a business owner."

"No, no, no." I toss the document at him like it's riddled with disease. "I don't want the Café. I accepted the job in Barcelona. It's too late to back out."

Rumbling dark clouds form in my head and echo in my ears. I can't feel my fingers and toes.

"Are you sure?" Kirk offers back the will.

"Absolutely. This place—and bless Jones for all his hard work— needs an owner with vision and lots of cash."

Kirk points to a line of the will. "Did you read this?"

My eyes skim the page.

If any beneficiary under this Will does not survive me by 90 days, then the property shall be sold and money given to charity.

If any beneficiary under this Will does not accept the terms, then the property shall be sold and money given to charity.

"If you don't take it, Caroline, I'm legally required to sell it."

Oh my gosh, Jones, what did I ever do to you? "This is not happening. *Not* happening." I pat my cheeks. "Wake up, Caroline; it's just a bad, very bad, dream."

"If you refuse the terms of the will, I'll start proceedings to shut down."

His matter-of-fact tone irritates me—like inheriting a man's life is an

everyday occurrence for me. "There must be some mistake." I flip
through the pages, scanning for any small *"Just kidding"* clause. "Just
because I don't want it doesn't mean we shut it down."

"According to the will, there *is* no alternative. Jones specifically
requested the Café be given to you, or closed down and sold."

"What about just sold? To the highest bidder."

Kirk exhales, sending a puff of hangover-mouth-mixed-with-coffee
breath. I turn my nose. "You can argue all you want, Caroline, but my
options are you or shut it down and sell it for charity."

"But *I* am charity. This whole place is charity. What about Andy,
Russell, and Mercy Bea? The breakfast-club boys and Miss Jeanne? Our
other regular customers? The Vet Wall?" I poke the air with my finger.
Kirk twists to see behind him.

"Very inspiring. Are you accepting the Café or not?"

"Are you telling me Jones wanted these guys to lose their jobs? That
it's me or no one?" I shake my head. "It doesn't make sense. This is the
man who gave money away faster than he made it."

"Caroline, I don't have the time or patience to dialogue about Jones's
heart or motivation. Yes or no."

"This isn't fair." My heart pulses. Beads of sweat break out over my
neck and back. The future of the Café cannot be left to me. It cannot.
"Don't I get twenty-four hours to think about it? Or a couple of days?
A year? How about when I get back from Barcelona?"

The Donald Trump of Europe is calling me in twenty minutes.

"Fair enough. I made you wait; guess I can give you a couple of days.
Shoot, take a week. I'll be back next . . ." He whips out a PalmPilot.
"Tuesday. Meanwhile, let's go over some details."

For the next fifteen minutes, Kirk rattles on about taxes, probate,
creditors, and a personal representative. But I can barely hear him for
the internal turmoil.

Head: This is a fine mess.

Heart: You're not sending me positive thoughts. I neeeed positive thoughts. I'm feeling weepy.

Head: Stop badgering me. I'm doing all I can to listen and not freak out.

Heart: [Sniff] Do you have any tissues?

Back to Kirk: "Doing business shouldn't be a problem since your name is on the accounts. But if you need a loan from the bank . . . ?"

"A loan?"

He gulps the last of his coffee and reaches for the pot to refill. "A loan . . . to pay bills, fix up the place. I've seen the books, though. You'll be hard-pressed to convince a loan officer to back you."

"Mr. Mueller runs when he sees me at the teller window."

"I'm not surprised." Kirk caps his pen. "Do you have any questions?"

"Only a thousand and one. Kirk, why me?"

He shifts in his seat, tucking the unruly sides of his wrinkled shirt into his waistband. "He never said."

"You didn't ask?"

"It's not my business."

"But, I—" The Christmas bells chime, and I look to see Miss Jeanne coming in for her late-lunch-early-supper.

"Hey, Miss Jeanne."

"Warm day, Caroline." She makes her way to her favorite spot—a two-top by the fireplace. She's slightly hunched and gray headed, but hip looking in her mom-jeans and terra-cotta-colored blouse. Time-earned wisdom lines her broad features, but her cherubic smile reflects the youthfulness of her soul.

"I left Ebony in the car. Do you think it's too hot?" She gazes out the window as if it can help her gauge the heat index.

"You left the windows down, didn't you?"

She grimaces. "Don't go insulting my intelligence, young lady, or I'll tell this young man how you almost burnt down Beaufort High School."

Kirk's brow crinkles. "Burnt down?"

"There you go." I flip up my hand. "Another reason Jones should've never left the Café to me. I'm a fire hazard."

Sliding out of the booth, I hunt down Russell, carrying with me the shock of the will. He's in the kitchen helping Andy prep for tomorrow's special. "Miss Jeanne's here."

Without missing a beat, Russell recites her order. "Pot-roast casserole, fresh Bubba's Buttery Biscuits, side dish of strawberry jam. Side salad with blue-cheese dressing."

"Perfect. I'll get her tea . . . Oh, Russell, she'll want a slice of rhubarb pie."

At the wait station, I fix Miss Jeanne's mason jar of sweet iced tea while the idea of owning the Café flies around my head looking for a place to land.

But all the runways are closed.

When I return to the back booth, Kirk's downing another mug of coffee and eyeing the biscuits.

"Let's say I take the Café. Can I sell it?"

Kirk removes his glasses and rubs his bloodshot eyes. "After probate, I don't care what you do. Neither will the law."

"Kirk, are you sure Jones was sane when he signed this will?"

He laughs for the first time since he walked in. "More sane than you and I are right now." He puts on his glasses and exits the booth. "Caroline, get advice, talk to your priest, visit a Gullah spiritualist, do whatever it is you do for guidance. But next Tuesday I need an answer."

6

To: Hazel Palmer
From: CSweeney
Subject: Stop the call!
Hazel,

Jones's lawyer just left. Are you ready for this? The old man left the Frogmore to me.

I said no, right? But Haz, if I don't take the Café, Kirk will shut it down—after fifty years of business. Andy, Mercy Bea, and Russell will lose their jobs. Faithful patrons will lose a friend. Beaufort will lose a piece of history.

You'd think Jones could've given me an "Oh, by the way" in the last year or so, but nooo. What an odd, insane little man. I feel sick. Really I do. My emotions are all over the place, my thoughts divided. Please cancel the Carlos call. There's no way I can convince him I'm his first apprentice. Hazel, what should I do? What would you do?

C

When J. D. picks me up a little after six, I'm edgy and distracted, fussing with my hair, putting it into a ponytail, then pulling it out again. He watches me by the back door as I attempt to transfer stuff from my backpack to my purse. Keys? Check. Lipstick? Check.

"Bodean called and said a bunch of folks are going to Luther's." He comes up behind me and smoothes his hand over my shoulders. "You game or do you want to go to the beach?"

"Luther's is fine." I jam a fat, square brush into my handbag.

"Caroline, are you okay?"

"Yeah." *Just peachy.*

"Do you need this?" He pinches my work apron, sprouting from the top of my purse.

"No, I guess not." Nor the one black clog.

"You're sure nothing is bothering you?"

I smile up at him. "I'm good to go."

J. D. leads me to his truck, opens the door, and leans close with a protective I'm-your-man stance. "Caroline . . ."

"J. D.?" His spearmint breath brushes my face. Our eyes lock for a heady moment and all thoughts of the will drain from my mind. My lips quiver.

For some reason, the deputy with the ladies'-man rep has yet to kiss me. Three dates, three handshakes. Maybe he heard about Daddy's blue-light-special speech.

The old blue light.

"Something funny?" J. D. backs away with a deflated expression.

"Oh, J. D., no, no, it's not you. Flash memory from high school." I conk my palm against the side of my head. "Danger, Will Robinson. Random thoughts firing."

He cocks his head to one side. "And just when I was going to kiss you."

I tug on his shirtsleeve. "Don't I get a do-over?" While I heeded Dad's warning about backseats and overzealous teenage boys, I did take quite nicely to the art of kissing.

"Nope, too late." He nudges me inside his truck.

"Spoilsport."

Driving toward downtown, J. D. gets me laughing about an old drunk he had to pick up this afternoon.

"'Please, sir, just get in the car. We'll get you some help,' I said. But, no. What does he do? Call me a pig and whiz over the backseat."

"J. D., no." Laughter is good. Keeps me from dwelling on the Café. Or the kiss I lost.

Worrying about my decision tonight won't solve anything. I'll sleep on it, and by some miracle, when I wake up, the answer will be *right there*—I tap my forehead. Crystal clear.

As we cross the river, a blue heron rises from the marsh grass and disappears into the slanting sunlight.

Wish I could go with you.

Luther's Rx, Rare and Well-Done is a converted pharmacy with exposed-brick walls, high round tables, great food, and a spirited atmosphere. Especially when Elle is around.

"Caroline, back here!"

My BFF since grade school, Elle Garvey, is standing in her chair, flailing her arms over her strawberry-blonde head, sending her trademark bracelets clattering down to her elbow. It's been weeks since I've seen her, and my taut emotions seem to relax at the sound of her voice. How could I even consider such a life-altering decision—Barcelona or Beaufort—without her wise input?

Unlike me, Elle's had her life planned out since she was thirteen: go to college, study art, then open an art gallery on Bay Street.

Two years ago, she accomplished her goals. Well, except one: find Mr. Wonderful.

With his fingertips hooking lightly onto mine, J. D. leads me to our gang in the back left corner. Once there, he runs his hand down my back and around my hip. It's an intimate move, sending a shiver of surprise down my legs. "Diet Coke?"

He remembered. "Yes, please. Oh, and a burger."

He grins. I never noticed how one side of his mouth hooks to the left a little. It's saucy and I like it. "Want some fried pickles?"

"Yum, yes."

He sets off to find our waitress, Tracey.

"Here, Caroline, sit." Ray Cimowsky hops out of his chair. He's another Beaufort high alum, married to one of my other BFFs, Jessica. "My wife has been dying to talk to you, and I'd like to see this baseball game." He motions to the TV hanging in the corner.

Elle lunges across the table, grabbing my arm as I sit. "Soooo, J. D. How's it going?" Her luminous green eyes are painted like Liz Taylor in *Cleopatra*. Totally works for her. She's gorgeous.

"Good. So far," I say between clenched teeth, giving her a warning look. *Want to keep it down?*

"I hear he's a great kisser," Jess says.

"Jess." I check to see if Ray heard.

"Who do you think told me? Didn't you, babe?" She looks around at him, but he's fixed on the TV screen.

Elle slurps her Coke. "Wonder how Ray knows?"

"He's full of useless information." Jess flicks her hand at her husband like she's brushing lint from her jeans. "You know what he asked me the other day? If we had any more bathroom tissue." She twists her lips in how-do-you-like-that? fashion, waiting for Elle and me to recoil or something.

Elle looks at me. I shrug. "So, did you?"

"Ladies, did you not hear me? *Bathroom. Tissue.*" Jess is incredulous. "What kind of man says 'bathroom tissue'? It's toilet paper."

"The same kind that says 'laundry detergent' and 'feminine products,'" Ray interjects, eyes still glued to the game.

Jess swats at him, laughing. "Didn't your mama tell you it's rude to eavesdrop?"

"Don't be making fun of me, baby, 'cause if you want to compare stories . . ."

Jess shushes him. "So, Caroline, J. D., huh?" she whispers, squeezing my arm.

I scrunch up my shoulders. "Yeah, J. D."

Speaking of . . .

"One diet." J. D. sets my drink in front of me. "Fried pickles and a burger coming up. Having fun?" he asks in my ear.

"The best."

He joins the boys watching the game—Ray and fellow deputy Bodean Good—while Elle angles toward me, whispering, "Dang, Caroline, first Mitch O'Neal and now J. D. Rand. Where do I get in the I-only-date-drop-dead-gorgeous-men line?"

"Too late," I tease. "The ship has sailed."

"See?" She sits back. "And this is why I end up on a date with Butch Moore."

My mouth is full of drink, and I spew a little, trying to laugh, swallow, and breathe at the same time. Fizz burns the back of my nose. "Butch Moore. You cannot be serious."

He was the resident nerd for Beaufort High's Class of '97, and proudly so. When last I saw him, not much had changed. He's still into video games and *Star Trek*. I wish him life, health, and happiness, but not Elle.

Jess sighs with a nod. "She did."

"Just dinner." Elle *Z*'s the air with her finger. "And I drove myself."

My beautiful, artistic, educated, compassionate friend. Reduced to dating nerds. It's not right. "Are you really that desperate?"

"Well, we can't all be you, can we?"

Touchy. "I've dated two men. If—and it's a big if"—I lower my voice—"you count J. D. This is only our fourth date."

"Oh, you're dating," Jess says with confidence. "I see the way he looks at you."

"What look?" I sneak a peek at him. Oh, he's watching me. I smile. He winks. Tingles rush over me.

The truth is there aren't many pages in my dating-history book. Before this "thing" with J. D., there was only Mitch. He was—*er*, is— spectacular. Last year, *People* magazine listed him in the top ten of "Most Beautiful Men of the Decade." The decade!

For far too long, I clung to Mitch as my true love, completely lost in the hope of "us."

At nineteen, he moved to Nashville with the intent of becoming a country music star, eager to shed his preacher's kid stigma. I was also nineteen and confident that all the promises we made to each other were real, passionate, and for life. I had no idea we'd keep—he'd keep—none of them.

After several years of back and forth, caring and not caring, roller coasting between tears and nail-spitting mad, Elle drove me down to Savannah for a nice dinner and hard talk. "Come down off Mount Still-Hoping. Look around—you're in the land of It's-Never-Gonna-Happen. Mitch has moved on. So should you. You're living a spinster librarian life while he dates Hollywood A-listers and the latest half-starved beauty from Madison Avenue." She shuddered. "And I saw him take the True Love Waits pledge at youth church."

As though to take my mind off bad memories, J. D.'s hand brushes along my shoulders and under my hair. His baritone rises and falls in conversation with the guys.

"Okay, be honest." Elle taps her forehead. "Does it say 'Geeks Stand a Chance' right here?"

"What?" I lean into J. D.'s caress. Jess's high twitter explodes around us.

"Ladies, I'm asking a serious question." Elle squares her shoulders and gestures to her slender frame. "Anywhere on here? Does it say 'Geeks Stand a Chance'?"

What is she talking about? Homecoming Queen, Most Popular— the guys had to book a date with her, months in advance. One of my joys in high school was standing in her shadow and watching the parade. And at the University of South Carolina, she was president of *this* club and chairman of *that* committee.

"You're beautiful and intimidating," I conclude. "The geeks are too clueless to realize they're hunting in the wrong field."

Elle slides down in her seat. "Y'all, I'm serious. The other day I was at the gym and this gorgeous guy with long black curly hair and great arms walked slowly past me. He looked. I looked." Elle demonstrates her *look*. "He smiled. I smiled. Then, out of nowhere, this geekozoid in Velcro sneakers and a T-shirt that says 'Too many women, so little time' is right in front of me, asking if I want to go to Luther's for a beer."

Lowering my head, I laugh into my drink. Jess's twitter deepens.

"I think to myself," Elle continues, "*Oh, my stars, I know people at Luther's.*"

Tracey appears with Diet Coke refills and the fried pickles.

"What did you tell him?" Jess manages between snickers.

"I told him I don't drink. Which is true, so I don't feel guilty." Elle snatches a pickle and munches down. "I'm telling you, times are getting desperate."

As we talk the perils of dating for a lowcountry single woman, the rest of our food arrives. I'm polishing off the last bite of burger when the lights dim. Tonight's singer, Branan Logan, steps into the spotlight burning down on the very small, front-corner stage.

"How's everyone tonight?" He's greeted with a mix of cheers and whistles. "Glad you all could make it out." He slips on his guitar. "For those of you who don't know, I'm Branan Logan and—"

As he speaks, Luther's atmosphere changes. I see people start to whisper and point, and the hair on my arms prickles. Without seeing, my intuition tells me who's entered the room. There's only one person who could electrify a local crowd like that. *What's he doing here?*

Loud and excited voices roll back from the front. Elle stands on her chair to see what's going on. With wide eyes, she looks down at me and Jess. "It's Mitch."

7

In tenth grade, Mitch walked into homeroom—much like he is doing now—and zapped the air. My eyes followed him as he walked down the rows, looking for a seat. Every girl prayed he'd pick the one next to her. But with proton pulses blipping around him, he stopped by me and asked, "Is this seat taken?"

I *eek*ed or something, shook my head no and he sat, knocking the wind right out of me.

And he's doing it again. I draw a deep breath and exhale slowly, savoring the air.

Branan, seeing the commotion swirling around his audience, spies Mitch among the faces. "Mitch O'Neal . . . Come slumming, man?" He laughs and gestures to the country star with a sweep of his arm. "Come on, sing for the home folks."

Mitch hesitates. "I just came in for a burger. Do we have to sing for our food now?"

The room exhales with laughter.

Elle cups her hands around her mouth. "Sing, Mitch."

Mitch shields his eyes from the lights and gazes in our direction. "That's got to be Elle Garvey."

"You got it, baby."

Mitch smiles easily as he's urged to strap on Branan's guitar. "Elle Garvey . . . head cheerleader . . . used to get me laughing in Spanish class when she answered Mrs. Gonzales in Pig Latin."

"Ouyay ememberedray."

"How could I forget?" Mitch tunes the guitar.

J. D.'s closer now than before, his leg gently resting against mine. "Good to see Mitch, isn't it?" I say.

"Yeah, it's been a while." He grabs my hand and doesn't let go.

The moment Mitch begins to play, everything stops. The TVs, the voices, the movement.

"I love the lowcountry," he says over the light picking of the guitar. "As soon as I hit the Beaufort County line, I rolled down my window and breathed deep. It's good to be"—his eyes stop on me—"home."

J. D. clutches my hand tighter.

A shout comes from the front entrance. "I'm in the house." Wild Wally barrels into the room.

Our little crowd in the back hoots. "Wild Wallyyyyy."

Wally spies Mitch. "Oh, man, look what Nashville sent back." Jumping onto the stage, he wraps the country crooner in a thick-armed hug—guitar and all.

"Wild Wally," Mitch claps him on the back. "For those of you who don't know, he's the best offensive lineman Beaufort High and S.C. State ever turned out."

"Yeah!" Wally pumps his tan, muscular arms over his head. He owns a massive landscaping and lawn-care service. His face is perpetually sunburned.

"Good to see you, man." Mitch faces the mike again. "I forgot what I was saying."

"Good to be back in Beaufort," someone shouts.

"Right." Mitch's tone is warm and introspective. "In the spring, the band and I toured Europe. How many of you have ever been to Paris?"

A few hands go up, followed by a light smattering of applause.

"City of Lights. Beautiful. But my favorite place on earth is right here."

Listening, I prop my chin in my free hand. Having seen Mitch only briefly in the last year, I watch him, wondering. Something's . . . different.

"We had a scary encounter in Paris. Sometimes fear is the only thing that makes us wake up and realize we've drifted way over life's yellow line."

Humility is reflected in his transparency.

"This song is called 'Yellow Line.'"

Jess jiggles my arm. "Do you know what he's talking about?"

I shrug. "No."

"Me neither. And I keep up with news about him."

Mitch's song floats over us.

And I've crossed over the yellow line.
Gone beyond where it's safe to roam.
I've gone too far with this will of mine.
And I don't know if I can ever come home.

The melody resonates with hundreds of other Mitch-melodies that have painted my soul over the years. The ones he sang for me on his daddy's porch, or mine, before Nashville lured him away. Tears surprise in my eyes. Behind me, Jess whispers to Ray for a napkin. Yes, definitely something's changed with Mitch. Boundaries used to be the enemy, but this song reflects a different attitude.

The population of Luther's has probably doubled in the last five minutes. The air is stifling. I stand to shake the closed-in feeling of a crowded room. When I do, J. D. wraps his arm around my waist and holds me close. His chest is warm against my back.

"You okay?" He whispers in my ear. The scent around him is clean and spicy.

"Yes."

"Let's get out of here," he suggests.

"O-okay."

Taking my hand, he leads me out the back door. I wave good-bye to Elle and Jess with a backward glance at Mitch. He catches me with a nod of his chin.

Outside, the river breeze feels good and blows the sentiment of Mitch off of my senses.

"I hope you don't mind leaving early," J. D. says, "but I work a double tomorrow and wanted some time alone with you."

"It feels good to be outside."

Sailboats drift by, beautiful with white lights. On nights like this I wonder how I could ever leave home.

But Barcelona . . . *I didn't have a chance to talk to Elle.*

"So . . ." J. D. falls against the waterfront's cement pylon, crossing his arms. "What's the deal with you and O'Neal?"

"Deal?" I lean next to him and watch a schooner bob on the river's surface, waiting for the bridge to open.

"Are you two, still, you know, close? A thing?"

"Would I be here with you if we were?"

He shrugs. "Maybe. You didn't know he was going to be at Luther's."

"Exactly, Deputy Rand." I hip butt him. "You're making my point."

J. D. scratches his hand over his close-cut dark hair. "Just checking."

"It's no secret about Mitch and me. I loved him. But we didn't work out, and after a bunch of years, I'm over him."

"Good to know."

We walk in silence toward his truck except for his boot heels scraping against the walkway to the rhythm of my flip-flops. As we near the truck, he steps in front of me.

"Can we do this again?"

"Talk about me and Mitch?" I grin.

He laughs. "No, go out."

"Do you have more in your repertoire than the Plaza and Luther's?"

J. D. pops open the passenger-side door. "I think I might."

Daily Special

Wednesday, June 6

Love Your Waitress Day

Stuffed Peppers with Gravy

Mixed Green Salad

Bubba's Buttery Biscuits

Pluff Mud Pie

Tea, Soda, Coffee

$7.99

8

To: CSweeney
From: Hazel Palmer
Subject: Re: Stop the call!
Caroline,
*When I told Carlos, I made up an excuse because I do NOT want you
to lose this opportunity. Remember, no small-town or family emergency?*

*This is what always happens to you. Someone needs you and
your life becomes theirs. When is it going to be your time? Elle's studied abroad and traveled. Mitch went to Nashville and found the pot
of gold at the end of his rainbow. I hired on with SRG International
and the great Carlos Longoria. And now you have an opportunity to
do something extraordinary and what happens? Break this cycle and
come to Barcelona.*

*Remember the time we sat up all night talking out on your dock?
Right before I left for Florida State? You said you didn't have any idea*

of what you wanted to do with your life, and you were half-afraid you inherited whatever made your mama weird out and run off, but you also didn't want to wake up at forty and wonder where the years went.

Wake up. Take a chance. You're not your mama, Caroline. Nor will you be. You're already light-years different. Ten times sweeter. Kinder. Smarter. Sane.

Do you realize how many Hah-vard grads would kill for an opportunity to work with Carlos? Literally. First-degree murder. Risking twenty to life. Please don't let this opportunity pass you by. I really did push Carlos on this. He's traveling this week, so he's distracted, but he wants to talk to you.

What do I think about you owning the Café? It's a run-down, has-been dinosaur. A Beaufort knickknack. It needs investors with vision and money. Is this really where you see your life going? Is owning the Café the thing you'll regret not doing? I don't think so, Caroline.

Hazel

CFO, SRG International, Barcelona

There's a fast knock outside the office, and Mercy Bea pops in before I can call, "Come in."

"So, what'd the snooty lawyer say yesterday? Are we in business or not?" She crosses her arms. An unlit cigarette protrudes from her fingers.

"We're in business." I click out of Hazel's e-mail, then stand, stretching. "Is it still slow out there?"

It's a little after eleven a.m. The breakfast crowd was solid this morning, and now I'm hopeful for a lunch rush.

"Dead as a doornail. So, girl, come on. Are you going to leave us hanging? What'd the old coot put in his will?" Mercy Bea motions for me to follow her to the back porch, where she lights up her cigarette. "Do I have a job? Youngest young-son came home with a list longer than Clinton's ex-girlfriends of stuff he needs for a basketball camp. As if money ain't tight enough." A wispy trail of smoke slithers upward. "Picked up an extra shift at the nursing home, though."

"Yes, you still have a job." *For now.*

The blonde bombshell taps her ashes toward the ashtray, but misses. Gray flakes flutter to the concrete porch. "Dang their daddy. Gave them his athletic ability, but not one plug nickel to help them out."

"Plug nickels aren't worth anything, Mercy Bea."

"You know what I mean."

Figuring now would be as good a time as any to tell them about Jones's dying wishes, I peer through the kitchen's screen door to see what Andy is doing. Cleaning under the ovens. "Come inside, Mercy. Let's talk about the Café."

I ask Andy to take a break from the toothbrush and bucket of soap, then call Russell from the pantry where he's cleaning shelves. Mercy Bea joins them on the other side of the prep table.

"As you know, Kirk was here yesterday." I face my small band of people. Their expressions make my heart thump.

As if listening in, the Café creaks and groans. The AC kicks in, and the lights brown out for a second. Then the entire Café goes black.

"Ah, no, not again." Andy shoves past the prep table toward the fuse box. "Jones should've fixed this mess—all this old wiring. I tell you, Edison was alive when they installed these glass fuses."

Electrical problems. Definitely a negative for saying yes to Jones's will.

Andy pops open the fuse box and in the soft light coming through the windows, bangs around, pulling fuses and putting them back in.

With a buzz, the lights flicker on.

Then off.

Then on.

I exhale, unaware I was even holding my breath. For years, Jones knew the Café needed an electrical overhaul. He just never got around to it.

One more reason the Café needs a moneyed owner.

"Spit it out, girl. You're making me nervous." Mercy Bea brings me back to the business at hand.

"Right, the will. Well . . ." I glance at my loyal crew. "You see . . ."

"Ain't got all day, Caroline."

Man, Mercy is pushy. "Jones left the Café to . . ." My voice bottoms out. "Me" is barely audible to my own ears.

"To who?" Mercy Bea's head tilts to one side. The fingernail drumming stops.

"Caroline, Jones left the Café to *you*?" Andy stoops over for a clear view of my face.

Our eyes meet. "Yes, Jones left the Café to me."

Tension and silence fall like hailstones. Hard and fast.

Mercy Bea fires up another cigarette right there in the middle of the kitchen. "Great day in the morning. You? Of all the . . . What in Sam Hill was he thinking?"

"Mercy Bea, take that outside." Andy points to her cigarette. "Caroline, do you want the Café?"

"I don't know." I grip my hands together. "There's this other job opportunity . . ."

"What job opportunity? What happens if you don't take the Café?" Mercy Bea exhales a stream of smoke in my direction.

"Well . . ." Oh, now, this is unfair. Why do I have to be the one? "Kirk will close it down, sell the property, and donate the proceeds to charity."

Andy's broad shoulders slump ever so slightly, and for the first time I see a break in his confidence. "Well, that's that." He slips the towel off of his shoulder and snaps the air. "Ten years. Not a bad run. Are the want ads lying round?"

"Un-freaking-believable." Mercy Bea's puffing and blowing smoke. "I protest the will."

"You can't protest the will, Mercy Bea. You ain't kin." Andy's big bicep tightens as he lifts the trash can, searching for the *Beaufort Gazette* classifieds.

"Now hold on, y'all. I haven't decided."

"There goes youngest young-son's basketball camp." Mercy-Bea-the-Positive unties her apron, clamping her red lips around the filter tip of her cigarette. "Since it's dead here, I'm going to run down to Panini's Café and Plums. See if they're hiring. Maybe I'll cross the line over to Paul Mulroney's."

Hear that, Caroline? Jones rolling over in his grave.

"Wait," I holler. "Did you *not* hear me? I haven't decided yet. Kirk is coming back next week for my decision."

"I'll be holding my breath." Mercy Bea balloons her cheeks with a backward glance and kicks open the kitchen screen door.

"Let her be." Andy sets the trash down. The want ads are rolled in his hand. "She needs to blow off steam."

"What about you?"

"Lost my head for a second. I'll find something to do in this town. Gloria's back isn't bothering her as much these days. She can go back to work until I get a job."

"I'll stick around, Caroline." Russell speaks for the first time. "I'll find work after we shut down."

"Shut down. Come on, y'all. I haven't decided." *Yet?* "Andy, what should I do?"

"Can't tell you." He taps his chest. "Only you know what's in your heart."

Mitch sits on the back porch when I pull up home Wednesday evening.

"Hey," I take the steps slowly, watching as he rises from the bench swing. "How long have you been here?"

"A few minutes." His easy stride is accented by his baggy shorts, oversized shirt, and flip-flops. "Well, maybe like thirty minutes. Okay, forty-five." He stops in front of me, smiling. "Actually, I have no idea. I dozed off."

With a laugh, I squeeze past him. Even now, he's electric and exciting. "Dork. Why didn't you come to the Café?" I unlock the kitchen door and head inside.

"I figured you'd be home sooner or later." He stands by the door, his blond hair loose about his face.

"Are you coming in or just holding open the door for the flies?"

There's a note in Posey's handwriting tacked to the fridge. *Gone shopping in Savannah. Dad & Posey.*

"Guess I'll sit for a bit." Mitch walks the rest of the way in, taking a seat at the table. "Does your dad still have the soda fridge? He kept the drinks so cold, ice chips floated on top."

"You know some things never change."

"Like you." His album-cover smile knocks at the closed, locked door of my heart.

Head: Go away.

Heart: Yeah, no one is hoooome.

"I've changed." *Haven't I?* Yes, definitely. How, I'm not sure, but surely I've changed. Yes, lookit, I'm ready to move way over to Spain and take a job I have no idea I can do. "Do you want root beer, diet, or what?" I shove open the mudroom door. The hinge is loose, so the bottom scrapes across the board floor. Dad's tackle keeps the room perpetually perfumed like rotten fish. "How long are you in town?"

"Root beer sounds good. Most of the summer. Taking some time for myself."

"Nice." Jerking on the leverlike handle of the old fridge, I take out two root beers. When I set his down in front of him, he says, "So, you and J. D. an item?"

Slowly, I pop open my drink. "We've gone out a few times." Talking to Elle and Jess about my love life is one thing. Talking to Mitch? Awkward.

"He's a decent guy."

"Decent? Kind of a bland thing to say about your old buddy."

Mitch grins. "Is it? I thought it was a compliment."

"What about you? Last time I saw the cover of *Country Weekly*, you were engaged to that new singer Mallory Clark."

Mitch pops the top off his root beer and slurps the foam oozing over the top. "We broke up six months ago."

Curling my leg under me, I sit in one of the kitchen chairs and sip my icy soda. "I'm sorry. Who's your woman now?"

Looking contemplative, he shakes his head. "Flying solo these days."

"Mitch O'Neal, running around Nashville untethered? What is the world coming to?"

"Confounding, isn't it? I'm working on a few life adjustments."

"You seemed different to me last night."

His exhale is half laugh, half regret. "Took God knocking me upside the head, but I'm waking up to some realities."

"Realities?" Mitch hasn't referenced God since before his Nashville days. I'm curious about the "realities" belonging to a distant, leave-me-to-my-business God. (Mind you, if there is a God. Jury is still out.)

Mitch fiddles with the root beer can, looking as if he can't formulate an answer. Finally, "Frank Sinatra's wrong. 'My way' isn't all it's cracked up to be."

"From where I sit, your way has worked well."

"Let's just say I'm a long way from the preacher's kid who walked an aisle and begged Jesus to live in his heart—whatever that meant. I just knew He was real."

"Isn't this what you wanted? Escape from the life of a small-town preacher's kid?"

He taps his finger over his heart. "Yes, but nine years later, it's left me pretty empty."

The emotion in his voice moves me. *Yeah, I know exactly what you mean.*

Hungry, we decide to cruise down Highway 21 to the Shrimp Shack for a shrimp burger. And, Mitch wants to drive Matilda. "It's been a while."

The Shrimp Shack is busy, and when Mitch steps out of the car, he creates a stir. Customers dining at the picnic tables, and those waiting to pick up, buzz, "Is that Mitch O'Neal?"

Beaufort County has changed so much, the newcomers are not used to seeing one of our favorite sons.

Mitch graciously signs a few autographs—he doesn't seem to mind this part of his reality—before we take our food to an outside picnic table and sit in the shade of a tall palm tree.

"All right, what's new with you?" My friend regards me with his sandwich between his teeth.

I pinch off the tip of a french fry. "Jones left the Café to me. You heard he died, right?"

He stops twisting open his water bottle. "Read about it online. Then mom called the day of his funeral. So, you weren't expecting to inherit the Café?"

"Are you kidding? I had absolutely no idea."

Mitch is always easy to talk to so I tell him the story of the Café and Hazel's Barcelona offer. He listens without interrupting, munching on his food like it's the best thing he's eaten in a while. The wind blows his hair away from his face. His cheeks appear leaner than the last time I saw him.

When my story is done, he asks, "Do you *want* to move to Barcelona and work for Carlos Longoria?"

His simple, upfront question requires a deep, philosophical answer. "I don't know."

"You feel responsible for the Café, don't you? I can see it in your eyes. You always did carry the weight of the world on your shoulders."

"Well, aren't you free with the grand sweeping generalities?"

"Am I wrong?"

"No." Smart aleck. He knows me too well. Even though our romance soured, our friendship remains. It was one aspect of our relationship I thought would keep us forever in love. "You try not feeling responsible when your mother abandons the family."

He wipes his hands with his napkin. "I'm not accusing you."

"I know." Absently, I dip a fry in a puddle of ketchup as my shrimp burger gets cold.

"What are you going to do?" He shoves his food basket to the center of the picnic table.

"I have until next Tuesday to decide."

"Translation, you have no idea."

Holding up my hand, I curl my fingers into an *O*. "Zippo."

"Barcelona . . . what a great city. But owning a lowcountry café can't be all that bad."

"The Frogmore needs a lot of tender loving care, Mitch. Money I don't have."

"I'd love to help you out, but—"

"No, no, no, I'm not asking."

"My label and I parted ways. And I just dumped a ton of cash to pay the bills and wipe out the mortgage on the Fripp Island house. I'm living light until I sign a new deal."

"Is that the reality God hit you with? Your label dropping you? After, what, five years?"

"One of the realities. Sales aren't what they were for my first two albums."

"So?"

"So . . ." His wry laugh is not airy, nor easy. "Record companies are in the business of making money. Not stringing along a party-too-hard artist whose album is tanking, while he barks about getting back to his roots."

Mitch, not electrifying the music charts? Unbelievable. "I'm sorry."

He stares off toward the road. "I brought in a bunch of songs they hated, including 'Yellow Line,' hoping to record like I used to before 'commercial appeal' took over my music."

"Their loss." I take a big bite of my shrimp burger. Even cold, it's fab. "What are you going to do?"

"Same as you."

"Decide next Tuesday?"

Daily Special

Friday, June 8

Frogmore Stew

Green Salad

Bubba's Buttery Biscuits

Scoop of Choc/Straw/Vanilla Ice Cream

Tea, Soda, Coffee

$7.99

9

Caroline, phone for you." Andy jiggles the kitchen's old wall receiver in the air.

It's Friday afternoon. Business is steady, but the Café feels old and tired to me. I feel old and tired. The Café dilemma is brutal. Do I fight to keep it open or call it a good half century and close down?

"Caroline, this is Melba Pelot over at the *Gazette*. How are you?"

The press. "I'm fine, Melba. What can I do for you?"

"Confirm a rumor." Her tone is airy, like this is no big deal, but I can tell when I'm being fished.

"What rumor?" I fall against the kitchen wall and stare out the back door toward the carriage house. It would be nice to live there, in town, close to all the downtown action.

"Did you inherit the Frogmore Café from Jones McDermott?"

"Yes, I did. How'd you—" *Ahh.* As Mercy Bea comes around the kitchen corner, humming, I know. Wonder who all she's told?

"What are your plans?" Over the line comes the *click, click* of Melba's keyboard.

Am I supposed to be honest with the press? I know Melba from around town, a *comeya* from Pennsylvania. "I'm still making my decision, Melba. There are conditions and terms to be considered."

"Really? Like . . ."

"Well—" Ignoring the big fat *nooo* in my gut, my mouth rattles on. "If I don't keep the Café for a certain amount of time, it will be shut down, sold, and the proceeds donated to charity."

"Really?" *Clickity, clickity, clickity.*

Instant regret fills my chest. Why did I tell her? "Melba, listen, this is between you and me. Off the record."

"Umm-hmm. Well, good luck with your decision."

"Melba, what are you—"

The dial tone speaks to me. That *comeya* has hung up on me.

Saturday I sleep in, tired from a long and somewhat emotional week. Andy and Mercy Bea are opening the Café today while Russell and I take closing.

Saturday business is schizophrenic—mind-numbingly boring to hectic. We've been managing to keep all the balls in the air without Jones, but we miss his extra set of hands in the kitchen. If I keep the Café, I'm going to have to hire help.

In a half-dreamy state, I hear Dad banging down the hall with his suitcase. Oh, it's wedding-trip day. I kick off the covers and swing open my bedroom door.

"Ready to go, Dad?" My shaggy hair slips over my eyes.

Dad looks back from the second stair down. "Sorry to wake you, Caroline."

"Off to get Posey?"

"Yeah, and I'm late."

I wrap my arms around my waist and lean against the banister, peering into the great room below. "Have a lovely wedding and a wonderful honeymoon."

Dad grins sheepishly "I'm planning on it." I do believe I'm blushing. "The hotel name and number is on the refrigerator door. Call if you need anything." He starts down the stairs, then pauses. "If the Mustang breaks down, drive the truck. Keys are on the kitchen hook."

I prop my chin in my hand. "Do you get tired of taking care of me?"

"Suppose I could ask the same of you." He stares off and away, clearing his throat. "I can't count the number of times you kept me this side of sane after your mama left. Those nights you watched TV with your old man instead of going out with friends . . ." Laughter gurgles from his chest. "Know what came to mind the other day? The summer you hired the lawn service. 'The dang grass is cutting my calves.'"

The memory is a soft favorite. "It became apparent no one in the Sweeney household could fire up the mower."

"Caroline, you all right? You don't seem yourself lately. I heard Mitch is back in town . . ."

Daddy knows me well. Watched me ride the Mitch roller coaster a few times. "No, it's not Mitch, Dad. Actually, I'm sort of dating J. D. Rand."

"J. D.? Didn't he have a crush on you in junior high?"

My sleepy eyes pop wide. "Where'd you hear that?"

"Careful around him, Caroline. I hear he's a ladies' man. He's—"

"Treating me very nice, Daddy. Don't worry. Go get married. I'm fine."

Why tell him about the Café and Barcelona? It'll only add to his load. And on his honeymoon. I can't be responsible for that.

"Well, guess you're grown. I'll leave you to your business." He takes the last of the stairs down, bumping his old suitcase the entire way. "See you in a week."

Once he leaves, I decide to take advantage of the morning and pon-der my options from high up in my live-oak sanctuary. It's a lovely but warm June day, fragrant with the scent rising from the dewed ground.

Between the ages of eight and nine, I begged Daddy to take us to church. All the kids in my class went.

Daddy refused. "Caroline," he'd say, pointing me to the front yard, "if you want to talk to some supreme being, climb the old tree. You've got more chance of communing with the Almighty out there than in some stuffy sanctuary."

It was the beginning of the Mama Years. When she started slipping away from us.

So I climbed the tree. Especially when Mama went missing or acted out—screaming with Daddy about her *horrendous* life—and I didn't want her to see me cry. The tree became my refuge. When I was fifteen Mama left us for good. I probably logged more hours in the tree than in school.

Now I sit here pondering how one man died and, in a way, changed my life.

If I refuse Jones's inheritance, I'll be the one responsible for the demise of the Frogmore Café. Reminiscing old-timers will shake their heads and click their tongues. "Remember the Frogmore Café? That Sweeney girl shut her down."

Okay, so they might not remember me as the one. But I will.

If I keep the Café and give up Barcelona. I'll forever be the one who passed up an incredible, amazing opportunity with Carlos Longoria. The envy of Hah-vard grads. Years from now, Carlos won't remember.

But I will.

"I need an answer."

Closing my eyes, I rest against the trunk and form a picture of the God Mitch claims slapped him with some reality. Oh, this Deity is frowning. I refuse to talk to someone who frowns.

I force the image in my head to smile—like Granddad Sweeney used to do when he'd tell me stories about growing up in the lowcountry, hunting quail on St. Helena Island. There, that's better.

Now, where's the peace I felt the other night when I decided to go for Barcelona? Maybe it's because the sun is out instead of the stars.

God, if You're real and can hear me, tell me what to do.

"We're busy?" I rush past Mercy Bea into the dining room, tying on my apron. Every stool at the counter is occupied and almost a third of the booths and tables.

"You got eyes. What do you see?" The ice she's frantically scooping clatters into four iced tea jars. "Russell came in early for a bite to eat and ended up clocking in. Did you see the paper?" She tips her head to the bottom counter shelf.

"No." I take over behind the counter. "Hey, Mr. Feinberg, I haven't seen you in a while. More coffee?"

Mr. Feinberg taps his cup with his fork. "Sure, Caroline, freshen her up."

I fill Mr. Feinberg's cup, then tend to the rich-looking, retired couple's iced teas and clear away a plate of half-eaten fries shared by three teen girls. When the lull comes, I sneak around the wall with the newspaper and stand inside the kitchen door.

Front page. Below the fold. A story on the Café with a then-and-now picture. The headline makes my heart jump: "Saying Good-bye to the Frogmore Café."

Answer to my early question? I should *not* be honest with the press. Small blurb in the Living Section, my eye, Melba Pelot.

I skim the article. Stuff about Jones, the history of the Café, and the old doctor's home. Then:

Sweeney, twenty-eight, who inherited the café from McDermott, is undecided about its future.

Town Councilman Davis Williams: "I'd hate for Beaufort to lose the Frogmore Café. It's true lowcountry, part of our rich heritage. And where else can hungry folks find Bubba's Buttery Biscuits?"

In the early '60s, McDermott defied Jim Crow laws by removing the separate eating sections for blacks and whites.

"It caused quite a stir," Williams said. "But if I heard Jones once, I heard him a hundred times. 'If I can share a foxhole in Korea with a colored, I can certainly share a meal in public. Jim Crow laws be damned.'"

I crinkle the paper to my chest. "Oh, Melba, why'd you do this to me?" It's one thing to shut down a beat-up old diner no one remembers. It's another thing to shut down a man's legacy.

Mercy Bea zips around the corner with her arms loaded with dirty dishes, almost crashing into me. "There you are. Mr. Feinberg is calling for you." She nods toward the paper. "Well, you done it now."

"I suppose."

"If you haven't made up your mind, there you go. Folks aren't going to want the Café to go away, Caroline." She drops her load on the counter for Russell to wash later.

"Yeah, well, then folks are going to have to find their way here to eat once in a while. Sentiment doesn't pay the bills."

I sound brave, but inside, I'm terrified.

Sunday I have the whole day off. After sleeping in late, doing a load of laundry, and surfing cable channels, I call J. D. to see if he wants to go fishing or down to the beach. I don't want to sit home all day, thinking, fretting.

"I'm working, babe," he says, "filling in for Lem Becket."

Babe? The intimate reference makes me feel googly. "Guess I'll talk to you later, then."

"I'm glad you called."

After a twittery good-bye, I absently dial Mitch's cell, but hang up before the first ring. Do I want to risk my securely closed heart doors by hanging out with his easy, familiar manner? Being good friends is what caused me to trip and fall in love in the first place. It was all Mitch and nothing but Mitch for far too long.

I smile at the memory. Hard to believe my friend and first love was voted by *People* magazine "The Man You Want to Be Stranded with on a Desert Island."

Oh, how wrong they are. If Mitch can't shower at least once a day, he considers it barbarian living.

No, if I'm stranded in the middle of the ocean on some two-by-four island, it best not be with Mitch. Not if I want to survive, anyway.

Heart: We should give him a call.

Head: No, we're moving on. Just like he's done.

Heart: But it's Mitch—best friends and all that.

Head: But it's Mitch—left us high and dry without so much as a "how do." Let the past be the past.

Heart: You . . . are no fun.

Head: Yeah, and when you get hurt and bruised, who has to relive it over and over? Me.

I dial Elle. "You up for a movie or something?"

"Meet me at my place. I'll drive. Last time I road-tripped with you, I was picking bugs out of my hair until the next morning. Really, you should get Matilda's top fixed, C."

"I'll get right on it." *Picking bugs. She's crazy.*

We choose a Drew Barrymore romantic comedy playing at the Plaza. During the drive over and in between buying tickets, popcorn, and large sodas, Elle rattles on about ways to find a good, decent, marriageable man, and when she pauses to breathe, I fill her in on Jones's will and the opportunity with Carlos Longoria.

She's appropriately stunned—"No, I didn't see Melba's article in the *Gazette*"—and gawks at me with wide, round eyes while nabbing a kernel of popcorn from the top of her ginormous bag. "Carlos Longoria. He's on the cover of *Forbes*, like, every other month. Look at me; I'm green with envy."

She whips her arm in front of my face. In the dim light of the movie theater, I can't make out the color of her skin, but I'm pretty sure it's not green. Elle is doing what she loves: photography and art. Owning an art gallery is her passion. A week—no, a day—as any businessman's apprentice and she'd pull out her hair. His too.

"Elle, O wise one, I'd love your thoughts on this." The theater lights fade to black and advertisements roll across the big screen.

"No-brainer. Barcelona."

"Really?" Why can't I have her confidence?

She turns slightly toward me. "It's your true Tarzan vine."

I snort-laugh. "Oh, brother, Elle, my Tarzan vine broke and dropped me face-first in the dirt."

Elle covers her laugh with the back of her arm, popcorn pinched between her fingers. "But you believed. You climbed that live oak, grabbed a handful of Spanish moss, and with a rebel yell, leaped."

"And hit the ground like a sack of dumb dirt."

"I've been waiting twenty years for you to believe in yourself like that again."

"Death would've been sweet relief that day." I slide down in the chair, propping my foot on the row in front of me.

The Tarzan experiment was a defining moment in my life. The

entire third-grade class watched me plummet twenty feet to the ground, finding it all too hilarious that I believed and preached Spanish moss to be as strong as Tarzan's vine. When I went home to Mama for sympathy and Band-Aids, she said, "Good grief, Caroline, don't you have a lick of horse sense?"

"Caroline, go to Spain," Elle whispers.

"Even if it means the Café closes?" In the light of the movie screen, I peer into my friend's eyes, searching for strength, for hope.

"Yes, even if it means the Café closes. Jones should've thought of that before he left the place to you. You've lived your life for everyone else far too long. It's Caroline time. What is your destiny?"

"What about J. D.?"

She twists toward me. "C, he's gorgeous, but he's not Barcelona-Carlos-Longoria gorgeous. If you were a serious couple or about to be engaged, maybe you'd have to reconsider. But you've been on four dates. If he's yours, he'll be here when you get back, *if* you come back."

"Did he have a crush on me in junior high?"

"The quiet, observing Caroline who sailed through puberty unscathed? Probably."

"Unscathed? I was voted worst dressed."

"Yeah, but to a junior high boy, that's cool."

"You had a mama at home."

"Right."

I sneak in one last question as the opening score fades for Drew Barrymore's dialogue. "What about Mitch being home? I mean, do you think it's some sort of sign?"

"You don't believe in signs."

"Exactly."

Daily Special

Tuesday, June 12

Stuffed Peppers (Pork or Beef)

Green Salad

Rice

Bubba's Buttery Biscuits

Cherry Pie à la Mode

Tea, Soda, Coffee

$7.99

10

Tuesday· D-Day.

Didn't sleep a wink. Last night I ended up at the city council meeting where they discussed the future of the Frogmore Café.

"The Café is part of our historical heritage," one man argued. "It's the council's job to watch out for our preservation."

After the meeting, I spent two hours in parking-lot consultations with the old-timers.

"Keep the Café, Caroline."

"Don't saddle the girl, Tom. She's too young. The place is run-down. She ain't got money to keep it up. Get rid of it."

But my favorite line of the night came from Darcy Day: "I never eat there. The food stinks."

At eight-oh-two this morning, the breakfast-club boys arrive. Their presence comforts my tilting emotions.

Dupree is at the ready with his opening bathroom story. "I've been irregular, if you know what I mean, so the wife gives me an enema. Now if that ain't something that will—"

"Dupree, stop, stop." Pastor Winnie slams his long hands on the table. "You've gone too far, friend. Enemas? No. I want to enjoy my breakfast. We've got to get you telling other stories. Ain't you got more going on in your life?"

"Sadly, no."

"Have you decided, Caroline?" Luke asks in his gentle manner.

"Not yet." Okay, here it comes—their opinions and advice. I brace myself. But nothing. Instead, they study the table menus from which they never order.

Kirk shows up at the Café just after ten. His rumpled dark suit is replaced with white golf attire, wrinkled but clean.

"Hitting the links today?" I pour him a cup of coffee as he sets up his office in the back booth again.

"Drove down last night with a couple of buddies. Got a room at the Beaufort Inn." He checks his watch. "We tee off at eleven."

Andy and Mercy Bea hover around the kitchen door. The breakfast-club boys linger, nursing their fiftieth cup of coffee. Dupree has worn a new path in the old carpet to the men's room.

"What's your decision?"

Setting the coffeepot on the table, I slide into the booth across from him, gazing out the window to my right for a long, trembling second. "As much as I loved Jones, and appreciate what he must have been trying to do for me and the Café, I cannot accept it, Kirk."

"All right." He adjusts his slipping glasses with the tip of his fancy pen. I wring my hands.

"Caroline, Jones didn't mean to torture you with this. Stand by your decision."

"Then what did he mean, Kirk? Hmm? Tell me? You can't leave a girl your life's work and expect her to not agonize over it. Do you realize the Café was the center of discussion at the city council meeting last night?"

"Caroline, calm down. Go to Barcelona. Forget about the Café. People will live. Life goes on. Change happens." He pops open his brief-case. "But listen, here's an option to consider. Hang on to the Café through probate, *then* sell it. The guys I'm golfing with today like to invest in *projects*."

"Then what, Kirk? The job in Barcelona will be gone."

Kirk leans over the table. "You'd have enough money to vacation anywhere in the world."

"Again, then what? Call Paris Hilton for a shopping spree? Money isn't going to give me a future."

"Then sign." He taps the papers he handed me. "Here . . . and here."

Taking the pen, I pause to read the form. Sure enough, I'm handing it all over to Kirk for him to close down. I breathe out. *Am I sure?*

Another gaze out the window. Through the trees, I spot the back of Paul Mulroney's bistro. Fifteen years ago, he and Jones used to compete for business, running cheesy radio spots with stupid jingles that got stuck in our heads. Over time, Jones grew complacent and lost his will to fight.

I flip the pen back and forth against my fingers. *Yes, I'm sure.* Breathing deep, I sign. Five seconds later, it's done.

The Frogmore Café is no more.

The others respect my privacy after Kirk leaves, letting me sit alone in the back booth, fighting an odd emptiness.

Where's the relief of making a decision? The excitement of what lies ahead? Two minutes ago, I felt confident. Now, it's like I spent my last dollar for a stupid fairground toy when I could've stopped for cheese fries on the way home.

The breakfast-club boys finally mosey over. "You let her go, didn't you?" Luke pats my shoulder.

"Yes."

They stare off in different directions, coughing, hacking, and sniffing until Dupree claps his hands on Luke and Winnie's shoulders. "Well, it was a good twenty years, boys."

My stomach knots. My skin is both clammy and hot. "Dupree, Luke, you understand, right? Pastor Winnie?"

Winnie juts out his chin and rolls back his shoulders. "S-sure we do. Sure." His sad expression tells me otherwise.

They stand around for another awkward moment; then Dupree remembers he has to take his wife "somewhere."

So, this is what it feels like to be a heel. Not that I ever really wanted to know. But I can't keep the Café. When will a man like Carlos Longoria ever want to work with me again?

As I head for the kitchen, I spot Mercy Bea on the other side of the waiter's station, wiping her eyes.

"Hey—"

"Eight years, ended, just like that, with a flash of a hundred-dollar pen."

"It was the right thing to do."

"For who? You?" She storms off.

Ho, boy. Mustering my courage, I hunt for my big-hearted cook. "Andy?"

No answer. I check the pantry. "You here?" Still no answer. The kitchen feels cold and abandoned. Regret strangles my heart from some dark inner place.

In the office, I flop down in the chair, which rocks back with a jerk, almost dumping me to the floor. This chair I won't miss, nor the clutter and dust.

I glance at the clock. Ten thirty.

Why isn't Andy banging around in the kitchen?

I get up and stand in the doorway. The Café is spooky and silent—as if no one ever lived here, laughed, or loved here.

The foundation isn't moaning, nor the eaves creaking.

My heartbeat drums in my hears. "Andy?"

The electricity buzzes, then browns out.

I can't do it. I can't.

Running through the dining room, I jerk open the front door so hard the Christmas bells crash against the glass. "Kirk." *I've changed my mind. Wait.* I dash to the curb, looking both ways down Bay Street. But the lawyer's Lexus is long gone. "Kirk."

Phone. I'll call him. I pat my pockets. Where's my phone? A dash back inside, tripping on the carpet by the wait station, then crashing into a lowboy.

In the office, I jerk my backpack from the bottom desk drawer.

"Kirk, Kirk, Kirk," I mutter, searching my cell-phone book for his number. Dang, it's not in there. I launch Outlook and scroll through the address book. "Kirk Harris, Kirk Harris . . . there." My hands shake as I dial.

7 . . . 6 . . . 3 . . .

It takes forever to ring—I could've rocketed to the moon—and bounces right away to voice mail. Sweat breaks out under my arms.

"Kirk, it's Caroline. I-I've changed my mind. I-I can't close down the Café. It's not too late, right? Please tell me it's not too late. It's only been a few measly minutes." Tears fizz in my eyes. "W-we can talk about selling. To the right person. You know, when the time is right. After the probate. Kirk. Please. You should've seen *their* faces."

The message beeps and cuts me off. I press End and toss my phone to the desk.

To: Hazel Palmer
From: CSweeney
Subject: The Frogmore and me
Dear Hazel,
I tried to do it. Let the Café go. But I couldn't. As soon as I signed the papers and the lawyer left, I felt sick. Hazel, you should've seen their faces—the breakfast-club boys, Andy and Mercy Bea—the expression of abandonment. I've seen it on Henry's face a dozen times. Whoever said responsibility was fun or easy? But it's honorable, right? After probate, I can look into selling it. Who knows, maybe I'll take to the Café life.

Hazel, don't be mad. Please, give my apologies to Carlos. I am grateful he wanted to work with me. But, in the end, I felt the old Frogmore deserved better than being sold at auction.

Regretfully, Caroline.

At four thirty, I'm alone in the Café. Kirk hasn't returned my call and I'm pleading with the stars that he didn't file the papers on his way to the golf course.

Andy, Mercy Bea, and Russell finished their side work and left without saying good-bye, and frankly, I don't blame them. I cost them their jobs.

The Café rebukes me now with moaning and creaking. The old AC bangs and rattles.

"All right, Caroline," I coax myself. "What's done is done. Stand by your decision."

So, I finish the day's deposit with my eyes welling up and blurring the numbers. Before shutting down the computer, I check to see if Hazel e-mailed. She didn't, but there's an incoming from Sheree over at the Water Festival.

To: CSweeney
From: ShereeLambert@bftwater...
Subject: Water Festival Raft Race
Caroline,
Saw the Gazette *article. If you're actually the new owner of the Café,*
think about pulling together a team for the Raft Race. The applica-
tions are due the end of June so you have a little bit of time. You need
eleven people.

   The raft race is well attended, fun, and would be great public-
ity. Might be a way to get the Frogmore Café back in everyone's
mind.

   Back in the day, Jones was a big supporter of the Festival.
   Think about it. I've attached the application.
      Sheree

The Water Festival raft race? Who's she kidding? Eleven people?
Where would I . . . A grin springs reluctantly to my lips. Actually, the
race would be fun. Too bad I didn't get to Kirk in time.

I click Reply.

Thanks, Sheree. I'll think about it.
   Caroline.

"Anyone here?"

I bolt out of the desk chair. "Hello?"

"Caroline?" A muffled voice calls from the dining room.

"Who's here?" Passing the prep table, I snatch a spatula for protec-
tion. Just in case. "Kirk?"

Yep, it's Kirk, at the back booth, rear in the air. I'd recognize his
wrinkles from any angle.

"What are you doing?"

His head pops up. "Oh, Caroline, have you seen my phone? I dropped it somewhere."

"So that's why you didn't return my call."

"Aha, here it is." Kirk dives below the table, retrieving his RAZR phone. "What call?"

"I changed my mind." The words fire out of my mouth. "I don't want to close down the Café."

Kirk glances up from checking his missed calls. "Are you sure?"

"Y-yes, for now. Like you said, after probate I can see about selling, right? But I can't let you put her on the auction block."

He flattens the phone to his ear, holding up his finger, listening. Then, clapping his phone shut, he walks right past me. "I'm late. Got to go."

"Kirk," I holler, incredulous. "Did you hear me?"

"Yes, you changed your mind."

"And?"

"I figured you would." He grins. "You wear your heart on your sleeve, Caroline. I'll shred the documents when I get to the office."

"Thank you, Kirk. Thank you." I rub my bare arms.

"Listen, just so you have a mental back door, I told my golfing buddies about this place. They love Beaufort and are keen on investing here. It's the new retirement haven. And, Caroline, their pockets are very deep."

"Really. Okay, then, so"—I fan out my arms—"the Café is mine."

He jerks his thumb over his shoulder. "And the carriage house. Have fun."

Daily Special

Congratulations, Caroline!

Monday, June 18

Country-Fried Steak

Taters and Gravy

Bacon-Wrapped Green Beans

Salad

Bubba's Buttery Biscuits

Sweet Caroline Pie

Tea, Soda, Coffee

$8.99

11

Dad and Posey arrived home from the Bahamas Sunday with very big smiles and beautiful tans. I like what I see in Dad's eyes—love. It gives me hope.

After shocking them with the I-own-the-Café-and-gave-up-Barcelona story, I revived them with CPR and asked if they'd like to help me move into the carriage house Monday evening.

"Newlyweds don't need the man's grown daughter hanging around."

Monday, Mitch calls while we're packing up to see "what's going on," so I tell him to come to the house. "We need your truck."

Since Mrs. Atwater cleaned and spiffed up the carriage house and left most of Jones's wood and leather furniture, all I have to do is haul over my clothes, personal items, and the antique armoire I promise I'm going to restore someday. We load Mitch's truck with clothes, books, and *stuff,* then he and Posey head over while I take one final pass of my room.

"Caroline?" Dad calls upstairs. "I've got the armoire roped to the truck bed. You ready?"

"Yes, ready." At twenty-eight, I'm moving out on my own for the first time. It's a lovely, long-overdue, frightening experience. Perhaps even more than taking on the responsibility of the Café.

Yet, as I take in my faded yellow room, I wish little girls never grew up.

"Your mama promised to paint the room pink with blue clouds, remember? And buy a lacy canopy bed." Turning, I see Dad in the doorway.

"Don't forget the pony galloping out of the corner." I sweep my hand from right to left across the room. "Because all princesses need a pony."

He smiles. "All princesses need a pony."

Since she died four years ago, Dad and I haven't said more than ten words about her. "Why didn't she do it?"

Crossing his arms, he leans his shoulder against the door frame. "To spite me. Your tenth birthday was coming up, and I pressured her to fix up your room like she promised. Thought it'd be the perfect present. So we sent you and Henry to your grandparent's for a weekend with the plan of painting your room. But Trudy spent most of the time . . . I don't know . . . frittering. She was in one of her moods. Late Saturday, I got on her about it, said I'd do whatever she needed me to do to get it done. She exploded, said some choice words, and disappeared. I woke up Sunday morning in the recliner to her banging around up here. She'd painted the room yellow and was putting together that crummy daybed."

"When we came home and I walked into my room, I knew. No blue clouds or pony would ever happen. I climbed the tree and cried."

Dad clears his throat. "I'm sorry, Caroline. Your mom and I fought for weeks about it, but I had to let it go. Blue clouds and ponies didn't seem worth the price of our relationship or what it was doing to you kids. I would've painted it myself if I had the talent. Trudy could work wonders with a paintbrush."

I look over at him. "I'll take my yellow room any day as long as you're my dad. Talent or no talent. You stayed when she didn't."

"I wasn't the best dad, but I did love you kids."

"It was obvious." I check the closet one last time. Empty. "So, Dad, on another note, do you have any idea why Jones left me the Café?"

He absently shakes his head. "Wish I did. When I was growing up, Dad and Mama didn't socialize with him. But after she died, Dad started his regular Friday nights down at the Frogmore."

"I wonder if I'll ever know. Ready? Mitch and Posey are probably there by now."

Dad stops me in the hallway. "Caroline—" He presses his fist to his mouth, clearing his throat. "I want you to know, you were a source of comfort to me, and to your granddad. I never said thanks."

Behind my eyes, a bottle fills with unshed tears. "No need. I only did what I saw my daddy doing."

Moving my armoire into the carriage house is like wedging Drizella's fat, corny foot into Cinderella's glass slipper.

Ugly. Impossible.

"Caroline, are you sure you want this thing?" Dad mops his brow with the edge of his T-shirt sleeve. "Looks to me like the bedroom has a big closet."

Mitch peers around the beat-up, dried-out oak armoire from outside the carriage house. The large wardrobe is stuck in the front doorway. "We could leave it here and hope someone steals it."

Propping my hands on my hips, I sigh. "Bunch of whiners. Just move it in, please."

Meanwhile, Posey works in the kitchen, putting away the glasses and dish towels she had left over from combining her life with Dad's. "All this avocado and rust decor is giving me seventies flashbacks, Caroline."

"Well, Mitch," Dad says, with a sad, sorry twang of resignation, "let's do this. One last shove."

"All right. Like birthing a baby."

With a low, growling grunt, Mitch shoves the wardrobe through the door, scraping off the sunflower antique-brass doorknobs. They fire like shiny bullets across the room.

"Hey, those cost me $9.88."

Dad doesn't call *whoa*, so Mitch just keeps driving forward.

"Mitch, Mitch, Mitch . . ."

Dad stumbles. The armoire tilts. I dart to catch it, but it crashes to the polished hardwood floor.

Posey scurries in from the kitchen. "What is going on in here? Land sakes." She anchors her fist against her hips, a dish towel dangling from her grip. "Why didn't you bring it in through the French doors?" We look beyond the kitchenette. "Open them up and you can drive in a tank."

Well, a-hem, now we know.

It's late. A tick or two before eleven o'clock. If I had known pizza tasted this good in my own place, I'd have moved years ago. At least considered it.

But today I've taken the first steps toward becoming the person I'm meant to be. And contrary to my lifelong belief, I'm not the Elmer's Glue of the Sweeney family.

Who knew?

The ornery armoire is backed up against the wall between the front door and the kitchen. "We're not getting this thing through that bedroom door," Dad surmised earlier, mentally measuring the width of the doorway against the size of the armoire.

We decided it looked just lovely and knobless in the great room.

The carriage house is just right for a single girl. Or an old bachelor like Jones. A large bedroom and a bath off the great room, opposite the kitchen. And a smaller room that doubles as an office/den/guest room. Beside the kitchen is a built-in dinette, then a set of double French doors out to a covered brick patio.

It's not Barcelona, but it's better than my ten-year-old-girl's bedroom.

Sitting next to me on the western-style leather couch, Mitch flips through my old photo albums, snickering, munching on the last slice of pizza.

In high school, I went through a phase. For two years, I shot everything that crossed my path with a Nikon F3. I'd signed up for a photography elective with Elle, dug out Mama's old camera, and, I don't know, went berserk. Maybe I was desperate to capture my fleeting youth, or just trying to tick people off, but I was obsessed with snapping pictures.

"Wild Wally . . . and that orange jersey." Mitch taps one of the pictures, his laugh rattling around in his chest. "He wore that thing every day for months to win a bet with Sam Evans."

I wrinkle my nose. "How could I forget? He was so mad when his mom made him wash it after the first two weeks."

"In every picture, Caroline, all football season, he's wearing that freaking orange jersey. Even under his pads. When the opposing team's defensive linemen got a whiff of Wally—" Mitch falls against the couch cushions, slaps his leg, and laughs, laughs, laughs.

I grin and snicker a bit, trying to laugh along, but after a few seconds I admit, "Guess you had to be there."

"Man, I've got to get with Wild Wally." He flips to another page and laughs all over again.

"He'd love to hang out, I'm sure." It's a good moment for me; to see

Mitch relaxed and reminiscing. He'd gotten egotistical and intense for a while. My eyes slip closed and I hear the photo album being set back on the built-in bookshelf next to the fireplace. "Barcelona will always be there, Caroline."

"Not for me. Not with this opportunity. But I couldn't—it's weird, Mitch, inheriting a man's life."

"I can imagine. For what it's worth, I think you did the right thing."

"It's worth a lot. And for now, I stand by my indecision." Opening my eyes, I sit forward. "So, tell me, what happened in Paris? What happened to make you see the mysterious yellow line?"

His lips form a half smile as he settles back against the couch. "A fan threatened to blow up the hotel we were staying in. At first we thought it was a terrorist attack." He stares off. "Caroline, you can't know your heart, your fears, until . . . Thinking terrorism had found me changed me. I thought I was so invincible. While the police investigated, I did a lot of praying. Turns out the threat came from some insane fan wanting to get close to me."

"Oh my gosh, Mitch. What happened to her? Very John Lennon, by the way."

"Never envied the man. They arrested her, which made me feel both relieved and sad. She was completely whacked, but I felt compassion for her. She risked her life for a man she didn't know—a flawed, weak, broken man."

He looks over. Something flickers between us, eye to eye. *Oooh, weird vibe.*

"Hey, don't sell yourself short, Mitch. I see why you felt for her. You always did have a tender heart."

"I've done a lot of talking to God, examining my life." His confession is humbly intense.

"What did you conclude?"

"Several things." In one graceful move, he's off the couch, carrying the empty pizza box to the kitchen. "One, I'm too far away from my faith. Two, the landscape of my life is barren and brown. Too many parties, too many women—" He stuffs the box in the trash with vigor. "My career became my God—my name, my fame, Jesus who?"

"Aren't you being hard on yourself? I mean, God's got a world to run and all. Maybe you're not as high up on His list as you think."

"No, Caroline, just the opposite. I'm way higher on His list than I wanted to be."

I draw my knees to my chin. If such a loving Deity exists, it would be nice if He's like Mitch describes. "What else did you conclude?"

"That I owed a few people apologies. Dad for one. I created such bad blood between us that in nine years he's never come to one of my shows."

"I didn't realize."

He lowers himself to one of the kitchen chairs. "Then there's you." The bass of his voice vibrates in my chest. *Oooh, the vibe again.*

"Mitch, you don't owe me—"

"Yes, I do." For a split second, our eyes meet; then he looks down. "I'm sorry, Caroline. I made a lot of promises to you that I wanted to keep, but wasn't man enough to follow through on."

"It's okay. We were young—"

"Stop. Don't let me off the hook. I told you I loved you, I wanted to marry you. We were going to buy a farm in Hendersonville or Franklin county, raise horses and kids, hobnob with the country music elite. Not one promise was kept."

"But don't you see, those are pie-in-the-sky dreams. We didn't really—"

"Are you telling me you didn't believe what we said?"

My eyes tear up, and I can't look at him. "I believed."

Mitch rejoins me on the couch. "I'm sorry I broke your heart."

"You think highly of yourself, Mitch." I yank one of the throw pillows to my lap and fiddle with the short fringe.

"Well, then I'm sorry I made a bunch of promises I didn't even try to keep. Please forgive me."

"I told you, there's nothing to forgive."

"Caroline, stop throwing up walls. Say you forgive me."

I slap him with the pillow. "I forgive you."

"Thank you. Geez, you're getting more stubborn with age."

With the clearing-the-air behind us, we sit side by side for a long, contemplative moment. "I'm glad you're home."

He looks over at me, his blue eyes full of light. "Come to church Sunday."

My heart pulsates. "What? I have a church. The old live oak."

"Caroline, I'm serious. Come with."

"Why? Mitch, don't tell me one terrifying moment now makes you want to save the world."

"No, only you."

"In twelve years of friendship, you never once asked me to church."

His gaze is intentional and intimate. "I'm asking now."

Daily Special

Thursday, June 21

Ham w/ Pineapple

Potatoes, Mashed or Fried Green Beans

Bubba's Buttery Biscuits

Cherry or Pluff Mud Pie

Coffee, Tea, Soda

$6.99

12

To: CSweeney
From: Hazel Palmer
Subject: Re: The Frogmore and me
Caroline,
Your decision is sound. I'm disappointed for you to have to pass on such a rare, great opportunity. But, I understand, I do. Now, to tell Carlos. Do you suppose I can tell him you were in a tragic accident? No, no, of course not.

On a personal note, I was looking forward to dropping movie lines in conversation and Saturday movie night. I quoted a great line from A Few Good Men *the other day—not one flicker of recognition. Blah.*

All the best with the Café.

Love, Hazel

CFO, SRG International, Barcelona

P.S. Have a date. Fernando. Will let you know.

Midafternoon Thursday, while decluttering Jones's office—I reckon the new owner won't mind—Andy comes in with an inventory sheet. "We're low on everything."

I blink away the dust cleaning has stirred. "I'll get to it when I finish filling this trash bag."

Andy snatches up the two already filled. "I'll cart these out. How's the money?"

"Not great." What did Jones want with all these broken oven knobs? "But I have a credit card and I'm not afraid to use it."

Andy chuckles. "Caroline, thank you. I appreciate you saving the Frogmore." He shuffles around. "Never realized how attached I was to this place. Jones hired me when I was really down on my luck, about to lose my family."

"Andy, I never knew." The weight of responsibility sinks deeper.

He's off to the dumpster. A second later Mercy Bea pokes her head around the door. "Mrs. Carrington is here."

"Who?" Menus from nineteen eighty-four? *Jones, what in the world?* Into the trash they go.

"Reese Carrington." Mercy Bea snatches a clipboard off the wall and points to a name and number. "Caroline, the Carrington birthday party."

"What . . . Oh, crud, when is it?" Truth is, I never intended to be the one hosting the Carrington birthday party.

Mercy Bea passes me the clipboard. "Not this Sunday, the next. July first."

A shadow falls over Jones's old event schedule and I look up to see a regal Southern woman in the doorway. "Mrs. Carrington." I wipe my hands on my apron and motion for her to come in. "Please, have a seat."

She perches on the edge of the office guest chair. "Thank goodness, someone is here. I've been trying to call for weeks. *Weeks.*"

Mercy Bea shoots me a good-luck glance as she hustles out.

"Weeks. Really? I'm sorry we've—"

"And you are?" Mrs. Carrington demands in a clipped tone.

"Caroline Sweeney, ma'am." I sit tall like a good third grader, hands clasped on top of the desk.

"Caroline." Mrs. Carrington clutches her rich-leather handbag. "I heard a horrible rumor. Is the Frogmore closing?"

"No, ma'am. We're staying open."

She exhales, resting her manicured hand at her throat. "Thank goodness. Now, who's in charge since Jones passed on?"

I pop a smile and motion to myself.

"You?"

"I'm the new owner, yes." The confession already feels familiar.

"Oh, dear," she mutters. "Well, I suppose I have no choice." She snaps open her handbag and produces a list. "As you know, my husband's family is coming in from the four corners of the earth to surprise his mother for her ninetieth birthday. And *against* my better judgment, we booked the party at this establishment. Apparently, my father-in-law proposed to Mother Carrington here seventy years ago."

"The Frogmore Café wasn't around seventy years ago, Mrs. Carrington." I launch Outlook. I'm going to need a Task List.

"It was a boarding house. My father-in-law lived here after being discharged from the Marines. Now, are we on for July first or not? And don't you dare say no. It's way too late to rebook."

"We're on for the first, Mrs. Carrington. Sunday evening," I peek at the clipboard and type "6:00" into Outlook.

"Now, what food do you have planned? Shrimp is a must, naturally. My mother-in-law adores shrimp."

"Yes, yes, we've planned several shrimp dishes." At least we have now. I type "lots-o-shrimp."

Andy appears with a large slice of cake. "Here you go, Miz Carrington. Would you like coffee?"

"Oh, lovely, yes. One Splenda, two creams."

I mouth a thank-you. When Andy returns with Mrs. Carrington's coffee, he hands her a menu. "Anything on the menu, Mrs. Carrington, we can make for your party."

The menu. Of course. Mental slap to the forehead. "Yes, Mrs. Carrington, pick anything from the menu. Did Jones negotiate a price with you?"

"Four hundred dollars."

"Okay, and how many people?"

"Fifty-eight."

"Four hundred? For everything?" One quick glance up at Andy and I read his thoughts: we're going to eat it on this one. Four hundred dollars for fifty-eight people to eat lots-o-shrimp?

Mrs. Carrington is *um*-ming over the cake. "This cake is divine. Add it to the menu."

I type in "Andy's butter cream cake." "Mrs. Carrington, Andy makes a wonderful—"

"Caroline." Mercy Bea barges in. "You're needed in the dining room. Pardon the interruption. Mrs. Carrington, do you remember me? I went to school with your girl, Sharon."

"No, I don't recall—"

"Mercy Bea Hart."

"Right." Mrs. Carrington has no idea who is standing in front of her.

Mercy Bea looks stricken. "Caroline, Kirk's out there with a couple of bright-teethed, tanned dudes."

I make a face. "Did you tell him I'm busy?"

"Yes, but he said he only needs you for a sec."

Of all the . . . "Excuse me, Mrs. Carrington."

Mercy Bea falls in stride with me, growling, "I only spent the night at the Carringtons' house a dozen times. Snotty, snobbity snob."

Sure enough, in the middle of the dining room stands Kirk with two men. Bright-toothed and tanned like Mercy Bea said. "Kirk, hey."

"Ah, there you are. Caroline, I'd like you to meet some friends of mine. Dale Westmoreland and Roland Hill, otherwise known as Buzz Boys, Inc."

"Nice to meet you." Handsome, probably in their midthirties, the Buzz Boys reek of old Charleston money.

"We came down to golf again and take in the town," Kirk says. "Dale wanted to stop by the Café."

"Great place." Dale rubs his palms together. "Buzz Boys is looking to invest in restaurants. This looks to be the right size for starters."

"O-oh, okay. Sure." What do I say here?

"They know it's all tentative," Kirk says, "and we have to wait for probate to close. But they wanted to check it out."

The front door's Christmas bells jingle. Miss Jeanne enters. Like the breakfast-club boys, she's right on time. Three fifteen. A sense of satisfaction settles over me. Keeping the Café is a good thing, for now, if only for the breakfast-club boys and Miss Jeanne. And the crew.

"Hey, Miss Jeanne, how are you this afternoon?"

"Sore. Started tap classes."

"Tap classes? Goodness."

"Ain't getting any younger."

Back to Kirk, who's leaning into me, motioning to the Buzz Boys, who are studying the Vet Wall. "Deep pockets, very deep."

"O-oh, well, yahoo." I admit, I feel slightly jerked around. A few days ago I had to either take the Café or close it down. The decision kept me awake at night. I left a good friend in the lurch. Finally, I've made peace with my Beaufort life, and now Kirk is bringing around these tire kickers.

He reads my expression through his dark-rimmed glasses. "No one's asking you to sign on the dotted line. They're just investigating."

Dale pokes his head into my powwow with Kirk. "The Vet Wall is incredible. The place is everything you said, Kirk. Charming, homey, but—" He sniffs as Mercy Bea passes with a basket of Bubba's Buttery Biscuits for Miss Jeanne. "Needs a lot of work."

Roland walks the length of the dining room. "What's capacity? Sixty, seventy?"

"Seventy." They're browsing and Mrs. Carrington waits. "Kirk, I have a customer in the office."

"Fine, we'll just look around. I'll call you later."

"Nice to meet you, Dale and Roland."

However, Mrs. Carrington didn't miss me. She's in a lively conversation with Andy about the changing shrimping industry. The cook has her completely charmed.

"Sorry for the interruption." I take my seat behind the desk.

"We got the menu planned out, Caroline." Andy hands me a slip of paper with a got-you-covered grin. "She's going with Jones's popular mushroom casserole, batter-fried wings and sauces, pot roast, and chicken casseroles . . . Well, you see it all there. Some platters of veggies and cheese. Of course, shrimp in all forms."

Yes, I see the more-than-four-hundred-dollars' worth of food here. *Should I tell her?*

Mrs. Carrington addresses me. "This is a huge event, Caroline. I cannot stress enough that everything must go perfectly. The family is spending a great deal of money to be here."

"She said Mr. Carrington's people have names on the Vet Wall," Andy says.

"Really, now."

"Winston's parents ate at the Café once a week for thirty years until his father died. His mother hasn't been here since, but she speaks of it so often, my husband insisted we hold the party here."

Mrs. Carrington's words sober me. This is not a casual hey-ho-it's-your-birthday-hope-it's-happy kind of party. This is celebrating a woman's life. I reach for a wadded napkin tucked under the computer monitor and pat my brow.

"All of Claire's—that's my mother-in-law—children, grandchildren, and great-grandchildren will be here, plus her sister and brother, and their children." Mrs. Carrington passes me a list of names. Andy reads over my shoulder. "We'd like nametags *printed* out. Some of the second cousins haven't seen each other in years."

Nametags? Printed? I look around at the printer on top of the filing cabinet. Is it a Dell or HP? I can't tell under the three inches of dust. "We'll take care of it, Mrs. Carrington." I add it to the to-do list.

"Winston's sister insists on bringing one of her atrocious cakes, so, Andy, make sure we have plenty of your divine masterpiece. Caroline, we'll need candles, a cutting knife, and cake plates, of course."

"Right." More entering on the to-do list. "Will you want to come early to decorate?"

"Yes, yes, of course. Around four would be perfect."

"You can count on the Frogmore Café, Mrs. Carrington."

She stands tall, handing me a check for four hundred dollars. "See to it."

13

Sunday morning J. D. rides with me toward Mossy Oak and Beaufort Community Church. We bob our heads to the rhythm of Keith Urban on the radio.

Oh, wait . . . I reach out and snap it off. Maybe I shouldn't listen to Keith on the way to God's place.

"Hey, what are you doing? I like that song." J. D. says. He's sporty and handsome in a cream-colored Polo and navy Dockers.

"I don't know. Shouldn't we be humming a hymn or something? Like the first verse of 'Amazing Grace.'"

J. D. flashes me his charming smile. "No, we don't have to sing a hymn." All right, he should know; he grew up Baptist. "Relax, Caroline, it's church. Not the IRS."

As we arrive, the last of the front-porch talkers are wandering inside. I slip my hair out of its ponytail, smooth out the tangles with a quick brush, then fix my lip gloss.

J. D. walks around to open my door. Taking my hand, he escorts me forward, but at the church steps, I jerk him back. "I'm nervous. It's been ten years since I went to church—some youth event with Elle."

The brawny deputy hooks his arm around me. "Caroline, you don't have to go in. We can cut out and drive down to Hilton Head. Walk on the beach and eat at some old dive by the water."

"Dive by the water? In Hilton Head?" I turn to the church doors. "I promised Mitch."

"I appreciate that, Caroline, but skipping Sunday church when you haven't been in over a decade isn't going to stun anyone. You can change your mind."

"I know—"

Actually, it's not changing my mind that's bothering me right now. It's my hypocrisy. Most of the time, I doubt God. He's the superior of the make-believes: Santa, the Easter Bunny, and Superman.

Yet, here I come, stepping into His territory.

"Y'all coming in?" An older gentleman in a suit and bolo tie stands in the door. "Service is starting."

"Um, yeah—" I peer into J. D.'s eyes. "Hilton Head will always be there."

"Hey, it's your decision. I'll do whatever you want to do."

Mitch signals to us from the back pew. "You made it. Hey, J. D." He doesn't seem put off that I brought a guest.

"Look at you. Suit and tie." I nudge Mitch with my elbow. "My, my."

He hands me a bulletin. A thick, worn black Bible rests on his knee. "Is this seat okay or do you want to go up front by Mom?"

Surely he jests. "This seat is just fine."

J. D. slips his arm around me as I face forward. My legs feel feeble, and my insides quiver as if I'm cold.

Mitch eyes my stiff posture. "Are you planning on running?"

"Maybe." *I know, I know, I'm sitting on the edge of the seat, stiffer than a dead coon. I'm a fish out of water here.*

Up front, an overly gregarious woman in a *really* green suit welcomes us all to Beaufort Community. "Just a few reminders. Wednesday evening is potluck for the community. Be sure to invite—"

A hand touches my shoulder. I swerve around to see the dark, tender face of Pastor Winnie. "Good to see you here, Caroline."

I clap my hand over his. "Hey, Pastor Winnie."

"Mitch, son, good to see you home." Pastor Winnie approves of him with a wink and shuffles down the aisle to a front row seat. He whispers to Luke, who turns around, scouting the back pew. When he spies me, his expression brightens.

In the surprisingly peaceful atmosphere of the church, I discover how much the breakfast-club boys feel like family.

A few rows up and over I spot Elle with her family. She has four sisters. Three are married with kids. Throw in her folks and they claim two whole pews.

The lady in the green suit is still talking, walking across the platform. "Do we have any visitors today?"

Tucking in close to J. D., I do my best to scoot down from view. *This* is a good reason to never go to church. They want to embarrass a person. *Stand if you're a visitor. Walk the aisle if you're a sinner.*

Glancing up at Mitch, I shake my head and mouth, "Don't say a word."

Technically, I'm not a visitor. I've been here before.

"No visitors?" Green Suit sounds disappointed.

In the next second, a familiar voice echoes all over the sanctuary. "I'd like to introduce a visitor."

Oh, no. Andy. I slide down another inch and cover my face with the bulletin. "Does the whole city attend Beaufort Community?"

Mitch whispers. "They heard you were coming."

"My boss is here. Caroline Sweeney." Andy announces.

J. D. nudges me to sit up, and with a glare, I do. Andy beams like it's all good.

"Welcome, Caroline." The lady points to me. People look. The men next to me snicker.

"Tomorrow, Andy is *so* fired."

We sing a bunch of songs I've never heard before, but rather enjoy. The song leader is a young kid with long hair and lots of multicolored wristbands.

When the singing is over, Pastor O'Neal takes the stage. He's an older form of Mitch, handsome but with more seasoned, kind features and wisdom-polished words.

Mitch watches his father intently. Love and admiration have replaced contempt and impatience.

"Let's open in prayer." The resonance of the pastor's words to God sober me. They're confident. Intimate. My heart beats in rhythm to his words. I lower my chin to catch my breath.

"Are you okay?" J. D. whispers.

I nod. The sensation in my chest is odd and scary. I want to leave, but am afraid to stand.

When the sermon starts, my adrenaline rush ebbs, and I relax a little. Pastor O'Neal's sermon sounds practiced and thought out, but he uses words like *sanctification* and *justification* in ways I don't understand. Every once in a while Pastor Winnie shouts an amen, which is followed by the green-suit lady jumping to her feet and flapping her hand in the air. "*Weeell,* come on now, Pastor."

So far, the shouting is my favorite part.

Then, in the middle of a sentence, Pastor O'Neal stops. It feels like the whole congregation is tossed forward—like slamming on the brakes when the yellow light flashes to red. He walks to the edge of the platform, taking a step down. I get the feeling he doesn't do this every week.

"Do you want to know a real inconvenient truth? Jesus. Who do you say He is? The Christ? Savior? King? A good man? Yet He called Himself the Son of God. Is He? Truth or lie?" He feigns a shudder. "Makes people uncomfortable, doesn't it. Why? Because if He is who He says He is, we have to do something about it. He's the God-Man who loves you. All He requires is for you to believe in Him alone as the way to the Father and eternal life."

Both Pastor Winnie and Green Suit are off the pew, shouting, waving their hands in the air. "Go on, say it like it is. Truth is truth. Let's get real, Pastor." I don't think Pastor O'Neal needs encouragement. He appears to be revving up.

J. D. shifts around. I'm not sure he's any more at home than I am. Mitch props his chin in his hand and watches like a kid at his first *Star Wars* flick.

"Jesus gave up the untold, unimaginable splendor of heaven to become like you and me. Elle, it'd be like you becoming one of your paintings. Not just for a little while, but for all of eternity. For. Ever."

My eyebrows flip up. Never heard that before.

"It's all about love. For God so loved . . . Colby Tanner. He loves you."

Green Suit hollers, "He do. He do. Go on, Pastor."

Mitch's father points to another parishioner. "He loves you, Sheila Dawson."

Sheila Dawson is here? I crane my neck to see. Four years ahead of me in school, her rep with the boys was legendary, even to the incoming freshmen. Her head hangs low, and the woman next to her hugs her shaking shoulders.

A warmth fills my middle. This is not how I imagined church.

Pastor O'Neal grows more energized. "His love will set you free, Gary Allen."

Five rows up, Gary sits straight and hard as a board. Next to him, his wife covers her face, but I feel her tears. Gary's been an alcoholic and abuser for years.

Pastor pauses to gaze around the hushed room. He doesn't seem to mind the weighty silence.

The congregation shifts after a few more seconds. Restless.

Am I the only one aware of a Presence?

In fifth grade, April Crammer's mother held a séance during her slumber party, and a very chilling "thing" crept past me. I ran screaming into the next week, and never went to April's house again.

Yet what I sense today is . . . well . . . *holy.*

"Darlene Campbell, Jesus knows your past and He loves you." She's a highbrow lawyer who prides herself on civic duty. But this morning, she weeps.

The pressure inside me bubbles and builds. Tears swell behind my eyes, but I refuse to release them. I'm fearful Pastor O'Neal will call my name, yet terrified he won't. What if this all-knowing, all-seeing God doesn't love *me?*

"We're leaving," I whisper to Mitch, speaking for J. D. and me. The man's halfway out of the pew anyway.

With his eyes still closed, Mitch grabs at my arm. "No, wait."

"Caroline Sweeney . . ." My head snaps up. Pastor O'Neal has zeroed in on me. "I've been wanting to tell you this for years: Jesus loves you. Passionately. Since you were a little girl waiting for a pink room with blue clouds."

My heart explodes, knocking the breath right out of me. A spark ignites on top of my head and runs down my face and neck, setting my torso on fire.

How did he know?

"Do you believe, Caroline?" Pastor asks.

Is he still talking to me?

"Caroline, do you believe He loves you?"

Slowly, I rise to my feet. J. D. settles back while Mitch bends forward, hands clasped over his head. "I-I don't know."

Pastor O'Neal is not rattled. "Fair enough."

The moment all eyes are not on me, I stumble over J. D., exiting the pew and making for the sanctuary doors.

Daily Special

Monday, June 25

Mushroom & Ham Casserole

Yellow Squash and Onions

Bubba's Buttery Biscuits

Ice cream

Tea, Soda, Coffee

$6.99

14

Let's go over the Carrington plan one more time."

Andy groans. I'm sure he would love to leap over the prep table and strangle me. He tugs his white beanie low on his forehead. "Caroline, we've gone over and over the plan. Honey, we're set. Stop fretting."

"Did you see her face when she talked about this party? We— I can't screw this up."

"You ordered the food and supplies, right?" Andy thumps his forefinger on the paper in front of me.

"I created an account with Sysco this morning and ordered with my credit card. Might as well bring our ordering into the twenty-first century."

He shoves his beanie back on his head. "Sounds good. Now, I best be getting home. Gloria went back to work today and I want to help out with supper in case she's all tuckered out." He strides for the back door. "Sure did my heart good to see you in church."

"Thanks for embarrassing me. I meant to fire you for it."

"Well, so glad you didn't, boss. Mighty Christian of you." Chuckling, Andy bids me good night.

J. D.'s cruiser swings into the parking lot Monday evening as I step out of the carriage house on my way to meet Elle and Jess at Firehouse Books & Espresso Bar.

"Hey, beautiful." He pops open his door. "Want to grab some dinner?" His brown eyes bore into mine as he wraps his arm around my back and hugs me against his bulky bulletproof vest. "You recovered from yesterday?"

"I've recovered."

After we sped away from church, J. D. rode with me out to Daddy's, where we launched my old boat, *Bluecloud*, and drifted on the Coosaw River for several hours. Daddy built the boat the year Mama left for good, keeping his hands busy so his mind wouldn't go crazy. At night I'd lay awake as long as I could, peering out the window at the light coming from under the garage's old swinging doors. Eventually, I'd drift off, then wake with a start to find the light still burning as darkness rounded the corner of night and faded toward the dawn.

But J. D. had no answers for my questions. Like, how did Pastor O'Neal know about the pink room with blue clouds?

"Maybe Mitch told him."

I slumped down against the side of the boat, pillowing my head against a life jacket. "I'm not sure Mitch ever knew."

J. D. cradles my jaw in his hands. "I had a good time yesterday, out in the boat."

"Me too." I hook my hands over his arms and he steps closer.

"Is it okay with you if—"

"Yes."

J. D.'s very kissable lips touch mine. Soft, tentative, then fierce.

When he lifts his head, I inhale sharply. "Y-you s-sure know how to . . . *ahem* . . . That was worth the wait."

He brushes his hands over my shoulders. "I about kissed you a hundred times in the boat yesterday, but every time I went to make my move, the boat rocked or you started spouting off about God again."

"Sorry, mental processing includes running my mouth."

"Caroline, I'm not sure Mitch is over you."

"J. D., he is way over me. We're just good friends."

"I don't know. He gave you a look yesterday . . ."

"Are you jealous?"

"Maybe." Dispatch beckons J. D.'s attention. Still holding me, he cocks his head to listen. "I've got to go." He kisses me again with tender purpose. "Let's finish this thing later."

Elle's in the Firehouse loft where she's reserved the chairs around a coffee table.

"Did you walk?" She pats a cushioned chair arm next to her.

"It's a beautiful night."

"It's going to rain."

I plop down. "I don't melt." However, I do sweat. The walk over was warmer than I thought and I've perspired myself. The AC feels good.

Dappled evening light flows through the high windows and falls across the banister and bookshelves lining the old brick walls.

"Did church freak you out yesterday?" Elle sips her espresso.

"A little."

"I loved it. Pastor O'Neal doesn't prophesy like that often. You'll get used to it." She sets her cup down and digs into a large tote, producing a notebook and what appears to be a couple of our high school yearbooks. "Tonight, we are talking about my future love life, tentatively entitled Operation Wedding Day. Here's our starting point."

"What makes you think I'm going back to church?" I reach for the top book. Class of '94. Elle has some of the pages marked with multi-colored sticky flags. "What is all this?"

"Of course you'll be back. Caroline, Jesus told you in front of three hundred people He loves you. After you ran off like a scared hen, Pastor only spoke to two more people. Okay, the yearbooks. Last night—"

Elle's explanation fades to the background as "Jesus told you in front of three hundred people He loves you" loops over and over in my mind. Is that what happened?

"So, what do you think?"

"Um, what? Sorry, you lost me there for a second. What are we doing?"

"Caroline, holy cow, pay attention. Look, I went through and marked all of the pages with men I (a) once had a crush on, (b) would like to have had a crush on, (c) know are still single and acceptable for at least one date, (d) don't know a status on but would like to find out, and (e) definitely would want to get something going with if available."

I'm speechless, really, for at least a nanosecond. "You're crazy."

"Why? Why does this make me crazy? Speaking of, here's my celebrity list. I limited it to five men, figuring it to be a realistic number."

"Realistic? Elle . . . Matthew McConaughey?" I drop the list, letting it float down to the table. "When are you going to meet Matthew McConaughey. Isn't he, like, fifty or something?"

"Fifty? Girl, he's only, like, thirty-eight or -nine. And a lot of celebs are visiting the lowcountry these days. He might just happen into my gallery."

"I don't dream like this when I'm asleep."

"And you've never had a plan and look where it got you."

Ouch, bringing out the big guns. Well, right back at you, El. "J. D. kissed me today."

My friend pops up straight with surprise. "And . . ."

If she'd offered me a million bucks, I couldn't have stopped smiling. "Very yummy."

"Jess was right? He's a good kisser."

"Very."

"That does it; I'm finding someone." Elle reaches for a notebook and flips open to the first blue-lined page. "I've color coded the categories of the sticky flags. Red is 'once had a crush on,' see? Blue, 'would like to have had a crush on,' and so on."

"Elle, you need serious help. Color coding?"

"If eHarmony can match people on a computer, based on some psychological test, then I can color code a few known prospects."

Exchanging my sophomore yearbook for my senior yearbook, I remind my friend of a few points. "Aren't you the one who told me God is in control of your life? How is this letting Him run the show? You claimed to trust Him when you studied in Florence. When you decided to go on a mission to Guatemala. Even when you opened your gallery. Now that you're ready to get married, He's off the job somehow? Gone fishing?"

Elle swats at my knee. "No, He's still in control, Caroline. I'm just lining up some men He and I can discuss."

"Oh, really? I'm sure He was just stumped without your help." Flipping over to our senior class photos, I see the pages are loaded with lots of sticky flags.

"Look at you, one Sunday in church and you're all about how God thinks."

"I'm just repeating what you've said over the years." Truth is—and I can't explain it—I've felt strong today. Confident.

"I don't know, Caroline. Maybe I'm restless." Elle falls back against the large, overstuffed club chair. "I love owning the gallery. Shooting weddings is a great joy for me. I'm never jealous, you know, of the bride. But after a while I realized, this is it. I'm home now. A businesswoman. Where am I going to meet a man to share my life with?"

Closing the book over my thumb, I face Elle. "Believe me, I understand. I felt the same way each time I took some admin or clerical job just to help out the family or a family friend. I wanted a passion for something, you know? Then I get the Café. Elle, it's not my passion, but I'm doing what I have to do."

"You're so brave, Caroline."

"Not really. But, listen to me, you're too beautiful, inside and out, for a man not to find you and lose himself in your deep, green eyes. You're the brightest star when we're all out together, outshining all of us. If you weren't so genuine, Hazel, Jess, and I would loathe you."

She picks at a loose thread on the hem of her top. "That was lovely, Caroline. Thank you." Then she sits forward. "Look, I'm not going to do anything stupid. But isn't it fun to dream? Pretend?"

"Then let's get to it. Matthew McConaughey, Elle has you in her sights, bubba."

"Oh, one more thing." Elle jabs her finger in the air. "Must have compassion for the arts and be able to pronounce and spell *renaissance.*"

"You go, girl. Set that bar high."

"Sorry I'm late." Jess hurries toward us, breathless, her hair tousled. "Ray called and I couldn't get him off the phone." She flops down in the chair opposite Elle. "What'd I miss? Why are these yearbooks here? With stickies?"

Elle flattens her palm on the stack of yearbooks and explains the whole process to Jess, who, to my surprise, thinks it's brilliant.

"Let me grab a latte and we can get started." Jess flashes her sweet smile at both of us while digging money from her handbag.

"Oh, bring me a chocolate biscotti," Elle says.

"Caroline, what about you?" Jess pauses beside the handrail. "Latte, espresso?"

"Nothing for me just yet, thanks."

Getting comfortable, I scan the faces on the glossy yearbook page, wondering how ten years went by in a day. "Oooh, Rocky Galloway, good choice. I heard he's a sports agent, living in Miami Beach."

Elle lifts her eyes from the yearbook she's perusing. "I could definitely go for the jock type. Miami? Not so sure. But he could move, right? Telecommute. Fly out of Savannah for business." She taps her page. "Carter Daley. What about him?"

"Married, four years ago."

"Rats."

"Tim Norton."

"Married."

"Ah . . ." She flips her wrist. "I didn't want to be Elle Norton anyway."

I freeze when my eyes fall on the next page. Elle has every color flag pointing to one picture. Mitch O'Neal. My pulse rushes. She can't be serious.

"Elle, you have every flag around Mitch?"

"Yeah, I know." She leans over. "He's single, right? And he doubles on my celebrity list."

She can*not* be serious. An instant picture of them kissing, cuddling, sours my stomach. *Oh, I don't feel well.* How could I deal with my best friend married to . . .

The love of my life.

Stop right there, Caroline. Mitch is only your friend.

"Two of my best friends, married." I swallow. "H-how cool."

Or not. Getting over Mitch was the hardest thing in my life—other than dealing with Mama.

Yet, I never considered the next phase—falling in love and getting married. It's one thing to know he's dating celebrity women who are more like movie characters than real people, but falling in true love?

"Caroline, you're over him, right? Moving on with J. D."

I squirm. "Yeah, but that doesn't mean I want you to go out with him."

"So you'd rather see him with a Hollywood skank or some bimbo groupie."

"So? You want to be with a man who has such poor taste in women?"

Elle rolls her eyes. "As I recall, he loved you first. Look, don't get your panties in a wad. He's one of a dozen great choices, Caroline."

Um-hmm. But so far he's the only one with all arrows pointing to him. "You'd be crazy not to list him as number one, El. He's kind, romantic, amazing to look at, rich, and apparently a renewed man of faith. Besides, who's to say he'd go for you anyway." The words sound harsher than I mean.

Elle's eyes darken. "Why wouldn't he go for me?" Her bracelets slip down her arm with a clatter as she brushes her silky hair off her shoulder.

The tension between us could hold up a gorilla and her babies. "It's Mitch, Elle. *My* Mitch. Yes, you're beautiful and talented. Any man would be lucky to have you, but . . . Mitch? What do you want me to say?"

"That you'd be happy for me. And you forgot educated and well traveled."

The blood drains from my cheeks. "I see. And I'm not. So you'd be a better match for the famous and well-traveled Mitch O'Neal."

"Caroline, no, that's not what I meant."

"Look—" I close my eyes and take a deep breath. "Mitch is available. So . . ." I force myself to look in her eyes. "Go for it."

The truth is, in perfect Caroline-world this conversation would never happen. My mama would've never run out on us, nor died at the youthful age of fifty. I would've gone to college and graduated with honors and certainly never inherited an old man's café. Mitch would be a P.E. teacher at Beaufort High, with a football championship trophy. Not one, but two. Still a star. And we'd be married with two-point-one kids.

Jess breezes into this mess with a large latte and a couple of chocolate biscotti. "Okay, what did I miss?"

Elle drops me off at the carriage house a little after eight because, as she predicted, it's raining. Operation Wedding Day went well—after the Mitch tension—and we laughed at old pictures and read the inscriptions our classmates wrote to Elle.

Elle, you are the sexiest girl in fifth period P.E. even though you are weird. Call me. Mark Hammond.

We sure had some laughs in Mrs. Gonzales's class. Oodgay ucklay alwaysway. Jenny Barrett.

When are you going to marry me? Steve Parker.

I tapped his signature. "Hasn't Steve been married, like, four times?"

"And getting divorced. Again." The Jess-and-Ray connection is great for scooping on old classmates. If we don't know what's up with someone, Ray does. Or he can find out. "Ray says he posted on MySpace he wants to beat Liz Taylor's record."

"He's banned from the list. I don't care how rich, kind, or good-looking." Me, being bossy.

"I'll be an old maid first," Elle said.

After two hours of poring over yearbooks and talking, Jess, Elle, and I came up with a list of ten wedding-day possibilities. Single, attractive, relatively successful, eligible men.

"With deep faith," Elle always added. "I need a man who knows Jesus."

We were one shy of ten after the list was compiled, so I tossed out Kirk's name to round out the field. Outside of wrinkled suits and obnoxious glasses, he's quite handsome. And, I believe, a Presbyterian, though don't quote me.

Elle taps my arm as I start to get out of her car. "Are we okay?" She shifts her car into park, leaving the motor running. Rain softly *ratta-tat-tat*s against the windshield.

"Yes, we're fine." I smile, reaching for my door handle. "It's just weird to think of you with Mitch. Or Mitch with anyone, really."

Elle's soft laugh tells me she understands. "Seems weird to me, too, actually. I always pictured you two as the Ross and Rachel of Beaufort."

"Are you my Emily?"

"The one Ross should've never married? I hope not. Caroline, listen, if you really want him off my list, say the word."

"El, it's fine . . . Yes, it makes me uncomfortable. But that's my problem, not yours. If I'm really over him—and I am—then I can't tell you, 'Hands off.'"

"Tell you what: if I'm not married by thirty-five, and the coast is clear with you, and Mitch just happens to be available, *then* I'll make my move."

"Mitch is your backup?"

"Secret backup. Won't he be surprised when I come calling in seven years?"

Laughing, I lean across to hug her. "Deal. Thanks for the lift."

As she pulls away, I dash between fat raindrops to the dark porch, and, as if scripted for an *I Love Lucy* episode, my right foot lands in a deep puddle. I'm suddenly hurtling forward. My purse goes airborne and the contents fly like New Year's confetti.

Face-first, I splash into a mini pool of rain. And curse.

"Caroline." Strong hands lift me off the ground. *Oh, my.* "Are you all right?"

Mud slips down the inside of my top. "Mitch? What are you doing here?"

"Porch lurking. Gave you a nine-point-five for the mud-hole trip."

"Nine-point-five? Oh, dude, that was a perfect ten." Stooping, I gather up the scattered contents of my purse.

"Take off point-five for the *word.*"

"Ha. I've heard ten times worse out of you. Again, why are you here?"

Mitch rescues my keys as they sink in a distant puddle. "Where'd you run off to yesterday after church?"

"The Coosaw." He passes me the keys. I offer my pinky finger as a hook. "Took the old boat out."

"The *Bluecloud* still floats?"

"She does."

"A little overwhelming, wasn't it?"

I swallow a sudden rise of emotion. "A little." Water drips from the ends of my hair. Goose bumps crawl over me when the damp breeze blows. "Elle claims Jesus told me He loved me in front of three hundred people."

"He did." Mitch smiles.

It baffles me how he always feels like coming home.

"So, do you want to come in?" I start for the door.

"Sure, if I'm not intruding." He seems a little lost. Lonely, even.

The wind drives the rain under the porch eaves. I can't unlock the door without dropping everything. "Mitch . . . Here . . . my keys." I jiggle my pinky. "The long, weird one opens the door." My brush slips to the floor. When I try to adjust my load, my phone breaks free. I grapple to catch it.

Next thing I know, my secret tampon holder is lying at Mitch's feet. He looks down.

"Mitch, hey, I'll get that. *A-hem* . . . Don't bother. My bad."

I reach down. Except, hurrying to rescue my girl-privacy, I don't see the porch post . . .

Wham.

"Ow." I slap my hand to my forehead. The rest of my stuff clatters to the old board floor, and the porch light flashes on—all the commotion activating the motion detector.

"Caroline, didn't you see the post?" Mitch grabs my wrist. In the small, white light, I see his furrow of concern, but he's not fooling me. His voice is fat with laughter.

"Of course I saw the porch post. I love smacking my head every now and then." I peek up at him. "Dork."

"You should've seen your face . . ." He chuckles. Politely. Which I appreciate.

"Oh, go ahead and laugh. I'll just be over here in extreme pain."

"Caroline, come here, to the light. Let me see this wound. You bleeding or anything?"

"Bleeding? Yes, pride, not blood." I remove my hand as he tilts my chin toward his face and the light.

"Ooooh, big red and blue mark."

"Tell me, Doctor, will I live?" Without making a big to-do, I stretch my foot forward, trying to kick the secret tampon holder into the shadows. Instead it slides sideways, further into the light. Forget it. I've known Mitch forever. Guess it's time I realize he knows about girl needs.

"Caroline . . ." He presses his thumb lightly to my boo-boo. "You've got a nice bump going."

As my face is cupped in his hands, headlights gleam against the carriage house. I look over to see J. D.'s cruiser rumbling into the Café parking lot.

"Oh, J. D.'s here." Half shoving Mitch out of the way, grinding the tampon holder into the board with my heel, I wave to J. D. But his car doesn't stop. Instead the engine roars to life as he peels away.

Daily Special

Tuesday, June 26

Beans & Greens

Cornbread

Bubba's Buttery Biscuits

Blackberry Cobbler

Mint Julep, Tea, Soda, or Coffee

$5.99

15

Mercy Bea, I'm going to try printing out nametags for the Carrington party. Call me if we get busy."

"Or if I win the lotto?" She stacks the refilled salt and pepper shakers on a tray.

"Definitely call me if you win the lotto."

In the office, I dust off the printer, wondering if J. D. has returned one of my half dozen calls. The one time he answered last night, he was pretty upset.

"He was kissing you."

"No, he wasn't. I bumped my head against the porch post. He was checking out my wound."

"I knew you weren't over him, or him over you."

And he hung up.

I check my cell. A message. Please be J. D., cooled off and ready to reason.

But it's from Mitch.

"What happened with J. D.? Does he think something is going on? Should I call him? Sorry, Caroline."

Elle is crazy to attempt relationships with more than one man at a time. I make a mental note to bring this up at our next Operation Wedding Day gathering.

With a sigh, I power up the computer, load paper in the printer, open the Word doc of Carrington family names I compiled this morning, and click Print. The printer wheezes to life and miraculously begins chugging out row after row of nametags.

Meanwhile, I check e-mail. Sheree from the Water Festival reminds me *again* to sign up for the raft race: *Great publicity, girl. Come on.*

I reply: *Still thinking about it.*

Wednesday at closing, Mercy Bea corners me as I sweep by the corner cubbies.

"What'd you do to the deputy? I haven't seen him all week."

"Misunderstanding."

She rolls her eyes. "Whatever you did, apologize."

"What makes you think it was me?"

Mercy Bea pats my shoulder. "Fix him a nice dinner and—Wait, you don't cook. Well, do whatever it is you do to make nice. A Café owner who don't cook . . . *mm, mm, mm.* It's a mad, mad world."

I lost count, but I think she insulted me about five times in this exchange. "Good night, Mercy. See you tomorrow."

"Call the boy. Do you intend on being an old maid? Don't follow in Jones's footsteps and never marry."

"Mercy Bea, please, I'm a long way from . . ." *Being like Jones. Aren't I?*

Broom in hand, I duck in the office and dial Bodean. He has a nice place with a few acres that is the official deputy hangout. "Do you know where J. D. might be?"

"*Fred*, I'm so glad you called."

"He's right there, isn't he?" I drop the broom in the corner, grab my keys, and flick off the office light.

"10-4."

"Is he mad?"

"What? Your car *broke* down?"

Oh my stars. This is stupid. "Bodean, just put him on." I lock up the Café and beeline toward the Mustang.

"Sure, that'd be great. Just come on over. A bunch of us are hanging out."

Okay, so this has to be face-to-face. "See you in a few."

When I park next to J. D.'s blue Ford F-250, I hesitate before getting out. Upon reconsideration, this is an astronomically stupid idea. What if he rejects me when I walk in? In front of his buddies?

I wipe my palms down the side of my skirt, debating. Never mind I'm not at my best, still wearing my work clothes and clogs. I didn't even think to change. As a matter of fact, I don't even have my driver's license.

Sneaking a fast peek in the rearview mirror, I grimace at my shiny face and tangled hair before giving my underarms a quick sniff. Secret is working as advertised.

I fluff my hair, adjust my top and bra—everything is contained—and head for the house.

"Hello?" I call weakly, shoving open the front door.

Shouts echo from the back room. "Bodean?"

The slender but wide-shouldered deputy comes around the corner. His blond hair sticks out in all directions. "Caroline, hey, *what* are *you* doing here?"

I exhale, grinning. "So not fooling anyone, Bo."

"J. D., your girl's here." With a wink at me, Bodean disappears, leaving me to wait alone in the stark living room.

The clink of pool balls is chased by raucous laughter. A fridge door opens and there's a call for beer. Then the hiss of bottle tops.

What am I doing here, invading his turf? I should go. Gripping my keys—*Is he coming?*— I'm about to turn for the door when . . . There he is. Dark, masculine, and sober.

"Hey," I say.

"Hey." His checked shirt hangs loose over his jeans.

"Enjoying your day off?" I smile.

"Yeah, sure. Some of the guys wanted to play pool." He steps around the leather couch, but remains on the other side of the room.

"Sounds like fun." Five feet away and I can't reach him. "Guess you'll be here all night, then."

He shrugs. "Most likely. Have a few too many beers and crash on the couch."

More nodding. Then an awkward silence. Yes, coming here was a mistake. Bodean's is J. D.'s safe place, like the live oak is for me, and I wouldn't have appreciated Mama interrupting as I tried to process my feelings about her.

"I'd better get going." I back toward the door. "See you."

"It looked like he kissed you."

"Well, he didn't."

"When I drove up and saw you two together, it was like—" He balls his fist, and his expression tightens. "Fire. I can't ever remember being so jealous."

"I told you he didn't kiss me. I conked my head."

J. D. takes a few steps toward me. "What was he doing there?"

With a shrug, I say, "I don't know, looking for company, good friends."

"Caroline, I'm not an insecure man, but he's *the* Mitch O'Neal. Your ex-boyfriend to boot."

"He hasn't been my boyfriend for many years, J. D." I think of Elle. "Here you go: Mitch is on Elle's short list of possible husbands. And it's okay with me."

The deputy laughs reluctantly. "God help him."

"Mitch is my friend, J. D. He always will be, but—" I take a step toward him. "Is there a you and me?"

In a few strides, J. D. crosses the room, grabs my hand, and pulls me outside. The moment we pass through the door, I'm in his arms, barely catching my breath before his lips cover mine.

Daily Special

Sunday, July 1

Happy 90th Birthday, Mrs. Carrington

By Sunday, we're all set for the ninetieth birthday bash.

J. D. and I went to church again. I just had to know if it felt the same as last week. It did. Surreal. Clean. Peaceful. Mitch waved to us across the sanctuary, but kept his distance.

Andy arrives at the Café a little before two. "Ready for your first party, boss?" He slams the door of his old green truck parked along the Harrington Street curb. Just seeing him fortifies my confidence.

A lowcountry menu is yummy and easy to prepare—dough, batter, and grease—so a few hours' lead time is plenty. Saturday afternoon, Pastor Winnie clocked in to help Andy and Russell prep the casseroles, batter, and sauces. All we have to do today is bake and fry.

"Let's get the air on," I say. "Check the bathrooms and dining room, make sure they're clean." My foot splashes in water. "Why is the floor wet?"

"Boss, the lights won't click on." Andy pushes past me for the fuse box.

Pain rips through my chest. My arms go completely numb. "Andy," I gasp over his shoulder, "please tell me you can fix this. You're the fixer."

"Jones . . . I told him to get the rewiring done. Said this would happen. It keeps shorting out the box." Andy punches the wall by the fuse box. "I can't get it to come on. Other than tampering with these old glass fuses, I don't know what else to do."

I panic. "This is not happening. Not. Happening."

"It's happening, Caroline. We have no power."

Scotty, if you're there, beam me up.

Andy tugs open the walk-in. "Starting to warm up in here."

In the daylight of the door and windows, I read the taut lines running across Andy's face. We're snafued.

"The ice under the shrimp is melting, but if we get more ice, the shrimp will be good. All this water on the floor is probably from the ice machine. But, Caroline, without power, we can't cook."

Yes, I'm aware. "Okay, we have shrimp. That's a start." I dig deep for some cheer. "I'm calling an electrician."

Ducking into the office, I retrieve the phone book and stand in the light of the window, looking up Buster's Electric. If Mrs. Carrington shows up to a dark, warm Café, she'll stroke out.

As I dial, I hear Russell's tenor voice. "Fuse box blow again?"

Mercy Bea pokes her head in my door, an unlit cigarette dangling from her lips. "Caroline, you best call Buster."

I point to the phone stuck to my ear. "He's not answering." The machine clicks on. *You've reached Buster Electric . . .* I leave a message, but I'm void of all hope to hear from him today.

Flipping through the book, I call every electrician. Nothing. Apparently Sunday is not a big workday.

What am I going to do? I gather my small crew. "I'm open to suggestions here."

"How about a candlelight party." Mercy Bea leans out the back door with her cigarette. "Throw open the windows. Click on the fans."

"The ceiling fans?"

"Right." She chews on her bottom lip. "No power."

"Our main problem is the menu. How're we going to bake the casseroles? And the cake?"

Heart: Oh, head, we are so dead. Mrs. Carrington adored Andy's cake.

Head: For once, you don't exaggerate.

Heart: Thanks, I think.

Head: Good job, by the way, on resolving the J. D. issue.

Heart: You think? I was unsure. You could've spoken up, you know.

Head: Am I ever silent when you go astray?

Heart: Good point.

"What about another restaurant?" Russell suggests.

"On such short notice?" I press my palm to my aching head.

"Find a generator and hook it up?" Russell tries again.

"Sure, Russ, run on down to the corner store and buy an industrial-sized generator. Get two. What are they, ten grand each? Grab my wallet there, will you?"

Russell makes a face. "You asked for ideas."

"I'm sorry. You're right, but I was hoping for good ideas."

Andy bursts out laughing.

"Don't be confused. I'm not trying to be funny." This is my attempt to not completely melt down. "Russell, really, I'm sorry. But, y'all, a ninetieth birthday, a family celebration, ruined."

"What about going across the street to Waterfront Park?"

I glance at Mercy Bea. "The park? Andy, what do you think? With the breeze, it might not be too bad."

"We got those old gas grills out back under the tarps. We could run to Bi-Lo for food, barbecue up some nice shrimps, chicken, and steak. The sauces are prepped too."

The four hundred Mrs. Carrington paid disappeared long ago, but right now, I'd gladly sell my precious, knobless armoire to make this event happen.

"Okay, okay. Now you're talking. What else?"

"The grills have burners. We can put on water for Frogmore Stew. Grill some veggies."

"Right, plus we have chips and drinks. We could buy cheese-and-meat platters from the deli. Get ice. Russell, can you get the mop and start cleaning this up, please?" I point to the floor.

"On it."

Okay, a plan is shaping up. I can breathe without pain. "I'll call the city to see if we can have emergency access to the park. Andy, work up a new menu. Mercy Bea, call—"

"Caroline—" Andy interrupts with a flash of his palm. He tips his nose toward the ceiling. "Do you smell something?"

Russell, Mercy Bea, and I sniff.

"Smoke."

Beaufort Fire and Rescue firefighters walk inspection as I stand in the middle of the Café dining room with a sense of deep, deep dread. Andy doesn't relieve me any when he says, "No go on the park."

A familiar flood of hopelessness springs from the deep well of tried-and-true past experiences. Every time something good is about to happen . . . If this is God loving me, then . . . forget it.

I'm on my own.

The fire inspector motions for me to follow him to the kitchen. "It's the wiring." He sips from a 20-ounce bottle of Coke beaded with condensation. "The wires in the attic are exposed and chewed up by squirrels or rats. And this place is so old you still got exposed wires running under the house. Raccoons have been feasting on them for years. I'm surprised the whole place hasn't gone up in flames."

Critters? In my Café. Oh, my heart. "So, what do we do? Please don't tell me you're shutting us down."

He swigs from his Coke again. "If you get power back on, then I'll give you thirty days to get the place rewired. If you need more time, let me know, but get it going, Caroline. This place is a hazard."

"Tomorrow. First thing. I promise."

The inspector packs up and stops at the back door. "I was at the city council meeting. I'm glad you're keeping the Frogmore open. My dad was a son of a gun, and on hard days, I'd sneak out and ride my bike down here. Jones gave me chores to do and in his subtle way reminded me that men sometimes behave in a way they don't mean. He was the most compassionate man I ever knew."

The inspector's transparency startles me. These little glimpses into Jones's life make me realize I inherited more than a man's work. I inherited his reputation.

And a house full of bad wiring.

It's midnight· Sunday surrenders happily to Monday· I fall into exhaustion and exhilaration. The Carrington party was a smash.

Thanks to Mitch, the perfect host.

After the fire inspector left, Mrs. Carrington showed up. I did what our old beagle used to do when he was in trouble—rolled over and tucked my tail over my privates.

"What kind of electrical problems?"

"The kind where there's no electricity."

"Caroline, that's unacceptable."

"Yes, I would agree . . ."

"My mother-in-law found out about the party. It's all she's talked about."
(Gripping her chest like she's going to keel over.)

Clearly, it was too late to run away screaming. Too late to bury my head in the marsh pluff mud. Then, it came to me—exactly what to do.

Mitch opened his Fripp Island manse and treated the entire Carrington clan like they were his closest friends, sprinkling his magnetic charm and Nashville stardust over everyone. He completely tamed a furious Mrs. Carrington.

"These things happen, Caroline. Don't worry. See how it all worked out for the best."

The younger Carrington women couldn't contain their cool and swooned a little when Mitch serenaded their grandma. The birthday girl, Claire, seemed less impressed with her star host, preferring to sit on the back deck overlooking the ocean and reminisce.

"We didn't have bridges to connect the islands when I was a girl, you see, so we caught a boat to go to school. There was only one theater in them days out to Parris Island. We took the movie boat over."

More than telling her stories, I believe the older woman enjoyed having the rapt attention of her family.

Around eleven, a tired-but-happy Claire asked to go home, and slowly the family trickled out. I dismissed the Café crew, telling them I'd clean up.

Now the house is finally clean and quiet. I collapse on the deck steps, letting the ocean's breeze wash my face.

"Here you are." Mitch plops down next to me, bumping me with his shoulder. "It went well, don't you think?"

"No, it went splendid. Because of you. I can't thank you enough, Mitch."

He stares straight ahead. Tiki lamps glow along the walkway down to the beach and around the pool. Waves coming ashore serenade us. The landscape is serene and beautiful. "I'm glad to help." With a chuckle, he adds, "Feels like penance for having this great place all to myself."

"You earned this place, Mitch. When did you start selling yourself so short?"

"You think I was kidding when I told you Paris changed me."

"No." Clearly, he's viewing God from a different angle than I am. "Did you smooth things out with J. D.?"

"We talked the other day. It's good."

He twists open a bottle of water. "Are you in love with him?"

"Too soon to tell."

"I'm passing on love for a while." He swigs his water.

"Because why?" Good thing Elle moved him to her reserve list. She wouldn't like this news.

He tears at the water-bottle label. "Clean up my heart and soul. Get some perspective. See what God has for me next." He laughs. "Some people fast from food to seek God. I'm fasting my career, my love life, my reputation, my future, everything."

I always suspected Mitch's faith ran deep—like a thread of gold embedded in a cave wall. "You're serious about this God thing, aren't you?"

"Dead serious." His eyes meet mine. "If I could redo the last nine years, I would."

"Really?" I knew the familiar sting of regret, but Mitch?

"In a Nashville minute."

Daily Special

Monday, July 2

Limited Menu

Due to electrical problems

Ask your waitress what's available

16

Come on up here, Caroline."

I squint up the attic ladder, trying to minimize my view of Buster's bagging breeches and all they're *not* covering. "Really? You need me up there? I trust you."

He peers down at me, shining a flashlight in my face. "Want to be an ignorant girl?"

I drop my forehead against the wooden ladder rung. Trumped by the ignorant-girl card. "No, I guess not."

Buster disappears inside the attic. I climb up after him. He arrived at the Café this morning a little after six, did his electrician magic thing, and restored power just in time for the breakfast-club boys to come strolling in.

Andy set up a limited menu since we don't want to run the risk of burning out the fuses, or worse.

"Looky here." Buster jiggles the flashlight beam over chewed wire.

"Eaten clean through. And see this wiring here? Older than my granny. I hounded Jones for years to bring this place up to code."

"Do you know why he didn't?" I'm a bit stiff, slightly paranoid a rat might run across my clogs. *Note to self: Do not jump in Buster's arms if you see a rat.*

Buster, a narrow-built man with generous facial features, curls out his lower lip. "Reckon he didn't have the money, or plain ol' forgot." He floats the yellow flashlight circle over the rest of the attic floor and ceiling. "A few water spots. May have to fix those while we're at it." He stomps his foot on the insulation. "All of this needs to be replaced."

"Buster, if Jones didn't have the money, how am I supposed to have the money?"

"Don't know, but you best find it. Can't put this off any longer." He sweeps the room one last time with his flashlight. "You're on the inspector's radar."

As the light falls in the front corner, I spot a small box. "Buster, put the light over in the corner again. What's over there?" Bending down, I point just beyond the trusses. "See the box in the corner?"

"That shoebox thing?"

"Yes, *that* shoebox thing." Grabbing onto a support beam, I work my way over.

The dull-finished pine box is not heavy, but when I shake it, something moves from side to side. There's a lock on the front, and I think I know where to find the key.

Back in my office, I set the box by the file cabinet by the printer for the time being while Buster writes up his job estimate.

"We'll do the best we can not to disturb your business."

I flick my hand at him. "It's already disturbed."

He scribbles his signature, then places the paper in front of me, slapping his hand over the final number. "It's a big job, Caroline. I cut corners where I could, but I figured you'd want the best materials. We're going to have to go under the house, and these walls—" He points with his pen. "They're plaster, half-inch thick, and the dickens to flush wire through."

"Okay, good to know." I pry up his pinky finger. "How much?"

He removes his hand, and I gasp. Holy bad wiring, Batman. "Buster, there's a twenty-five and three zeros on this line."

"I cut every corner I could. Did a job similar to this last year. Forty grand."

Twenty-five thousand dollars? That's more than my entire annual income last year. Where am I going to get twenty-five thousand dollars? I don't like this. Not one bit.

My clothes and hands smell like attic dust and grease when, in fact, every pore of me should smell like coconut oil as I tan myself by the Mediterranean.

The wind whips my hair around my face as I speed down Highway 21 toward Dad's fishing hole on the Coosaw. My foot leans on the gas. *Twenty-five thousand.*

I swing into the landing where Dad always puts in and park next to his truck. I can see him out there, floating in his favorite spot. Reaching inside the cab, I pound the horn a few times.

Dad looks up. A second later, I hear the boat's engine fire up and grind toward shore.

"Are they biting?" I call.

"Not one." He inches the boat alongside the dock. "What brings you out here? Everything okay?"

"No, everything is not okay. Dad, I need money." No use beating around the bush.

He hops out of the boat. "*You* need money, or the Café?"

"Is there a difference?"

He chuckles. "Always did love your humor in bad situations. Remember the year I told you and Henry there wouldn't be any Christmas presents?"

I rake my tangled hair away from my face. "Dad—"

"You said, 'I knew that fat Santa spent our Christmas money on McDonald's.'" He throws back his head and laughs freely.

Normally, I'm game for a skip down memory lane, but my thoughts are locked in the desperation of the here and now. "Dad, I need twenty-five thousand dollars."

He stops laughing. "What for?"

"Rewiring. It's pretty serious. It's amazing the Café hasn't burnt down."

Dad carries his tackle box over to the truck bed. "I'd love to help you, Caroline, but I spent all the cash I had on the wedding trip to the Bahamas. We lived pretty high on the hog, decided to enjoy ourselves. The rest, which was shabby, Posey and I sunk into an invested account. I suppose I could—"

"No, Dad, no. You're not emptying your accounts." I tuck my hands in my skirt pockets.

Dad props his elbow on the rim of the truck bed. "Guess you could go to Henry and Cherry."

"No way. The last time I borrowed money from Henry, the payback pressure kept me awake at night. One night I ordered pizza just as he came through the door and he drilled me about how much it cost, giving me a lecture on 'this is why you never have any money.' And all he spotted me was a hundred dollars. I can't imagine what twenty-five grand would do to him. Or me."

I stare out over the water. My thoughts bob along the waves of my emotions, refusing to go deep and hook reality—what am I going to do if I can't come up with the money?

"Caroline, I'm sorry. Guess I'm not much of a dad in times like these."

I focus on him. "Dad, this is my life, my problem. Don't feel the burden of it. It's enough you're here to listen."

He clears his throat and looks away. "Coming to dinner? Henry's working late, so it's just us and Cherry."

I jerk open the Mustang door with a glance at my watch. Five fifteen. "I'll try."

"What about Mitch?"

"What about him?"

"Money."

I answer with a vigorous shake of my head. "I'll figure this out. See you in a bit."

To: Hazel Palmer

From: CSweeney

Subject: Re: The Frogmore and me

Hazel,

Did you fall off the face of the earth? Fall in love with Fernando and elope? Get fired by Carlos because your hometown friend is a flake?

Café update: Almost burned down. Horrendous wiring problems. Called Buster and got him to bubblegum us together until he can fix everything proper. Guess what the tab totaled up to be?

$25,000.

Yeah, you read it right. If I'd been standing when I read the quote, I'd have keeled over.

Did I ever tell you J. D. Rand and I are dating? As of a few days ago. He was jealous of Mitch—long story—so we had a heart-to-heart and made it official.

Elle roped Jess and me into a harebrained scheme: Operation Wedding Day. Don't ask. Actually, we had fun coming up with ten prospects for her future husband.

"Houston we have a problem."

Love, C

Daily Special

Happy 4th!

BBQ Ribs

Macaroni and Cheese

Cole Slaw/Potato Salad

Chips

Andy's Apple Pie à la Mode

Coffee, Tea, Soda

$7.99

17

Mr. Mueller, please, I'm begging you, lend the *Café twenty-five thousand dollars. I'm desperate."* On my knees, I weep and beg.

"Desperate? You've come to the right place." The bank manager's eyes darken, then flash red. He crawls over the top of his desk and drops down in front of me. "For your firstborn. And your second." He holds up a blood-stained document. "Sign here."

"No, no . . ." I stumble backwards.

His wicked laugh rings out, sending a parade of chills across my body. He snatches up my hand and pricks my finger.

"No!" I wake with a jolt. Panting. When I realize I'm safe at home, I plop back down to my pillow. "A dream. Just a dream."

From the living room, light from a table lamp halos the bedroom doorway. The clock on the nightstand clicks to midnight.

It's not enough my twenty-five-thousand-dollar need haunts me during the day; it now visits me at night.

Two days ago, I went to the bank to ask Mr. Mueller, the manager, for a loan on behalf of the Frogmore Café.

My very appearance about got him laughing. *"The Frogmore's too great a risk, Caroline. What can you offer as collateral?"*

I boldly offered the best I have—a broken-down '68 Mustang convertible.

That did it. He guffawed. Without so much as a good-bye, I let myself out, his condescension kicking me all the way down the street.

Tossing back the covers, I slip out of bed and away from the dream. I grab a bottle of water from the fridge, plop down on the couch, and click on the television—the one household appliance Jones managed to upgrade in this century. Flipping channels, I land on a late showing of CMT's *Inside NashVegas*. The show's host, Beth Rose, stands in front of a big building I think is the Gaylord Entertainment Center. I've seen pictures of Mitch there.

Fans shove around behind Beth to get in a camera shot.

"Lots of star activity in Nashville this week," Beth says. "*Inside NashVegas* caught up with a few of your favorite stars performing for the Fourth of July celebration at the GEC."

Wonder if Mitch is bummed he's not at this event? I snuggle with a throw pillow. He can't be that far out of the mainstream already, can he? Artists break away from record companies all the time. The rest of what's going on with him is self-induced.

The shot cuts away to a black-tuxedoed Scott Vaughn, Beth's cohost, who is inside the auditorium.

"Thanks, Beth," Scott says, "I'm here with country-music favorite Mitch O'Neal."

Whoa. I scramble for the remote to up the volume. He looks amazing in a black tux. I hate to admit it, but a there's-my-man smile hits my lips. So what? It's late, I'm alone, and just had a Mr. Mueller nightmare.

"You're performing tonight at the GEC." Scott holds the mike out to Mitch.

He flashes a movie star–like smile. "I am. And I'm very excited to be a part of this tribute to our nation's birthday, and to country music and country music fans."

I scrunch up my shoulders and almost giggle. Mitch is so cool and poised. So . . . so . . . starlike. I'm proud, and totally crushing. After all, he is *the* Mitch O'Neal. "You go, Mitch."

This is exactly what I needed to soothe away the terror of the dream. Upping the volume, I keep my eyes steady on the screen.

Then *she* glides into view. A willowy, breathtaking, golden brunette, linking her arm through Mitch's.

Scott greets her. "Miss Tennessee, Elaine Solem, exquisite as always."

Miss Tennessee? When did Mitch meet her? I tuck my knees to my chest and stretch my pajama top over my legs. She's a walking feather. Just watching her on TV makes me feel like an engorged slug. I'm never eating again.

"When can we expect a new album from Mitch O'Neal?" Scott asks.

"I'm working on a new project, spending time in the South Carolina lowcountry, reconnecting with my roots, writing. The new project will have the elements of my first album."

"Can't wait to hear it." Scott turns to Elaine. "How do you like the lowcountry?"

Her smile blings like perfect pearls. "I haven't been." She snuggles up to Mitch. "Yet."

A few more questions, some yada-yada *this* and yada-yada *that* before Scott thanks them for taking the time to talk to *Inside NashVegas* and wishes Mitch a good show.

"Thanks, Scott. Give my love to your lovely wife, Aubrey." Mitch slips his hand into Miss Tennessee's and leads her away.

What was all that baloney about fasting life, passing on love?

"You're a fraud, Mitch O'Neal." I toss the pillow at the TV. "A fraud."

Sheree sends another Raft Race reminder on Thursday afternoon: *It's past the sign-up deadline, but I think you can still get in if you hurry. Great publicity.*

This time the words *Great publicity* jump off the screen and do a little soft shoe across my brain. This is a good idea. Time to put the Frogmore Café back into the community's eyes.

I print out the entry form and walk into the kitchen. "Andy, how do you feel about the water?"

"It's wet." He slides the grill's cleaned grease trap into place.

"Har, har. No, I mean, being in the water. Boating. Fishing."

"Grew up on the water, girl." His eyes narrow. "Why you asking?"

Walking over to him, I flop my arm over his huge shoulders. "The Frogmore Café is entering the Water Festival's raft race."

His eyes widen. "Who you got to race?" He takes a look at the entry form. "We need eleven strong people."

"How about eleven people, period."

"Well, if you ain't particular."

Setting the entry form on the prep table, Andy and I go over potential rafters. I write in their names. "Russell and Mercy Bea, if she can get her hair wet."

"Got to race," Andy insists. "They're employees. How about my boy, Jack? He's a defensive lineman. Strong back and arms."

"Excellent." I jot down Jack. "Six more."

Tapping the pencil eraser against my chin, thinking, I watch Mercy Bea walk through the kitchen with a heavy tub of dirty dishes. *Hmm.* Did she always have Olive Oyl arms? I look at Andy, who's looking at me.

"Okay, we need seven more," he says, going toward the pantry as I erase Mercy Bea's name. "What about J. D. or Mitch? Your daddy and Henry?"

"Yeah, maybe . . ." Though I can't see Henry leaning into a raft oar.

J. D. rows with the sheriff department; they've already been talking and planning. Dad has a temperamental back. And Mitch? Mr. Date-A-Feather. I write his name down.

"What are you doing?" Mercy Bea hovers over my shoulder. "The raft race?"

Is that glee in her voice?

"I love the raft race." She claps her hands. "Hey, Caroline, I don't see my name."

"That's because"—*Mercy Bea Hart*—"I'm writing it right now. See?"

She makes a wry face. "You weren't going to put me down, were you?"

"Mercy Bea, honey, sorry, but look—" I pinch her narrow arms. "Really, really skinny."

Fire shoots from her hazel eyes. I jump back as the feisty waitress drives her elbow into the prep table. "Right now, you and me, Caroline. Arm wrestle. I'll show you 'really, really skinny.'"

Ho, boy. "I'm not going to arm wrestle you. You're on the team."

Andy comes back from the pantry, his arms loaded with dinner fixings, breaking up our almost girl fight. "Mercy, move out the way. Caroline, Jack's got a buddy, Donny Vetter. He'll probably row for us."

"Good, good." Seven all told now. "We need four more."

"How about the breakfast-club boys?" Andy actually suggests them with a straight face.

I laugh and fill out the blanks. "Sure, and Miss Jeanne too."

"You said eleven people, Caroline. You didn't care who or what. Those boys would be honored. So would Miss Jeanne. We don't care if we win, do we? Let's just get out there, have fun, and remind folks the Frogmore is alive and well." Andy takes a roasting pan from the hook overhead.

"When you put it like that . . . We have eleven. We're a team." I slap

Andy and Mercy Bea a high five, then hurry to fax the entry form to Sheree.

Eleven illustrious names. Caroline, Andy, Mercy Bea, Russell, Jack, Donny, Mitch, Luke, Dupree, Winnie, and Miss Jeanne.

We're doomed.

"Anybody home? Caroline?" Mitch's chiseled face pops around my office door as I shut down the computer. His sky-blue eyes are bright and a light beard dusts his cheeks.

"Back from Music City already?" The image of him with *her* flits across my brain.

Mitch ducks his head. "You saw, huh?"

"Miss Tennessee is very beautiful."

His brow tightens. "I'd asked her to go with me months ago. She's just a friend. I flew up for the event one day and flew back the next. Don't bust my chops."

"She told all CMT viewers she's waiting to visit you here."

Mitch picks up the squeeze football Jones kept on the desk. "Elaine is a walking sound bite. It's her pageant training—smile and agree with everything."

"So, she just ran off at the mouth?"

"Pretty much. When I asked her about it later, she didn't even remember saying 'it.'"" He walks around the desk, eyeing the attic box. "What's in there?"

"You know, I forgot to look. Found it when Buster was giving me a tour of the damage."

"What was the damage?"

"Twenty-five thousand."

Mitch whistles. "That's cheap, Caroline. These old buildings are a bear to work on."

"So I heard." Opening the middle desk drawer, I fish for the key I'd found taped to the file cabinet. To my not-so-surprise, it works. The lid pops open. Before peering inside, I close my eyes and make a wish. "Twenty-five grand, twenty-five grand."

Mitch arches over the desk to see. "What is it?"

"A picture." A black-and-white, curled-edge picture of six twenty-somethings lies alone on the bottom of the box. The date is stamped on the white photo border. "June forty-eight."

Mitch comes around the desk for a closer look. The scent of Hugo Boss is distracting. "Isn't that your granddad in the middle?"

"Yes, and Nana." Her smile is very distinct. Sweet and unassuming.

"There's Jones on the other side of your nana." Mitch taps the young, angular face of my old boss. He grabs my hand to turn the picture over. "Nothing written on the back."

"So, that's it. A locked box with one old picture? Very weird."

Mitch taps the picture. "A betting man would say there's more to the story."

"Caroline? Ready to go?" J. D. stops short when he sees Mitch. I watch his face, expecting to see a flicker of jealousy, but if he is, he cloaks it well. "Hey, Mitch."

"Good to see you, J. D." The country singer offers his hand. "What are y'all up to tonight?"

"Going to see *Grease I* and *II* at the drive-in." J. D. angles over the desk to kiss me. I accept it, though it feels weird in front of Mitch.

"Look, J. D., an old picture of Jones. There's Granddad and Nana."

J. D. bends down to look, pressing his cheek against mine. "Another world."

"So, a *Grease* double feature at the drive-in," Mitch says.

J. D. clears his throat. "W-why don't you join us?"

The loud *thunk* is me hitting the floor.

"No, thanks, I don't want to impose." Mitch turns for the door.

"No, man, really. It'd be nice to hang out. It's been a while." The deputy smiles, resting one hand on my back. "Jess and Ray are coming. Wild Wally and his girlfriend, Holly. We could call Elle. Right, Caroline?"

Oh, I see. "Sure."

Mitch hesitates with a glance at J. D., then me. "You talked me into it."

Daily Special

Friday, July 6

Frogmore Stew (all you can eat)

Cornbread

Bubba's Buttery Biscuits

Pluff Mud Pie or Pecan Splendor Cake

Tea, Soda, Coffee

$8.99

18

I signed you boys up," I announce to Dupree, Luke, and Pastor Winnie as they come in at eight-o-two.

"Signed us up for what?" Dupree asks, sliding into the booth. "Toilet overflowed at two this morning. Been up ever since. Bring extra coffee, Caroline."

"The Water Festival raft race. I needed eleven in the boat and . . . you boys are eight, nine, and ten."

Luke squares his shoulders. "The Frogmore is putting a raft team in the race?"

"That's the idea. What do you think? Get our name out there, show the town we're alive and well."

Dupree laughs. "Alive, maybe. I'm not so sure about well."

"Never mind. Are you gents up for rafting?" I give them the details. They grunt and nod.

"Looks like we're all in, Caroline," Dupree says.

Good. Ten down, one to go. Mitch. I meant to ask him last night, but the gang dispersed after the movie. During intermission, Elle hauled me off to the ladies' room and announced she'd booted Mitch from her back-up list.

"Every time I look at him, I see your face."

"Wait seven years. When you call for backup, it'll be different."

She lined her lips with fresh gloss without looking in the mirror. "No, I can tell, Mitch is not for me. While charming and loverly to look at, there's no spark—if you know what I mean."

"Not really." Spark is definitely—well, *was* definitely—not a problem between Mitch and me. "Elle, then why are you still primping and glossing?"

"I want to look good when the paparazzi pop out of the trees or swing down from the Spanish moss."

Her expression had me laughing. I wish I owned life like Elle.

In the office, I dial Mitch's number. *Hey, have I got a job for you. Mitch, pullease, I need a favor . . .*

"What's up?" This is how he answers the phone.

I blurt. "I need a favor."

"Is it legal?"

"Far as I know. Will you row with us in the Water Festival raft race?"

He chuckles. "Who is us?"

"The Frogmore Café." I run down the team names.

"The breakfast-club boys?" he says slowly. "Miss Jeanne?"

"I know, I know—"

"I'm in. Now, will you do me a favor?"

"Is it legal?"

Mitch laughs. "Far as I know. How about letting me sing at the Café during the Water Festival? Try out new material. Might help draw some business."

I lurch forward. "You're kidding? All nine nights?"

"That's the offer. Two shows a night. Look, I know it's a lot to ask, but—"

"Yes, yes. Sing at the Frogmore. Mitch, that will be so great for business." Maybe twenty-five thousand dollars great. Or close.

"Well, I've filled a few stadiums."

"What do you—"

Buster's toothy grin appears around the office door. "Look what we found in the attic wall, Caroline." He swings an electrified, petrified squirrel by the tail.

"Buster, did you carry that thing through the kitchen? I'm running a food business here."

He frowns. The poor dead squirrel tick-tocks back and forth. "Don't get your nose out of joint. Just thought you'd want to see what's in the wall."

"Please, take it to the dumpster. Don't let any customers see you."

"Caroline?" Mitch's tone is deep and serious. "What's up?"

"Buster and a petrified squirrel."

"His dinner?"

"No. What's wrong with you? He found it in the wall. Okay, you were saying? Something about filling stadiums?"

"You will get a crowd. A very large, crazy crowd."

This is just what the old Frogmore needs. Someone to say, hey, it's cool here. "How much should I pay you?"

"Nothing. You're doing me a favor. This gig is back to basics for me. Just a man and his music."

"Okay, okay, great." I smile, then fade to a frown. "What if we don't get a crowd?"

"I'll shoot myself." He laughs. "You'll get a crowd. How about for the two shows, just have drinks and appetizers on the menu. Keep it fast and simple."

"Tell you what: you worry about the music, I'll worry about the food."

With the Festival kicking off in a week, I decide to place an ad in the *Gazette*.

Exclusive @ the Frogmore Café

Country Sensation Mitchum O'Neal

Live!

Beaufort Water Festival Week

Nightly shows @ 8:00 & 10:00 p.m.

Drinks and Appetizers Only

Reservations open an hour before each show

Monday, I hire Andy's boy, Jack, and his buddy Donny to work afternoons and evenings during the Water Festival.

"Good, good," Andy says when I tell him he's in charge of their training. "I'll work them hard, get them ready for football camp."

Russell mentions his friend Paris Truman. "She loves Mitch O'Neal." He jots her name and number on a napkin.

"Fine, but does she work hard?"

He nods. "Putting herself through school, and so far she carries a four-point."

"She's hired."

Tuesday, Andy reminds me of another Café problem. A stinky one. "If we're going to pack this place with people, you're going to have to get the toilets fixed. Only one of two works in the ladies'."

"Right, right."

"And you best make sure Buster gets done, or close to it. I've worked up an appetizer menu—baked bread and cheese, shrimp, chips and salsa, cheese fries—but we're going to need the Café at full steam during the day."

"Right, right again."

So I missed a few details. Maybe it's a good thing I'm not working for Carlos Longoria. *Caroline, you're fired.*

I check with Buster, and he promises me he'll get the rest of the wiring done before the Water Festival. "So, Mitch O'Neal is going to sing here, huh? Don't tell my wife."

"You better hide the newspaper. I put in an ad."

Next, I call Stu Green to come out and fix the toilets. He hammers around the bathrooms, shouting and cussing all afternoon, then finds me in the office.

"I hate to tell you this, Caroline"—he drops to the guest chair—"but I've patched up those pipes for the last time. The bathrooms need complete redoing."

My shoulders droop. "I'll put it in my letter to Santa. Can we survive the Water Festival?"

"I reckon. You don't get a big crowd here—" He hands me a bill.

Holy can't-flush. "This much for patching old pipes?" I look up at him. "And I *am* having a crowd here during the Water Festival. I hope. Mitch is singing."

"Mitch? Whatcha know. I'll have to find a date and come out."

I arch my eyebrows. "Front-row seating for you and your date . . ." I pass the plumbing bill back to him. "For a teensy-weensy discount."

"Tell you what, I'll check the pipes for you the night I come to a show. How's that? This"—he flicks the bill sticking out from my fingers—"I'll take in cash or a check."

"Spoilsport." Plopping down on the squeaky chair, I pull out the book of rubber checks and pray this plan with Mitch works.

Stu takes the check, twisting his lips into a smile. "How's Henry these days? We had a lot of fun playing smashmouth football back in the day."

My brother and the plumber were offensive guards for Beaufort High, seniors when sophomore Mitch O'Neal became a star quarterback.

"Henry's good. He took over Granddad Sweeney's construction business a few years ago. Married his college sweetheart, Cherry." I put the checkbook away, then double-click on QuickBooks.

"We lost touch after your mom died." He stares at the floor. "I'm sorry about that too. Death is not a good time to desert a friend."

"It happens, Stu."

People don't know how to respond to tragedy. Especially tragedy like ours. A mother who just doesn't want to live up to her responsibilities and commitments. A free spirit forever roaming. What kind of woman in her right mind chooses to abandon her children? But she did, then died of her own devices.

"Call Henry, Stu. He'd love to hear from you. Beaufort isn't big enough to avoid him for long."

"Yeah, you're right." Stu taps the check against his palm and for a brief, oh-hallelujah moment, I think he's going to tear it up or something. He stands. "I'll redo the bathrooms after the Water Festival."

"I suppose you'll want to charge me for it."

He reaches for the door. "That's how it usually works."

Wednesday morning, Luke offers to work the Festival. "I'm getting tired of sitting around all lonely. I can run the dishwasher, Caroline, or mop floors. Run food."

I pump his hand with a firm, CEO shake. "You're hired."

"I'm pretty handy in the kitchen," Pastor Winnie offers. "Put me on the schedule too."

We simultaneously look at Dupree—who growls. "Oh, all right. Put me down, Caroline. Bunch of bullies, y'all are, the lot of you."

Weekly Special

Country Sensation Mitch O'Neal!
Appearing Nightly 8:00 & 10:00

19

$\mathcal{G}$ood evening." Mitch rests his arm on his guitar, smiling, his eyes surfing the faces of the room. Friday evening and we have our first full house.

Dupree, new-hire Paris, and I squeeze between the crowded tables, taking orders. The house lights are down, and I can't see—*ouch*—where I'm going.

A crowd has been on the porch and in the Café yard for most of the afternoon. The off-duty deputies I hired for security—an unexpected expense—were kept busy with crowd control.

Two fights.

One auto accident.

One near hit-and-run.

And a lot of flirty-flirts with the scantily clad women waiting to see Mitch.

"Um, *helloooo*, miss, I need a large Diet Coke over here." A blonde stabs me with her claws as I hurry by.

"Large diet? Would you like an appetizer?"

Nothing. She's so glued to Mitch, she doesn't bother to answer. The Café is stuffed to the brim with gorgeous, sexy women vying for one man's attention.

If only they knew. Mitch is off the market.

"This is the Frogmore Café, a Beaufort treasure owned by my good friend Caroline Sweeney." He points to me. "The gorgeous brunette serving you tonight."

The blonde leers at me as I set down her soda. I smile. "Enjoy."

"I'm in the midst of writing new material," Mitch says. "Y'all are my guinea pigs."

Gorgeous blonde tosses her hair over her shoulder, beaming her sex-ray vision Mitch's way.

No wonder he needs a break from "love."

"I've been making changes in my life, coming back to my faith, reconnecting with friends and family." He gazes around the room. "We're living in a time where we can't be dispassionate about what we believe or we'll end up driving down the yellow line of life."

Mitch is being transparent in front of standing-room-only strangers. "Anyway—" He starts a chompy beat on his guitar. "Here's a song to get us started. One you'll remember. It hit number one on the country and pop charts."

The song energizes the room, and when he starts to sing, every voice rises with his.

The Frogmore Café Raft Race Team
Saturday, July 14
Come cheer for us

Saturday morning. Raft race. Nine o'clock. The Frogmore team gathers on the riverwalk with all the other rafters.

Andy, Russell, Mercy, Luke, Dupree, Pastor Winnie, Jack, his friend Donny, me, Mitch, and, last but not least, Miss Jeanne.

Walking among my very tired-looking team, I try to stir them up. "Look around; we size up all right with the competition." I smile broadly. Paul Mulroney's team looks older and more tired than mine. "We might just win this thing. Wouldn't that be something?"

They moan. Ho, boy. What a ragtag bunch. Maybe it was a bad idea to draw my raft team from the senior-citizen set and the crew I'm working half to death at the Café.

"Can't believe I let you do this to me." Miss Jeanne is the only one who looks half-awake. And she's sipping coffee. "I could die today."

I hook my arms around her shoulders. "What? You die? I know you're going to cheat death many times."

Sheree, the race coordinator, finds me. "Good news. Y'all are in the first race."

I whirl around to my team, cheering. "Woo-hoo, gang. We're up. Let's go."

They respond with a weak and sloppy, "Woo-hoo."

"Come on, y'all, wake up." I bounce around, patting each one on the back. "We're outside in the sun and wind. Life is good." I'm really believing we can win this thing. Why not? The underdog spoilers. "Sheree, who do we race?"

Wincing, she points beyond my shoulder. "I'm sorry, Caroline, it was the luck of the draw."

My eye follows the line of her finger. The team gasps collectively as we watch eleven muscle-bound men move in one stride toward us as if in synchronized slow-mo.

The few, the proud . . .

"The Marines?" I whirl around. "Sheree, you have us racing Marines?"

She curls away from me. "We drew names from a hat, Caroline."

"What about the teen girls, the Pirettes? Or the OB-GYN team? I want publicity, not humiliation."

Sheree cringes. "We drew from a *hat*."

I can't take my eyes off of the "dogs." "We're dead." The plan was to put us back on the Beaufort map, not wipe us out.

Andy drapes his arm around my shoulder. "I think we can take them."

"Take them?" I say, shaking Pastor Winnie's shoulder. He's sleeping standing. "We can't even stay awake."

"Have faith, Caroline," Andy says into my ear.

Faith? There's not enough in the world. I huddle my team. "All right, so our first race—"

"And last," Dupree says with confidence.

At that moment, our opponents' voices boom over us. "Death dogs, booya."

Yeah, they're going to cream us.

One by one, the Marines pile into their raft with disciplined order as if executing a military exercise. Their faces are painted with black and green stripes. Not one of them smiles.

Their raft captain—they have a raft captain—commands them in a solid, even voice as they row to the starting line. "Stroke, stroke, stroke."

Eleven strong backs and shoulders shoot the raft across the water.

"Caroline, my back went out." Dupree hunches over, pressing his hand to the small of his back.

"You don't have back problems, Dupe."

"Just came on me, suddenlike."

Mitch whispers in passing. "You know they've got to be disappointed we're their first heat."

"Caroline, let's go." Sheree motions for us to get into our raft. Mitch and Andy take the front, while Jack and Donny anchor the back. Waiting their turn, the breakfast-club boys watch their younger military counter-parts with hard glares.

"I looked like that once," Dupree mutters.

"Sure you did," Pastor Winnie says. "When your eyes was closed, dreaming."

Luke guffaws.

"I'll have you know, I was a champion welterweight boxer."

Focused on his past physical prowess, Dupree missteps off the dock while getting into the raft and flops into the drink with a big belly splash. Pastor Winnie and Luke double over, slapping their knees. Dupree shoots out of the water, cursing and sputtering.

Andy angles backwards. "Dupe, give me your hand."

But the old retired Marine refuses. "Coming aboard." Dupree hooks his arms over the side of the raft and with a strenuous "ugh" tries to hoist himself up. He struggles and kicks, his white, skinny legs flailing in the air.

I'm positive one of the Death Dogs cracks a smile.

Finally, Mitch yanks him aboard by the back of his shorts. He flops inside the raft and picks up his oar.

Pastor Winnie goes next, gracefully landing in the boat. Then Luke.

"All right, Miss Jeanne, you're up."

She hops in with a cheery "Weee," which makes Dupree's mishap all the more humiliating.

"Dupree, how're you doing?" I ask.

"Let's get this race started." He smacks the water with his oar.

Mercy Bea and Russell go next. And last, me. I assume the role of captain. "All right, stroke, stroke, stroke." Lowering my voice. "Stroke, stroke, stroke."

We turn in a circle. Mitch and Andy pull forward to back, Jack and Donny stroke back to front, and I'm not sure what the rest of us are doing.

I cut the air with my paddle. "Stop. Stroke front to back, front to back. Ready? Stroke, stroke, stroke." A sneak peek over my shoulder. The riverwalk crowd saw the whole thing.

Great publicity, Sheree said. Wait'll I see her.

We move toward the starting line with some amount of ease and precision. Once we're in place, I smile over at our competition. "Good luck."

Their eyes are forward, faces set. Not one response. Not a wave or how-do.

I pump up the team. "Everyone ready? Let's go. We can do this."

On the riverwalk, a man holds up an air horn. "Ready?" he calls.

"Oars up," I call like a good captain.

The Marines are stiff, poised with their oars about a foot above the water.

I refuse to be intimidated.

The air horn blasts. My heart careens into my chest. "Stroke, stroke, stroke." Adrenaline spikes my voice an octave or two. And I don't care.

We move forward, *wow,* with surprising swiftness, gliding over the water.

"Stroke, stroke, stroke," I repeat.

"My oar! I dropped my oar." Mercy Bea. Good grief. Behind us, her paddle floats on top of the water. "I can get it."

"Mercy Bea, no. Leave it."

Too late. As she stretches back, her hand slips off the side of the raft, and in she goes, head first.

"Start treading, Mercy Bea." The Jet-Ski guys will rescue her. "Stroke, stroke, stroke."

A few more strokes and we are halfway to the finish line. I look back to see the Death Dogs have not left the start line. *What gives?*

"Keep going." I cheer my team. "We're winning."

The breakfast-club boys stroke hard, putting their lean muscle into it.

"Stroke, stroke, stroke." Hope abounds in my heart. We're going to win this thing.

The crowd watching along the riverwalk goes bananas. The weaklings from the Café are smoking the Marine Death Dogs. Even if they launched right now—

"Stroke!"

I whip around to see the Death Dogs oars in the water, pulling in unity.

"Stroke." The captain's voice explodes in the sunny, Beaufort air. Another unified pull and the Death Dogs are practically halfway to us.

"Stroke, stroke, stroke," I yell, sounding every bit like a doggy chew toy. "Go, y'all. Go."

The muscles in Mitch and Andy's back ripple. The breakfast-boys grunt. We surge ahead. The finish line is right in front of us. I can *taste* it.

"Stroke." The Death Dogs' raft glides alongside ours.

"Stroke, stroke, stroke," I holler, my voice weakening along with my hopes.

"Stroke." The Death Dogs shoot past us.

My mouth drops as I watch, stunned.

"Stroke." One last pull and they power right over the finish line. The waterfront crowd watches in stunned amazement.

Dupree jumps up. "I'm bringing y'all up on charges of insubordination."

Miss Jeanne yanks on his swim trunks. "Sit down, old man, and hush up."

Being bossed by an old woman doesn't sit well with Dupree any more than being beat by a raft of younger Marines.

"Don't touch me, Jeanne." Dupree jerks away from her, twisting to his right, catching his foot on Luke's paddle. He stumbles. Arms flail. And over the side he goes. He comes up sputtering and cursing—again.

The Death Dogs celebrate in macho silence, raising their oars over their heads and barking, "*Semper Fi.*"

Dupree wags his fist. "*Semper Fi* this."

Pastor Winnie leans over, plants his hand on Dupree's head, and shoves him under.

Saturday-Night Special

July 21—Final Performance
Mitch O'Neal at the Frogmore Café
Last Day of the Water Festival
Appetizers, Tea, and Soda

20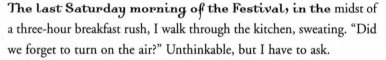

The last Saturday morning of the Festival, in the midst of a three-hour breakfast rush, I walk through the kitchen, sweating. "Did we forget to turn on the air?" Unthinkable, but I have to ask.

Between last Saturday's raft race and Mitch's nightly appearances, the Frogmore Café is back on the Beaufort dining circuit. Business picked up Tuesday and we've been busy all day, every day since.

We've done nothing but work and sleep. J. D.'s popped in most afternoons, dragged me back to the office for a little light necking, then left me breathless and, well, slightly heated. The man does things to me. *Clearly, I'm not fifteen anymore. Wonder if the blue-light special speech has a statute of limitations?*

But right now, I have heat issues of a different kind. Mercy Bea hovers over Andy's oscillating fan, arms spread like bird wings. "Caroline, I think the air's broken."

"You're not serious." I check the thermostat while Luke drags a step stool under the vent. "Eighty-eight."

"Nothing coming out, Caroline." Luke jumps off the stool.

"No, no, not today." I head out the door. "Not today." Sure enough, the rusty AC unit sits in the afternoon sun, frozen.

We throw open the doors, click the ceiling fans to high, and send Dupree out for emergency fan buying. But by the evening, the Café is just too hot.

I call Dad's AC guy, but his cell message says he's "Boating. Back on Monday."

So, in the very hot Café, Mitch prepares for his final night. He's so gracious and fantastic about the heat. In fact, he's been great all week. Last night he even helped carry out the trash—I let the crew clock out a little before eleven— and gave me a God talk.

Slinging the first trash bag into the dumpster: "Just because things aren't going well, Caroline, it doesn't change the fact He loves you. Don't assign your mama's weaknesses to God."

I handed him the next bag. "I'm not. But when will I know God is on my side or whatever?"

He tossed the second bag of trash. "Just takes faith." Dusting off his hands, he stared toward the amber bloom of the street lamps. "When I was twelve Dad signed me up for church camp. Did I ever tell you this? He really ticked me off and I stayed ticked off. On the last night of camp, there was a consecration meeting. All the parents came to witness their children pledging their lives to Jesus and His service.

"Dad was one of the speakers and I determined *not* to pledge my life. I wouldn't give Dad the satisfaction. The preacher's kid—" He exhaled. "What a brat."

I dug my clog's heel into the sand-and-shell parking lot. "Did you embarrass your dad?"

"No, actually, God embarrassed me." He gazes down. Half his face is lit by the moon glow through the trees. "And I deserved it."

"So much for the kind, loving, compassionate God your daddy talks about."

"Don't get confused, Caroline. God is all of those things and more, but when an arrogant teen digs in his heels, sometimes a good exposing is the only thing that gets his attention. There I was, standing stone still during worship. But one song into the set, God whacked me. I mean, *wham!*" He slapped his chest. "He invaded every pore of my being. Next thing I know, I'm face-first on the ground, bawling like a newborn calf." He laughed. "They could hear me all the way down to the lake. After that night, Caroline, I knew. Jesus loved me and there was no denying Him. But I sure as heck could run."

One last bag of trash. "You never told me this before."

He tossed it. "And you never told me about the pink room with the blue clouds."

"It's not a fun memory. Who do you think told your dad?"

He slung his arm around my shoulder and walked me toward the Café. "Jesus, I reckon. You're going to have to give on this Jesus thing, Caroline. He's pursuing you. Now, you can accept it, or be like me. A running fool."

Easier said than done.

Back to the death of the AC—if it had to break, tonight was the best night. The Water Festival's Commodore's Ball is going on across the road at Waterfront Park, and even the wonderful Mitch O'Neal can't draw a large crowd. By eight, my crew is sweating and begging to meet their family and friends at the Ball.

"Go, go. Have fun." We had to shut down the kitchen anyway on account of the heat. I can handle serving a few iced teas and sodas.

"Looks like it's just you and me in the room tonight." I hand Mitch an ice-packed mason jar of tea.

He pauses from tuning his guitar for a gulp of tea. "I've faced worse."

"It's been a great week. Thank you."

"Did you make money?"

"We've been so busy I haven't had time to sort it out. I've just been putting the money in the safe each night. But, I've gone to a third money bag."

Mitch raises a brow. "A third money bag?"

I laugh. "I know, big deal, right? But before this week, I could keep an entire month's revenue in one money bag and hardly tell the difference between the empty ones."

A little after eight, the house is half-full. I set pitchers of water, tea, and soda on all the tables and tell folks to help themselves, on the house.

After that, I perch on a counter stool with a mini fan blowing directly on me, ready to listen to Mitch, undistracted for the first time all week. I would've liked to have done something with music—learned an instrument. But Daddy worked long days and Mama was too unpredictable to schedule lessons.

"Thank y'all for coming out tonight," Mitch says, starting the set.

The audience applauds.

"Caroline is your server. Take good care of her. She's an excellent woman." His gaze fixes on me. *The vibe again.* What is up?

The Christmas bells ring as the front door opens. Pastor O'Neal crosses the threshold. I hop off the stool.

"Pastor, welcome."

He tips his head toward my ear. "I came to hear my boy. Is there a table?"

"Y-yes." I motion to a table near his son.

Mitch hesitates for the slightest second. "Everyone, please welcome my dad, Pastor Eli O'Neal."

Again, the crowd applauds.

"Can I get you anything?" I whisper to Pastor O'Neal.

He shakes his head. "Just want to hear my famous son."

My gaze locks with Mitch for a moment. I'm almost disappointed the Café isn't packed like the previous nights. But by the expression on Mitch's face, this moment is worth more than a packed Café or even a stadium of fifty thousand.

"Dad . . ." Mitch's voice fades a little, but he holds on. "It's an honor to have you here." He looks out over the dining room. The guests' smiles seem permanently fixed. "Anyway, I want to play this new tune for you. It's called 'Caroline.'"

Back on my stool, I sit straight. *Me, Caroline?*

The bells clank and jingle again. In walks Elle, whom I haven't seen all week, with Chris Barry. One of the victims on her list.

I smile and give her a thumbs-up. She gives me a curled lip. I wince. *Sorry, not good?*

No . . .

As Mitch plays, the music swirls around me, and I feel like I'm taking a cool dip in a clear, blue pool at the end of a hot day. His voice is rustic, yet sophisticated, and perfectly pitched. I forget time and space. Mitch's music reached into the unseen and capture the melodies of the lowcountry.

Sing to me, Caroline
A lowcountry lullaby

Sunday afternoon a banging on the front door wakes me from a sound sleep. Groggy, I stumble to the door. Able to finally pull the plug on a whirlwind Water Festival, I crashed a little after one this morning and am not yet ready to face the day.

Dad stands on the front porch. "I came to check out the Café's AC unit."

"How'd you know?"

"Ran into Elle."

"Ah . . . I called the AC guy, Dad. Hopefully, he'll be able to stop by tomorrow." My brain is fuzzy, my thoughts thick. "Want something to drink?" Schlepping to the kitchen, I jerk open the fridge door. It's empty. Not even a bottle of water.

"No, I'm good. Let's go look at the AC. I bet all it needs is a swift kick. Save you a repair bill."

A swift kick? "But of course." Dad's solution to everything is a swift kick. Even for Henry and me on occasion.

Still in my pajamas, I follow Dad across the Café parking lot. He circles the rusty AC unit, stooping and squinting. Sniffing.

"Dad, you're ridiculous." I cross my arms and yawn. "I don't see how a swift kick is going to fix this thing, but, hey, free meals for a month if you get it running. Andy won't last long in a hot kitchen without central air."

"Shh." Dad presses his ear against the grate over the unit's fan, then shakes the rusty monster, analyzing the rattle. "Hmmm . . ."

My dad, the AC whisperer.

Nevertheless, he has me curious. I tilt my head to listen. *Speak to me, AC.* Nothing. I hear nothing.

"All right, here we go." He draws back his leg, then—*BAM!*—drives his foot into the side of the metal.

With a screaming laugh, I jump sideways. "Dad!"

The monster shudders. Dad draws back and swift-kicks again. *WHAM!*

Unbelievable. "You're going to break your toe."

The monster shudders. The fan spins once, then stops. "Come *on*," Dad yells with a precise pound on the unit with his fist.

Whishhhh. The fan starts to spin and a nice, gentle whir fills the air.

I stare at him. "No way." In all his swift-kicking days, I've never seen Dad do this.

He dusts his palms. "Had a twig or something in there, gumming up the works."

"Dad, this is nothing short of a miracle."

He hitches up his shorts while puffing out his chest. "Ain't nothing to it."

Since he's here and *fixing* things, might as well see if he can swift-kick the plumbing.

In the soft light of day, I discover the Café is a disaster. Three broken chairs, a hole in the front wall, a cracked mirror in the ladies' room (I don't want to know), a sink coming off the wall in the boys' room (I really don't want to know), and a tear in the threadbare carpet. A tear!

In the ladies' room, I flush one of the toilets to show Dad how it floods. As we watch the water swirl over the rim of the bowl and onto the floor, Dad settles his hands on his hips. It's then I notice he's not wearing faded, holey jeans, nor his trademark plain T-shirt and loosely laced work boots.

No indeed. He's wearing an ironed, oversized button-down with khaki shorts and Top-Siders. My stepmother is a miracle worker.

"You best call Stu," Dad says.

"Stu? What about a swift-kick?" Toilet water oozes around my flip-flopped feet. "Come on, Dad, give it a good kick. Maybe all it needs is to loosen up a stuck twig or, you know, a *log*." I can't help it, I had to say it.

Dad looks at me with wide-eyed disgust. "Good grief, Caroline. Mind yourself."

Crawling back into bed a few minutes later, I'm still laughing.

The closing credits roll on *White Christmas* as J. D. and I cuddle on the couch, singing at the top of our lungs, arms and legs intertwined.

"With every Christmas card I write . . ."

Candles flicker from the end tables and bookshelves. The carriage house is cozy and romantic.

"Only you, Sweeney." J. D. tugs me onto his lap, pressing his hand around to my back.

"Only me what?" His touch sends fiery tingles racing down to my toes. The past week's quick interludes of passion in the Café office have left me smoldering and stirred.

"Watch a Christmas movie in July."

"Why not?" Reaching for the remote, I aim at the black-and-white fuzz on the TV and click it off. "Why wait all year to watch a great"— his hot breath swirls around my neck "[*swallow*] romantic movie."

His hand is sliding under the edge of my shirt as his lips caress my neck. *Ho, boy.*

"You are so beautiful, Caroline. Sexy as the day is long."

Apparently, we are not talking about Christmas movies in July anymore.

"J. D. . . ."

Slowly he lays me back on the couch, his hands finding skin, his lips finding mine. He drinks deep, then whispers in my ear. "Let me stay over, Caroline. Please."

How is it possible to burn at the sound of his desire? But I do. His wanting blankets me, and, oh, surrender seems sweet. My breathing becomes rapid and deep.

"I don't know, J. D. We've only been dating a few weeks."

Raising up, he flashes his luminous, square smile. "Eight weeks, Caroline. My parents were married in six." With a laughing growl, he rolls me off the couch and onto the floor. "Don't you care about me?"

I brush my hand over his hair. "You know I do. And you?"

"Would I be here if I didn't?"

Grinning, I press my lips on his. "You *do* have a rep."

"Okay, okay, I was a scoundrel once. But Caroline, you've reformed me."

"Oh, what power I have. Hmm . . ." I touch my finger to my chin. "What else can I get you to do for me?"

Wiggling his eyebrows, he says, "Let me stay and I'll show you."

He's trying to be funny and light, but a tremor of trepidation causes me to shove him aside and sit up. "J. D., this is, um, well, new territory for me."

"Baby, it's okay, I know." He runs his hand along my jawline. "You won't regret it."

The passion burning in my middle begins to cool and solidify. "Oh, you are so tempting, J. D., but I need more time. I'm the girl with the blue light in her car, remember? The girl with the daddy who said, 'Wait for the ring and the wedding.'"

"Sure, babe, but you're not that fifteen-, sixteen-year-old girl anymore. You're a woman with your own business, your own life." He traces his finger along the neckline of my top. "Your own desires."

For a long moment, I study the curves of his face. Am I in love? Do I need to be in love for him to stay over? How will I feel in the morning when I can't undo the night? "J. D., please let me think about it." I grab his hand away from its journey.

He hesitates, then kisses me slowly, softly. "Okay, I don't want to rush you, but Caroline, decide yes. You don't know what you do to me."

For a long time after he leaves, I lay in bed, staring at what would've been his pillow, thinking about life, Daddy and Mama, Mitch and his camp-God story. Despite the ache J. D. stirred in me with his kisses and touch, an overwhelming peace comforts me that tonight I sleep alone.

After a five-minute inspection of the bathrooms Monday morning, Stu calls me into the office. Summation: It's bad.

"How bad?"

Sitting at my desk, he writes out a quote, referencing a thick book from time to time. I tap a pen against the faux-wood desktop.

"Annoying . . ." Stu says without looking up.

"Sorry." I jam the pen into the holder and start to pace back and forth. My clogs thud against the floor. *Aren't plumbers, like, millionaires? What does Stu earn—eighty dollars an hour? My gnarly plumbing is going to buy him a new truck, I just know it.*

First Buster, and now Stu.

After Dad left Sunday afternoon, I showered, met J. D. at Panini's for a quick bite—he was on duty—then spent three hours going over the Water Festival revenue.

We did well, and I even said, "Thank you, Jesus," but once I calculated the extra payroll, the food charged on my credit card, paying for the rent-a-cops, plus standard monthly bills, like electricity and water, there was only enough left over to pay half Buster's bill. Never mind whatever damage Stu is planning.

My heart is ready to wave the white flag, but my head shouts not to surrender yet.

Meanwhile, Stu fishes out a prehistoric calculator from his toolbox.

"Where'd you find that thing, caveman, under a rock with the fire?"

"Oops, look, I added too many zeros."

I frown. Plumbers have no sense of humor. Better make myself scarce. "Wonder what Andy is doing in the kitchen?"

"Yeah, go see what Andy is doing. And Caroline, if a basket of Bubba's Biscuits showed up right here . . ." Stu points to a spot on the desk in front of him.

"Gotcha."

"Well, what's the damage?" Andy looks up from mixing a couple of Pluff Mud Pies.

"He's calculating it now. But I have a feeling it's going to be bad."

I grab a basket, layer it with a napkin, and drop in a few fresh, hot biscuits.

"We had some plumbing done at the house awhile back. It ain't cheap."

Worry creeps in. How am I going to pay for this? If I'd have known all this would come down on my shift, I might have opted for Kirk to put the Café on the auction block.

Next to me Andy hums. A hymn, I think.

When I return to the office with the biscuits and an added bonus of iced tea, Stu is finished with the plumbing estimate.

"I cut where I could."

Exchanging biscuits for a bill, I close my eyes. *Think cheap. Think cheap.* With one eye, I peek at the bottom line. Holy cow. My other eye pops open. "*This* is your bargain price?"

"Have you been in those bathrooms?" Stu snatches the estimate from me and points out detailed expenses. "I'm not just fixing a few toilets and sinks. We have to tear up the floor and wall. Replace all the pipes. Get new fixtures. Replace the plaster with drywall, retile."

I grimace. "Right, of course. When can you start?"

Monday evening I lock up the Café with Jones's box from the attic tucked under my arm. It will look nice on the carriage house bookshelves. I can prop the picture against it.

In the parking lot, Mercy Bea leans against Matilda, taking a final drag on her cigarette before mashing it into the dirt with the toe of her clunky shoe. "Did we clear the tower last week? Make some money?"

"We did very well, but we still owe Buster, and now Stu." I fall against the car door next to her. "You wouldn't happen to secretly be a rich heiress would you?"

She tosses her head back with a laugh. "No offense, I wouldn't be here if I were. Guess Jones checked out just when the ole Money Pit started sinking deeper." She picks at the Mustang's peeling paint. "My brother had an old car like this. A '71 Dodge Charger. He and his friends would race down 170."

"The good ole days when there was no traffic after nine o'clock. Dad has a few racing stories. Almost got killed once."

"My brother too. Probably more than once." Mercy Bea pats Matilda's door. "So, has she broken down lately?"

"I haven't been driving as much. Guess she just wanted to retire and sit in the shade."

"Sounds good to me." The dyed and painted waitress taps another cigarette from a crumpled pack. "You have plans with J. D. tonight?" She flicks her lighter and touches the flame to the cigarette. "Don't you just like to look at him? I think his face is just about perfect."

The memory of his face from last night is etched in my mind. My heart skips one beat. "Just about perfect, yes."

"You know, I never took to handsome men for myself."

"What kind of men do you like?" I shift the box from one arm to the next.

Smoke billows from her nose like she's a steaming kettle. "Roughed-up looking, but with soft hearts. The boys' daddy was sweet, but he could rumble if need be. Broke his nose in three places, had a crushed cheekbone that never got fixed, and a scar right here." She slashes her red nail across the side of her face down to her neck. "Never would tell me how he got that one."

"Where's he now?" This is the most Mercy Bea's ever opened up to me.

"Only God in heaven knows. He got weird and ran off."

"I'm sorry."

Her cigarette crackles and burns as she takes a long drag. "Your mama *was* a loose nut. Prettiest girl around, too, but—" Mercy whistles *cuckoo* and makes the crazy circle with her finger. "Ever get scared you'll turn out like her?"

"Once a day and twice on Sunday. But I try to think of her good qualities. Creative, uninhibited, free . . ."

"Your mama did one good thing." Mercy flicks her second cigarette to the ground. "You."

The compliment surprises me.

"Guess I have to give your old man most of the credit for you turning out so nice." She gestures toward the Café. "Your mama would've never kept this place if she'd had a chance to fly off to Barcelona. Didn't look after her kids, why would she care for a dang Café?" She shakes her head. "I wouldn't fret none over it. You're not like her. Not that I can see."

A light wash of tears blurs my vision. Go figure. Encouragement comes from the strangest places. "Good to know."

"Well, better head out." Mercy Bea starts to walk off but stops, digging the toe of her shoe into the gravel. "I lost my job down at the nursing home. Wanted you to know."

"What happened?"

"They said I was snippy with the old folks."

Not surprised. "I'm sure it's not an easy job."

She flicks her wrist at me. "Shift happens, doesn't it? So, I'm available for more work if you aren't keeping that skinny gal Paris around."

"Paris wants to keep working. For now."

Mercy Bea clicks her thumbnail against her middle fingernail. "If you need me, let me know."

"Will do." I wait for her to walk off, but she stares off toward the river for a long moment. "Is there something else?"

She purses her lips and shakes her head. "Naw, I'm good. See you in the morning."

Daily Special

Tuesday, July 24

Meatloaf

Choice of Three Sides: Baked Beans, Cole Slaw,
   Mac and Cheese, Mashed Potatoes, Green Salad,
   Turnip Greens, French Fries, Okra, or Peas

Bubba's Buttery Biscuits

Sweet Caroline Pie à la Mode

Tea, Soda, Coffee

$6.99

21

To: CSweeney
From: Hazel Palmer
Subject: Re: The Frogmore and me
Caroline,
Sorry, got swamped with end-of-fiscal-year accounting. Meant to e-mail about Fernando. Charming, lovely Fernando. Oh, Caroline . . .

He took me to Semproniana, a muy *romantic place in L'Eixample. It's converted from a '60s factory. Has these great iron columns, old furniture, paintings. A very cozy atmosphere.*

Handsome Fernando (think Antonio Banderas without the wrinkles) is all habla, habla *in* español *with his arm lightly around my waist, body whispering. I might have swooned a little because I don't remember walking to the table.*

He knew everyone, including the owner, who sat down with us for a few minutes.

We ate, talked, drank a little wine, but not too much. I'm still a Southern Baptist girl, but when in Rome—in my case, Barcelona . . .

We strolled the shops, and C, it felt like we'd known each other for years. His English is perfect, yet sprinkled with the most delicious accent. He tried to coach my Spanish along and we laughed so hard we couldn't speak at all.

He kissed me tenderly good night and said, "Hasta luego."

Apparently, his "luego" was ten minutes later. He dropped me off and called me on his way home! Shocked me so much, I didn't even know it was him for the first minute of the call. I'm like, "Who is this?"

LOL. I'm meeting him again for dinner tonight.

So, J. D., huh? I haven't been around much in the last four or five years, but isn't he a ladies' man? The more the merrier? Big surprise to hear you're interested in him.

Didn't he have a crush on you in junior high?

I keep up with home by reading the Gazette *online and loved seeing you on the front page in the raft race. I loved the quote you gave Melba Pelot: "The Frogmore is here, bubba." Cracked me up. I called Carlos "bubba" the next day. Didn't get it. (Thank goodness.)*

And Mitch singing at the Café? Brilliant. By the way, what is he doing in town? I e-mailed the story links to Carlos. Your stock soared with him. I swear, he drooled. He loves that you're saving an old Café, helping people keep their jobs. If you're loyal to the Café, you'd be loyal to him.

If you need $25K, go to the bank. It's a business loan. No biggie. Please tell Elle and Jess I love them. I owe them both e-mails.

"Here's looking at you, kid."

>*Love, Haz*
>
>*CFO, SRG International, Barcelona*

Kirk calls Wednesday. "How's it going?"

"Besides the bathroom plumbing being ripped out as we speak? Peachy. What's up?"

"Do you know someone named Elle?"

"Yeah, I might. Why?"

"It's weird, but the other night I had this garbled voice mail, and all I could make out was her name, yours, and a wedding?" His voice goes up on the end.

What is wrong with El? Did she completely abandon *cool* when she launched Operation Wedding Day?

"I'll talk to her."

Confiding she's on a manhunt would be wrong, right?

"Thanks. Also, I wanted to let you know Roland and Dale spent a couple of days down at the Water Festival with their wives. Loved it. They are more interested in Beaufort than ever. Roland's wife heard Mitch O'Neal at the Café one night, and I think she envisions becoming his best friend or something."

"Did you tell her he doesn't live here most of the time?"

He snickers. "No. Listen, Caroline." His tone sobers. "They saw other properties they liked. There's a restaurant on Lady's Island for sale. Needs way less work than the Frogmore. Their business is ten times better. It's close to the beach, tourists, and retirees with money. Are you getting the picture?"

"Grimly, yes." My heart sinks, dragging with it my chance for freedom.

"I'm sorry, but listen, I'll keep looking for a buyer. You do the same, okay."

"Come out, come out, wherever you are. Olly, olly, oxen free."

Kirk's laugh is warm. "Don't get discouraged. The Buzz Boys are still interested. It's just you have some competition. If they don't buy now, maybe they will in a year."

"In the meantime, Kirk, did Jones happen to leave a secret cash stash behind?"

"Sorry, no. Why?"

"We're broke and the Café repairs couldn't wait." I reach for the straightened paper clip that's always on the desk and twirl it between my fingers.

"You'll get the money back when you sell."

"When. I'm more in a *now* need."

"Hang in there. I think we can close the informal probate by Christmas, bar any unforeseen roadblocks."

"Christmas?"

"Ninety-nine percent chance, yes. If you still have the Barcelona opportunity, you could be there by January."

The burden of a few grand over plumbing doesn't seem so bad now.

"One more thing, Caroline. I was going through some papers, looking at copies of bank statements, and I found Jones's property insurance policy."

"Finally, I'm rich. How much?"

"Ha, you're funny. The Café is currently uninsured."

I plop my head down to the desktop. "You're kidding, Kirk." Jones, you quirky little man. "Why'd he let the insurance lapse?"

"He probably forgot, Caroline. Just call the agent. I'll overnight the policy to you. Get it renewed quick. You don't want to be caught with fire or storm damage. Plus, any buyer will want to know you have a current policy."

I scribble a note on a yellow sticky and tack it to the computer monitor: PAY INSURANCE. Not that I'd forget.

As I hang up, a loud crash, a resounding thud, and a booming voice seep in from the other side of the wall. Stu is tearing up the bathrooms, telling the pipes what they can do with themselves.

The second meeting of Elle's Operation Wedding Day is at the Café after closing. From behind the counter, I fill three glasses with soda. "El, did you call Jones's lawyer, Kirk?"

She scrunches up her nose. "You gave me his number."

"I didn't think you'd actually call him."

"Why not? He's on the list. I liked his voice. He sounds smart and sexy."

At this, I laugh. "He looks like a rumpled Ross Geller."

"Oo, does he whine?"

"Not that I've noticed." I pass around the drinks. "But if you call him again, do not mention me, please."

"What? I have to mention you. You're the only thing we have in common." Elle holds up her manhunt list. More than half the names are scratched off. "Water Festival pretty much took care of the list. I'm down to three names. And I can tell you right now, two of them will be a no go. I'm merely giving them a courtesy date."

Jess gives her side glance. "Desperate girls can't be so picky."

"Speaking of . . . Elle, is your meeting over?" I ask. "I need advice."

She pounds the handle of a butter knife on the counter. "Temporary pause of Operation Wedding Day discussion to deal with Caroline's problem. You have the floor, Miss Sweeney."

"Okay, well . . ." Gee, I'm nervous. I didn't think this would be so embarrassing. "First of all, Jess, wherever Ray gets his information, he's dead-on. J. D. is a great kisser."

Jess flashes her palm for a high five. "You go, C."

I slap her a light five. Not sure this is a real celebratory moment. "Yeah, well, as you know, kissing leads to other things—"

A bang and clank come from the ladies' room, where Stu is still working and swearing. Jess and Elle lean back and stare toward the bathroom.

"What's going on in there?" Jess asks.

"Stu Green, bathroom pipes, old plaster walls." I point to Elle. "Hey, he's single. Add him to the list."

"What? No." She leans and whispers. "Mean-machine Stu Green?"

In high school, he had a wicked mean streak, which unfortunately influenced my already angry brother.

I tap Elle's paper. "He's really nice now, and he's eligible, fairly handsome, and I saw him without a shirt. Great abs. Come on, add him to the list."

"All right, smarty britches, I'll add him. Even though his potty mouth matches the toilets he fixes." Elle grunts as she writes *Stu Green*. "But I'm not worried. There's no way he can spell *renaissance*."

"Fine, Stu's on the list. Caroline, back to J. D. What's up?" Jess props her elbows on the counter and chin in her hands.

"Yeah, well, he wants to stay *ooover*."

Elle gasps. "What? He said that?"

Jess remains unchanged. "Can't blame the guy, Caroline. He's been there, done that, if you know what I mean, and you're a very sexy, beautiful woman."

Elle gapes at her. "So what, Jess? How does her beauty give him a free pass to the Caroline show?"

"It doesn't, El. Bring it down a notch. I'm just not surprised."

"So, what do I do?" I glance between Elle and Jess, who simultaneously answer.

"Tell him to take a hike." Elle.

"Go for it." Jess.

Hearing Jess's response, Elle launches out into Incredulous-Indignation Land. "Jess, didn't your mama raise you better? Caroline, no way. You're willing to give it up for a good kisser?" She huffs. "What happened to the blue-light queen?"

"For crying out loud, El, she's not fifteen anymore. And my mama raised me just fine." Jess focuses on me. "You're a grown woman. This is the twenty-first century. Do what you want."

"Who cares what century it is? Some things do *not* change with age or time." Elle shakes the knife at me. "If he wants you that much, why can't he commit?"

"Ring and a date seem like a lot to ask," I say. "I'm not sure I want those things from him."

Fire flares in Elle's eyes. "Oh, really? Then what's the point of this discussion? Caroline, giving the most precious part of yourself, a one-time gift that can't be undone or taken back had better be worth a heck of a lot more than a sleepover."

Well, there's a point.

Another crash resounds from the bathroom, and Stu bursts into the dining room, lugging a rust-stained, water-dripping toilet. He stops when he catches us staring.

"Afternoon, *laa-dies*." He drops the once-white ladies' throne right in the middle of the dining room. I gasp. Elle and Jess jump against each other.

"Stu, what are you doing?" I run around the counter. "You can't put that nasty old toilet in the middle of the Café."

"Don't worry, Caroline, it's only temporary."

"Move it now, Stu. If the health inspector sees this—"

"Health inspector?" He clicks his tongue and winks, holding up crossed fingers. "He and I are like this."

"Stu, come on, think of my customers."

"You're closed, Caroline."

"Move the toilet."

"Bossy." Stu hoists the toilet and carries it out back.

Returning to my place behind the counter, I distract myself by rolling silverware for tomorrow's business. "So, no sleepover."

"No. Caroline, respect yourself." This from Elle. Emphatically.

"I have to admit, she's right, Caroline. If you're not sure, wait. Please, don't let J. D. talk you into something you'll regret."

I nod, still unsure. "Right. Right." Truth is, it's enticing and alluring to be wanted by someone like J. D. All-out handsome, sexy, built, macho with a little-boy cuteness.

After a moment of silence, Elle pounds the counter again with the end of the knife. "Are we done with Caroline? Good. Back to the meeting at hand."

As she bangs her makeshift gavel, Stu rounds the kitchen corner. I rush to pour him a glass of iced tea. "Tea, Stu?"

"Yeah, Caroline, that'd be great. Hotter than blazes out there."

"Say, Stu, the girls and I were arguing over a word." I peek at Elle. "You wouldn't happen to know how to spell *renaissance*, would you?"

"Renaissance, huh?" He lifts his chin in the air, eyes squinting. Elle snickers, and I hear a pencil scratching. "Great revival of art and literature in Europe, beginning in the fourteenth century, lasting well into the seventeenth. Launched the world into the modern era out of the medieval. R-e-n-a-i-s-s-a-n-c-e. *Renaissance.*"

We all blink at him. He's looking at us. *Is that all?* I clear my throat. "See, I told you there were two *s*'s, Elle."

Stu snaps up his jar of tea and heads off to the ladies' room. "You'd think you'd know that, Elle, being an artist and all."

"Yeah, you'd think I would." Elle slowly rewrites *Stu Green* on her list.

"I'm more than a simple plumber, ladies." Stu spreads his arm with a bow, walking backwards to the bathroom.

When he's out of sight, I fall against the counter, laughing.

22

On a remote part of St. Helena's, the beach is lit with dozens of sandbag candles. "J. D., how beautiful."

"Thought you'd like it." His chest is warm against my back as he cradles me in his arms and kisses my cheek. "Beyond the palmettos is the house my great-granddad built. We use it for family events, and Mom comes out here sometimes. Did I tell you she's trying to become a novelist?"

"Really? What's she writing?"

"Who knows?" Wrapping his hand around mine, he leads me down the sandy, candlelit path. "She won't show anyone. Hungry?"

"Starved. Bubba, this is amazing. Your first major romantic date . . . scoring big points here."

He glances over his shoulder. "My plan is working."

Smiling, I cuddle his arm, pressing my face against his bulky muscles. "Ah, there's a plan? We shall see if it's working."

Since our hot-and-heavy Christmas-movie night, he's been respect-ful and patient. Tonight, though, looking over the romantic beach set-ting, a fleeting thought of his patience wearing thin breezes through my mind.

At the end of the candles path, a small fire burns. There's a blanket, a picnic basket, and a boom box playing something soft and classical.

The serenity of the twilight sky and ocean surround us.

"Sit here." J. D. points to a spot on the blanket with a bow. "How does milady feel about steak and shrimp?"

"Your lady feels wonderful about steak and shrimp." I shake the sand from my flip-flops before stepping on the blanket.

"How do you like your steak?"

"Medium." I open the picnic basket to find treasures from the Café. Andy's apple crumb cake, baked beans, Bubba's Buttery Biscuits. And a jug of tea. "You sneak, how'd you order this without me knowing?"

He raises his brow. "I have my ways."

He grills and I set up. As usual, he gets me laughing over some deputy story and I tell him about Mercy Bea finding a critter in the pantry.

"She went screaming through the dining room. Like she's never seen a rat before."

I have to admit, it freaked me out too. But not for Mercy Bea to see.

"Don't tell me, the exterminator comes in the morning."

"First thing. Darn the cost too."

Talk is light through dinner. J. D. is fun to hang out with, but when he sets his plate aside and scoots in behind me, wrapping his arms around me, all the dormant passions ignite. I'm not sure how long "no" can linger on my lips. We are very alone here.

His chin rests on my shoulder. "Caroline, can I ask you a question?"

"Sure." I twist to see his face. His brown eyes reflect the fire's flame.

"I was wondering . . ." He plants a warm kiss on my neck.

My heart pumps. Is he going to ask me to decide tonight? Here? Now? "Wondering?"

He smiles, slowly, peering into my eyes. "Let's move in together. I care about you, Caroline. We're good together, and I'd like to see if we could make a life of us."

If my heart wasn't pumping before, it is now. "Live together? You and me. Like, move in over the weekend or sometime?"

The wind brushes my hair over my face. J. D. smoothes it away. "Yeah, the weekend or sometime. Look, babe, I understand your hesitancy in letting me stay over. This is just a way to let you know I'm going to be there in the morning. I don't think we're ready for marriage, so this is a great compromise. See how we do together, you know?"

Do together? So far, except for sex, we *do* together just fine. Laugh at each other's jokes, listen to end-of-workday stories.

"I don't know, J. D." My stomach cramps a little. Can we go back to just sleeping over?

"Think about it." He holds my face to kiss me, as if reminding me what awaits if I say yes.

"O-okay, I will." I whisper to the God I hope exists. *Help.* "Do you love me, J. D.?"

"I'm getting there."

A soft knock sounds on the door. "Caroline, it's Stu."

The plumber pops through the office door and collapses in the chair opposite my desk. He runs his rough, dirty hand through his dark, thick hair so it stands on end.

"Well?" I brace for the blow. The bad news. *Needs more work. Costs more money.*

"The twa-lette rooms are done." Stu shakes his head slowly. "I think Houdini installed the plumbing first go-'round."

"Hard job?" As if I didn't know. Any closer to his liturgy of four-letter words and I'd have curly hair. I shouldn't have teased Elle into putting him on her list. "What's the damage?"

Reaching in his hip pocket, Stu pulls out the bill and tosses it to the desk. "It cost a little more than I thought."

"Naturally." Squinting, I unfold the paper. *Boing!* "A little more. Stu, it's an extra nine hundred. Thirteen thousand dollars."

Over the past few weeks, I managed to save three thousand for this auspicious day, plus pay Buster a grand, barely wheedling down his bill. I stare so long at the bottom line, my vision blurs.

"Caroline?"

I snap to attention. "Yeah, sorry, just thinking. Can you come around for the check tomorrow?" Because tonight I'm going to pull out all my teeth, stuff them under my pillow, and expect the Tooth Fairy to pay big dividends.

"Sure. I'll be by in the afternoon."

"Thanks for everything, Stu."

He leaves and I close the office door, plop down in the desk chair, and run my fingers over my tired eyes.

Jesus, can You help me? Please.

How does one listen for an answer from the Almighty?

"Caroline, need you out here." It's Andy. Yeah, for a nanosecond, I thought Jesus sounded like a friend of mine.

Guess He's leaving this problem in my bailiwick. I shove out of the chair. "Coming."

By the time we close, I still don't have any idea how I'm going to pay Stu. I walk across the parking lot, noticing how the sunlight dances across the Mustang. Poor girl, been sitting there so long. I should take her out . . .

I stop. From nowhere, an alien thought crashes over my heart. My gut tightens. *No.*

As I stand staring at Matilda, the wind gushes from the river, lifting the limbs of the car's live-oak canopy. Matilda is draped in sunlight. I glance overhead. *Did someone cut down a tree?*

More light. More wind. The thought streams again. *Sell.*

No! "Listen, Jesus, if this is You, forget it. Dad couldn't convince me, nor Henry, and quite frankly, I'm positive they exist and love me—well, Daddy does; jury's out on Henry—so don't come knocking on this door. If this is some divine idea— You're off by a country mile."

But even after a quick, refreshing shower, I'm still nagged by the earlier encounter. *No*, I say to no one. My own stubborn thoughts, maybe.

Slipping into a comfy Liz Claiborne top and skirt, I wander into the living room. The evening seems empty and ominous. I walk along the bookshelves, reading the spines of Jones's collection.

Dickens, Twain, Faulkner, James, Austin— I stop. *Austin? Jones, you old romantic.* He has several of her works. A couple of Steinbecks, and Grisham, Clancy . . . figures. The Bible. Jones's Bible.

Hesitating, I reach for the worn leather book. Pages slip, almost falling to the ground, when I look inside. Just about every one is marked with scribbles in Jones's broad, round script. The back half of the book is so marked I can barely read the text. Almost every verse is highlighted with yellow, blue, or green.

"Jones, how did you read with all of this coloring?"

The old man practically devoured a book I've never even read. Dickens and Austin, yes. Steinbeck and Faulkner, yes, but under duress. American lit class. But the Word of God (or so it claims to be)? Never.

I don't know one verse . . . Wait, I do. John 3:16. The football-game Scripture. Where is John? John, John, John. The tissuelike pages crinkle and slide as I hunt around pages labeled Deuteronomy and Exodus. Where is John?

Finally, I sit on the edge of the coffee table, find the table of contents, and turn, gently, to John.

Chapter 3. Verse 16.

The words are printed in red. Interesting. *For God so loved the world, that He gave His only begotten Son, that whoever believes in Him should not perish, but have eternal life.*

I read them over again, liking the sound of being "so loved" and "not perish." Then my eye skips over the next page.

Jones circled and colored over verse 36. *He who believes in the Son has eternal life; but he who does not obey the Son shall not see life, but the wrath of God abides on him.*

Wrath of God? What happened to not perishing? Slamming the book closed, I jump up. "God, please—"

Mitch's camp story springs to mind. *"He's pursuing you. Now, you can accept it or be like me, a running fool."*

What if I don't want either? Middle of the road is good, right? What I need is some company. Get my mind off things like boyfriends wanting to move in, selling cars, and God's wrath. Wonder what Dad and Posey are up to?

I grab my keys and purse and head out the door. "Wake up, Matilda, we're going out."

The wind in my face feels good. The Toby Keith song on the radio is one of my favorites, and by the time I brake for the stoplight on Carteret, I feel like myself again.

Then I spot Mercy Bea on the corner with a fleshy-faced, rotund man. *What is she doing?* I move to the left turn lane instead of going right, over the bridge. *Is she all right?*

Flesh-face jabs the air around her, running off at the mouth. In return, Mercy Bea wrings her hands, a pantomime of explaining and pleading.

My head doesn't like what my eyes see. With a quick glance up at the light—still red—I cup my hands around my mouth. "Mercy Bea."

She whirls around. Her expression is intense at first, but she lightens it with a casual, "Hey, Caroline."

The light flips to green faster than I thought and the guy behind me is immediately on his horn. I shift into gear and slowly take the corner. "You okay?"

Mercy Bea motions for me to keep driving. "I'm fine. Go on, now."

"Are you sure?"

The guy behind me lays on the horn. *Beeeeeeeeeeeeeeeeeeeeeeeeep.*

"Mercy?" I'm not moving until I'm sure . . .

"Get going. You're holding up traffic. I'm fine."

Liar. Something is up.

23

I never make it to Dad's. After turning left to check out Mercy Bea, I just kept on going toward Boundary Street and found myself at Beaufort Memorial Gardens.

The Sweeney tombstone stands guard over Mama as she sleeps, hopefully free from all her demons. I ease the Mustang around to the near side of the grave and come to a stop. Slipping out from behind the wheel, I reach to the passenger seat for the bouquet of lilies I stopped and bought at Bi-Lo once I figured out where I was headed.

"Hi, Mama." I flash the flowers from behind my back like a surprise. "Lilies. Your favorite."

Her grave is sad and dark. Weeping weeds creep along the smooth, gray stone, searching for a place to take root. Mud embeds the chiseled letters of her name: *Trudy Sweeney, Free Spirit.*

Picking at the weeds, I find the vase for the flowers tipped over and clotted with mud. My heart smarts at the family's neglect. The Harper family stone next to Mama's is clean and refreshed with flowers. Their departed are loved and remembered.

"Next time I see Henry, we're making a plan to spruce things up around here, okay? I don't care how busy he claims to be."

I brush away the mud from her name—T-R-U-D-Y—then smooth my skirt under my bum, sitting on the edge of the granite and angling my toes together to keep from slipping. I tuck the lilies in the vase and dig up the few good memories I have of my mother.

Dancing to the kitchen radio while fixing dinner.

Painting the side of the garage with giant, colorful wildflowers.

Taking pictures of Henry and me sitting in the spring grass.

Her soft, pulpy palms absently rubbing my arm.

"So, I guess you're wondering why I'm here." It's almost as if Matilda drove herself. "Funny thing. Jones McDermott died . . . Actually, that's not the funny thing. He left the Café to me. That is the funny thing."

I pick at the grass beneath my feet.

"Maybe you know this already. Heck, you and Jones might be sharing a good laugh over it."

When I open my hand, the wind knocks the grass blades to the ground.

"Then there's this guy, a cute deputy. He wants us to move in together. Maybe that's what you wished you'd done with Daddy instead of marriage and kids." In the quiet, I release a prayer to the wind. "But that's not why I'm here. The Café needs money. Everything but the kitchen sink needs to be fixed or replaced. Truth be told, even the kitchen sink. I'm going to sell the car, Mama—"

Forgotten sentiment springs from a fallow part of my heart. I'm surprised by my own smile.

"I'll never forget the day you drove Matilda into the yard, all the way from California. The top was down, and your hair stood out to kingdom come. The radio blasted some rock tune over the whole of Lady's

Island. Then you popped out from behind the wheel. 'Caroline, bay-bee, look what I brought you from Cal-i-forn-i-a.'"

The scene rolls in front of my mind's eye, making me laugh.

"Hazel, Jess, Elle, and I had a lot of fun with Matilda, driving all over town, down to the beach, over to Hilton Head. You would've liked us, Mama, I think. We were fun."

Sitting half in the sun, half in the shade, I linger, searching my spirit, my soul, the texture of the wind for confirmation. Sell?

When nothing comes to change my mind, I get up, make sure the vase of lilies is secure in the holder, and lean to press my lips to her chiseled name in the sun-warmed stone. "'Bye, Mama."

Wayne at CARS walks around Matilda as the evening light settles over us. The air is thick with humidity. "I don't know, Caroline." He kicks tires.

I flop my head forward with an exaggerated sigh and wiggle my body like an impatient four-year-old. "Stop fooling around, Wayne. You've wanted this car for years."

"Sure, but you never even *hinted* at selling. When did you get this dent here?"

This is ridiculous. We both know he's going to buy it. "High school. I backed into a parking post."

"Hmm, I reckon I can give you seven thousand for it."

"Seven thousand? Wayne, Wayne, Wayne." I pop my hand on his shoulder. "You can do better."

He juts his foot forward with his hands on his belt and shakes his head. "Caroline, give a guy a break. The whole car needs refurbing. New top, new interior, new paint. I don't even have to go into the engine troubles."

"Ten thousand."

He gapes at me. "Ten grand? Girl . . . Eight."

"Ten."

He shakes his head. "You're robbing me."

"Come on, Wayne, I need the money." I walk to the front of the car and prop my hands on the hood. "Besides, who is really robbing who here? You'll fix this baby up on your own time, using your contacts and discounts for parts, then sell her for four times what you're paying me."

He circles the car again, chuckling. "You got me there. Why are you really selling?"

The reason comes easy. "To buy a little piece of my future."

Wayne studies me for a moment, then motions for me to follow him to the office. "You drive a hard bargain, Caroline."

I smile the whole time he writes the check. When he hands it over, I do a double take. He wrote it out for eleven thousand. "Wayne, we agreed on ten. I don't understand." I offer back the check.

He stuffs his checkbook back into the file cabinet. "You're right, Caroline. I'll fix it up and sell it for four times. Make a killing. Don't see why I can't help out"—he clears his throat—"your future."

Without hesitation, I wrap him in a hug. "You old softy." My eyes mist as I open the office door and pause to look back at the wiry mechanic. "Take good care of her."

Outside CARS, I dial J. D. I'm confident I did the right thing, really, I am, but what's the point of moments like this if a girl can't cry on her man's shoulder?

Besides, I need a ride home. Clearly, I did not think this all the way through. Carlos Longoria would've had my hide. *The devil is in the details,* chica.

"Hey, babe." J. D.'s voice is tucked in low. "Bodean and I are finishing something."

"Big something?" I breathe deep to keep my voice steady.

"A domestic situation."

Wayne closes up behind me.

"Then why'd you answer the phone? Never mind. Call me later. 'Bye."

Next, I dial Dad, but he and Posey are out to dinner with friends. Forget Henry. He'd throw confetti in celebration and sneer, "You've finally come to your senses."

"Need a ride, Caroline?" Wayne stands by his truck, jiggling his keys.

"Not sure. Hold on."

I autodial Elle, but remember she's in Charleston at an art show. Wayne waits. I take a second to ponder my last option—Mitch—before giving in and dialing.

"Are you busy?" My voice warbles. Of course he's busy. I mean, the man has a life.

"Yes, I'm sitting out on the back deck, watching the last of the sunset."

He has a *nice* life.

"Can you pick me up at CARS?"

He laughs. "Sure. Did Matilda break down again?"

"Not really."

"I'll be right there."

Unbidden tears come as I wave for Wayne to go on. "I have a ride." He toots his horn as he pulls away, leaving me alone on the side of the road, waiting for Mitch, clutching Wayne's check, the answer to my prayer.

Starting August 3rd
LIVE Music
Friday & Saturday Nights
8:00 and 10:00

24

Friday night Mitch sets up for our first weekly music night. "Let me kick things off," he said.

At the front podium, Paris takes reservations for the next show. Elle is here with . . . Stu.

Holding out my hands and wrinkling my forehead, I ask how and when behind his back. She grins and slides into a booth. Stu catches sight of me and flashes me a broad white smile. He is very unplumbery tonight, rather dapper in his jeans and Polo.

A hand slides down my back. "Ready to go, babe?" J. D.'s quick kiss is familiar.

Mitch walks over, offering his hand. "Good to see you, J. D. Where y'all headed?"

J. D. slaps his hand into Mitch's. "Bodean is throwing himself a birthday party. Too bad you're singing tonight. Love to have you join us."

Mitch smiles so sincerely. "Tell him happy birthday for me."

J. D. clutches me close. "Will do. Stop by later if you can. I'm sure we'll be there until the wee hours. You know Bo and his parties."

Mitch listens with an agreeing nod, but his body language tells me he's not even considering J. D.'s invitation. No doubt, he's changed.

"Mitch if you need anything, ask Mercy Bea. She's in charge tonight."

"Aren't you full of courageous moves this week."

"Yeah, well, a girl's got to do what a girl's got to do."

J. D. questions me with his gaze. *What?* He's been working since the great car selling, and our conversations have been via phone or between fast Café kisses. I'm about to answer, "I'll tell you on the way to Bo's," when Cherry bursts through the Café's door, bolting past Paris.

"Excuse me, ma'am, you need a reservation tonight. Ma'am?" Paris tracks her through the tight row of tables.

"Caroline, can I speak with you?" Her normally perfect hair flies about her face. Mascara residue collects under her eyes, and the hem of her blouse blooms from her waistband.

"Paris, it's okay. This is my sister-in-law, Cherry."

Paris's cheeks flush pink. "Oh, sorry."

Cherry spins around. "Don't be. You were just doing your job."

With a pleading glance at J. D., I say to Cherry, "Let's go to my office."

Cherry collapses against me, crying, as I nudge the door closed. My blood runs cold. "Honey, what's wrong?" I've never, ever seen her ruffled or even slightly emotional.

"Oh, Caroline, it's all messed up. All of it." She sniffs and shudders.

"What's messed up? Surely, it's not that bad, whatever it is."

"H-hen-n-er-ry." Cherry's shoulders shudder with each syllable.

"What about Henry?" Angling backwards, with Cherry's forehead still buried against my shoulder, I wiggle my fingers at the tissue box until I tap the edge enough to pull the box forward. "Cherry, here."

She steps away to blow her nose. "I'm probably making something out of nothing." Pacing the length of the narrow office, she pauses, looking around. "Caroline, it's lovely in here. You cleaned it up. I love the lamps."

"I couldn't stand the mess, or the overhead fluorescent light." Crossing my arms, I lean my backside against the desk. "What'd Henry do?"

Cherry folds herself into the chair across from my desk. "I think Henry's having an affair."

"Cherry, no." I shake my head. "Never. Not Henry. He loves you."

She sniffs through a fresh batch of tears, tucking her hair behind her ears. "Things happen, Caroline, love fades. It's just he's been so elusive lately. I call him and he's busy, distracted. A couple of nights a week, he comes home really late."

"Honey, you know him. He's a workaholic, trying to rebuild Granddad's business."

She dabs under her red, puffy eyes with a fistful of wadded tissues. "Typically, yes. But over the past few months there have been inconsistencies. A few times, I even forced myself to drive by the office, and he wasn't there."

"Okay, then he's with a client."

"If only." She shifts her gaze to my face. "The other night he told me he was meeting Foster Spears for dinner. Said I should eat without him. So, I put on my comfy clothes, ordered take-out, and went to Blockbuster. Who do I run into? Foster Spears."

Cherry's too sensible to see things that aren't there. "Cherry . . ." I whisper. "Surely, it's not what you think." *That rotten brother of mine. He best not . . . to Cherry.*

"Caroline, please. Then tell me what to think. I'm begging you." My steely, no-nonsense sister-in-law pleads with her tone, with her eyes. I'm unnerved. If Henry and Cherry fall apart, whose love can stand?

"I-I don't know, Cherry. It has to be a misunderstanding."

She jerks up from the chair to pace again. The heels of her designer pumps thud against the floor, hitting a loose board every time. *Thud, clank, thud, thud, clank.* "Every time I bring up the future or kids, he shuts me down, changes the subject. Sometimes, he pretends he didn't hear me."

"He's always been skittish about kids."

There's a small knock on the door followed by the appearance of J. D.. "How's it going?" He holds up his wrist with the watch.

"I'm sorry, J. D." Cherry bends down for her handbag. "I interrupted your evening."

"Wait, Cherry. J. D., we need a minute." I leave him no room for debate.

With a reluctant pause, he pulls the door closed, and I face Cherry. "Henry's got issues. Mama's wildness impacted him hard, different than Dad and me. But sweetie, he's not a cheater."

My sister-in-law presses her hand over her middle. "How do you know? Are any of us exempt? If Henry's not cheating, then what is he doing?" She drops her hand to the doorknob, but it slips off as if she doesn't have the energy to hold on. "I've watched other women when he's around. They're fascinated by him. He's charming, good-looking, successful." Her gaze lands on some obscure point beyond my shoulder. "He's only a man, Caroline."

I'm unable to connect with the idea of a cheating brother. "Henry has his issues, I'll be the first to admit, but. . ." I want to think of something to lighten the moment. "Maybe he's taking French cooking classes or training to have rock-hard abs and wants to surprise you."

The suggestion barely garnishes a sad smile from the hopeless woman at my office door. "I need to let you go. Thanks for listening." She turns the doorknob with one huge effort. "Do you think the gestapo chick at the podium will let me sit behind the counter and listen to Mitch? Order an appetizer? I don't want to go home yet."

"Absolutely. Hey, Cherry, you're welcome to join J. D. and me. It's Bodean's thirtieth."

"Thanks, but right now, sitting alone at the counter, eating something deep-fried and listening to Mitch sounds really, really good."

"Tell Mercy Bea you can stay as long as you want." I follow Cherry into the kitchen where J. D. waits, leaning against the wall with his arms crossed. "Keep me posted, Cherry. I-I'll—" This part feels weird. I've never said it to anyone before. "I-I'll pray for you."

As J. D. and I climb into his truck, the air between us is taut. "Sorry, J. D. She needed to talk."

He cranks the engine and shifts into reverse. One gun of the gas and we shoot backwards out of the Café parking lot. Dirt and sand billow in our wake. "It's fine, Caroline."

Then how come it doesn't seem fine? I decide to wade in. "Is something bothering you? I mean, if we can't pause to help family and friends because Bo's having a party, then we need to—"

"Please, that's not it." The truck lurches forward as he presses the gas. "Then what?"

"Why didn't you tell me about selling the Mustang?"

Oh. That. "Who told you?"

"Mitch."

Oh. Him.

"Why didn't you tell me? I felt stupid standing there while Mitch told me about my girlfriend's ordeal."

All right. I turn sideways in my seat. "J. D., um, I sold Matilda for eleven thousand dollars so I could pay Stu for the plumbing."

He pinches his lips. Flexes his jaw muscle. Then bursts out laughing. "You're such a smart—"

"Hey, now."

"I thought you'd have that thing dismantled and buried with you."
He taps the brakes as the light on North changes.

"Yeah, well, speaking of growing up and making womanlike
decisions . . ."

"Why'd you go to Mitch?" There's only a terse hint of jealousy.

"I needed a ride home."

"He said you snotted all over his shirt." The portable pack set on the
dash tells us there's a hit-and-run on Robert Smalls Parkway.

"Okay, I needed a ride *and* a really large Kleenex."

The quick burst of J. D.'s laugh bounces around the cab, but fades
quickly. "Caroline, how can we build our relationship if you don't come
to me when you need help?"

"You were busy."

"You sold the car two days ago. I've talked to you on the phone half a
dozen times, stopped by the Café twice. Made out with you in the office."

"I know . . . It just didn't come up. I was going to tell you tonight."

J. D. reaches for my hand, kissing the tips of my fingers. "So, how
are you going to get around now?"

Twisting my lips into a goofy grin, I pull my hand free from his and
poke his arm. "You?"

"Bodean, happy birthday."

"Finally, the prettiest woman in town has arrived." Bodean
approaches as we walk across the yard toward the music and lights, his
arms wide, his smile mischievous. "Caroline, you look amazing."

J. D. tightens his arm around my waist. "Don't come fishing in
another man's pond, Bo. Isn't Marley here?"

"It's my birthday. I'll flirt with whomever I want." Bodean kisses my
cheek, pointing in the direction of the party area lit with lanterns and
party lights. "Okay, here's the lay of the land. Mars—the men—is over

there, by the game area. Venus—the women—there, under the trees, by the food. Go figure."

"Very junior high. I like it," I say, spotting Elle on the Venus side gazing toward Mars. Naturally.

"Hurry to the games, J. D. We need you. The rookies are whupping us at the beanbag toss game thing you invented."

J. D. laughs. "Never fear, I'll show them how it's done. Be there in a second, Bodean."

But Bo is off greeting more newcomers. "Rachel Kirby. At last, the prettiest girl in the county is here."

She giggles. *Tee-hee.* "Shush, Bo."

"So," J. D. says as we stand on the edge of the parked trucks and cars. He scoops his fingers into my hair, sending chills down my neck. "Before we end up spending an entire evening on different planets—"

I kiss him lightly. "Save a dance for me."

"Maybe tonight we find 'our song.'" His mood is light and infectious. "What you said in the truck . . . about me driving you around . . . Does that mean what I think?"

Slowly we sway in a circle to our own rhythm.

"Maybe. Still thinking."

He draws me tight. "Tell me during our song?"

"Stacking the deck, are you, J. D.?"

"I'll do whatever . . . Caroline, say yes."

25

J. D. tracks for Mars, where a bunch of Martians call to him, yuk-yuk-yukking, announcing him as the creator and champion of some beanbag tossing game and goading him into playing.

I track for Venus. *What is my answer?*

"Caroline, hello." The wives, girlfriends, and friends of the Beaufort County Sheriff's Department and Bodean greet me in chorus.

"Hey, y'all."

"Girl, your hair has gotten so long. It's beautiful."

"We've been meaning to get by the Café since you took over."

Elle pats a vacant spot next to her on the picnic table. Jess dips into the cooler for a Diet Coke. "Here you go, Caroline. Icy cold like you like."

"Thanks, Jess." I bump Elle with my shoulder. "Who are you here with?"

"No one. I'm trolling."

I pop open my coke and sip. "Any bites?"

"A few, but I tossed them back. Didn't meet the weight limit."

"You weighed more?"

"What is it with all the skinny men?"

"Ray's put on twenty pounds since we got married. Pure fat, mind you, but I like it. He was so thin before," Jess says.

The conversation drifts to skinny versus fat and the latest fashion fads. Fun girl talk, but I can't concentrate.

J. D. wants an answer. And he deserves one. If I say no, are we over? If I say yes, then what?

Can I still go to church? I'm pretty sure they still frown on the whole sex-without-marriage thing. I'm really starting to enjoy Sunday mornings. Even braved another read of Jones's Bible.

Is J. D. the one to give the gift I can never get back? Am I over thinking this?

Yes.

But if he wants to live with me, make love to me, why can't he marry me?

Laughter and shouts rise and fall under the lights draped among the tree limbs. The band is setting up on the empty lot next to Bodean's place. Torches burn along the path to the dance floor. (A couple of pieces of plywood.)

I scan Mars for the sight of J. D.

"You're quiet." Elle says.

"Tired, I guess." Explaining J. D.'s living-together proposition will only ignite Elle. Why fire her up when I'm undecided? She'll do something crazy, like rocket over to Mars and perform the first intergalactic execution. At the very least, castration.

"I've seen your 'tired' face. This isn't it."

So I throw her a bone. "Cherry came into the Café just as we were leaving. She's worried about Henry. Thinks he's having an affair."

"What? Oh my gosh, Henry? Never. He's too uptight. Besides, he's mad about Cherry."

"Not Henry," Jess echoes.

Swig of Diet Coke. "That's what I said. I told her I'd pray for her."

Elle bumps me with her shoulder, beaming. "I'll pray too."

Bodean's on-again, off-again girlfriend, Marley, joins the triangle of Jess, Elle, and me. She's five-eleven, athletic, and commanding. Bo keeps going back to her because she's the only one confident enough to handle him.

"Look at that, will you?" Marley nods at one of the younger deputies' girlfriends wiggling by and sublimely predicts the demise of low-rider jeans.

"Definitely on their way out," Jess agrees. "Must make way for the high-waisters of the eighties. They'll soon be the rage."

"Oh, girl, please." Marley cuts a sharp glance over at me. "My mama's butt looked like a small island for an entire decade."

Elle chokes on her gulp of soda. Her bracelets clatter. "Mine too. And two of my sisters. What a sad fashion decade."

From the men's huddle comes a roar. I look over to see J. D.'s hands raised over his head. At that moment, he looks over at me with a for-your-eyes-only smile and quickens my heart with a warm gush.

I smile back—for his eyes only. "*Maybe.*"

Jess asks for an update on Elle's Operation Wedding Day. So far— and big surprise—Stu Green is the front-runner. Bodean's party is a bust for new prospects.

An electronic screech pierces the air as the band runs a sound check. Scoping the Mars surface again for J. D., I decide it's a lovely night for a slow dance and to tell him, "Let's do it."

"Anyone for a trip to the ladies'?" Marley stands.

"Me." I down the last of my drink, toss it in the trash, and tag along with Marley to Bodean's guest bathroom—which we find occupied.

Marley falls against the wall. "You and J. D. seem tight these days."

I smile. "Getting there. He asked me to—"

Voices seep under the bathroom door. I give Marley a quizzical glance. "Is someone crying?"

We lean close.

Sniff. ". . . *she's* here tonight. With him." *Wail. Moan.*

Marley mouths to me: "Who?"

One can only guess. There's always a romance saga or two going on among the deputies.

"Look, he's a jerk. I told you not to go out with him. Good-looking guys are always bad news."

I snap straight. Marley touches my arm, shaking her head. *No.* But the swirl in my gut says *yes.*

"J. D. is *not* bad news, Trisha."

Marley's fingernails bite my flesh.

"I can't stay here, watching him dance with *her*, kiss *her*, tell *her* all the things he's said to me."

"Beat him at his own game, Lucy," Trisha pleads. "He promised you a dance or two, right? Make him want you over her. Be your gorgeous, sexy self. One dance and J. D. will forget that Caroline Sweeney ever existed."

Marley claps her hand over my mouth. Beyond the door, we hear scuffling.

"Is someone out there?"

Jerking free from Marley, I bang on the door. "Lucy, it's Caroline."

Silence.

Marley takes over the door hammering. "Lucy, Trisha, we heard you."

The door snaps open and two very beautiful young women wearing low-riders and tight tops face us with defiance.

"Didn't your mamas teach you not to listen to other people's conversations?" Trisha shoves past Marley. Lucy follows, her head high, eyes averted.

"Lucy, are you dating J. D.?" I am not ready for this showdown, but here goes.

She whirls around. "Caroline, if you have an issue with J. D., take it up with him."

A surprising calm spreads through me. "Lucy, it's a simple question. Are you, or have you recently, dated J. D.?"

"Answer the question." Marley demands.

The shapely brunette juts her chin. "Yes."

"Once, twice? A month ago, a few weeks?" As the tension builds, I'm reminded cornered kittens scratch.

"A few times, over the past few weeks." Lucy's shoulders droop slightly as her defiance wanes. "He'd stopped by our apartment." She gestures to Trisha.

"Did he spend the night?" *Don't answer. Yes, answer. Wait . . .*

Lucy's bright cheeks speak louder than words. "I love him."

"And he loves you?" Marley asks. By her expression, I think she wants to deck Lucy and be done with it.

"He cares about me."

The words ring with haunting familiarity. *Oh, I'm sick.* Fifteen minutes ago, I was a breath away from saying yes—to a man who . . .

"Lucy," I *eek* out. "If he cheated on me, he'll cheat on you. Don't start out as the *other* woman."

"What makes you think *I'm* the other woman?" She shivers though the hallway is hot and airless. "I told you, Caroline—" Her voice breaks. "I love him."

Marley grabs my arm and drags me toward the door. "Good night, ladies."

The patio doors swing wide and a laughing Bodean and J. D. step in with Mack Brunner.

Shielding me like a celeb bodyguard, Marley glares at J. D. "Excuse us."

I can't look at him. I might spit.

"Caroline, hey, what's up? Where are you—" J. D. stops wondering. My guess is he's spotted Lucy.

Marley steers me out the door, then pauses, leans back, and proceeds to cuss J. D.'s face blue.

26

Full astern," I whisper to Elle, finding her near the dance floor, talking to John Exley, which is an enormous waste of time; he's famously antimarriage. "Full astern." Gently, I shove her from behind, steering her away from John toward the cars.

"Caroline, what are you doing?" Elle shuffles along in front of me. "'Full astern'?"

"Take me home." As I feared, tears surface. I don't want to cry. Not over a cheater like J. D.

"What? Why? I was talking to John."

"Elle, John? Please. He'll ask you out, analyze the whole relationship before you even go on the date, conclude it'll never work, and treat you like gum stuck to his shoes the entire evening. You'll be forced to be nice to him so he won't tell people he dumped you because you were a witch."

She slaps her forehead with her palm. "Oh my gosh, Caroline, I wasn't—"

"Right. You're welcome." Weaving among the trucks, antique and classic Mopars, I can't spot her BMW. "Where did you park?"

She takes the lead. "Over there. Caroline, why are we full asterning? Did you hit an iceberg? See a ninety-foot tidal wave?"

Pulling her keys from her pocket, she aims her fob. The BMW blips and blinks. Quickly, I slip inside. Elle fires up the engine but doesn't engage the gas. "Now, what is going on?"

"J. D. is also dating Lucy McAllister."

"Caroline, no, he's not."

"Marley and I heard her through the bathroom door, lamenting about being the other woman tonight." I collapse against the cool leather seat. "She confessed they'd been together . . . if you know what I mean. Just get me out of here."

The blackness of the whole ordeal starts to settle over me.

"He what? In the midst of wanting to sleep over with you?"

"Worse, El—he wanted to move in."

"Caroline." My friend's voice is wispy with sympathy. "You're kidding."

"Don't I wish." I recount the evening at the beach, J. D.'s proposition, my nervous hesitancy, but almost-decision to go for it tonight. Enter Lucy.

When I conclude the tale, Elle flops back against her seat. "You are so blessed, Caroline. Look at me. I mean this: God is watching out for you." Elle shifts into reverse. "Can you imagine finding out about Lucy *afterwards?*"

Bile rises in my throat. Then I think about the first night he asked, and how I slept alone . . . the peace I felt. Now I understand. The peace that comes from doing the right thing.

"Let's just go, please." I cover my eyes, fighting a headache.

But as we pull away, a hand slams against the window. "Caroline, she means nothing." J. D.'s face looms in front of me.

Elle starts to gun away, but I hold out my hand. "Just a second," I say, getting out when she stops the car. Let's just end this here and now. I face J. D. square on. "Means nothing? Did you tell her that, J. D.? Because she thinks she's in love with you."

He reaches for me, but I snap away from him. "We went out a few times . . . I met her out one night—"

"Before or after the afternoon we talked, declared ourselves a couple? Before or after you asked to . . ." My teeth clinch. "Sleep over? Move in together?"

The darkness of the night irritates me. Where's the moon? The starlight? The only light is the man-made glow of Bo's party.

"Babe, I never told Lucy I loved her. I never asked her to move in."

"Funny thing here, J. D.—you never told me you loved me either."

Bing. Lightbulb overhead. I see clearly now. I almost gave myself to a man exactly like Mama. Selfish and cowardly. "And when were you going to tell me you were sleeping with Lucy? Tonight, when I thought living with you might be worth a try? After you slept with me for the first time?" Nausea slithers up my throat.

A dozen yards away, Bodean and Marley watch from the picnic area. Elle blares the car radio. The bass vibrates against the glass.

"Okay, I admit it. I've been with Lucy. But it meant nothing. We were just hanging out."

I jerk open the BMW's door. "And you freaked because you *imagined* seeing Mitch kiss me. See you, J. D."

"Caroline, come on, this is ridiculous." He comes at me like a cornered dog, but Elle hammers the gas before I'm all the way in and peels out of the yard.

"Easy there, Steve McQueen." I'm quivering all over.

The light we're careening toward switches to red, and she mashes the brake so hard I'm tossed toward the dash. My seat belt engages. "Steve McQueen, please."

"Sorry."

While we wait at the light, Elle thumps the steering wheel alongside comments like, "What is wrong with him?" or "Caroline, I'm so sorry." When the light changes, she hits the gas. We're off.

The homes and businesses along Ribaut whiz by. "Funny in light of Cherry's fear about Henry," I muse aloud. "He would never . . . and here I was completely trusting J. D. who, truth be told, would."

"Caroline, I'll say it again: God is watching over you. What are the odds of you finding out about J. D. on the night you planned to say yes? Women go years without discovering infidelity."

"Sad part is Lucy. She's trapped. God should look out for her too. J. D. probably didn't think he was hurting either one of us."

"How do you do it?" The next light catches us, and Elle brakes again. Gently this time. "Always find the good."

"Lots of practice." Tears ease down my cheeks. I brush them away. "J. D. has a way about him. Makes people feel special."

I blow my nose on a napkin Elle passed over.

My cell rings, and when I fish it out of my handbag, the tiny screen tells me it's J. D.

Pressing End, I blink away a rush of tears, toss my phone into my bag, and pray that part of my summer never rings again.

To: Hazel Palmer

From: CSweeney

Subject: The hits just keep on coming

Hazel,

I can top your Fernando story. Here's the mini-sode. Went to Bodean's birthday party with J. D. He wanted to make our relationship more permanent. He suggested living together.

Hazel, I was seconds away from saying yes. Then, as if the cosmos needed a good laugh, I found out J. D. has a little cookie on the side. Lucy McAllister.

And unlike with me, he had overnight privileges at her place. When I think about it, I feel ill. Yet, I miss him. He made me laugh and made me feel wanted.

In other news: I sold the Mustang to pay for Café repairs. Can you believe it? Know what I miss—the memories. That car was a rolling memory machine. We had some laughs in that thing, didn't we? Remember when Carl Younger and Peter-John Hayes filled the inside with sand? And when Elle hung out the window to flirt with Alex LeBoy and spilled her soda all over her lap just as we were driving up to school, late. Oh, and the time we went camping. LOL. It rained and we lived in the car for three days.

Now I'm sad. I miss all that broken-down heap stood for. Well, we always have the photo albums of '96 and '97.

"It's a Blues riff in B, watch me for the changes and try to keep up."

       Love you, Caroline

Daily Special

Monday, August 6

Fried Steak

Squash Casserole, Baked Tomato

Bubba's Buttery Biscuits

Banana Cream Pie

Tea, Soda, Coffee

$8.99

27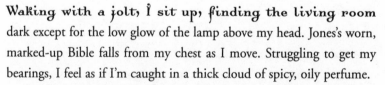

Waking with a jolt, I sit up, finding the living room dark except for the low glow of the lamp above my head. Jones's worn, marked-up Bible falls from my chest as I move. Struggling to get my bearings, I feel as if I'm caught in a thick cloud of spicy, oily perfume.

Who's here? Running the heel of my hand over my eyes, I shove my hair away from my face and reach down for Jones's Bible. The pages I'd been reading about a man named Moses slip from the binding.

Holy ground.

A pain ripples between my shoulder blades from sleeping with my head propped against the couch's arm. Stretching, I try to stand, but a heady, weighty fragrance settles over me.

Holy ground. The fragrance intensifies. *Someone's here.*

My pulse races. "Hello?" A quick glance at the door tells me all is secure. The deadbolt is turned, and the chain hangs across the door.

A swirling sensation engulfs me and the fragrance strengthens. Did I spill something last night?

No, I've never owned anything like this. It's strong. Pure. Unlike anything I've ever breathed, but so familiar. The hair on my arm rises.

Holy ground.

Closing my eyes, I slip to my knees, half-afraid to open them and see some angelic apparition standing before me.

I'm one hundred percent sure I'd soil myself.

Swallowing hard, catching my breath over a racing heart, I clasp my hands at my chest, unsure of what else to do. My body sways slightly back and forth.

With each breath, the fragrance intensifies until I almost can't take it anymore. It burns through my nostrils and into my lungs. An indescribable pure, weighty love wraps around me. I feel unworthy and ashamed, yet desperate for it to remain.

Finally, I whisper, "Jesus?"

Without seeing or hearing, I know.

"Yes."

Terror mingles with awe. *Think of nothing. Think of nothing. He's pure and holy. Moses, how did you do it?*

The fragrance drips on me, soaking dry, barren places in my soul. A puff of air hits my forehead and my eyes well up. My torso expands as my chest heaves for air.

"You are so loved, sweet Caroline. So loved."

The declaration washes over me, and a wail escapes from some deep, hidden place. The dam bursts. All these years of giving up my dreams, my plans, for someone else, feeling responsible for the happiness of the whole world—all of it has been about being loved.

I can't stop the tears now, even if I wanted. Love and hope consume me. My thoughts awaken, fighting to rescue my right to be hurt and angered. But the heat of the fragrance is burning it all away.

Falling onto the coffee table, I let everything go. *Have it all.* My throat burns, and my nose runs, but I don't care. Jesus—this God-man Mitch, Andy, Elle, and others know—loves me.

And now I know. If He promises to love me like this, I'll follow Him to the ends of the earth. Who can compare?

"I believe."

"You are so loved, sweet Caroline."

Mercy Bea eyeballs me. "Did you color your hair? Oh. My. Gosh. You waxed your brows."

Giddy, I shake my head and scoop ice into a mason jar. Dupree wants iced tea this morning instead of coffee. "No, and big fat no on the eyebrows."

"Well, something's different. You look . . . brighter. You lost weight, didn't you?"

"Yeah, five pounds overnight." *And a hundred pounds of burden.*

Sarcastic exhale. "You're wearing new makeup?"

"No, again. Same ole Cover Girl."

My wee morning encounter with the Prince of Peace has affected more than my insides, it appears.

Mercy Bea pops her hands together. "Got it. You're in love with J. D. Am I right? It's love. I knew it." She squeezes my arm. "Just had to give it some time."

I grab the basket of Bubba's Biscuits and Dupree's tea. "Stop guessing."

"Oh my stars, it's Mitch." She slaps her thigh. "I knew that country crooner had his hooks in you."

Mercy Bea follows me over to the breakfast-club boys. I address her over my shoulder. "Mercy Bea, don't you have customers?"

She snaps a clean towel at my rump. "For once, you're more interesting."

Mercy Bea tries a few more times to get a word out of me about being in love with J. D. or Mitch, but I confess nothing. A scent memory teases my nose and almost makes me weepy.

"Leave it alone, Mercy Bea." I retreat to the office and lock the door. My emotions are raw and tender, on the surface. Last night's encounter is a sacred thing between God and me, and I'm not ready to discuss it yet.

By midafternoon, rain clouds gather and break over Beaufort, washing away the muggy heat of the day—if only for a moment. Miss Jeanne comes running in for her early supper, shaking the rain from her permed gray hair.

"Couldn't run in fast enough from the car, daggum. Got all wet. And I used to run track."

She sits at her table by the defunct fireplace. When I bring around her order, she motions for me to sit.

"I have an idea for you."

"All right." I perch on the edge of the seat. "What's your idea?"

"Reminisce Night. Let folks come around and tell their stories. I bet there are a lot of memories to be shared about Beaufort and the Frogmore Café. I'm sure there's even old pictures floating around. Pick a Sunday or Monday evening, get a microphone, and let people talk. You got your Friday night music, now add this. Mark my words, you won't be able to seat them all."

Miss Jeanne spears a hunk of her pot-roast casserole, a pleased look on her cherubic face.

"Good idea. I'll talk to the crew." We could use business. We need money.

I gather everyone together and lay out the idea, and Andy, Mercy Bea, and Russell jump on it like flies on cake. Mercy Bea's been wanting to pick up an extra shift. Paris too.

There's a collective "Yeah," and bobbing of heads.

"All right. Let's do it." I pick a date in September for Reminisce Night, call the paper to place another ad, then phone Mitch.

"Can I impose on you once more?" I hunt around the desk for my paper clip, hoping I didn't throw it away in the big cleanup. "Can we use your sound gear for other musicians? And we're having a Reminisce Night."

"Be my guest."

"Awesome." I sound a little giggly.

"What's up with you, Gidget?"

"Nothing. Happy, I guess."

He's silent for a moment. "What'd you do, elope?"

"Elope?" I love how he's fishing without any bait. "No. Definitely no. Mitch, J. D. and I parted ways."

Silence. "Are you okay?"

"If you'd asked me a few days ago, I would've said 'Getting there.' But, today—"

Leaning over the desk, I tip the door closed. "Mitch, this really bizarre thing happened to me last night."

I recap the whole God encounter, because, I have to confess, in the sensible light of day my head is starting to question the experience. I've never heard of such a thing happening to anyone before, not even a preacher's son.

"That's amazing, Caroline," Mitch says when my story is done. "Jesus visited you. Not the first time in history He's done that, but I don't know of many who've experienced what you did."

"W-what do you think it means?"

"Lots of things. Mostly to let you know in no uncertain terms He loves you. Don't look now, Caroline—I think you got saved."

I jump up in my seat as an image of a TV preacher I once saw crosses my mind. He must have said *say-ved* a thousand times. "No, no, I don't want to be a Holy Roller."

"Then don't. Be a lover of Jesus. Pray, read your Bible, go to church, love others."

"Lover of Jesus? I don't know, Mitch, that sounds weird. Who would understand what I'm saying?"

"Plenty of people. But if you aren't comfortable with that, say you're a disciple of Jesus, or a follower of Jesus. Take your pick."

I can feel my face scrunching up. Who knew church came with so much terminology. "What do you call yourself?"

"A prodigal." He laughs. "Caroline, either way, you've met Him. Read the red words in your Bible and do what He says."

A chill runs over me. "Okay." Then, "What are the red words?"

"Jesus' words and parables. His instructions to us."

"Oh, I see."

"Caroline—" Mitch's voice warbles. "This news is better than any award I've ever won."

Elle rushes me after church the following Sunday. "We're going shopping. New clothes will cheer you up."

"All my wealth is tied up in bathroom plumbing." I shake my hair over my shoulders. "And, I don't need cheering up. Really, I'm fine."

"Okay, okay, I confess, I need cheering up." We head straight toward her car. "I've been thinking: must find the planet where it's raining men."

"Again," I say as she aims her key fob and bleep-bleeps her car, "I have no extra *dinero*."

"My treat." She flashes her palm. "No protesting."

Forty-five minutes later we walk into the Savannah Mall and beeline it to The Limited. The store is bright and fragrant with the new-clothes smell. A very slender blonde with Jennifer Aniston hair approaches.

"Everything on this side of the store"—she gestures right—"is half off. Can I help you find anything?"

Elle-the-shopping-guru appears slightly insulted. The salesgirl should've recognized her designer clothes. "No, thank you."

John Mayer sings to us via the store Muzak while Elle and I riffle through the half-off rack.

"Elle, look, why don't you buy me lunch and call it a good day, hmm?"

She sighs, peering over her shoulder at me. "One top. Or a skirt. Both, maybe. Please. You love skirts." Spinning around, she slaps a sage-green top against my chest. "Matches your eyes. And the scoop neck is sexy, but not too . . ." She arches her eyebrows. "If you know what I mean? Mom always said to leave them wondering."

The soft material under my fingertips deactivates my ability to protest. "Well, maybe one top."

"And one skirt." Elle's melodic laugh floats around us. "Remember when we went shopping for bathing suits and found that old blue light outside the old Kmart—"

"We convinced Larry Olsen to hook it up to work in the Mustang," I say while surfing the sales racks.

"You got cocky one night and flashed an unmarked police car."

For the next few minutes, we're lost in giggles. Since the night Jesus visited, it seems easier to laugh. Even to cry.

Elle shoves several tops and skirts at me. "Don't look at the price tag. Just try them on."

Of course, I look at the price tag. Even at half off, the cheapest top was thirty dollars.

In the dressing-room mirror, I wince at my ET-like complexion in the harsh dressing-room lights. Despite the fright of my reflection, I slip on a top and sporty skirt. The fabric feels cool and soft against my skin. When I glance in the mirror, the creature from outer space is gone. Instead, a pretty girl with rosy cheeks, pink lips, and bright green eyes stares back at me.

The top and skirt are perfect. But letting Elle buy for me seems . . . somewhat pitiful.

"Caroline, let me see." Elle knocks on the dressing-room door once, then barges in.

"Ta-da."

"Lovely," she says. "We're getting it. All of it."

"Elle . . . Thank you," I whisper to my friend. "You're too kind."

Elle doesn't leave herself out of the fun. Her new tops, slacks, and undies slide into The Limited bag right along with my things.

Since shopping and hunger go hand in hand, we head for the food court.

"Japanese?" Elle suggests, motioning to Sakkios.

"Sounds good to me."

We order, then carry our trays around until we find a clean table. "I have a date tonight." She gives her shoulders a prissy shake.

"Tonight?" I'm in mid-rip on my straw paper. "With who?" I'm suspicious. "Operation Wedding Day is suddenly going well?"

"If you must know, yes." Elle can't keep her delight hidden. "The new associate pastor at church asked me to dinner."

I jam my straw into my soda cup. "Jeremiah Franklin? You're kidding. I thought he was married."

She laughs, biting into her garlic chicken. "Me too. How does a man that cute go through Bible college and come out single? It's a miracle."

I stir my chicken and rice together. "So, do tell. How'd this happen?"

"He came by the gallery; we started talking and this morning he asked me to dinner. Caroline, I think this could be it."

"It? Oh my stars, you are too much, Elle. Can he spell *renaissance*?"

"Forward and backward."

Laughing, I toast her with my soda cup. "Kudos and congratulations. You'll make a good pastor's wife."

Elle freezes, a piece of fried rice sticking to the edge of her mouth.

"What? Wait . . . I never thought of it like that. Being a pastor's wife." Her expression slowly morphs from exhilaration to terror.

"Well, if he's the one—"

"Stop, Caroline, stop. It's one dinner. What do I know? I'm getting ahead of myself here. There're still more men on the lists, right? Jeremiah and I may have nothing in common but art." She gulps a calming breath. "It's one innocent date. No big deal."

"Right, NBD."

As quickly as the terror overtook her, it fades. Our conversation returns to normal. Until . . .

Elle jumps from her chair, her gaze fixed on some point across the food court. Her bracelets clank as she cups her hand around her mouth. "Conroy Bean, over here!"

Whipping around, I scan the mall shoppers. Where's Conroy? Sure enough, ducking under a Titans baseball hat is Conroy Bean.

Grinning, I watch as he tries to maneuver the crowd without being noticed. Years ago when Mitch first went to Nashville, Elle invented a code name for him so when he gained mild notoriety, we could address him without creating a stir.

One afternoon, we took my little boat out to the sandbar, and Elle smacked Mitch in the head with a pluff mud ball. "I dub you Conroy Bean."

"Conroy Bean? No way." He smacked her back. A baseball-sized chocolate mud ball slid down her hair.

"Too late. Your alter ego is Conroy Bean." She smacked him dead center in his chest with a softball-sized mud ball.

Hazel and I hovered together in the marsh grass like tall, featherless egrets. J. D. was with us that day. He called the mud fight like a sports announcer.

"Mitch O'Neal's pitch is high and outside. Oh, Elle Garvey, strike one. Clean over center plate."

Then a drunk guy came paddling by in a dinghy. "Wrestle her down, boy; it's more fun that-a-way."

Eight years later, Mitch-Conroy strolls across the Savannah Mall food court toward us without the slightest flicker of irritation over his alias. Under the shadow of his hat, I see his jaw is dusted with a light beard. He's wearing jeans and an oversized white pullover. He exudes a masculine aura that makes it hard to imagine him singing a love song with power and emotion. But, boy, he does.

A picture forms in my mind. Mitch as a daddy, strolling down Bay Street, grasping the hands of his little girls. One on each side. Each with blonde curls and Precious Moments blue eyes.

And me.

No. I squirm and shovel rice and chicken into my mouth and try to ignore the cloud of butterflies beating around inside my chest. I never pictured Mitch as a daddy before. Never, ever pictured me as a mama. I was always half-scared I'd inflict my kids with the pain Mama inflicted on Henry and me.

That's Henry's problem, I know, when Cherry brings up the subject of children. But he's too proud to admit it.

"Hey, you two." Mitch-Conroy slides into the seat next to me.

"What have we here?" Elle rubs her palm against his light beard. She is brazen against personal boundaries. Re: the dressing room earlier.

He ignores her question, turning to me. "Hey, Caroline."

"Conroy." I smile, though my middle quivers. Ever since J. D.'s been out of the picture, the air between Mitch and me deepened—it zaps and pops with electrons as if something's brewing.

Elle points to his shopping bag. "Conroy, you've been to the Family Christian Store."

Mitch scratches his forehead with his thumb and turns his Titans hat so the bill is in the back. "I have."

Elle snatches the bag from him. "What'd you get?"

Mitch grabs it back. "Nosy."

But it's too late. She's already dipping her hand inside. "A Switchfoot CD, a Max Lucado book, and, oooohh—" Elle pulls something from the bag. "A new Bible. I *looove* new Bibles." She pops the lid off the box.

"Elle." I cover the Bible with my arms, glancing back at Mitch. "She's can't help it; she's part puppy."

He laughs. "Where's a rolled-up newspaper when you need one?"

"Hey—" Elle shoves my arms off the Bible. "I'm right here, listening. Oh, Mitch—"

The Bible is a beautiful burgundy leather with a name inscribed on the bottom right corner.

Caroline Jane Sweeney, Beloved

With wide eyes, Elle snaps her gaze up at Mitch. "You're unbelievable." With one fast-forward motion, she plants a kiss on his furry cheek. "And incredibly sweet."

The country crooner blushes.

Taking the Bible, I smooth my palm over the leather cover. *Beloved.* "This is the best gift I've ever received."

Mitch shifts around as if he's embarrassed by his own charity. "I didn't know if you had one, and . . ." He shrugs, then whispers, "I hope you like it."

"I love it." I kiss his cheek. "Thank you." Hugging the Bible to my chest, I tell them about Jones's worn-but-loved Bible.

"Remember, read the red words, and pray hard." Mitch hooks his arm around my shoulders and gives me a tender squeeze. "Maybe we can do a Bible study or two."

"I-I'd like that." Ho, boy! Down, girl. I recognize the feeling in my heart.

We're only friends. Just friends.

Munching on a broccoli floret, Elle yips, "What'd you buy me?"

"Nothing."

"Really? So what I needed."

Mitch gets up for something to drink and Elle peers at me like, *See.* "He's your lobster. Your Ross."

"More *Friends*? Elle, we're just friends. Don't make more out of this."

"I just love lobster."

"What are we talking about?" Mitch asks, sitting next to me, sipping from an iced latté.

"Friends," Elle puts out. Yes, definitely puppy.

"Friends? As in you and me or the TV show?" Mitch shifts his gaze from Elle to me and is waiting for an answer when we hear a rumble from the other side of the food court. Gasps of recognition. *Mitch O'Neal. Where? Over there.*

I feel the stares on my back and the suffocation of a gathering crowd. Peering at Mitch, I realize with his hat on backward too much of his face is exposed.

"They're onto you, Conroy," Elle whispers, cleaning up the last of her garlic chicken.

The Mitch O'Neal rumble grows louder. I slip the Bible back into the bag and grab my purse.

Mitch turns his hat bill around. "It's the thunder before a storm. Ease away from the table." He rises slowly. "Act casual."

But the clouds break. "Mitch O'Neal." *Screeeaaam.*

In synchronized motion, Elle, Mitch, and I take off down the main mall thoroughfare. My toes grip against the soles of my Clark's clogs as they *thunk, thunk* over the terrazzo floor.

Elle immediately falls behind. "Wait, I'm wearing flip-flops. Wait."

A bird's-eye view of us running paints across my mind, creating a whirlwind of laughter. I can barely keep running.

"What's so funny?" Mitch asks.

"T-this," I *eek* out, glancing back for a visual of Elle. Oh no, she's surrounded by a sea of Mitch-crazed teenyboppers.

"Conroy, wait," she calls. I can't even hear her clattering bracelets for the squealing. "Watch out, kid. That is *not* Mitch O'Neal. It's Conroy Bean. Get back, you. Oh my gosh, what did you just call me? Does your mother let you eat with that mouth? Conroy . . . Caroline . . ."

Daily Special

Tuesday, August 14

Andy's Submarine

Chips or Fries

Cole Slaw or Molasses Baked Beans

Pluff Mud Pie

Tea, Soda, Coffee

$6.99

28

To: CSweeney

From: Hazel Palmer

Subject: Re: The hits just keep on coming

Caroline,

J. D. and Lucy McAllister, huh? Rat-fink. Guess he's not changed at all.

I baby-sat her. What is she, eighteen, nineteen? You're better off, C. Once a ladies' man, always a ladies' man.

Fernando update: He hasn't called in a while, then I ran into him the other night. He was body whispering with this waif of a thing I believe was once a blonde Swedish woman. Who can tell with all the protruding bones and translucent skin. (Thin is so overrated.)

And Caroline, I ignited with jealousy. I couldn't believe it. The pure evil green stuff. Until now, I thought he was rather pushy and overbearing. It so surprised me I wanted to run, but he saw me and called me over.

I tried to be cool, but I blathered and tee-hee'd like an American Idiot and almost groveled at his feet.

I need help.

Matilda: Gone! I can't believe it. A tidal wave of homesickness crashed over me when I read you'd sold her, leaving behind old shells echoing of good memories. I dug out my photo albums and for about an hour lived in Beaufort, nineteen ninety-six, -seven, and -eight.

You know, if I go in tomorrow and tell Carlos your latest sacrifice for the Café, he might just hop on a plane and fly over to meet you. He's really on this kick of back-to-basics business. He's tired of formula marketing and tricky practices. He's not picked an apprentice, yet. You're his Cinderella, fleeing the ball. Prince Carlos is convinced he won't find someone as perfect as you. Even if half of what he believes is his own created fantasy. (No offense.) I'm not sure he'd hire me after envisioning a hardworking, self-sacrificing, business-savvy woman like Caroline Sweeney.

It's late. Better get a few hours sleep.

"I said good day, sir. I said good day!"

> *Hugs, Hazel*
> *CFO, SRG International, Barcelona*

The second week of August starts off slow, but by Wednesday, business picks up enough that I call Paris to come in and help with lunch. Luke notices how busy we remained after the breakfast-club boys take off and ties on an apron.

Miss Jeanne arrives precisely at three, wearing a big smile and a pill-box hat.

"Nice hat."

"Thanks." She walks toward her favorite table. "Found it in the downstairs closet."

"Very Jackie O." I pour her iced tea at the waiter's station.

"Bought it the day after I saw her wearing one." Miss Jeanne sets her pocketbook on the tabletop. "Just came from the film-committee meeting. Tom Cruise might film a movie in Beaufort."

I set down her tea and a straw. "Tom Cruise? Well, well."

"Sure enough. Now, where's my pot-roast casserole? Add a salad today, Caroline."

"Sure thing, Miss Jeanne."

In the kitchen, Andy stands in front of the convection oven, grumbling and growling. I frown as I stick Miss Jeanne's order on the slide.

"Miss Jeanne's here. Are you okay?"

"Thought I'd see if I could get this old convection oven working, but it's shot." Andy looks square at me. "Caroline, we've got to get a new one."

"Why? We never used that one."

"Look around, girl. We're getting busy. I can barely keep up with making biscuits now. A good convection oven will speed up cook time and keep the kitchen cooler."

I exhale through tight lips. Where the money will come from, only God knows, but I've managed to save a little for emergencies. If Andy says we need a new convection oven, then we need one. I hate to turn him down. He works so hard for so little.

Andy plates Miss Jeanne's pot-roast casserole. "There's a place going out of business down in Port Royal, Caroline. Casa Verde. We can get their oven for a song."

"A song? Should I send Mitch then? He can sing a song or *two*." I pick a couple of hot Bubba's Buttery Biscuits from the baking sheet.

Andy chuckles. "Wouldn't hurt."

Heading out with Miss Jeanne's order, I answer over my shoulder, "If I can get a ride, I'll check it out this afternoon."

An hour later, I'm sailing toward Port Royal in the good ship *Miss Jeanne*, a '56 Plymouth. The windows are down, and the wind gushes past, whipping up the ends of my hair. My knuckles are white as I hang on to the door handle, keeping my eyes peeled for signs of a possible collision. *Out of our way—land yacht coming through.*

And I have absolutely no faith in the antiquated lap seat belt, which I'm trying to wear up around my ribs.

Miss Jeanne's faithful companion, a border collie named Ebony, hangs out the back window, nipping at sunbeams and licking the wind.

My dear senior citizen friend offered to drive me to check out the convection oven when I mentioned it in passing. In passing! Daddy and Elle were busy—Daddy with a job in Bluffton, and Elle scouting out a new artist. Wonder how it went with the associate pastor. She never called me afterwards. *(Note to self . . .)*

Mitch left a message yesterday saying he was going up to Nashville for a few days. Jess is back teaching. And Andy—the one I'm doing this for—promised his youngest boy he'd stop by football practice.

Up ahead, the light changes to red, but Miss Jeanne barrels toward it like she's playing chicken. "This is the first car I ever bought," she says. "About a year after I started my law practice."

"Y-you were a lawyer?" The car in front of us brakes, slowing to a stop. I inhale sharply and brace for impact.

"For twenty-five years. Had an office right on the Bay. Then Mother died and I closed the office to take care of Daddy."

"What kind of law practice?" My foot grinds into the floorboard. Houses and trees whiz by my window. *Miss Jeanne, brake . . .*

"Taxes, wills, real estate, and neighborly disputes. Back in them days, folks didn't have wills like they do now. Land was simply passed from father to son, father to daughter, what have you." Two inches from the car in front of us, Miss Jeanne mashes the brakes, hard. "But as families grew and spread out, disputes started happening, and I found myself a nice little niche."

I exhale with a gush as my taut stomach muscles release. How she stopped this monster on a dime, I'll never know, but thank you, Jesus. "I'm impressed." In more ways than one. "How many women were in your law class?"

Her seasoned laugh fills the car. "I was the only woman in the law class of '54, University of South Carolina."

Propping my elbow out the window, I mutter, "Amazing. And here I am in the twenty-first century, fumbling through life."

"Fumbling? Dear girl, you're running a town institution. I'd hardly call it fumbling. Don't shortchange yourself, Caroline. You're just getting started. Life is far from over."

The light changes to green, and Miss Jeanne ambles along, picking up speed, maneuvering the boxy car around a slow-moving Toyota.

Casa Verde is in a strip mall. The outside is green stucco walls with a Guatemalan man painted on the outside. *Bienvenidos, amigos!*

Inside, the restaurant is cool and dark. I squint as my eyes adjust to the low light.

"May I help you?" A lovely, brown-skinned woman comes out from the back.

"I'm here to see Mario. I'm Caroline Sweeney."

"Excuse, please, for a moment."

Miss Jeanne stands next to me, digging in her pocketbook, shoulders squared. "I forgot to freshen up my lipstick."

Miss Jeanne is full of surprises. "You look lovely."

"How about you? Want a little lip paint?" She swishes the open lipstick tube in the air in front of me.

"I'm trying to cut back."

She cackles and snaps the lid on. "So, where's this Mario fella?"

Now that my eyes have adjusted, I see the restaurant is very quaint, with a Central American decor—colorful walls, wood trim, brick walls, tile floors, rustic furniture.

From a side dining room, a man's laugh mingles with the high, fast chatter of children. The sound is fun and carefree, so I peer into the room, curious. At a four-top in the far corner, a man sits with three boys. One white, one black, one Hispanic. They're munching on tortilla chips, swinging their legs, reaching for too-full coke glasses. The man is dressed in khakis and a pullover. His shoulders are lean, and the back of his dark hair is neatly trimmed.

My heart is touched by their affection—a man and his sons, perhaps, taking after Brangelina.

One of the boys notices me and stops giggling long enough to wave. The man turns slightly in his seat.

My breath catches.

"Miss Sweeney, sorry to keep you waiting."

I spin around. "Mario? Hello."

"Very nice to meet you." He gestures toward the kitchen doors. "Please, come see the oven."

"What kind of oven did you say it was, Caroline?" Miss Jeanne asks, hurrying along beside me.

"A convection oven," I answer automatically through swirling thoughts. What is he doing here? With three boys? "The Café's is broken, and my cook really wanted a new one." Holding the right side door open for her to enter ahead of me, I pause to glance toward the small dining room.

Casa Verde's kitchen is small and hot. A cook gazes over at us. "*Buenos dias.*"

"*Buenos dias,*" I reply with a forced smile, trying to focus on the situation in here. Not the scene out *there*.

Miss Jeanne walks up to the oven in question and opens the doors. "Single stack? How old is it, Mario?"

His brow furrows and I read his expression. *Who is this woman?* "The oven, it is one year old."

"Is it electric?"

Mario clasps his hands together. "Yes, electric."

Miss Jeanne pats the polished stainless-steel side. "Tell me the truth, now, is it a true convection?" Where'd she get all this detail?

"The very best. I pay four thousand dollars." Mario glances at me to see if I approve.

Miss Jeanne purses her lips. "How much do you want for it?"

"Three thousand dollars."

"Sorry to have wasted your time, Mario." Miss Jeanne snatches my hand and whips me toward the door. "Call us when you're ready to sell."

"Wait—" Mario runs to block our exit. He flashes his even, white teeth. "We're just getting started here. Ladies, please, we can talk."

"One thousand." Miss Jeanne's offer is firm with a nonnegotiable quality.

"Twenty-five hundred dollars."

Miss Jeanne steps around him. "No deal. Caroline—"

"Miss Jeanne, hang on, now." Gently, I restrain her with a soft tug on her elbow.

"Caroline, you heard the man." She flicks her hand in his direction. "Twenty-five hundred for a used convection oven? Highway robbery."

I make a face. "No one's robbing any highway. Mario, the price seems fair."

"For that piece of junk?" Miss Jeanne interjects. "Twelve hundred or we walk."

"Miss Jeanne—" I whisper in her ear. "What are you doing?"

"Getting you a deal," she whispers back.

Back to Mario, who is not quite as amiable as five minutes ago.

"This oven is top-of-the-line, I assure you. Only one year old. Two thousand." He crosses his arms. "And I'm being robbed."

"Fifteen hundred."

I step in between. "Can we stop all this Wall Street negotiating? I only wanted to check the oven out. I'm not sure I want to buy."

Miss Jeanne jabs me in the ribs and mutters. "Nice move. Disinterest."

"No, seriously, I'm not sure . . . I'm new to this biz and wonder if it's best to shop—"

Panic flickers through Mario's eyes. "Eighteen hundred dollars."

"No, Mario, please, I'm not trying to—"

"Okay, okay, fifteen hundred." He sweeps his hands in front of us. "Final offer."

"Deal." Miss Jeanne thrusts out her hand.

Mario shakes, then wags his finger at me. "Very clever. You bargain well, *señorita.*"

Hello? "Wait just a cotton-picking minute. Miss Jeanne, you can't say 'deal' with my money." I feel a bit railroaded here.

Mario's expression hardens. "A deal is a deal."

Miss Jeanne mutters again. "Caroline, you're embarrassing me."

"I'm sorry. I don't mean to be difficult, but I thought I'd shop around."

"A deal is a deal," Mario repeats with a white, smarmy smile.

Miss Jeanne lays the back of her hand to the side of her mouth and whispers, "You're giving us white folks a bad name."

Oh, well, in that case . . .

Sigh. To Mario: "Do you take credit card?"

Mario beams. "Right this way."

After squeezing fifteen hundred dollars onto my credit card, I sign my name with a whimper. An oven. For fifteen hundred dollars, I could be on a shopping trip to Madrid with Hazel, purchasing a very small piece of original art from the Prado.

Humming to himself, Mario asks, "When can you pick up oven?"

"When I have a truck."

Mario escorts Miss Jeanne to her car while I peek again into the small dining room. They're still here.

I walk across the room, the heels of my clogs tapping against the tile, announcing me. The little boys stare with cute expressions. "Hey, Henry."

My brother jumps up, tipping over his chair. "Caroline, what are you doing here?"

"That's what I wanted to ask you. Hi, boys."

"Hello," they say.

Henry smiles at them. "Boys, this is my sister, Caroline. Caroline, this is Roberto, Trey, and David."

"Very nice to meet you boys."

With the pleasantries over, Henry grabs me by the arm and steers me away from the table. His posture is stiff as if I caught him in some heinous act. "Don't say a word to Cherry."

"Why not? Henry, she thinks you're having an affair." I lean back to see the boys again. "Are you? Whose kids are those?"

"She thinks I'm having an affair?" His tone and expression deny any sort of hanky-panky.

"Henry, talk to her. What are you doing here with these boys?"

"It's no big deal. What are you doing here, anyway?"

"Buying a convection oven, and it is a big deal if your wife believes you're cheating."

"Okay, look, I didn't want to tell anyone or make a big fuss about it, but I'm a Big Brother. I'm hanging out with these guys because they don't have a dad."

Shut my mouth. "Since when?"

"Few months."

"Oh my gosh, Henry, does Cherry know this?"

"No." He runs his hand over his head and looks back at the boys. "She'll flip and want to start trying for a baby." Henry switches his gaze up to meet mine. "Part of this is me testing the kid waters. You know, seeing if I even want kids. So, please, don't tell her."

"Henry, I won't, but you have to. She can't go on thinking you're cheating."

He flinches. "I'll tell her."

"Do you realize the night you told her you were having dinner with Foster Spears, she ran into him at Blockbuster?"

He utters a sour word.

I press my hand to his arm, a soft spot forming in my heart for him. "You best fix this." Then I smile and pat his cheek. "Well, well, Cindy Lou Who, my brother the Grinch has a heart after all."

Daily Special

Wednesday, August 29

Chicken Pot Pie

Green Salad

Yeast Rolls or Bubba's Buttery Biscuits

Sweet Potato Pie

Tea, Soda, Coffee

$7.99

29

Andy, Mercy Bea, Paris, Russell, Luke, and I stare at the TV Dad installed a few days ago in the back corner of the Café. "Got to have Fox News running or something," he insisted.

Now, bad news depresses my dining room: "The National Hurricane Center has issued a hurricane warning for north-central Florida. And a hurricane watch for coastal southern Georgia and South Carolina. You can expect high winds and torrential rains over the weekend."

"A hurricane." Mercy Bea twirls her cigarette between her fingers. "Don't that beat all. Caroline, there goes Reminisce Night."

"Just pray, y'all." I mean what I say too. It beats all those years I spent talking to the stars from the ancient limbs of our live oak. How great to know Someone loves me and is truly listening. "Come on, we've all been through storms before."

Paris's hand goes up slowly. "Not me."

Wide-eyed and white-faced, Russell squeaks, "I'm terrified."

"It's wind and rain." I clap my hands. "Buck up, bubbas. Tell you what, we'll have a hurricane party at the carriage house. We're going to be fine. Just fine."

She says, she says, she says. All my cheering is sugarcoated bravado. Russell said it best: *"I'm terrified."*

Andy turns the TV volume down as early lunch customers walk through the door. Paris grabs a couple of menus and seats a group of young professionals. They are smart and classy in their business attire and thick-heeled pumps.

Standing behind the counter, I absently run my hand over my soiled apron (I dropped a plate of pancakes). Isn't my top the one with the Tide-resistant stains? I subtly check. Yep.

One of the women, Catherine Hale, is director of marketing for the Chamber of Commerce. The other woman, Stephanie Burke, works for her dad's insurance firm and drives a high-horse-powered, sporty convertible. I know this because she stopped behind me one day at a traffic light, bobbing to the beat of her stereo while Matilda coughed up black smoke.

On the heels of Catherine, Stephanie, and their male counterparts, I notice a dark, fleshy-face man enters the Café. A heebie-jeebie nips at me.

Mercy Bea is waiting on the professionals, so I come from around the counter. "Can I help you?"

The man points to Mercy Bea. "Waiting for her." He settles in booth 2.

Somehow I don't think Mercy Bea is waiting for him. She jerks back when she sees him and cuts a wide berth around booth 2 on her way to the kitchen, her gaze down the entire time.

"Caroline," she whispers as she passes me. "Take my tables."

"What is going on?" I stop Mercy Bea inside the kitchen door.

"Nothing. I just need to go." She slips the professionals' order on the slide, then unties her apron.

"Mercy Bea, hold the phone. Where are you going?"

"Caroline, you ask too many questions." She stuffs her apron into her cubby, exchanging it for her big tote. "Andy, easy on the butter with that order."

"Too many questions?" My forehead wrinkles. "Mercy, you're walking out, in the middle of a shift. A very strange man is waiting for you. What is going on?"

"Caroline, leave it be." With that, she exits the back door, lighting up a cigarette as she goes.

Andy and I exchange a look.

"What was that?" he asks.

"You tell me." I head to the dining room to tell the gentleman Mercy Bea's gone for the day.

After lunch, I snag one of Andy's slow-roasted beef sandwiches—he's developing his own menu items and sauces, and this one's a little bit of heaven touching earth—and head to the office with the money bag full of the lunch receipts.

But I'm stopped short. "Mitch."

He rises from the spare chair. "Afternoon."

"I thought you were in Nashville?"

"Got home yesterday, late."

"Do you want something to eat?" I motion to the kitchen. "Andy's new sandwiches are to-die-for."

"I know. I've had the turkey and the roast beef. Are you free tonight?"

"Sure." I plop down in my chair. "Do you notice anything weird going on with Mercy Bea? Seems she's working on a relationship with a beady-eyed goon. What do you have in mind for tonight? Want to hang at my place? Watch a movie? Otherwise, you'll have to pick me up. I'm sans car."

"I'll pick you up around six." He pauses at the door. "Dress nice."

My teeth are buried in my sandwich. "Dress nice?"

"Yeah, dress nice." His sparkling smile bursts the cocoon of warm fuzzies I keep stored behind my ribs for special occasions.

"Hmmm?" I mumble, sauce-dipped roast beef dangling down the side of my jaw.

"See you at six." And Mitch is gone.

Wait, Mitch. Munch-munch-munch. How much meat is Andy putting in these things? Better do a cost analysis. *Munch-munch-munch.*

Swallowing, I run after him, yanking a napkin from Russell's pile as he refills the table dispensers. Mitch is halfway to his truck parked out back.

"Hey, what's going on?" I walk toward him. Rain clouds dominate the early afternoon. The hurricane's calling card? "Do you mean movie-jeans-and-top nice? Sunday-skirt-and-clogs nice? Or evening-wedding-dress-with-heels nice?"

"Evening-wedding nice."

My shoulders jerk back. "Really?"

He pops open the cab door. "See you at six."

With sandwich sauce sticking to my hands and face, I watch Mitch drive away.

Head: Interesting development.

Heart: For once, I agree with you.

Head: What do you think he's up to? And, we've agreed before.

Heart: Do we risk it?

Head: No. Stay in neutral heart.

Heart: But he's changed. Really.

Head: Don't make me come down there.

Heart: Ha! Like you'd win, you big bunch of gray matter.

Evening-wedding nice, huh? How much can a girl dress up a new top and skirt from The Limited?

Back inside with my sandwich, I ponder over Mitch's mysterious invitation. Being around Mitch is one of my all-time favorite things. Yeah, it's risky, but hope floats, doesn't it?

Heart: We can always dream and pretend, can't we?

Head: You get five minutes. Go.

Washing the last of my sandwich down with a slurp of cold, sweet tea, I dial Elle. Her closet is full of evening-wedding nice.

To: CSweeney
From: Hazel Palmer
Subject: Call with Carlos
Caroline,
Carlos would like to speak with you. What time would work?
    Hazel
    CFO, SRG International, Barcelona

To: Hazel Palmer
From: CSweeney
Subject: Re: Call with Carlos
Haz,
Why?
    Caroline

Elle is meeting me at five with a selection of dresses. But, really, Mitch should know better than to spring something like this on a blue-collar café girl like me.

My nails are ratty, my hair is long and uneven, and I'm a centimeter away from a unibrow.

As I'm closing up the office, Paris brings around a long, slender box. "These came for you."

I smile. "Flowers?"

Her smile lights her slender face. "Red roses. Oh, Caroline, don't be mad. I just had to peek."

"Who would send me red roses?" Weakly, I reach for the box. In twenty-eight years, I've never received flowers, let alone red roses.

"Maybe J. D. is trying to get you back." Paris surrenders the box, almost reluctantly.

J. D.? My hope sinks at the idea. It'd be a sweet, but futile gesture.

I slip off the red ribbon and lift the box's lid. Silky, fragrant red roses lie on a bed of baby's breath. Paris and I gasp together.

"They're beautiful."

"Who, who, who?" Paris bobs up and down, tugging at the tissue paper for a card or note.

Finding the card tucked along the side, I tear open the tiny envelope. There's only one line on the card. No salutation, or signature. Just one line.

"Oh, it must be good; you're crying." Paris wrings her hands, leaning to peek. Her long blonde ponytail slips over her shoulder.

I press the card to my chest. "Give me a moment, Paris, please."

"Sure, sure. Guess I'll get to my side work."

As she leaves, steamy and hot tears erupt like Old Faithful.

"*You are so loved, Caroline. So loved.*"

The words sink deep as I mutter them over and over. Daily, I'm growing to understand the life and power of these words.

Blowing my nose on the used sandwich napkin, I laugh to myself. Should I be freaked out? God sent me flowers.

Elle will be here any minute. I'm scurrying out the kitchen door, locking up and dashing for the house, when Mercy Bea pops out of nowhere.

I jump sideways. "Didn't you go home?"

"No, I just clocked out." She clicks her nails. A cigarette angles up from her fingers. The wind gusts shove tree branches around and stirs the dead leaves on the ground.

"What's going on?" I try to read the emotion in her eyes. "Is this about the man who came to the Café?"

She smiles, but her lower lip trembles too much. "I need money, Caroline." She jams the cigarette between her lips and takes a long, hard drag. A burning menthol fragrance fills the air. A plume of smoke exits her lips.

"And he's your banker?"

"Can we go inside? I need a tea." Mercy Bea taps ashes to the dirt and sand.

"S-sure."

We sit in the large corner booth, and while Mercy Bea fixes two iced teas and divides the last of an apple crumb pie into two pieces, I ask God to help Mercy Bea.

She slides into the booth, with our tea and pie. "Jones used to help me out now and then . . . with money. I'm sure it was one of his many habits that didn't help the Café."

"Why do you need money?" A thin light streams between the rain clouds, through the window, and over us.

"Caroline, do you have any idea how expensive two teenage boys are? No, I guess you don't." She puffs on the last of her cigarette, smashing it out on the edge of the plate. I hope it doesn't leave a burn mark.

"Mercy Bea, are you borrowing money from that man?"

She picks at the pie crust with the prongs of her fork. "See, my older young-son was stealing from me for a while, but we had a come-to-Jesus meeting and he's seen the errors of his ways. Then, younger young-son had basketball camp and every freaking little expense under the sun— shoes to underwear. I was hanging on until I lost my nursing-home job.

I've been doing some cleaning for folks here and there, but, well . . . I'm not the most thrifty gal in the world." She taps her sculptured nails against the table. "But next thing I know, every bill is past due and the collectors are knocking on my door."

"How much did Jones help you?"

She shrugs, flaking away more of her pie's crust. "A hundred here, a hundred there, as I needed it. Sometimes he just gave me money without having to ask."

"I see." My mind churns, figuring how much I have in the Café account. I don't feel right about giving her Café money when Andy works just as hard. And I'm still paying off Buster.

But my personal account has a small reserve now that I don't have to feed Matilda.

Mercy Bea drops her fork and shoves the pie plate forward. "Know what, Caroline, forget it." She moves to the edge of the booth. "I shouldn't burden you with this."

"How much do you need? I'd rather you take money from me than borrow from that goon. He's frightening."

Mercy Bea stares into the dark Café. "Tell me about it."

"So, how much?"

She shakes her head. "Too much. I can't—"

I snatch her arm to keep her from leaving. "Don't be stubborn. You've confided in me; now let me help. How. Much?"

"Ever seen that picture of the iceberg where the part above the water is like a small mountain, but the part below is a berg ten times the size? The part that sank the *Titanic*?"

I whistle. "Still need a dollar amount, Mercy."

"Three thousand." I only have half of that.

The figure just hangs in the air between us.

"Three . . . thousand."

Her hands shake as she fishes for another cigarette. "That's just to break even. Pay rent and electric. And don't you know that nasty trailer is the world's largest roach motel. They come in, sit right up to the table, and ask what's for dinner."

Think . . . Think . . . Borrow from Café and pay it back out of my check. "I'll lend you the money."

She lights the cigarette. "I can't pay you back. Not soon, anyway."

"Fine, I'll *give* you the money . . . on one condition."

A sad, unsure shadow darkens her eyes. But she waits to speak.

"Don't ever deal with *that* man again. You might be putting yourself and young-sons in danger."

Mercy crisscrosses her heart. She tries to speak, but emotion steals her breath. Then the tears come with streams of black mascara. I shove into her side of the booth to wrap my arm around her shoulders, trying hard not to peek at my watch.

Mercy Bea Hart buries her head against me and cries away her burden.

30

Mitch beats me to the carriage house.
After Mercy Bea's confession, she talked for another half hour, eating all
of her pie and the last half of mine. The tough broad from the South
needed friendship today as much as money.

I gladly wrote out a check, feeling even more satisfied to be giving
Mercy Bea a listening ear and a shoulder to lean on.

"Sorry," I say to Mitch, dashing through the front door, then stopping all forward motion when I see him. "Wow." The door clicks closed
behind me.

"Wow, yourself." He's smiling and teasing. Maybe flirting?

"Me? No . . ." I gesture toward him. "You . . . look . . . amazing."

Mitch stands tall and broad-shouldered in a rich black tux. His
blond locks are cut and styled, revealing every fine detail of his beautiful face.

"You cut your hair."

He runs his hand over his head. "Keeping it long got annoying."

My heartstrings pluck like a twangy old guitar—trying to make a song, but very out of tune. I toss my keys onto the table. "Is Elle here?"

"She ran back to her place." He steps toward me. "Muttered something about 'Black-tie is not the same as evening-wedding nice.'"

Crossing my arms, laughing, I face Mitch. "Trying to give the girl a heart attack. So, what's up, O'Neal? Where are you taking me?"

"The Performing Arts Center fund-raiser for the hospital. I bought tickets awhile ago, not planning to attend. Thought Dad could take Mom. Then I thought of you. Actually, Mom suggested you, and it seemed like a fine idea."

He steps closer, and all my senses move to full alert status.

"The roses are beautiful."

He raises his chin. "I didn't send them."

"Technically speaking, no. I understand that."

"I did *pay* for them, and gave the florist the address."

I kick off my work clogs. "Why'd you sign it the way you did?"

He steps closer. "Yesterday, I was working on a song, praying at the same time, and—"

"He told you. Like He told your Dad?"

"Does it mean something to you?"

"Yes."

"Good. I wasn't sure. Especially figuring you'd know I had something to do with the flowers." Mitch stops in front of me. "This is an official date by the way."

Just then, Elle burst inside, breathless, a pile of dresses draped over her arm.

"Caroline, where have you been?" She grabs my elbow. "Mitch, I don't have much time, but I'll do what I can with her."

For the next twenty minutes, Elle skirts the edges of my personal boundaries. She frets, fluffs, and weed-eats my eyebrows. I complain a lot, but seeing Mitch's face when I walked into the living room might just be the highlight of my year.

"You will be the envy of the ladies this evening," he says, rising from the couch.

My hand brushes down the side of Elle's black, off-the-shoulder gown with the A-line skirt. "Because of you."

"No, it's all you. Ready?"

I twist to check the mirror by the door. The red marks from Elle's no-pain-no-gain eyebrow waxing have faded. "Ready."

In the truck is one luscious white rose. "This one *is* from me."

The evening is divine· No wonder Cinderella forgot her curfew. Mitch never leaves my side. He walks beside me, resting his hand on the small of my back, or lightly touching my shoulder blades.

I feel found—like a precious treasure. My mind snaps mental pictures, then couples them with emotional impressions and stores them in a new heart corridor. When blue days come around, I'll visit tonight's memory hall for a ray of sunshine.

The evening is classical, with performances by the South Carolina Philharmonic and local quartets. I'm carried away by the beauty of the music . . . and Mitch.

During intermission, our Washington congressman beckons Mitch over to his large circle of people with a sweeping gesture. Yet I'm in mid-conversation with the head of child protective services.

"Caroline, let's definitely add the Frogmore Café to the Ghost Tours this Halloween."

"I'd love it." I nudge Mitch with my elbow. *Go ahead.* But he waits for me to finish. "I'll e-mail you about fund-raising for the Ghost Tours too. Maybe we can figure out something with Bubba's Buttery Biscuits."

"Oh, wonderful. Caroline, please, send along the information about the Vet Wall. Shame on us for overlooking it all these years."

When Mitch escorts me over to the congressman's circle, he introduces me as a respected Beaufort businesswoman.

The congressman shakes my hand. "The Frogmore Café. I've heard of it. Home of Bubba's Buttery Biscuits."

"Yes sir." Impressive.

He turns to Mitch. "How's Nashville?"

"Still there."

The circle laughs. *Yuk, yuk, har, har, phony, phony.*

Mitch body whispers, as Hazel would say, when he brushes his hand over my shoulders.

The congressman aims his charm on Mitch, asking him to help out on his next campaign. "Running for Senate this time. People would come out to see us with you on the ticket, hear what we have to say."

His impression of Shere Khan is fantastic. I glance at Mitch. He's no Mowgli.

"I'm flattered, Congressman, but I'm unimpressed with the celebrity-politics mix of the day."

Brief moment of shock and dismay. Mr. Congressman recovers with only a small blip in his smile. "Mighty narrow view, Mitch. People trust celebrities—they have a lot of influence."

Mitch smiles and stares the tiger down. "Exactly my point."

Touché, Mitchy.

The circle coughs and looks away. The congressman fixes his tie, adjusts his jacket with a shift of his shoulders. "Think about it. I look forward to hearing from you."

Mitch bows slightly and leads me away. "Enjoy the rest of the evening."

"Mitch, wow. You were amazing."

"Don't be impressed. The congressman is a liar and a cheat. I'd prefer to debate his inconsistencies, but this isn't the place."

"I remember a Mitch who wouldn't turn down any opportunity to perform, be the center of attention."

"Yeah, well, that's the old Mitch, and he's dead." He holds the auditorium door for me. As I pass inside, he touches my hand. I stop and peer into his eyes. "Caroline, you were by far the most charming and beautiful woman in that room. Everyone wanted to talk to you. You never have known how amazing you are."

Our relationship leaps to another plane.

As the house lights dim for the second half of the performance to begin, Mitch offers his hand. "May I hold your hand, Caroline?"

Gulp. I nod.

His hand is firm and broad; his fingers lock perfectly with mine. "Mitch," I say, barely above a whisper. "I'm afraid of falling."

He presses his lips to my ear. "Don't worry, I'll catch you.

"Caroline, it's Kirk."

It's Thursday evening and we are hustling. The town is starting to come out, little by little. "Yeah, what's up? Paris, refill the teas on table 10 for me, please?"

Exchanging the old wall phone, with the out-of-shape twist cord, for a portable was one of my best ideas yet, if I say so myself.

"Sounds like you're busy."

"Is that why you called?"

He laughs. "No. Listen, did you renew the insurance?"

I roll my eyes. "Yes. Why?"

"Don't be snippy; just checking. Keeping an eye on you. Looks like Hurricane Howard is tracking your way."

"Yeah, we're watching the news. I think Savannah is going to get the worst."

"Either way, you're insured. Good news—Dale and Roland are back on the Frogmore Café kick. The other deal didn't work out. They want to come down tomorrow, check out the Café, chat with you. See what you're thinking."

"Oh, fine, nothing like being second choice." I motion for Russell to run out the order sitting under the heat lamps, flashing the table number with my fingers.

"Don't be bitter. At least you're getting an invitation to the prom."

"Kirk, there's no prom."

"No prom? Are you saying you don't want to sell?"

"Don't talk crazy. See you tomorrow."

The Café is hopping when Kirk walks in the door with Roland and Dale, strutting like a Hollywood celebrity team. John Travolta in *Saturday Night Fever*. Cheesy yet confident.

Kirk shoves me toward the kitchen before I can barely greet them. "Give us a minute."

"Go ahead and take the booth in the back . . . Mercy, will you see to these gentlemen?"

"Sure thing."

Kirk leans close. Coffee breath. "What is it?"

"On the way down, they talked about how much they want to get in this area. You're looking at a million-two, maybe a million-three."

I glare at him. "H-how much?" In all the talk of selling, I never considered the price.

"Over a million."

My knees buckle a little. "W-wow."

Kirk grins. "Also, wanted to tell you I'm your lawyer on this deal. I told the Buzz Boys to hire representation. I don't want to be compromised."

"Oh, Kirk, thank you."

"Don't look all sappy. I'm doing it as a favor. Well, a little, but set aside a teeny bit of that mil-plus for me."

"Gladly." A million dollars. Jones McDermott, bless your old-coot heart.

For the better part of an hour, Kirk, Dale, Roland, and I sit in the booth, talking. They ask a lot of questions, and I answer them all: staff, menu, suppliers, average business day, average income, history, clientele, and potential clientele.

After a while, I go to the kitchen to get Andy. "Go meet the Buzz Boys. Tell me what you think. Then send out Russell, Luke, and Paris."

Luke protests. "I'll retire when you go, Caroline."

"Luke, no, you love working here. They seem really wonderful, and I do believe they'll take care of you all. Just now, they talked about incentive programs and employee insurance."

"Well, only for you, Caroline. I'll talk to them, but I ain't promising nothing."

"That's all I ask." I kiss his cheek. Don't know why; I just did.

His face reddens as he goes back to mopping the kitchen.

Over the next fifteen minutes, the crew parades out one by one to meet the Buzz Boys while I sit at the counter and watch. I can tell they're charmed. Even, reluctantly, Luke. But finally the party's over.

"Caroline—" Dale settles his hand on my shoulder. "We love this place. Love *it*."

Roland spears a bite of Pluff Mud Pie he's eating. "This is fabulous. Pluff Mud Pie. Fabulous. So local. Brilliant idea. Brilliant."

"Jones bought the mix from a Gullah store over on St. Helena."

"And that—" Dale gestures to the Vet Wall. "I mean, a wall with signatures. We love it. *Love* it. Incredible. Caroline, do vets still sign?"

"There are new signatures from last December. The wall was Jones's project. I haven't devoted time to it."

"Roland"—Dale reaches in to the pocket of his tennis shorts for his

Palm-Pilot—"call your buddy over at the History Channel; get a story on the wall. It'd be great publicity."

Roland stabs the air with his fork in agreement while chewing and swallowing a bite of pie. "Larkin TerBerg. Brilliant. Let's do it."

"The wall has already been on the History Channel," I note.

"Excellent, we'll use that info to get us on again." They talk as if the Café sale is a done deal.

Clearing my throat, I decide to ask a few questions of my own before they leave.

"Dale, Roland, I'm really glad you're interested in the Frogmore Café. She's a town treasure. But I'd like to ask a few questions."

Since Roland is still eating, Dale answers. "Absolutely. Ask whatever you want. We are an open book, Caroline."

"Absolutely, Caroline, ask away. We want this to be a comfortable arrangement for all of us." Roland motions to Paris as she hustles by with a loaded tray of drinks. *More pie.* She smiles and nods. Good girl.

"The Café founder, Jones McDermott, worked hard to develop an authentic lowcountry menu. Will you stay with the menu and motif of the business? Our cook has created some wonderful new dishes."

"Yes, yes, sure. Oh, absolutely. Can't see it any other way."

"What about the staff? Andy and Mercy Bea have been here a long time. They know this place and its customers. The other three work hard. They'll do right by you."

"See no reason whatsoever to jettison the staff. We believe in people, Caroline. The heart of every company is the people."

I'm starting to get a really, really good feeling selling to them.

Dale puts his arm around me. "Ease your mind. We'll see to the staff. Like we said earlier, our plan is merely to expand the hours, fix up the inside, and convert the carriage house into a dining area."

Roland is into the second piece of Pluff Mud Pie Paris brought. Or is it his third? And not even an inch of extra around his waist. "Maybe add a coffee bar."

"Now you're talking." Mercy Bea breezes past.

Dale reaches to the counter for a napkin. "We didn't plan on doing this today, but when you see a good thing—" He fishes a pen from his hip pocket. "It's unofficial, but here's something to think about."

It was one thing to hear a million dollars. It's another thing to see it. Dale wrote the amount on the napkin like a check. Even signed his name.

One-point-two million. My knees go weak again. "W-what if I decide not to sell?"

Yeah, and what if the world ends or Godzilla storms Beaufort?

"Then we'll have to call in our muscle." Roland laughs with a look at Dale.

"Our wives. They can get blood from a turnip. You think I'm lying?"

"They can't make you sell, Caroline," Kirk interjects softly. "They'll offer a letter of intent by weeks' end, right?" He glances at Dale, then Roland. "Bottom line, it means you won't sell out from under them."

"Okay." Clutching the paper napkin check, I watch them go. The first brick in the sale, and a whole new life for me, is laid in the dirt.

Daily Special

Saturday, September 1

Closed for Hurricane Howard

Will Reopen ASAP

Coming Soon: Reminisce Nite—First Monday in October

Come Share Your Memories & Pictures

of Beaufort and the Frogmore Café

God Bless!

31

To: CSweeney

From: Hazel Palmer

Subject: Re: Call with Carlos

Caroline,

Carlos has been out of country on business, so not sure when he wants to call, but I told him you guys were prepping for Howard. I've been singing your praises, still. Keeping hope alive.

Be safe, girl. Are you scared? I hate storms. Will keep up with the news online.

Update: Fernando called. Totally different tone and attitude. Upshot: dinner tomorrow night at 7:00.

"You can't handle the truth."

Ciao, *Hazel*

CFO, SRG International, Barcelona

Beaufort braces for a weak category-one Hurricane Howard. The news stations out of Savannah and Charleston urge us to execute hurricane preparedness. Howard is expected around midnight over Savannah, with the northeastern rain bands dumping buckets of rain on Beaufort. We spent Friday night, and so far most of today, prepping. Business is off anyway—folks are battening down or bugging out—so I closed the Café at noon.

"Howard!" Mercy Bea spits as she cleans up the last of the pots Andy used to make soups. "Why can't our hurricane be named Esmeralda or Lillian, or heck, Mercy Bea. No, we get Howard. Before this one, Hugo."

"What's wrong with Howard?" I pause to wipe sweat from my eyes. Andy, Russell, and I are bringing in five-gallon water bottles from Andy's truck. The prehurricane air is still, sticky, and hot.

Mercy Bea juts out her hip, plopping her bent wrist on her waist. "Have you ever in your life met a Howard remotely as exciting or wild as a hurricane?"

"Howard Hughes." I undo my ponytail, comb my fingers through my damp hair, then wrap it up again.

She snorts with an exaggerated face. "How do you know Howard Hughes, Caroline? He's dead." She stops and gazes toward the ceiling with a wrinkled brow. "Right? Howard Hughes is dead? No, wait, he's the guy who runs the Playboy mansion."

Andy drops two jugs of water to the Café floor, catching the sweat on his brow with a swipe of his shoulder sleeve. "Hugh Hefner runs the Playboy place. Howard Hughes was an entrepreneur. Made movies, was into planes. And he's dead."

"That's right. The DiCaprio boy played him in a movie. Too many *H*s around here. Howard Hughes, Hugh Hefner, Hurricane Howard." She shudders and reaches for a dish towel to wipe down the pots.

Andy came to me a few days ago with an idea. "Why don't we make up a bunch of soup, stock up on nonperishables and water. You know this storm is going to knock out power someplace. I'll have Luke bring out the big grills, clean them up, make sure the propane tanks are full and working. We wait too long, and we won't be able to get any supplies."

I loved the idea. "We can feed anyone who stops by. Even cook their food for them, stuff that might go bad if they are without a fridge."

Andy nodded. "That's what I was thinking. And, Caroline, let's not charge folks. Let them come on out, fellowship, and eat a good meal for free."

Great minds . . . "Yep. Help me get a list together and I'll send Russell and Luke shopping."

So, here we are, unloading supplies.

"Where do you want this stuff, Caroline?" Russell holds up several Wal-Mart bags. My credit card protrudes from his fingers. "I bought every battery packet I could find and cleaned out the flashlights. Got a bunch of matches too."

I slip the credit card into my shorts' pocket. "Thank you, Russell. Just put the bags in my office."

"Caroline, if you don't need me, I'd like to go," he says as he comes back out of the office. "I should get my place ready."

I check the clock. Four o'clock. Already. "Go." I hug him. "Be safe. See you when it's over."

I suppose he's not the only Café employee who has a hatch to batten down. "Do you need to go?" I ask Andy and Mercy Bea.

Mercy Bea waves her hand in the air. "The boys bugged out with friends last night. I plan to find a corner in a shelter and hope Howard blows away my roach motel."

The hollow ring of loneliness pings my heart. The echo hurts. *"Find a corner in a shelter . . ."* "Shoo, Mercy Bea, I'm so glad to hear you're footloose and fancy-free. I could use some company at the carriage house. How about it?"

She drops the damp dish towel in the laundry bin. "Well, if you're scared."

"What about you, Andy? Do you need to go?" With a working wife and children, there's bound to be work to do at his place.

"My boys are boarding up. I need to finish up here, but then reckon I should make sure we have water and food."

I motion to the gallons of water we brought in. "Take a couple of these."

He whips off his cap, scratches his head, then plops his hat back down. "What about boarding up the Café and carriage house?"

Oh. Crud.

Ten minutes later, Mercy Bea and I stack plywood boards from the shed in Andy's truck bed. Boarding up? I hate it. The Café and carriage house will be dark and claustrophobic. Then stifling when the power goes out. I'd almost choose to sit in the hammering rain and raging wind.

During Hugo, Mama went stir-crazy in our boarded-up house. She paced, then sat quietly before organizing a play of Broadway proportions, including set design, singing, and dancing— all to be Fred Astaire perfect. When we showed less-than-stellar enthusiasm, she crawled into bed and stayed there for two days. Daddy plied Henry and me with enormous amounts of junk food.

I stretch my stiff back with a deep arch and think of how that storm was the first time I realized darkness haunted my mama.

"Hey, Caroline, pay attention. No time for a break, girlie," Andy says with a chuckle, lugging yet another board out of the shed.

I love the many-windowed Café, but I have to confess, I'm a bit bitter at the moment. Boarding up is going to take forever. Howard will have come and gone.

Daddy calls as Andy helps me hang the first board using the Tapcons Jones drilled into the walls years ago. Mercy Bea goes behind us, screwing on the wing nuts.

"You doing okay, Caroline?" Daddy asks.

"Andy and I are hanging boards."

"And me."

"And Mercy Bea."

Dad hesitates. I'm sure he's trying to picture the daughter he couldn't get to hang up her clothes for more than a decade, lugging around plywood. "I'm still on a job. Posey's waiting for me at home to board up. Come to the house when you can."

"Thanks, Daddy, but Mercy Bea and I are going to hang out here. I want to open the Café as soon as I can for folks who need food or water."

"All right. Call if you need anything."

"See you when it's over."

Henry calls a few minutes later. "Cherry and I are helping the boys' families. Are you okay?"

Huh? I hold out my cell phone to check the number. Yes, it's Henry. "I-I'm fine, thanks. You told Cherry about the boys?"

"That night. I realized how stupid I was behaving. Time to grow up."

That sinks my last doubt. Indeed, there is a God. "Good for you."

"This time next year, you might be an aunt."

"Really?"

"Cherry said thanks; she felt your prayers."

My feeble, fumbling offerings worked? "Tell her hi."

"She loves the boys too. I'm not just a Big Brother now; we're more like a big family. So, how're you sitting there? All good? Need anything?"

I smile. "All good. See you when it's over."

A half hour later, Andy and I are halfway through boarding up the Café when his cell goes off. "Caroline, I got to go. The boys are arguing more than working. And Gloria wants me to stop by her mother's to bring in the outdoor furniture."

"Go, go, take care of your family." My arms are stretched to the sides of a large square board. "I can finish up."

Mercy Bea looks at me. "You don't figure on me helping with these boards, do you?" She spreads out her fingers. "I already broke a nail and am about to lose another."

The board slips from my grip and crashes against the Café. "Mercy Bea, why don't you go home and get your things. Secure the trailer, then come on back." I flick my wrist at the pile of boards. "Don't worry here." If I have to leave this side exposed, the risk will be minimal.

"I like your thinking, Caroline." She's off the porch and on her cell phone before I can say, "See you later." "Allison, thank goodness . . . I need a nail repair pronto."

A wind gust knocks against me. I lift my eyes to the darkening sky. Mountains of gray clouds loom over Beaufort.

I decide to hang a few more boards, or at least try, then see what I can do at the carriage house. Maybe I should buzz Dad back and beg, "Help."

Hoisting the board, I aim the drilled board holes at the top Tapcons. The right side hooks onto its industrial-strength screw at an odd angle, and I can't get it the rest of the way on, or off.

"Stupid board."

Anchoring it in place with my knee, I spy the hammer on the stool. I reach. The plywood splinters scrape my skin. My fingertips barely capture the hammer's handle. Finally.

Gripping tight, I whack the board into submission.

"Now what did that board ever do to you?"

I whirl around. "Mitch, hey."

"Need some help?" He slips his hand over mine, taking the hammer.

I hold his blue gaze. "I thought you were in Nashville." I haven't seen him since our so-called date. Seeing him now makes me realize I missed him.

"Seems I arrived home in time for the hurricane fun." He steps in front of me; I sniff his shirt, *yumm.* "You should get hurricane shutters. Push of a button, and my place is set."

"That'll be a chore for the new owners."

"You're selling?" He easily pulls the board free, then hangs it evenly.

"Yep. Buzz Boys, Inc., sent me a letter of intent." I spin on the wing nuts. "Want to join Mercy Bea and me for a hurricane party?"

He looks over at me. "I thought you'd never ask."

Midnight. Peeking out the bottom of the front window where the board didn't quite reach the end, I watch horizontal rain in the light of the street lamp—still glowing, thank God. The live oak limbs battle and twist in the surging wind, and the palmetto branches bend at a right angle.

Behind me, my little Hurricane Howard party is quiet and peaceful. Elle decided to join the festivities and is painting a hurricane scene in the corner by the boarded-up French doors. Mercy Bea flicks through *Cosmo*, reading embarrassing female anomalies out loud. Mitch pretends to watch the news, but the perpetual grin on his face tells me he's hearing every word.

He's so cool. When we finally hunkered down for the storm, he pulled out his guitar and sang a few hymns, then led us in prayer. The peace it generated reminded me of the night Jesus stopped by. Mercy Bea went through half a box of Kleenex.

A gust of wind crashes against the house. The lights flicker off. But before we can moan and complain, they flick back on.

"Howard best not leave us in the dark." Mercy Bea rises from the breakfast nook with a Wal-Mart bag dangling from her fingertips. "Caroline, I brought a surprise." She holds up the bag. "Hair coloring. Let's get you fixed up."

"Color my hair?" On impulse, my hand reaches to the edges of my rough, dry, once-a-rich-brown hair. "Now?"

Mercy Bea shakes the bag. "Miss Clairol with extra conditioning. Now, come on. Aren't you tired of that dried-out, mousy brown?"

"Who brings hair color to a hurricane party?" I sink my backside farther into the cool, leather couch.

"Mitch, convince her a little conditioning and color wouldn't kill her?"

Mitch munches on an Oreo cookie from the coffee table junk-food pile—MoonPies, potato chips, M&Ms, Oreos, boiled peanuts. "It *is* a little mousy."

"What?" I lean forward to see his face. "You would hand me over to this wanna-be stylist? Besides, what's wrong with mousy brown?"

"Caroline, let's *goooo*." Mercy Bea motions for me to march to the bathroom, like a kid doomed for a Saturday-night bath. "Come on; it'll be fun." She produces a pair of shears. "I'll trim the ends for you too."

"Don't you need a license for those?"

Elle calls from the kitchen, where she's washing out her brushes. "I'll do your nails."

"Now, wait a minute, y'all." I slide forward and slap Mitch's knee a few times. "We can't turn this into a girls' night. What about poor Mitch?"

He waves off my comment. "After hearing Mercy Bea read out loud from *Cosmo* the past hour, I'm pretty much immune to girlie stuff in all its forms. Besides . . ." He points to the built-in shelves, "I'm going to peruse Jones's old LPs."

"That's your last excuse, Caroline. Get cracking." Mercy Bea shuffles me off to the master bathroom.

Mumbling as I change into an old, I-don't-care-if-it-gets-stained T-shirt, I submit to Mercy Bea and let her dump a bottle of hair color on my head while Hurricane Howard howls over us like a hungry panther on a cold winter night.

"In twenty minutes, you'll have lovely auburn hair, Caroline." Mercy

Bea scoops my hair on top of my head, secures it with a big clip, and tucks a towel around my neck.

"If you say so." My skin tingles as the color slips down my scalp.

Mama was a naturalist. She gave up shaving her legs and underarms about the time I hit puberty. "Bondage," she claimed. "Makeup, hair color, false nails, tweezing, shaving—tools to keep women in bondage to man's idea of beauty."

So, any discovery for me about *bondage* came from *Cosmo*, Hazel, Jess, and Elle.

I emerge from the bedroom. "Ta-da."

Mitch looks around from the bookshelves, grinning, then laughing. "What? No mud mask?"

I pistol my fingers at him. "Shutty uppy."

"Caroline, Iamoverwhelmedbyyourbeauty."

"That's more like it."

Back to the albums lining the shelves, Mitch slips one from the row. "Have you looked at Jones's collection? It's amazing. Hundreds of albums in mint condition."

"Y'all want popcorn?" Mercy Bea hollers from the kitchen.

"Popcorn is good," I reply, standing next to Mitch, wiping my brow with the edge of my T-shirt. The strong scent of hair dye mingles with his fading cologne.

"The Carter Family, Bob Wills, Bill Monroe, original 78s and LPs." Mitch flips through the stack. "Buck Owens, Homer and Jethro, Dixieland jazz, Glenn Miller—this is incredible."

"Do you want to play one?" Jones's record player from the seventies is on the bottom shelf. I lift the lid and click on the fuzz-covered turntable. "Elle, can you mute the TV?"

Mitch eases a Buck Owens LP down the spindle, then sets the needle down on the spinning disc. The old speakers crackle and pop.

"Oh, that sound takes me back. The crackle of a needle on vinyl."

Mercy Bea leans across the kitchen counter, waiting for the microwave to produce a bag of popcorn.

Buck sings: *"They're gonna put me in the movies."*

Mercy howls along, almost drowning out Howard's eerie wind song. Elle and I wince. However, Mitch takes the high harmony.

"All I gotta do is . . . act naturally."

When the song ends, Mercy Bea jumps up for the popcorn. "Are there any Johnny Cash albums, Mitch? Now there's a *man* for you."

Howard shrieks with a surge of intensity. The muted TV screen shows us the hurricane's eye looking down on Savannah.

"Mercy Bea, what's the time on my hair?" I ask.

"Five more minutes."

Mitch pulls out an obscure-looking disc. "Here's a record marked 'State Fair, '49.'"

Elle gets up to see over his shoulder. Her bracelets clink softly as she reaches, turning Mitch's hand for a better look. "What do you think it is?"

Mitch slides the disc from the white paper sleeve. "Fairs used to have recording booths. For a few bucks, a person could record a song or message."

"Let's hear it." Mercy Bea tosses in a second bag of popcorn.

The old disc protests the needle with a pop when Mitch sets it down. In the next second, a very familiar voice emanates from the speakers. "This here is Jones Q. McDermott at the South Carolina State Fair, nineteen and forty-nine, singing a song to my true love."

Clunk, twang, thunk.

Elle and I exchange a quizzical glance.

Mitch chuckles. "He must be having a hard time with his guitar in the booth."

Mercy Bea comes over munching from her first bowl of popcorn. "He sounds so young." Her words fade away. "I miss him."

I grab a handful of white popped kernels. "Me too."

"This is for my gal—"Jones says.

("Hurry up, kid. Ya ain't got but two minutes!")

"Ah, hush up, old man. Here's for you, darlin'."

The guitar strings squeak and Jones begins his serenade.

You captured my heart
With your lovely smile
We was young
But for a while
I've been in love with you—

("Ha-ha-ha! What'd you do with the money your mama gave you for singing lessons, kid?")

Always loved you
Darling, will you marry—

("Not if she's smart. Time, kid. Time.")

The recording is over. Abrupt and rude. My emotions cry foul. Jones McDermott captured me with his heartfelt, fifty-eight-year-old song.

Mitch lets the needle scratch against the paper label for several long seconds.

"What happened? Where's the rest of the song?" Elle yips. "Mitch, check the other side. Who was that man yelling?"

"The booth operator." Mitch somberly flips the record over, but there's nothing on side B. So he plays A again.

"This here is Jones Q. McDermott . . ."

The four of us listen and fuss to each other about the rude booth operator, then wonder who in the world stole Jones's heart.

"Mercy Bea, did you ever hear him talk of anyone?" I ask.

She tosses popcorn into her mouth. "I may be the oldest among y'all, but I'm not that old. By the time I met him, he was a cranky, committed bachelor."

Mitch carefully slides the 45 into the white sleeve. "Sounds like he really loved this woman. But the man yelling . . . Not cool. Poor Jones trying to sing his heart to a woman he loved." He laughs lightly. "I remember my first recording session. I was petrified."

I jab his ribs with my elbow. "You were not."

"Yes, I was. Terrified. If someone yelled at me like that, I would've bolted. Never sung a note."

Mercy Bea rams her wrist in front of my eyes. "Time, Caroline. Time." She runs toward the bedroom. "Hurry, we best get you rinsed out."

"Mercy Bea—" Eight extra minutes have passed. "If I look like Lucille Ball . . ."

"You won't look like Lucille Ball."

Howard chooses that exact moment to shake Beaufort as if we are a tiny town encapsulated in a snow globe. The lights flicker.

"Come on, baby, stay on." Mercy Bea grabs a clean towel from my closet with a quick review of the coloring directions. As she grabs the shampoo, Howard bears down with another giant gust.

The lights flicker off.

And stay off.

Frogmore Café Feeds the Neighborhood After Howard

By Melba Pelot
Wednesday, Sept 5

By normal standards, Caroline Sweeney is an average twenty-something, lowcountry born and bred.

But Sunday, after Hurricane Howard blew through, she became the belle of Beaufort.

Along with the Frogmore Café's cook, Andy Castleton, Caroline and her crew fed more than a thousand people over the past two days at the Bay and Harrington Street café.

Many customers brought food from home to be fired up on the grill, contributing to the giant block party.

"Caroline shows extraordinary heart. Giving from the Café to people in need," said Councilman Dave Williamson. "She donated all the food, water, and time she had."

"I saw people Sunday night after the storm I hadn't seen in years," said Beaufort dentist Dr. Gerry Collinsworth. "Mini reunions happened all around me."

Sunday night became even more magical when country great and Beaufort son Mitchum O'Neal pulled guitars with local favorite Branan Logan and filled the hot, humid night with music. Later, they were joined by other local musicians, Penny Collins and Red Stebbins.

"In times like these, I'm reminded of how many great people live in Beaufort," said Connie Stern, a local realty receptionist. "Caroline Sweeney being at the top of my list right now."

Daily Special

Friday, September 7

Fried Chicken

Mashed Potatoes w/ Real Gravy

Green Beans or Corn

Andy's Raspberry Cake

Tea, Soda, Coffee

$7.99

Live Music

Penny Collins

32

Elle sits at the Café's counter, scowling over her Operation
Wedding Day list, scribbled with lines and notes. It's worn from being
folded and unfolded so many times.

"So, the preacher didn't work out?" I refill her mason jar of soda,
noting she's been consuming a lot of Diet Coke and very little food.

She lifts her shoulder with an exaggerated inhale. "No." Exasperated
exhale. "He hasn't called back since our date."

Squeezing her hand as if to ease her pain, I search for comforting
words. "Elle, you can't schedule love. Are you losing weight?"

"I'm not hungry." She slaps her paper to the countertop and draws
her soda close. "It's stupid, and I know God has the perfect man for me,
but I can't see it, you know? The future seems dim."

"Just believe. Look at all the things God's done for me, and I didn't
even know Him until a month ago."

Elle sighs. "Yeah, and it's wonderful to see." She folds the list.

"Enough of this for now. So, Caroline, what'd Mercy say about your hair?" She squints. "It's downright blinding."

I slip my hand over my very red ponytail. "She called her hairdresser, but they had some water damage from the storm. They should be open in a few weeks and Mercy's going to pay for my appointment."

"A few weeks. You want to look like Carrot Top for a few weeks?"

"It's not that bad, Elle, and everyone's already seen me. Shoot, I was photographed for the paper the day after. Splashed all over the front page."

Elle sips her drink, hesitates, then orders a cheeseburger with the works. When I come back from the kitchen she says, "I've never seen a grown woman so afraid of the dark."

"Well, the storm didn't help. All that banging and shrieking."

"That wasn't the storm, that was Mercy Bea."

The memory makes me laugh. "I thought Mitch would never get her detached from his arm. Don't tell her, but he has fingernail scars."

"He was amazing. Calmed her down with prayer and a few songs. In fact, I was feeling a little scared myself until he started playing."

"Too bad music couldn't save my hair."

The front bells ring as several customers enter the Café for a late lunch. I grab a couple of menus and lead them to a booth.

"How are you folks today?"

"Fine, fine. Been meaning to get by here since we saw the article in the paper."

"We're glad to have you. Can I get you something to drink?"

Beyond the Café windows, the sun is high and hot in a hazy blue sky, the memory of Hurricane Howard a small dot on the horizon. Yet, the storm did something for the Café no advertising, raft racing, or singing Mitch O'Neal could do: endear us to the heart of Beaufort.

Opening up to feed the neighborhood simply seemed like the right and honorable thing to do. Giving away food in crisis is what love is all about, right? I didn't even bother to calculate the cost.

Once power was restored and life returned to the mundane, our business boomed. Here it is Friday midafternoon, and ten of our twenty tables are full. And we've had a dozen calls from folks checking on our dinner hour.

I'm praying to add an additional five hundred in my payment to Buster this month.

"Paris, customers in your section, table 12," I say as I pass her on my way back to the counter. "Both want sweet tea."

"Caroline." Luke appears around the kitchen opening. "Phone for you."

"Be right there."

Ol' Luke. So faithful. Comes in for breakfast with the boys, then dons his apron. He keeps the floors mopped, the tables bussed, and the bathroom Lysoled without so much as a "will you?" from me. He sees what needs to be done and does it. With all his hustle, Luke's silently challenged Russell to put more into his work.

Smiling, I reach for the kitchen receiver. "This is Caroline. Can I help you?"

"I certainly believe you can." The timbre of his voice, the accented words . . .

"Señor Longoria?"

"What's up with you? Your cheeks are flushed." Elle's eye's follow me as I return to the dining room. Three more patrons have arrived at the counter. Mercy Bea indicates with a wild gaze she's done covering for me.

"Carlos Longoria called. Hi, Mr. Peterson, what can I get you?"

While I take care of my customers, Elle interjects questions. "What did he want? Why are you trembling like a scared pup? Is there any more raspberry cake?"

"He offered me a job. Hazel's still been talking me up to him like I'm some kind of diamond in the rough."

"You are a diamond in the rough. Anyway . . ."

I stick my tongue out at her and plate a slice of raspberry cake. "She sends him online links to the *Gazette* about me and the Café. The last one, where we served the city, really impressed him, I guess."

Elle licks the ketchup from her fork—from eating fries—and sinks it into the cake. "And he offered you a job?"

I lean in close. "Three times the money I make here. Plus moving expenses and benefits. All I have to do is commit to a one-year apprenticeship. After that, who knows?"

Elle drops her fork against the plate and grabs my hands. "Do it. Sell this place to the Buzz Boys and go. Caroline, it's now or never."

To: CSweeney
> *From: Carlos Longoria*
> *Subject: Offer*
> *Dear Caroline,*
> *It was a pleasure to speak with you the other day. Your answers to my questions were intelligent and delightful. Qualities I'm looking for in my first apprentice.*
> *Please find attached my formal offer letter. Feel free to e-mail me with questions.*
> *Saludos,*
> *Carlos*
> *President, CEO, Founder, SRG International*

I spend the weekend not thinking about my Friday conversation with Carlos, enjoying a good weekend crowd at the Café, then a lovely Sunday church service followed by a late dinner at Mitch's.

He told stories from his life on the road—only the G-rated ones, I'm sure—until I double over laughing. The intimacy from our fancy night out smolders beneath the surface of our relationship, but neither one of us seems willing to stir the embers. For now.

He asked how things were going at the Café, and I gave him the short roundup. When I told him about Carlos's offer, a funny look crept across his face.

"You're selling and moving?" Then he spent five minutes encouraging me to sell the Café and take this "amazing opportunity." He said "amazing opportunity" so many times I said he should write a song about it. I thought it was funny. Mitch? Not so much.

Now, he's in Nashville for a string of meetings, probably about to get his career back on track. His season home will end and . . .

I should go to Barcelona. Really, I should. I mean, why not?

"Jesus, what can I do here?"

After closing the Café, I walk down to Elle's gallery. I'm ready to toss her the hard question: do I really, sincerely, for real, no hesitation, this-is-for-all-the-marbles take the job in Barcelona?

Paul Mulroney is chatting with customers in front of his Bistro. He waves. Wait 'til he meets the Buzz Boys.

Fear is juxtaposed with excitement. Will I like Barcelona? Can I sincerely impress Carlos Longoria? Am I ready for such a big job when my greatest business feat is to give away several thousand dollars' worth of food after a hurricane?

What do I know about building projects, budgets? (Well, a little; I wrote a budget for Mrs. Farnsworth's. But that was for plants and dirt.) Will I get lost in the marketing jargon?

Ho, boy. Like the first day I braved Sunday school at Beaufort Community, I'll need a translator.

All that aside, as if it's not weighty enough, I have one buzzing-me-like-a-pesky-fly question: is selling the Café the best for everyone, not just me?

Will Roland and Dale honor the heart of the Café and all Jones poured into it? Will they treat the crew with respect? Will they love the Café as much as we do?

The late afternoon sky is blue with white-cotton clouds. Elle and I drift along the Coosaw in *Bluecloud.*

When I burst into Elle's gallery two hours ago, ready to talk business, she wanted to drift on the water. "I need inspiration."

"But I need to talk."

"We can do both. On the water."

Right now, she's reading Carlos's offer letter. Her hair is kinky from the wind and humidity, her forearms pink from the sun. She looks up when she's read to the end.

"What do you think?" I ask.

She slides her sunglasses from her forehead to the bridge of her nose, folds the letter, and hands it back to me. "Caroline, if you don't go, I'm going in your place. He doesn't have a picture of you, does he?"

"Saw me in the hurricane article."

"With all that red hair? And he still wants to hire you?" She laughs.

"I'm trying to make a serious decision and you're making fun." I tuck the letter into my skirt pocket, then dangle my arm over the side of the boat, letting my fingers skim along the top of the cool, thick water.

Elle lifts her face to the sunlight. "I'm hiding my extreme jealousy. Barcelona. How fantastic. What an amazing opportunity. You have to do it. Have to."

"But the Café—"

Elle adjusts her position against the side of the boat. "Sell the Café.

Sweetie, this is your time. You've done your duty here, Caroline. If Jones knew you had this opportunity, he'd demand you go. Maybe he left you the Café because he thought you needed focus, something to sink your teeth into."

"Am I that pitiful?" I bat away a surprising rinse of tears.

"No, no, that's not what I'm saying. Think of Jones as . . . as Beaufort's Donald Trump. Giving a girl a chance."

My heart spews a much-needed laugh and suddenly the decision doesn't seem worth all the worry I'm investing. "Kirk's relationship with the Buzz Boys seems timely and providential, doesn't it?" I slip down against the side of the old boat, resting my head on a life vest. "But is it the best decision for everyone involved?"

"For the hundredth time, yes. They will earn more money. Get benefits. The Café will be remodeled, the hours expanded."

"So, it's really better for *them* if I sell."

"Way better. Caroline, for the love of all that's good in life, go to freaking Barcelona."

"Okay, here's the deep, deep, can't-see-the-sun, buried question I haven't even asked myself yet." I sit forward, drawing my knees to my chest. "What about Mitch?"

"What about him? He's in Nashville, working his career. He'll be back there permanently before you close this deal with the Buzz Boys."

A loose string in the hem of my skirt blows in the low breeze. "Yeah, I know. We've been getting along so well. He's the Mitch I've always known and loved, only new and improved. Special, you know? And there's, this, like, smoldering thing between us. We ignore it as if reaching out will get one of us burned. "

Elle leans toward me. "Caroline, are you in love with him?"

I squeeze my eyes shut. "Yes . . . I don't know . . . maybe."

"You are the most patient, enduring, hopeful Pollyanna I ever met. Or, you're plumb crazy."

"So, I go. Forget Mitch."

"Forget Mitch?" Elle pulls a sketch pad from the canvas bag she brought along. "Impossible for you, I think. But God has put an incredible opportunity in your lap." She digs in her bag for pencils. "You've proven yourself to be faithful in the little things. Now prove to be faithful with the big."

"Want to hear something mind-blowing?"

"Why not? It's been a while." Her pencil scratches against the paper.

"Right now, I want Barcelona more than Mitch. Whenever I think of going, this funny, feeling flutters over me."

Elle grins. "My girl's going to Bar-ce-lona."

Daily Special

Tuesday, September 18

Fried Red Snapper

Baked Squash

Bubba's Buttery Biscuits

House Salad

Cherry Cobbler

Tea, Soda, Coffee

$8.99

33

Mitch calls midmorning. "How's my favorite redhead?"

"Ha-ha, very funny." I twist my ponytail, thinking I should ask Mercy Bea for an update on the waterlogged salon. Until now, I wasn't bugged by my redness, but my brown roots are starting to show. "How's my favorite country star?"

Hearing his voice stirs my longing for him. I love the texture of his voice, the way the scent of his soap mingles with his cologne, the way he shares his heart without restraint.

"Miss me?" he asks.

"My heart stopped beating."

"Mine too. I had to go to the emergency room."

He can't one up me. "They had to break out those paddle-shocky things on me."

He laughs. "You win. So, how's everything? Make any major decision?

Hey, Caroline, hold on . . . Jack, in here. I'm on the phone. Give me a sec . . . Caroline, sorry. I need to get back to this meeting. I just wanted to make sure you hadn't jetted off without saying good-bye."

"O-okay." Not what I expected him to say. "I'm still here. Can't go anywhere until probate closes anyway."

"I'll be home in a few weeks." He pauses, and the moment practically aches for an I-love-you, but we don't dare.

"See you soon."

Slowly I drop the receiver to the cradle, my affections suspended between friendship and love, our past and my future.

Monday, October 8
Reminisce Night 7:00
Come Share Your Memories & Pictures
of Beaufort and the Frogmore Café
Comeyas and binnyas

Weaving my way between the narrow aisle to the Café's stage, I take the microphone.

"Welcome, everyone, to the Frogmore Café's first Reminisce Night." I smile, confident. The evidence of Mercy Bea's hurricane lights-out panic is gone from the top of my head. Her stylist transformed my hair into a shiny chestnut brown and cut away all the dry dead ends. For about two minutes, I fumed over my short cut, until she showed me a picture of Cameron Diaz with the same style.

"You could be her twin," she said.

Okay, maybe I see it in the eyes.

"We're so glad you came out—" The microphone screeches. My *sound man*, Luke, fumbles to turn the knobs like Mitch showed him. When he nods to me, I start again.

"We're so glad you came out for Reminisce Night. Please don't be shy about telling your Beaufort or Frogmore Café stories." I lift my free hand. "Whatever is on your heart."

About seventy pairs of eyes stare back at me. *Ho, boy.*

"My name is Caroline Sweeney."

"We know," a male voice hollers.

"Dupree, was that you?" Squinting, I shield my eyes from the bright spotlight and scan the dining room for a sign of my breakfast-club boy. Instead of spotting Dupree, my eyes land on Roland and Dale, sporting wide smiles and Polo shirts, with a blonde, pale Amazon.

I continue with the formalities. "Mercy Bea and Paris will take care of you tonight. Be sweet to them."

"Where's Mitch?" a female voice calls this time.

"Dupree, was that you?" I ask again.

Laughter peppers the room. Roland and Dale tuck in next to the wall. Amazon chick studies the Café, firmly gripping her briefcase.

"Sorry, Dupree." I spot him off to my left with his wife, Helen. Next to him is Pastor Winnie with his Alva.

"I still love you," he says.

"Love you, too, Dupree. No, Mitch is not here, but I'll tell him y'all asked about him. Anyway, let me introduce the Café's fab cook, Andy Castleton." I motion to the back of the dining room where Andy tips his cap at the sound of applause.

"Also, Luke and Russell are on the crew tonight, bussing tables, washing dishes, cleaning toilets, and are all-around champs. But you didn't come to hear me talk. You came to reminisce. The ground rules are: one, share whatever's on your heart; and two, keep the stories as short as possible so everyone who wants to share has the opportunity." I gesture to the booth right of the stage. "To get things started, please welcome my dad, Hank Sweeney."

Applauding, I stand off to the side while Dad comes forward, smiling.

"Well . . ." He scratches his head. His voice warbles. "On my way here, I must've told Posey a dozen stories, and now I can't think of a one, other than the fact I was born here."

"The bridge," Posey prompts softly.

"Right, the bridge." Dad's face brightens. "In light of our high-tech, modern world, this seems downright primitive, but Tom Cantwell and I used to spend our Saturday nights watching the bridge open and close."

"Me too, Hank" echoes about the tight dining room.

"Of course, I remember things like the Village Pizza Inn. When Ribaut and Boundary were two lanes. Movies at the Green Lawn. Best thing for me was meeting my wife, Posey."

With that, he quickly exits the stage. When he slides in next to Posey, she kisses his cheek, leaving a red lipstick stain. Dad is proof: no one is too old or too wounded to bloom under the light of love.

The stage is empty. Seconds tick by. I glance around to see if anyone looks close to coming up. No one. More time ticks by. Seconds feel like forever.

Please, Lord, don't let Reminisce Night begin and end with Daddy.

"Well, guess I'll take a turn." A slender, seventyish woman maneuvers forward through the tables. "Hi, everyone. I'm Linda Stewart." Her voice is sweet and shy. "My daddy was a World War II Marine colonel. About as strict as they come. Pat Conroy and I could swap a few stories. He mellowed when I got into my teens, thank goodness, just in time for me to start dating. We moved here when I was sixteen, and not long after, Keith Randall, the cutest boy in school asked me to the movies. I thought heaven had come to Beaufort."

All eyes are fixed on her round, pink face.

"Daddy met Keith at the door, invited him in, and asked him his intentions." Her gaze is distant, as if she's watching the scene unfold in her mind's eye. "Poor Keith. But he was a good sport about it and agreed to Daddy's request to have me home by eleven. Sharp. Once ten o'clock rolled around, Keith checked his watch every two minutes, afraid time would mysteriously slip away from us. We headed home in plenty of time, but don't you know . . ." She pauses. "We got caught by the drawbridge."

Gasps rise from the listeners. Heads bob. Snickers chase around the room.

"Y'all know. Been there same as me. We sat there for thirty minutes while the slowest boat in the world sailed the Beaufort River. I could've walked home faster. Sure enough, when we pulled into the driveway at eleven-o-five, Daddy waited with rifle in hand."

Moans roll forward from a dozen or so ladies, followed by the laughter of what I assume are rifle-toting fathers.

"Since we were new to town, Daddy did not believe for one minute Keith and I were delayed because of a bridge. He sent me inside, fearing for my life, then gave Keith a tongue-lashing that curled hair better than Mama's home perms. Told him to never call his daughter again. Two days later"—she laughs, holding up two fingers—"Daddy was caught by the bridge, making him very, very late to a *very* important inspection."

The crowd bursts out laughing, applauding.

"A week later, y'all, guess who came to dinner?" With that, Mrs. Stewart bows, ending her story to great applause.

So, the pump is primed. One by one, young and old, newcomers and old-timers rise to tell their stories of life in Beaufort. Mercy Bea and Paris keep tea flowing, rotating in fresh baskets of Bubba's Buttery Biscuits. The camaraderie flowing through the room is heartening. I hate for it to end. But at nine, I take the mike. "Can't believe it, but it's nine o'clock already. I loved every story."

Whistles and applause.

"So, I'll take one or two more stories. Any of you have a burning story to tell?"

"Are you doing this again?" someone asks.

"Yes, in January." *I won't be here, but . . .*

The applause tells me January suits them fine. Take note, Buzz Boys.

"So, last call. Going, going . . ."

Still in the back, Dale and Roland and their long-legged blonde friend seem pleased and amused. Seconds tick by, and I'm about to say "gone" when an older man, thin and shaky, rises from a table near the front door.

I've never seen him before, but I like him. The aura around him is genteel. His chin is square. His shoulders proud.

"Evening." His voice is raspy, but strong.

"Evening."

"My name's Sebastian Fowler. I'm eighty-one this year, and like the first talker, Hank, over there, I'm a born and raised Beaufortonian. I got a story for this old Café and this young gal right here." He motions to me.

Me?

"Jones McDermott was like a brother to me. Our parents were friends, and they stuck the two of us in a crib together, don't you know. Our dads took us hunting and fishing out on St. Helena. We played football for Beaufort High, chased the same girls. But in our senior year, old Jones tripped and fell in love—headfirst—with a little ole gal from Port Royal."

Sebastian smiles, gently rocking the mike stand back and forth. "Never seen the boy so gone. Wrote to her every day while we was in the Army. He'd say to me, 'Sebastian, I'm going to marry her.'" The old man gazed down the length of the dining room. "Even recorded an original love song at one of them fairground booths."

I stand away from the wall. The recording we heard the night of the hurricane.

"This gal was a pretty thing. Sweet, a church girl, and loved Jonesy, but not like he loved her. The Army sent us TDY to Germany for six months. Hoo-wee, he was lovesick. But he had a plan." Sebastian jabs the air with his finger. "Save money, come home, buy a business, marry this gal, and live happily ever after.

"About our third month of TDY, he got *the* letter." Sebastian presses his hands over his heart. His eyes glisten. "She was engaged to another man."

The room is quiet, steady on the story. Even Mercy Bea and Paris have stopped working.

"He had a rough go of it for a while. I tried to tell him there'd be other gals. We saw lots of pretty ones in Paris and Berlin. But he wanted this one particular gal. You'd think a fella would get over his heartbreak, but not Jones. No sir. But he saved his money, bought this place, and lived a good life. Happily some days. Not so happily others."

Sebastian weaves his story with purpose, leading us to the dramatic end.

"The gal Jones loved was Gracie Kirby."

My jaw drops. Nana? I look over at Dad. His sharp expression tells me this is the first he's heard anything like Sebastian's story.

"Gracie Kirby married Hank Sweeney Senior before our TDY ended. The catchall is Jones had asked Hank to look in on his gal while we was gone, make sure no other fellas invaded his territory. Hank agreed, but he kept telling Jones to cut loose of that skinny, stuck-up gal. Hank didn't care much for Gracie, so Jones figured he was safe. But like Jones, Hank tripped over Gracie's charms and fell in love."

Nana was the object of Jones's love song. And a love triangle? Nana . . .

"Jones never quite got over Gracie. The Café became his wife. My job moved me across the country, and we only talked a few times a year. But, one day out of the blue, he calls up and says, 'I met the cutest gal.' I thought, Good, you're fifty-six, and it's about time you settled down. I was already a grandpa."

The serene Café ambience is pierced with laughter.

Sebastian turns toward me. "The gal he met was you, Gracie's grand-daughter. Something about you, Caroline, watered his dry heart."

The static questions from the summer have answers now—loud and clear. Jones's affection for me came out of his love for Nana. For the first time, I understand why Jones gave me the Café. But instead of being shocked and surprised, my heart responds, *Of course.*

"Jones regretted Gracie died before he came to his senses and mended a broken friendship. When I heard he left the Café with Caroline, I figured it was his way of saying, 'Gracie, you and me, we're all right.'"

Sebastian pauses with a glance at me. "Guess that's my story, and, young lady, how do I get off this stage?"

To: MusicMan

From: CSweeney

Subject: Reminisce Night

Mitch,

It's late. The Café is closed, the deposit done, tips paid out, and the first Reminisce Night at the Frogmore Café is over.

Ding howdy, did you miss it.

Remember the woman Jones sang to on the record? It was Nana Sweeney.

Granddad stole her from Jones when the Army sent him to Germany. Granddad was supposed to keep the other guys away.

Jones never recovered, Mitch. He loved Nana and no one else. Sebastian thinks he left the Café to me as his way of mending fences with Nana.

Afterwards, Dad, Posey, Henry, Cherry, and I talked with Sebastian and his daughter, Rose.

Daddy never knew about any of this. He just knew that one

*Friday after Thanksgiving, Granddad took me to the Frogmore Café
(I was ten) and hit it off with Jones.*

*So here I sit, the center of a love triangle. Jones worked out his
feelings for Nana by seeing me as a granddaughter.*

*One half of my heart is overwhelmed that Jones would entrust
his life's work to me. The other half angry. Why didn't he talk to me?
Tell me how he felt?*

*Odd, these small-town mysteries of who loved who. When and why.
Friendships lost, friendships found. Hearts broken. Hearts mended.*

*Contrast this story to the potential buyers making an appearance
tonight with their lawyer, an Amazon woman.*

*She said to me (in a deep voice), "Nice place." Remember Rocky
IV and "I must brrreak you"? She's definitely not from around here.*

There's more to that story, but I just ran out of typing steam.

Love, Caroline

Tuesday afternoon, Andy comes in the office as I count
down the cash drawer. "Here's the inventory for the day, Caroline."

I finish counting the one-dollar bills. *Forty-eight, forty-nine, fifty.*
"Hard to believe we're ordering almost every day."

He whips off his beanie. "Business is good. Can I sit a minute?" He
gestures to the empty chair across from me.

"Absolutely." I bundle the ones, smiling up at Andy. "Why do you
even ask?"

He strides over to the chair, swirling his beanie between his fingers.
"Mercy Bea overheard them Buzz Boys talking last night, Caroline." His
tone is sober.

"Yeah? What'd they say?" Rocking back in my chair, I hook my foot
around the desk leg to keep from tipping back too far. "They seemed to
enjoy themselves."

"Caroline, now, you know Mercy Bea can spin a yarn with the best of them, but she come to me this morning saying she overheard the Buzz Boys say things like 'change' and 'get rid of' about a hundred times. She looked scared, Caroline."

It's not like Andy to worry over the small matters Mercy Bea claims to be tidal waves. Something about her claim rings true with him.

"Why hasn't she come to me?" I ask.

"She's afraid you won't take the job in Spain."

An unsettled feeling twists in my middle. "Did she hear any specifics?"

"She heard them talk about a French chef up to Charleston that has folks talking. One of them, the tall dude, thought they could get him to come down here. Then, the lady with them suggested selling off the Vet Wall to the city."

I jerk forward so fast the chair lists to starboard, and I have to grapple for the desk's edge. "The Vet Wall is part of the building's structure. It's had signatures for a hundred and fifty years. It *belongs* to the Frogmore."

"Mercy heard them say something about the Wall reminding people of war and they don't want them thinking of war, but of eating and drinking. Then there's the folks who are against war, and the Wall might offend them."

I'm stunned. "A few weeks ago they were getting the History Channel on the horn."

"Well, the lady—she's their lawyer—suggested getting rid of the Wall." He looks over finally. "Mercy heard them talking about the Frogmore being the first in a chain where all the restaurants would look alike, serve the same menu."

Did they lie to my face? The Buzz Boys are over-the-top, but to smile and lie right to me? "Andy, I'll talk to Kirk. Clear this up."

He rises slowly. "I'd appreciate it. I'm kind of fond of this old place. I don't know nothing about French cooking."

I watch as Andy plops his beanie on his head as he goes out. His shoulders are rounded with his burden. And reaching for the phone to call Kirk, a myriad of summer images—from Hurricane Howard to Reminisce Night—form a picture I've never seen before.

Andy arrives early every morning.

Works all day without complaint, singing most of the time.

Talks about the Café with tender affection.

Keeps true to all of Jones's recipes.

Andy Castleton *is* the true heart of the Frogmore Café.

To: Carlos Longoria
From: CSweeney
Subject: Re: Offer
Dear Carlos,
Thank you for your offer. I am pleased to say I accept and look forward to working with you.
    Saludos,
    Caroline

Daily Special

Closed—Sunday, October 14

Coming Soon!
Bubba's Buttery Biscuits delivered to your home

Child Abuse Prevention Association
Ghost Tours Oct 21—Oct 30

34

To Caroline." Elle stands, raising her glass, taking in the faces around the table at Panini's Café. "To Hazel and beautiful Barcelona, to the reality of 'It's never too late' and 'Miracles still do happen.'"

My party guests, Jess and Ray, Bodean and Marley, a few new friends from church, and J. D. (Ray invited him; he wanted to come) raise their glasses.

"To Caroline." The salute is accompanied by the clinking of glasses.

The atmosphere of good wishes fortifies my confidence. I'm doing the right thing by selling the Café to the Buzz Boys, men with wealth and imagination. Men who can heal the wonderful but wounded Frogmore.

With my limited God experience, I believe He's leading me. My call to Kirk relieved me of Mercy Bea's fears. He assured me the Boys loved the Frogmore as is and the only changes they have in mind are cosmetic.

"When we close probate, they'll be ready to take over and you'll have a check for one-point-two million, Caroline." He whistled over the phone. "What are you going to do with all that money?"

That's when a brilliant idea hit me. Brilliant, I say. Just thinking of it warms me all over.

The table talk is lighthearted. We're laughing and bantering so much the server has a hard time getting our order. I am so relaxed. Even J. D.'s presence is soothing. He catches my gaze and smiles.

Forgive me?

I smile back. *Don't sweat it.*

In the middle of taking in a Wild-Wally story, a hand touches my shoulder.

"Sorry I'm late, everyone."

"Mitch, oh my gosh," I jump out of my seat, giving him a hug. "When did you get home?"

"Just now. Drove straight here." He keeps his arm around me as he sits in the empty chair, saying hi to the rest of the group. I glance at Elle. She's beaming.

Mitch's presence electrifies Panini's—no surprise—and awakens the mellow atmosphere with whispers, craning necks, and a dozen autograph seekers.

Finally, his attention is on me. "Missed you." He slips his hand into mine and kisses my cheek. The invisible fingers of my soul grasp at my evaporating confidence. *Maybe I shouldn't go to Barcelona.* "I missed you too."

His blue eyes search mine. "Want to hang out tonight, after we eat?"

"Absolutely."

Dinner at elegant Panini's ends with the gang standing around the table, saying "Good night," "Let's do this again soon," "What a great time," and doling out tip money. Mitch talks to Ray, standing so close to me we fit together like puzzle pieces.

"Ray, honey, come on. I've hit the wall." Jess tugs on her husband's sleeve with a sleepy-eyed wave at me. When she gets tired, that's it; the night's over. For everyone.

"Night, Jess," I say, leaning over the table to meet her hug.

"I'll call you this week."

Then Mitch and I are alone by the table. "So, first selling, then Barcelona?"

"I wanted to tell you in person. It all happened so fast." Facing him, I see two women approach from the opposite side of the dining room. "Mitch."

He turns as they ask, "Mr. O'Neal, can we have your autograph?"

Fame comes at a price. Public private conversations are a luxury. Two beautiful women hold out pen and paper, batting their eyes while sporting take-me-now smiles. Mitch is irritated, I can tell, yet he bottles it while talking with them.

"How are you two tonight?" His smile is slow, but sincere.

The large-bosomed woman arches her back so her exposed cleavage is right under Mitch's nose. "I'm wonderful. How are you?"

Ho, boy. If Mitch has this coming at him all the time, no wonder he strayed over the yellow line. But he barely seems to notice this woman and her two "friends."

"Thank you, ladies. Have a good night." He takes me by the arm and steers me toward the door.

"I think they wanted more than an autograph, Mitch."

"Those kind always do."

I snicker, and he breaks into a soft chuckle, steering us to the river-walk where the wind off the water presses against us in tender, cold gusts. "When do you leave?"

"January, I think."

He leans against the cement pylon and faces me, tucking his hands into his jeans' pockets and hunching his shoulders against the cold. "Are you sure? Don't you want to stay in Beaufort? The Café is doing well. You have family and friends. A church."

"Am I sure? Are you not the one who was singing the 'amazing opportunity' song a few days ago? Mitch, the Café will be in much better hands. The staff will have benefits as part of Buzz Boys, Inc. Paid vacations, insurance, even bonuses. I've signed papers, accepted Carlos's offer . . . Yes, done deal." I shiver in the damp, chilled air. I left my jacket in Elle's car. "The building inspector came on Friday."

"Caroline, all that 'amazing opportunity' stuff I said? Bull. Don't sell. Keep the Café. Stay here." The words come clipped and fast and drizzle me with a sense of desperation.

"Keep the—Why? And what do you mean 'bull'?" I stand back away from him. "What would you have me do? Grow old and alone like Jones? Be married to that old run-down money pit? Or, hey, here's an idea. Let's get married. You and me. You could live in Nashville, and I'll live here. How'd that be? Hmm?"

"Fine, but I'd prefer to live here. With you."

Heart: What'd he say?

Head: Live here.

Heart: Ears, is that right?

Ears: 10-4

Heart: Head, have mouth ask him again.

Head: I'll try, but mouth has a mind of its own.

"Live where? Beaufort?"

He shrugs. "Times have changed. I can commute to Nashville. I'd prefer it."

I laugh, wagging my finger at him. "Okay, I see what you're doing. Messing with me, right. You . . . you're funny. Mitch, I'm joking. Marriage. Ha-ha, good one, Caroline. You're joking too, right?"

"No." He pulls his hand from his pocket and pops open a small box. "I'm not kidding."

I blink. "Is that a ring?" A large, square diamond glimmers in the waterfront's light. "Mitch . . ."

"Marry me, Caroline."

The statement electrifies the hairs on the back of my neck. "Marry you?"

"I love you." His velvety confession suspends all doubts. "Very much."

"You want to marry me? For sure? No 'Say it now, forget about it later'?"

"Yes, I want to marry you. Now. Forever." His cocky, yet endearing smile beams. "I didn't want to even hint at this until I had the ring. I wanted to surprise you."

"I-I'm stunned. Mitch, really? M-marry you?"

I-I can't . . . Do I love him? In a flash, I compare my heart for Mitch to what I felt for J. D. *Oh, yes, I love Mitch.* Marry him? *Oh, yes.*

I throw myself against him. "I love you, Mitch. Yes, yes, I'll marry you."

Our first kiss in many years is deep and tender, passionate with years of love and friendship. I can hear his heart thunder. "Caroline." He reaches to slip the ring on my finger.

Wait. I back away, the heat of his lips still on my mine. The cool platinum ring lightly touches my finger. "I accepted the job with SRG."

"Can't you call back, turn it down?"

"Call Carlos back? And say what, Mitch? Oops—never mind, my high school boyfriend finally coughed up a ring?"

He drops his hand, cupping the ring. "That's not fair, Caroline."

"For you? Or me? Mitch, I gave my word. Of all people, you were the one cheering me on."

"Of all people, I thought you wanted to be with me."

"I did . . . I do. But not now." I step into him, grabbing his shirt. "I told Carlos yes. He held the position open for me, Mitch. He could've hired someone else when I had to take the Café, but he wanted to give me a try. Hazel went out on a limb . . ."

"Well, then, forgive me. You absolutely should take the job with SRG." He tucks the ring into his pocket. "What's a lifetime of love and commitment compared to a year with the Latin Donald Trump and fifteen-hour workdays?"

The muscles along the back of my neck twist, sending a sharp pain over my scalp. "Don't you dare, Mitch O'Neal. Don't you dare. Not after you walked away from me for your career."

"And I was a fool to do it. Learn from me."

My knees buckle when I look into his eyes. "Learn what? That you followed your heart and ended up with a stellar career? That you lived a dream life? Are the envy of men, the adoration of women?"

"No, that love cannot be replaced with fame, money, careers, or amazing job opportunities. Caroline, I love you. Carlos is a businessman who sees you as cheap labor."

"And what do you see me as? Easy lover. Poor Caroline, waiting at home for Mitch to return on his white steed?" A sour word spews between my lips. "Well, not this time, Mitch. I won't do . . . do what . . . what everyone . . ." The expression in his eyes dissolves every irate fiber of my being. "Everyone else . . . wants. Expects . . . Now's my chance to . . . explore . . . life. Be free."

"Am I offering bondage?"

"Did I say that?"

"Yes, in so many words." Mitch walks off, disappearing behind the curtain of night beyond the waterfront lamps.

"Where are you going?"

"Sooner or later, Caroline," his voice comes from the shadows, "we have to move on. Maybe we just weren't meant to be. I want to get married, settle down, have a family."

"Family?" A trigger word for me. I'd love to have my own family.

What am I thinking? Do I want the Barcelona job *that* bad? It's a stupid line in the sand. One crash of a wave, and it washes away. Mitch loves me. He's here, he's now and he's right—Barcelona is only for a season, but marriage is for life.

His steps scuffle back toward me, then stop. "Are you ready to go home? My truck is that way."

Loneliness explodes in my chest. In a hair's breadth, my future without hope of him plays across my mind's eye.

"Please ask me again." My ears drum with panic.

Mitch appears, half in the shadow, half in the light. "You don't mean it."

"Now you're telling me what I mean?" I can't stop shaking.

"You'll resent me."

"Only if you don't ask me again." Gripping my hands at my waist, I fight the trembling, warding off the fear that I almost lost the love of my life.

Mitch strides toward me, his eyes locked on my face. I think. *Drat the darkness.* Then, I see his smile. "Are you sure?"

"Will you ask me already?"

My man slips his arm around my back and tugs me close. Versace perfumes the air between us. "Caroline, will you marry me?"

I press my lips to his, then breathe out, "Yes, Mitch, yes. I'll marry you."

"No doubts?"

"None."

He scoops me up with a shout and whirls me around. When he sets me down, he traps me against a pylon so I can't escape.

"I'm going to love you like no one's loved you."

I loop my arms around his neck. "It's always been you, Mitch. I've never loved anyone else."

"I'm in it for real, Caroline. No record deal—I just signed a new one, by the way—can keep me from you. No world tours, no promise of fame or riches."

"Good, because I might just have to hunt you down and—"
He cuts me off with a kiss. *Oh, I see how it's going to be.*

To: CSweeney
From: Hazel Palmer
Subject: I'm stunned, but so very excited
Caroline,
Finally, you said yes. I can't believe it. To be honest, I was convinced something at home would come up to keep you from coming. But you proved me wrong. I actually did a jig in my office when Carlos told me. After he left, of course, and I closed the door.

I can't wait to see you. We are going to have a blast. Listen, we charge all travel and moving expenses to our corp AmEx, so e-mail me when you know your travel/moving day. Then I'll book the company villa on the Mediterranean for a few days.

Carlos is amazing, but he'll work you hard Monday through Friday. You are so very lucky.

Also, I looked at some apartments for you (see attached) thinking you'd rather live on your own. I keep very weird hours. And I'm a slob at home. Anal neat freak at work, but no time for it at home. Thank heaven for maid services.

Can't wait to see you.
"You're gonna need a bigger boat."
> *Love, Hazel*
> *CFO, SRG International, Barcelona*

Monday morning. 8:02. The breakfast-club boys slide into their booth as I set down their coffee cups. Pastor Winnie waves his hands in front of his eyes.

"Whoa, whoa, what is going on here? I'm blinded. Caroline, your finger . . . Heaven and all the angels, girl, you done got yourself engaged?"

"She sure enough did, Winnie." Mercy Bea says as she hurries past.

I'm exhausted from being up all night talking to Mitch, Daddy, and Posey, then collapsing into a not-so-deep sleep in my old room outfitted with Posey's new guest-bedroom furniture. Was it excitement, nerves, too much caffeine? I couldn't sleep. I watched each wee morning hour tick away.

Dupree picks up my left hand and examines Mitch's ring at close range. "Flawless?"

I take my hand away. "You think I asked?"

He dumps a creamer in his coffee. "At least three karats too."

Pastor Winnie spreads butter on his biscuit. "A man like Mitch ought to be able to afford a nice piece of a 'girl's best friend.'"

The tip of my thumb touches the shank of the ring. "Mitch is my best friend."

"Well, he's given you another." Pastor Winnie chuckles and shakes his head with a *tsk, tsk.*

"What happened to the job? Madrid, was it?" Dupree asks.

I don't know . . . "Barcelona." I hurry off for their breakfast.

But just beyond the kitchen door, Luke catches me by the elbow and railroads me toward my office.

"What happened?" Luke eases the door closed. "You were smiling wider than the Broad River when you told us about accepting the Barcelona job."

I've seen Luke on a near-daily basis for over two years, but never with the expression he's giving me now.

"I love Mitch, Luke. Always have, and I want to marry him."

"Suddenly this love between you has a time limit? Seems to me he could wait until after Barcelona."

"Marriage is forever. Why eat up Carlos Longoria's time, and take an opportunity away from someone else, when at the end of my year there I'll come home to marry Mitch?"

He grunts. "Waste of God's good potential."

A cold sensation runs through my insides. "What does that mean? Marriage is what makes the world go 'round, Luke."

"You never even tried, Caroline." He props his hands on the desk's edge, the skin around his eyes crinkled with wisdom lines. "If Mitch really loved you, he'd back off, encourage you to move to Barcelona. Carlos Longoria is a businessman. He'll understand investing time in you for only a season. Believe me, he'll get his money's worth out of you."

Unable to look Luke in the eye, I focus on the basket of paid bills. For the first time in months, the paid pile is higher than the unpaid. "If I go, I'm afraid it'll be the end of Mitch and me, forever."

"Well," Luke exhales, his voice soft, "marrying a man out of desperation is the best reason, I suppose."

My gaze shifts to his face. "That's not what I'm saying."

He raises his eyebrows. "Then what are you saying?"

Walking toward me, Elle smiles. Her gallery is lit with spotlights over her latest paintings. The one of me reclining in *Bluecloud* is a dreamy framed watercolor.

"Five hundred dollars." I blink to see if my blurry vision added a zero.

"Shh, keep your voice down. This isn't the flea market." Elle pinches my arm with a nod at browsing art enthusiasts.

"You're going to sell my face for five hundred dollars?" I whisper this time, but skirt the edge of loud.

"Sold one of my niece, Rio, last month for twice the amount."

"Then why am I only five hundred?" Astonishment to insult in under ten seconds.

"Stop already." Elle picks up my engagement hand. "I still can't believe it. Engaged. To Mitch. Oh, girl. We are going to have some fun planning this one. I'll be your photographer, of course, as well as maid of honor, right?" Her eyes twinkle.

"Of course." At this rate, all I'll have to do is show up.

"Have you picked a date yet?"

"No, still enjoying being engaged." I glance over at Mitch. He's on the other side of the gallery, head bent as he listens to a rich-looking tanned man wearing shorts and a Polo—collar flipped up. As if sensing me, Mitch looks up, catches my eye, and winks.

And what I feel terrifies me.

"Caroline?" Elle nudges me. "Did you hear me?"

Forcing a smile, I answer, "No, what?"

"I asked if you wanted Mom to come with us to shop for wedding dresses. She'd love to help. Besides, the woman has five daughters, three married. She's a pro."

"Yeah, that'd be great."

"So, any word from Hazel? How'd she take the engagement news?" Elle straightens one of her wall portraits.

"She said, well—"

"Excuse me, Miss Garvey," A slender brunette with sun-lined cheeks steps into our conversation. "I'd like to talk about this piece over here."

Elle excuses herself and walks off to make a sale.

I haven't told Hazel, yet.

Mitch joins me after a moment, slipping his hand along my shoulders. "Want to grab some dinner?"

I peer into his boundless blue eyes. "Sounds lovely."

"We can talk about setting a date. My schedule is booking up and I want to save plenty of time for wedding and honeymoon"—he gives me an intimate grin—"stuff."

Taking his hand, I follow him out the door, with a backward wave at Elle, who is taking the large painting down from the wall.

Mitch is so the opposite of J. D. Although I sense his passion as strong as J. D.'s.—maybe more—never once has he pushed the boundaries.

So why, oh, why, does my heart race every time I think of marriage? Why does my belly flip-flop every time I think of Barcelona?

Climbing a tree is not as easy as it used to be. When did my legs become cranky old ladies? Wasn't I just in this tree a few months ago?

"Omph." I hike my foot up to the first branch, stretching my arms toward a branch so I can pull myself up. The heel of my work clogs catches in the crook of the limb as I clasp my fingers around a thin limb and heave myself up. My skin crawls as I feel the platinum shank of my engagement ring scrape against the rough live oak bark.

"Come on, Caroline, sissy girl, get in the tree," I urge myself. But my hands slip. I tumble backwards, arms winging in the wind. My foot is stuck. "Ack!" My ankle twists one way while my body goes the other. There's nothing to catch me but the ground.

Face-first, I fall, leaving my shoe wedged in the tree and my skirt hiked up to my skivvies.

A few minutes later, sitting on the dock, I stare up at the twilight sky, wondering why the dream of a lifetime coming true doesn't feel as swell as I thought.

"What's going on?" I ask, not the stars this time, but the One who holds them in His hand. "This is Mitch. And me. Finally. The life I wanted."

I wanted . . .

The words slice gently through my soul, cutting away the cruddy feeling I've had since Mitch—oh, my man Mitch—asked me to marry him.

Since I said yes. When he asked me to pick a date the other night at dinner, I froze. Then, later, while cuddling on the couch, I fell asleep against his chest. He was so gracious and loving. But I feel guilty and need to give him an answer.

For the first time since I handed God the reins of my life and said, "Here, take all of me," I realize I just said giddy-up to three things I never really asked Him about.

Selling the Café. The job in Barcelona. And marrying Mitch.

"Okay." I cup my hands together and raise them toward heaven. "You can have it all. The Café, Mitch, Barcelona. And me."

I squint and turn my chin over my shoulder, bracing for the pain of having God rip out my heart. My arms shake as I stretch my hands higher.

And yet, as I take a deep breath, I feel relieved. Sincerely, profoundly, deeply relieved. While I sit in the chilly night, thinking and praying, clarity comes.

Daily Special

Wednesday, October 17

Fried Oysters

Corn on the Cob

BBQ Baked Beans

Side Salad

Bubba's Buttery Biscuits

Apple Fritters

Tea, Soda, Coffee

$8.99

35

The sun sets in a gold-red-orange-blue fall sky as Mitch
and I stroll arm in arm along the beach by his house. The crisp air has
me thinking of a warm fire and mugs of hot chocolate.

I burrow my face into Mitch's arm. "My nose is freezing."

"Let's go inside and build a fire." In one deft movement, he scoops
me up in his arms and carries me up the beach toward his home. The
stinging wind slips up the hem of my skirt and I kick and squirm to be
let down. He refuses, huffing and puffing up the deck steps to the back
French doors.

When he sets me down, his warm lips touch mine. "I can't wait until
we're married and I carry you across the threshold as my wife."

It's then that I know for sure.

"By the way," Mitch opens the left-side French door and starts gathering wood from the deck pile, "Mom wants to host an engagement tea

for you. Invite the ladies of the church. She knows you're working like crazy, but when would be a good time for you?"

"A tea party? For me?"

Mama wanted to give me a tea party for my twelfth birthday. She hand-painted fifteen invitations to girls in my class and called all their mothers. She painted the sunroom to look like a wild prairie meadow. We strung multicolored summer lights, shopped for a special tea set, and hired Mrs. Hogan to sew Mother-Daughter dresses. We ordered a cake from Mrs. Parker.

On the day of the party, I woke up in the house alone. Dad had taken Henry fishing, and I couldn't find Mama anywhere.

As the party guests arrived, I tried to pretend all was well—despite the fact we had no cake, no food, nor tea.

Convinced Mama would pop through the door at any moment, wearing her beautiful smile with an armload of presents, I did my best to hostess my confused guests.

When Dad and Henry came home, I sat alone in the dark living room, dirty tear tracks on my face.

The memory is old and rusty, and I'd rather die than attend a tea party, but I would endure for Mrs. O'Neal. "Your mother is very sweet, Mitch, but can we talk about something first?"

"Sure." He's gathering a second armload of wood. I crouch down next to him, gathering logs.

How do I say this, God? "About getting married, Mitch . . ."

He snaps to attention. The muscles in his arms bulge from the heavy pieces of firewood he cradles.

"Recently, I've made several decisions—selling the Café, accepting Barcelona, accepting your proposal—and I just, um, well . . ." My throat pinches closed. My hands shake as I add another log to my small stack.

"Caroline, say what you want to say."

Oh, please don't hate me. A nauseating swirl leaves me weak. "I can't marry you, Mitch. Not before Barcelona." I drop my firewood back onto the pile, as confidence begins to bloom. "Mitch, I love you. Most of my adult life, I've lived with the hope of someday being your wife. But, I'm learning and growing, coming to some idea God's given me gifts and talents I haven't begun to explore. Like when you moved to Nashville, hung with stellar musicians, and discovered you had the talent to play any instrument you pick up."

"I can't play the oboe."

He makes me laugh. "Yeah, well, who can?"

"Caroline, honey, you can do whatever you want with your life, even after we're married. Want to keep the Café, fix it up, and hire Andy to manage it? Great. Want to go to college? I'll help you cram for tests. Want five babies, I'll be more than happy to do my part." His grin is slightly wicked. "Think a month in the Brazilian jungle, learning about indigenous worms, will enhance your life? I'll support you."

"Mitch," *Oh, the look behind his eyes . . . I can't, God. I can't.* "I want to move to Barcelona and work for Carlos Longoria."

Standing there with his arms still wrapped around firewood, he studies me for a second. "I don't want a long-distance marriage. Being apart for a few weeks or a month is fine, but for a year with thousands of miles and a half dozen time zones between us? No."

"No? You're not making decisions for us, Mitch. *We* are." I circle my hand in the space between us. "This has been the hardest decision of my life. I haven't slept more than a few hours a night since you proposed. When I try to dream of wedding plans, I get cranky and snap at the crew." I press my hand over my middle. "I feel sick and confused."

Without a word, he pushes past me, taking the firewood inside. I watch him disappear, shivering. Night approaches with a distinct chill.

In a minute, Mitch reappears with a thick jacket. "Here, it's getting cold." He stoops for another load of firewood. "I suppose I could see about living in Barcelona." He glances up at me. "I could fly back and forth. It'd be awkward, just signing with a new label and putting out a new album, but it might work."

Tears bubble. "Oh, Mitch." I crouch next to him. "How the timing between us got so whacked, I'll never know, but I'm going solo, Mitch. Just Jesus and me. I need to do this . . ."

Holding my hands low at my waist, I slip his ring from my cold finger. When I offer it back, his countenance darkens, and his load of wood drops to the deck floor.

"I want to marry you . . . someday. If you still want me." My confession is thick and true.

He cups the ring in his hand. "Caroline . . . I—I . . ." His words wobble. "I can't believe this."

"I'm so, so sorry." Tears glide over my eyes and pool in the corners.

Mitch leans against the table, looking out toward the beach. Silence screams. It seems like minutes go by, but it's only seconds when Mitch gathers me in his arms.

We cry, holding each other tight.

"Best let me drive you home," he finally says.

"Mitch—" My heart yearns for him to know. "I love you, still. I'm trying to follow God here. I can't explain it, but there's something for me in Barcelona. Something intangible, something . . ."

"I know." He steps toward the door.

"I do love you."

"Just let me get my keys." He disappears in the house, and for one brief, frightening moment, I fear I've made the biggest mistake of my life.

To: Hazel Palmer
From: CSweeney
Subject: Better be worth it

Hazel,

Here's the nutshell update. I'm too emotional and exhausted to go into detail. But we are soooo talking when I get there.

Mitch asked me to marry him. I said yes. After I accepted Carlos's offer. For days, I couldn't sleep. I begged God for answers, laying it all out on the table. Selling the Café, accepting the job with SRG, and marrying Mitch.

In the end, I knew selling the Café was right. I knew working for SRG was right. I knew marrying Mitch was wrong. Not wrong, really, but wrong timing.

The night I gave him his ring back, he drove me home in complete silence. Oh, how I missed Matilda at that moment. As he drove away, I sank down to the parking lot and cried until there was a puddle of tears in the sand.

Hazel, I miss him something fierce. This is it for us. We're over. Not like the other times when he got busy with his career and we simply drifted apart.

This time when he dropped me off and said good-bye, I heard the clink of a door.

I'm sad and weepy, but I know I'll regret it the rest of my life if I don't try Barcelona.

Good night.

"**Letter for you, Caroline.**" **Mercy Bea** drops the **Café** mail on the counter.

"Letter?"

"Looks like Jones's handwriting. Want me to put the rest in the office?"

Letter? "Yes, office, thanks."

On the back is a note from Kirk. *Jones wanted this mailed to you after the ninety days. Sorry, just now found it.*

I tear open the letter and read.

Dear Caroline,

By the time you read this letter, I hope you've stopped cursing me. I suppose inheriting the Café came as a shock. Please forgive me if the deed unduly burdened you. That was never my intent.

On the other hand, if you're reading this, I've crossed over to the Golden Shore and am happy to be away from worldly troubles.

My prayer is for the Café to bless you. She's been around a long time, and as I write this letter, I'm filled with sentiment.

Why the ninety days? So you'd have time to think before acting. I didn't know what to do with the Frogmore. No kin to leave her to, or close friends.

Then, you came to mind and I knew you were the right one. Perhaps you're wondering why not Andy, or Mercy Bea? Other than the satisfaction I felt whenever I thought of you, I don't know. Andy is, in many ways, the soul of the Café.

I just knew you'd do the right thing by all of us.

The other reason is your grandma Sweeney. I loved her. She broke my heart when she married my friend, your granddad. But, over time I forgave her, but never humbled up to speak to her about it. I reckon this is all out of the blue for you, Caroline, but your Nana was the love of my life. After she died, your granddad came to me and said, "Gracie told me, 'Go see Jones. Don't let the bad blood linger.'"

Giving you the Cafe is my way of saying "All is well, Gracie."

I yank a napkin from the dispenser and blow my nose.

Best of everything to you, sweet Caroline. I hope you have a good life, full of love, family and well, a basket of my ole Bubba's Buttery Biscuits and Frogmore Stew. My chili weren't bad neither.

Yours truly.
Jones Q. McDermott

P.S. Never did know what the Q stood for. Best find my mother in heaven and ask her.

Daily Special

Thanksgiving Day—Closed

Friday, November 23

Turkey and Gravy

Stuffing, Mashed Taters

   Cranberry Sauce, Sweet Potato Soufflé

Yeast Rolls

Pumpkin, Pecan, Apple, or Cherry Pie

Tea, Soda, Coffee

$9.99

36

The crisp, bright Sunday after Thanksgiving, Mercy Bea and I string Christmas lights along the Café's front porch while Andy Williams sings from the boom box. *"It's the most wonderful time of the year."*

"Hmm, cinnamon." Mercy Bea draws in a large portion of air, turning her nose toward downtown.

"Makes me hungry and I just ate." I hold up the next string of lights. "Pay attention, Mercy Bea; we still have the inside to decorate."

She taps a small hook into the porch board with her hammer, then hangs the next section of lights. "What's your favorite Christmas memory, Caroline?"

I shrug. "Mama had a thing about *man-made* traditions."

"Like how? Hand me another hook, Caroline, please."

"Like she hated them. Daddy did his best to give us a nice Christmas, but without her participation, it was hard. He'd put up a tree Christmas Eve, buy us presents most years, but the tree went down two days later."

Mercy Bea shakes her head with an *mm-mm-mm*, tapping in the hook and looping the light cord over it. "Wonder what got into your mama."

"I don't know, but it's time for new memories and new traditions, starting with this Christmas. I have a feeling it's going to be my best one yet." A bolt of electric excitement zaps my middle as I think of the crews' surprise.

She glances down at me, her face pinched. "This Christmas? The best? Girl, after letting that hunk Mitch get away—which, by the way, I still can't believe. Today's the first day I've seen you smile without a frown behind your eyes."

"Yeah, well, life isn't always what we want it to be." Getting over Mitch is taking more sleepless nights than I imagined, but today during church, I decided: *God, I trust you.* Peace came, and so far it's winning the war on worry.

"What's so special about this Christmas?" Mercy Bea asks, dragging the box of Christmas decorations down to the next section of porch.

"You'll see." It's all I can do not to burst with the sheer thrill of my secret.

To: *CSweeney, JesslovesRay*

From: Elle Garvey

Subject: Operation Wedding Day

Okay, y'all, Operation Wedding Day is closed for Christmas. I want this to be a happy time, celebrating with friends and my family. Why purposefully risk depressing myself with a dateless holiday season. Or worse, remember it as How the Geeks Stole Christmas.

Caroline, I sold the sketch of you today. Half goes to you. Merry Christmas.

So, let's get this holiday season started. I say girls' Christmas party at my place, gift exchange, and fun food. What do you say? I'll make

up a party list and send it to you. I heard Carrie Campbell just
moved back to town. Too fun. Haven't seen her in far too long.
Love, Elle

By the first week of December, my flight to Barcelona
is booked. Hazel and I have chatted a dozen times about travel plans and
living arrangements. She hooked me up with the company that moved
her belongings. I don't have much, but the armoire is coming with. She
sympathized with me over Mitch, while commending me for making a
bold decision.

Naturally, she informed Carlos. My stock soared.

In the evenings, I'm cleaning out the carriage house. Daddy and
Posey agreed to take Jones's furniture for the sunroom they're adding
onto the house, and his books. When Posey got a close look, her eyes
rolled back in her head and she drooled.

Except the Bible. That goes with me.

Cherry wanted his antique chest of drawers and footlocker. She and
Henry are doing so well, and we never talk about the night Cherry came
into my office afraid for her marriage.

Tonight, I must decide about Jones's old records. Tapping my cell
phone gently against the palm of my hand, I pause, knowing what I
want to do, but nervous to try.

Inhaling, I dare myself to dial. I'm surprised when he answers.

"I didn't expect this call."

"Hey, Mitch, how are you?" As I walk toward the bookshelf, nervous tension chills my fingers.

"Doing well. What's up?"

The tenderness his voice used to carry for me is missing. Now his
tone is the one he uses with all his regular friends. But, I made my
choice. I won't lament it.

"I'm packing up the carriage house. I wondered if you wanted Jones's old LPs."

"Really? I'd love to have them. Thank you."

"Merry Christmas." I run my finger along the shelf's edge.

"Merry Christmas."

"Will I see you before I go?"

"I don't know."

I swallow. "Oh, of course. Well, then I guess this is Merry Christmas and Happy New Year."

"Guess so." There's resolve in his voice. "Take care of yourself."

"You too. I'll drop the albums off at your folks'."

"I hope Barcelona is all you want it to be, Caroline."

I want to remind him of how much I love him, but I don't. "So, see you around?"

"See you around."

Two days later, Kirk calls. "Judge granted our petition. Probation is closed. Congratulations."

My skin tightens with excitement. "So this is it."

"On to phase two. Dale and Roland want to set a time to come down and close the deal. They're ready to hand you a check."

"They divided the money, right?"

"Confirmed it with them yesterday. After taxes and my fee, taking out ten-grand bonuses for Russell, Luke, and Paris, the remainder is divided evenly between you, Andy, and Mercy Bea."

Is my smile breaking my face? "I'm putting their checks in their Christmas cards."

"They're going to flip."

"Thank you, for everything, Kirk."

"Caroline, it's been an honor. Never met anyone like you."

Daily Special

Monday, December 17

Country Omelet

Shrimp Grits

Bubba's Buttery Biscuits

Sausage, Bacon, Country Ham

Fried Apples

Eggnog

Tea, Soda, Coffee.

$7.99

37

At three in the morning, I'm wide-awake. Today is my last day as owner of the Frogmore Café. By the afternoon, Jones's legacy will be in the Buzz Boys' hands. Trying to sleep when I'm restless is annoying, so I get up. Andy will be along in an hour anyway. Might as well get ready and head over to the Café, get the coffee started.

The morning is calm and quiet, but clean, cold, and exhilarating. I plug in all the Christmas lights, then sit in the breakfast-club boys' booth.

The Café is quiet—no moans or creaks—as if sitting with me in solidarity. *Thank you, Caroline.*

In the warm, white glow of the lights, the worn places in the Café disappear. The vinyl booths shine like new, and the walls aren't dirty and dull. I'm lost in a sleepy thought when a loud bang resonates from the front door. Jumping awake, I peer through the window.

Mitch is on the other side.

Unlocking the door, I step aside for him to enter, leaning against the frame. "Hey." My heart *thud-thuds* when his clean, showered scent kisses my nose.

"Hey." He brushes my arm with his fingers. "I saw the lights . . ."

"You just happened to be up and about?" Should it feel odd to see him at the Café, so early, on selling day? Yes, but somehow it doesn't.

"Something like that. Elle e-mailed today was the day."

Figures. "Coffee?" I walk over to the counter, but he remains by the door. Is he going to leave? Stand there staring at me? Get hit in the back-side at 8:02 when the breakfast-club boys arrive?

"Last call for coffee."

Finally, he steps toward the counter. "If you have a pot going, I guess one cup would be all right."

The coffee's not going, but it will be in a second. He sits at the counter as I scoop sparkling grounds into the filter, watching me, man-aging confidence and vulnerability in a single expression. The race of my pulse slows so my emotions can rise up and take over.

Heart: He looks good. How can we leave him?

Head: And in twenty years, how will he look? Like the one who robbed us of Barcelona? Stay the course, heart. Stay the course.

"Everything's all set, then?"

"Yes, just formalities, signing papers . . . and stuff." Two feet from me, and I can't throw my arms around him or feel his lips caressing mine. Two feet from me and I "miss" him.

For a few seconds, only the coffeemaker speaks, gurgling and exhal-ing the fresh-brewed aroma of Santa's White Christmas.

"Say," I finally venture, "your new album is going well?"

He picks at the corner of the paper placemat. "The new songs are going down great. Recent events in my life make for great lyrics."

"Oh—" I reach under the counter for a couple of mugs. What am I supposed to say to that? "I wish you many number one hits."

"From your lips to God's ears."

Silence interjects itself again, though not strong enough to cover the subconscious murmur of wonder between Mitch and me. Like, *Is this it? We're over? What will we do in a year? Do you still love me?*

"I dropped Jones's records at your parents' last night." I had to say something.

Mitch circles his mug on the countertop between his hands. "Ah, my consolation prize: antique albums. Mitch O'Neal, what do you win? The girl? No, but a hundred scratchy vinyl albums of great country crooners bemoaning the loves they lost." He sweeps his arm through the air, his voice deep like a game-show host.

Daggum, but he ticks me off. Want to play jilted lover? I own the game, wrote the rules. "And what did I win all the years you were seeking fame and fortune in Nashville, hmm? When you took beauty queens to country tributes and award shows? Heartache, Mitch." I slam the counter with my hand. "Heart. Ache. You've had a few weeks of disappointment. I've had years of a dull, yet pulsating, longing. Like a toothache that can be ignored, yet persistent enough to make its presence known. Then, when I finally move on, finally do something for myself, here you come."

"Oh, don't play the 'poor me with no life' card. You could've left just like the rest of us. But you chose to stay and baby-sit your family, be Miss Goody Help Everyone. You didn't have to work for your dad, or Henry, Mrs. Farnsworth, or Jones."

"And you could've asked me to marry you nine years ago, Mitch. But you didn't. You wanted your freedom, your chance. Maybe I came to the game during the fourth quarter, but I'm on the field and can smell a touchdown."

"Caroline—"

Too late to "Caroline" me now. "No, Mitch, no. Don't you dare come in here accusing me, throwing your pity party. If you want me, then wait for me. Like I waited for you. Not knowing when or if you'd ever come back. Man, I'm sick of this—"

I jerk the full coffeepot from the BrewMaster and slosh steaming black java into Mitch's mug. "Still take it black, right?"

"You can change your mind." It's a statement buoyed with suggestion. "Yes, black."

I fill my own mug with black java. "Mitch, I never thought I'd say these words to you, but I don't want to change my mind. I'll go crazy if I stay here and pass up this chance. Every time I think of going, excitement bubbles up in me. A feeling I've never had before, and something tells me it's a God thing. As new as I am to God things . . . I'm going to give Him a chance to use me, change me."

He grips the mug without drinking. "That's how I feel every time I think of marrying you."

My wind rushes out like I've been punched. "Then, Mitch, wait for me."

Oh, for a heart-pounding second, I'm flushed with passion and consider grabbing his face and kissing him until he can't breathe. Instead I dump a pound of cream and sugar in my mug. "So where are we?"

Picking up his coffee, he still doesn't drink. "You tell me. Where does a couple go after, 'Will you marry me?' is followed by a 'No'? Feels pretty much like a dead end."

"Mitch, are you saying this is it?"

A loud tap at the door halts the conversation, piercing the tension. Mitch tucks away his response as I go to open the door. Dupree barges in. Seeing him causes my vision to blur under a watery sheen.

"Is it 8:02 already?"

"Close enough." The ex-Marine unwraps his muffler—thick enough to keep an Eskimo warm—and drapes it over the coat rack.

"Coffee?" I ask, following him to the counter.

"Does a sheik have oil?" Dupree takes the stool next to Mitch. "Couldn't sleep. Thinking about you leaving, Caroline. Good to see you, Mitch. I see you couldn't kiss her into staying."

Mitch shakes his head with a guarded gaze at me. "Gave it my best."

"Well, what're you going to do? Women are tough creatures to figure out."

Another tap resounds against the door as I pour Dupree's coffee, half wishing Mitch would leave. Otherwise, I might just break. *Jesus, a little help for Your friend, please.*

Pastor Winnie and Luke are at the door this time. "More early birds?"

"Dupree called."

"Caroline, thanks for the coffee." Mitch rises from the counter stool. "Merry Christmas, fellas."

"Leaving so soon, boy?" Winnie asks, taking the stool next to Dupree. "I was hoping for a Christmas tune when I saw you sitting there."

Mitch cuts a glance at me. "Another time. Don't feel much like music today, Winnie."

"I hear you, I hear you. Sad day for us all, losing Caroline."

"A sad day for us all."

Mitch leaves with a backward glance, allowing a flicker of good-bye in his eyes.

See you, Mitch.

By the time Andy arrives at four thirty, the four of us are good and caffeined up. I hide in the ladies' for a good, solid, snot-running cry—just couldn't hold it in any longer—then ordered a batch of eggs, bacon, and grits for the house. As dawn breaks over the lowcountry, I spend my last morning as owner of the Frogmore Café reminiscing with some of my best friends anywhere, while aching for the one who recently said good-bye.

At four p·m·, Kirk arrives for the signing-away-of-the-Café. He's jittery, never looking directly at me. His black suit is dotted with lint and dust.

"Are you okay?"

"Yep. Fine." He starts arranging tables and chairs. "Let's shove these two tables together. Sit here instead of the booth."

"Ah, Kirk, we can't give up the booth. We've done all our business there," I tease. "I'm sort of sentimental about it."

"It's ridiculous for us to slide in together. We can't get out without making everyone move." Kirk's briefcase thumps against the tabletop.

"Are you sure you're okay?" A terrifying thought crossed my mind. "The Buzz Boys aren't changing their minds are they, or lowering the price?"

"No, no. How about coffee and water on the table, eh?"

A few minutes later, the Christmas bells ring out. The Buzz Boys enter with their lawyer, Laurel the Amazon.

From the kitchen doorway, Andy, Mercy Bea, Russell, Luke and Paris hover, watching the big deal go down.

Dale is Buzz-Boy cheery. "Caroline, isn't this fantastic? Such a win-win." He looks over at the watching and waiting crew. "We're going to take care of y'all."

I gesture for Paris to bring the baskets of biscuits and jam.

Meanwhile, Laurel and Kirk exchange whispers and documents. Kirk's expression is tense. He mutters and shakes his head.

Laurel whispers to him in a way that sounds like flies buzzing.

Sitting tall, I ignore the sadness of saying good-bye by picturing the surprised faces of the crew when they open their Christmas cards. Elle designed the cards after we brainstormed something unique and special for each person.

Then tonight, I've planned a Christmas shopping spree that will make Bill Gates look cheap.

"Are we ready to get started?" Laurel speaks through her plastic expression. One blue peel too many is my guess.

"Sure." What is wrong with Kirk?

Taking command, Laurel distributes the papers we need to sign, giving us instructions.

Then she hands me six checks. "Divided up as you requested."

Smiling, I flip through to see if each amount is right—Andy and Mercy Bea receiving their third. Luke, Russell, and Paris their bonuses.

How fun to be Santa Claus.

I stack the checks and turn them facedown on the table. "Ready to sign."

Kirk remains disengaged, almost sulking. Ignoring him, Laurel tells Dale and Roland where to sign, then me, explaining the small print and conditions.

Shaking a little, I take the pen and aim for the signature line.

"Excuse me." Kirk fires out of his chair, almost toppling it over. "Caroline, I-I, I'm not happy with my fee. No, not at all." His glasses slip off the tip of his nose.

"Your fee?" He's gone mad.

"Yes. I need to see you in your office."

Laurel's eyes darken. "Kirk." She loses her fixed smile. "Sit down, please. I'm sure you and Caroline can renegotiate your fee after she signs. It's not an emergency."

Kirk lowers toward his chair, but buoys back up before his bottom hits. "Caroline, your office."

Laurel stands, towering over him. "Kirk, what are you doing? You. Can. Talk. To. Caroline. In. About. Ten. Minutes." Her jaw is tight. Dale and Roland chat among themselves as if unaware of Laurel and Kirk's cloaked battle.

Without answering her, Kirk takes my arm and leads me away.

As we head toward the kitchen, Andy, Mercy Bea, Russell, Luke, and Paris scatter like barnyard chickens.

38

Behind my closed office door, Kirk whips off his glasses. Is he sweating? "Don't do it."

"Don't do what? Sell the Café?" I cross my arms.

"What a bunch of . . . Caroline, I'm so sorry I mixed you up with those crooks."

"Crooks?" *Hello, not a warm-fuzzy word, Kirk.* "What crooks?"

"Those two yahoos." He flicks his glasses at the door. "Teach me to play golf with the country-club set. Poor kid from Charleston, wanting what *they* have. Who are *they,* anyway?"

"Kirk, please, save your identity crisis for the shrink's couch. What about the Café?"

"They're changing everything, Caroline. Everything Mercy Bea heard is true. Haute cuisine. After they remodel, the crew will go, even the name will change."

Shaking, I fall against the desk. "Why didn't they just tell me?"

"Why?" Kirk's wild-eyed look tells me he thinks I'm crazy. "Because you wouldn't sell to them if they 'fessed up. This location is incredible. There's not another deal like it in Beaufort. They lowballed you on the price and I knew it." He lands hard on the guest chair. "Here you are being incredibly generous with the staff. And I helped them cheat you."

Wait, wait . . . My thoughts are melting. "Kirk, I've leased an apartment fifty meters off the Ramblas, bought a plane ticket, bought new knobs for my armoire and shipped it."

"Greed. It's always been my kryptonite."

"When were you ever Superman?" Clark Kent glasses aside.

"Never. That's just it." Sighing, he rests his forehead against his palms. "Might as well confess: they offered me a bonus when the deal closed. A nice bonus."

"They paid you to betray me?"

He holds up his hand. "Don't. I already know what a lowdown louse I am—this is not my finest hour. I'd convinced myself it wouldn't matter in the long run. The Café would have its deep pockets. You'd be in Barcelona with the job of a lifetime. The crew would have their fat bonuses. Then I caught the light in your eyes when Laurel handed you the checks. I couldn't stand myself."

"That makes two of us."

"They were going to offer the Vet Wall to the city council for half a million."

"What? The wall already belongs to the city, by way of the Café. Oh my gosh."

Kirk's arms sweep wide. "Caroline, I'm begging you. Don't sell. Please. I'll find another buyer. Whatever you need. I'll contact Carlos for you. I'll work with the bank to get you a loan to redo the place. Please, don't let them win."

Sitting, I reach for the straightened paper clip.

Kirk mumbles, "Think you can trust old college friends? No."

Okay, God, this is a kink I did not expect in the works. What, what, what . . . At the moment, I care squat about myself. The money will be such a blessing to the crew. Mercy Bea can move out of her roach motel. Andy can wipe out Gloria's medical bills.

"What am I going to do?"

"Don't. Sell."

"Then what, Kirk? That's not an answer. We have to settle the Café—"

Then, the line from Jones's letter materializes before my mind's eye. *Andy is the heart and soul of the Café.*

Kirk stops mumbling and looks up at me. "What is it? You're smiling."

Christmas Eve

Daddy, Posey, Henry, and Cherry squeeze into Beaufort Community's back pew with me.

This is the best Christmas, ever. *"Freely you received,"* Jesus said. *"Freely give."*

When the choir leads us in singing "Silent Night," my heart remembers Mama, wishing she'd found deliverance from her demons enough to enjoy times like this. *Merry Christmas, Mama.*

Mitch sits up front with his own mama. When the children's choir sang "Let There Be Peace on Earth" he peered over his shoulder, searching the congregation. In the warm candlelight, his blue eyes found mine and held on for a moment. He nodded once, then faced forward again. A chill shimmied down my back and legs.

It's really over. I know it.

Meanwhile, Hazel is frantic for the holidays to be over. She e-mails daily. "I want to see you here, in Barcelona, so I know nothing else is going to delay you."

I decided to have some final fun with her and shot off an e-mail with only this subject: *The Café sale flopped.* She actually phoned at two in the morning to find out what happened.

The choir begins "O Holy Night." I join in, eyes closed, sitting very still, remembering . . .

"Here's your bonuses." I handed the crew their Christmas cards.

Andy gripped his chest when he read the certificate Kirk and I made up: "You are now the owner of 70 percent of the Frogmore Café."

Mercy Bea opened her card: "You are now owner of 30 percent of the Frogmore Café. P.S. Your debt is cleared."

She screamed and screamed, gave me, then Andy, a flying hug. *"Andy,"* she squeaked, *"you won't regret being my partner. I'll do some good stuff around here for you. I'll work hard. What should we do first? Hold a staff meeting. Let's plan—Oh, Andy, please, can I move into the carriage house? Please."*

Andy locked his misty eyes with mine. Then he shoved past Mercy Bea, still squealing like a poked pig, and buried me in a ginormous hug.

"God bless you, Caroline Sweeney. God. Bless. You." Then, without shame, he cried.

Russell, Luke, and Paris open cards to find thousand-dollar Christmas bonuses. Courtesy of Kirk, who discovered his hunger for the joy of giving.

Then we had the best Christmas party ever . . .

"Caroline," Cherry taps my arm softly. "The service is over." She smiles. "You were lost down some memory lane."

I stand. "It's a nice place to get lost."

"There's Mitch." Cherry nudges me. "Want to go over? Wish him a Merry Christmas?"

"Actually, we've said all we're going to say to each other. Besides, look, he's got a horde of lovely ladies waiting."

"Oh, Caroline, are you sad?" Cherry bends around to see my face, pausing just outside the sanctuary doors.

"If I wasn't, then Mitch never meant anything to me, right?"

"Nice thought." She brushes my hair away from my face.

"So, yes, a little, but mostly I'm happy, Cherry, looking forward to the days to come."

"Caroline Sweeney, you are my hero."

I laugh. "Cherry, you've *got* to get out more. Really."

Talking, we walk arm in arm toward the rest of the family in the churchyard. Elle calls "Merry Christmas" to me, waving as she heads off with her family.

"Ready?" Dad says, popping his hands together. He's excited. His first Christmas in eons without loneliness, angst, guilt, or regret. The presents under our tree rival any kid's dream.

But this year, I have a specific gift longing. Walking over to Henry, I link my arm with his. "Ready to give me my Christmas present?"

He balks. "Now? Tonight? Shouldn't we wait for Santa to come?" Since hanging out with little kids, he's fallen in love with this holiday.

"This is a special present I picked out for myself. From you to me."

He narrows his eyes, glancing at Cherry. "Don't look at me," she says.

Henry: "What's this going to cost me?"

Me: "Everything."

After a small debate—some things never change—Henry reluctantly agrees to drive me where I want to go. Cherry heads home with Dad and Posey.

"Where are we going?" Henry asks, starting his car.

"To see Mama."

"Sneaking around a graveyard on Christmas Eve . . . Sort of sick, don't you think, Caroline?"

Henry's protesting wears me down. But I refuse to give up my Christmas mission. "We're not sneaking around. We're visiting our mother's grave."

"This is ridiculous. She hated Christmas." Henry slows by her grave-site and cuts the engine. He remains stiff and stubborn behind the wheel.

Reaching to the floorboard, I pick up the wreath I bought at a closing-down Christmas tree stand. "Let's go."

"I repeat, this is ridiculous." Henry jerks on his door handle, chin up.

"Humor your little sister, then."

After placing the wreath on Mama's headstone, I stand back next to Henry. "Merry Christmas, Mama."

"She's laughing at us," he scoffs.

"Your turn."

"I'm not talking to a granite stone, Caroline. This is your deal. I only came because you claim this is your Christmas present."

"Tell Mama you forgive her." In the light of the street lamps, my brother's raw emotions coat his round features. He is the physical image of our mother. "That's my Christmas present—from you to me."

I go first. "Mama, it's Christmas. I know you didn't care much for holidays, but Jesus' birthday feels like a right time to forgive people. So, it's okay, Mama. Life just didn't deliver like you wanted, did it? I wish you could see how good Henry and I turned out."

Henry begins to tremble.

Stretching forward, I pat the tombstone. "Rest in peace."

He snorts, loudly, almost urgently. I wait for him to speak. When he doesn't, I squeeze his hand. "Let her go. Forgive her. Not for her sake, but yours."

He rolls his shoulders back and looks beyond her grave into the darkness. "Why should I?"

"Because being bitter hurts you, not her. Frankly, I'm tired of it. It shadows your relationship with Cherry, and your future kids. With me and Daddy. You're not saying she was right, you're simply forgiving."

Henry's turmoil increases. I can feel it, but I'm determined. "We're not leaving until you say something."

So we stand in cold silence.

Finally, as if punched from behind, he bursts out, "Mama, I used to sit up nights waiting for you to come home." His confession is pluff-mud soft. "Cried myself to sleep more times than a teen should. I missed your perfume, your voice, the soft touch of your hand on my cheek." He brushes his face with the back of his hand. "I hated you for leaving us. But I . . . I forgive you."

As a sudden gust of wind whooshes around us, Henry falls against me and buries his face in my shoulder, weeping. Rising up on my tiptoes to shoulder his burden, I pray quietly for the Christ of Christmas to heal my brother's wounded heart.

Welcome to the Frogmore Café

Andy Castleton, Proprietor
Mercy Bea Hart, other Proprietor
Open Monday—Thursday
6:00 a.m. to 9:00 p.m.
Friday and Saturday open till 11:00
Live Music!

39

January 2
Savannah Airport

I want to jump out of my skin. My first flight ever and it's
over lots of water. It's all sinking in now. The reality of what I'm doing.

Posey's hand rests on my arm. "How're you doing, Caroline? Excited?
I'm excited."

"I'm caught between thrilled-beyond-belief and I'm-going-to-freak-
out." My right leg jitters up and down. I felt fine until they announced
first-class boarding in five minutes. (Carlos had me booked in first class.
I'm going to like him.)

"Now, Hazel knows when to pick you up, right?" Dad asks for the
hundredth time.

I reach to squeeze his hand. "Yes. Do you want to come with me to
make sure I'll get there okay?"

Posey laughs. Dad hops out of his chair, slapping his hands against
his jeans. "You don't know the language, Caroline, the culture, the

people. A lovely woman, traveling alone, is a prime target. A prime target. The world ain't what it used to be. If Hazel's not there, what are you going to do?"

"Dad, if I know Hazel, she's already there."

He paces around in front of me. "You remember all the self-defense moves I taught you, right?"

"If not, I remember what Sandra Bullock taught the world in *Miss Congeniality*. SING."

Dad makes a face. "SING? What? How can singing . . . You been hanging around Mitch too long."

Posey shakes her head. "Okay, you two, stop. Hank, she's going to be fine. Caroline, you're his baby. Twenty-nine, yes, but still his baby. Give your old man a break."

"Daddy, I'll call the moment I arrive, I promise."

He squeezes my shoulder. "All right, then. I won't worry. Too much."

Posey takes his hand. "Let's give her a minute. Caroline, we're going to the newsstand to buy goodies for your trip. Magazines, chocolate, whatever fun things we can find."

"Remember, I'm only allowed two carry-ons." I wink.

With a weak exhale, I slump down in my chair and try to picture what the next few weeks will be like, but my mental landscape is blank. I have no idea what challenges and surprises wait for me in Barcelona. I picture angular, freckled, auburn-haired Hazel, with her energy and bright smile.

The Café good-byes were hard and tearful. Dupree arrived late for breakfast the first time in twenty years and handed me a card with his and Helen's picture.

"Don't want you to forget me. I'll e-mail you my bathroom stories."

I sniffed, laughing. "Please. I'll miss them."

Pastor Winnie prayed a blessing.

Mostly we tried to act like it was an ordinary workday. Andy spouted running updates on inventory, asking what I thought about trying a new vendor for fresh fish. Mercy Bea complained about the schedule—until I reminded her she took over the task last week. Luke avoided me most of the day. But at four, no one wanted to leave. This good-bye was a permanent good-bye.

"It's empty in here without the lamp and your things." Luke's face appeared in the office door.

"Andy will fix it up."

"Won't be right without you around." He cleared his throat, not bothering to hide his tears. "I love you, Caroline, like you was my own."

"You're one of the most honorable men I know."

So, we cried and hugged, then Mercy Bea busted in. One thing led to another, and the whole crew was wrapped around me, crying.

"Lost in thought?"

An unexpected voice shoots me out of my chair. "Mitch." There he stands, three feet behind me, handsome in a dark turtleneck and leather jacket. His eyes watch me with blue intensity.

"Hey, Caroline."

I don't care what he's doing here or why. I run into his arms. "I've missed you so much."

He scoops me up so tight it's hard to draw a deep breath. "I'm sorry I was such a jerk. I knew how much Barcelona meant to you . . ." He cradles my face in his hands and lowers his lips to mine. "I've missed you so much it hurt. How could I let you go to Barcelona without telling you one last time? I love you."

I cling to him, the heat of his confession melting the chill of our separation. "How'd you know when I was leaving?"

"Your dad called."

I smooth my hand over his chest. "He's turning into a softy."

"Ladies and gentlemen, we are ready to begin boarding Flight 801 to Barcelona."

Mitch's eyes search mine. "Maybe we'll never be lovers, but a life without your friendship is just too empty." He reaches inside his jacket. "Merry Christmas."

"Mitch." The box is small and velvety. "No, I can't—"

"Open it."

My fingers tremble as I pry open the blue lid. Inside is a beautiful, thin diamond band. "Oh, Mitch, it's beautiful. And really, too much."

He slides the ring onto my pinky finger. "When I was on *Oprah*, I noticed she had a ring like this. I liked it. Whenever you wear it, remember your best friend loves you. No promises or strings attached. I just wanted you to have something from me."

I didn't want to cry today. "I don't have anything for you."

He grins, then kisses my forehead so softly. "Friends?"

"Friends. Yes. Best friends."

The horizon beyond my small oval airplane window is like one of Elle's lowcountry paintings—wild with color and light. Gold and red mixed with the fading blue sky, reaching down to the dark line that is earth.

The power of the jet's engine makes my muscles rumble. When we lift off, I feel like I'm floating. I'm doing it. Leaving on a jet plane, as Daddy said, singing some old Peter, Paul and Mary tune.

Mitch stayed with me, Dad, and Posey until I walked down the Jetway. He promised to e-mail, perhaps see if he could get a gig in Spain this summer. Posey already has Dad saving for a spring visit.

When I paused and looked back before disappearing inside the jet, Mitch smiled, raising his hand to wave. That's when a new "*suddenly*" hit me.

Maybe we're not as over as I thought.

My life changed the day a man died. Seven months ago, I left a man's funeral, wondering what would be next for me. Because Jones died, a bunch of scary, yet wonderful things happened.

If I'd have known I would inherit the Frogmore Café, race the Marines in the Water Festival, deal with electrical and plumbing problems, and part with Matilda to pay for it, I would've run screaming against traffic down Robert Smalls Parkway.

If I'd known about J. D. and Mitch, I'd . . . well, do it all over again.

I saw Matilda the other day. Henry pointed her out. Wayne gave her a beautiful makeover. Then decided to keep her for himself.

Being home, stuck in Beaufort, tending Jones's legacy brought the best gift of all. Meeting Jesus. The God I hoped was real every time I climbed my live oak sanctuary, is. Sometimes I catch a whiff of His perfume.

With a freeing breath, I close my eyes and lean into the turn of the banking plane.

Acknowledgments

Every story requires a mountain of support. I'm very grateful to all who have shined their light on the journey of writing Caroline's story. Thank you to:

Catherine Hipp at the Beaufort, South Carolina, Chamber of Commerce. Thank you for showing me around your beautiful city.

Connie Hipp for being my quick and wonderful Beaufort and low-country resource. I so appreciate all your help. I couldn't have done this without you. All mistakes are mine.

Charles Gay, Gay Fish Co, for the pluff mud and shrimping stories.

Aaron Hinman and Jason Flores, for the great talk one afternoon at Luther's, and for standing on the wall to watch over our freedoms. *Semper Fidelis.*

A big thanks to the other Beaufortonians who lent their expertise:

Sherry Little for Water Festival information and the raft race idea. Bernie Kole for rewiring and plumbing expertise. William Winn for Beaufort hurricane details. Lisa Estes for will, probate, and other legal help. Anne Schumacher for insight into the life of a restaurateur, and Nicole Seitz.

Terry Dunham for writing a song about the Praise House, going on an adventure to Beaufort, and showing us your brief movie, which inspired the setting for this story.

Also, thanks to:

Jess Dang, Chris Cox, Bart Black, Chef Rob, the crew at La Patina's, Melbourne, FL.

Thank you to:

Leslie Peterson, for weeding through this manuscript with expertise, pointing out the holes, and asking me to go deeper. You make me a better writer. Thank you!

Ami McConnell, my editor and friend, for believing in me. And to Allen Arnold, Jennifer Deshler, and the great staff at Thomas Nelson.

Karen Solem, my agent, for encouragement and all-around expertise.

Christine Lynxwiler. What a gift and blessing from God you have been to me this year. You've encouraged me, prayed for me, brainstormed, and made me laugh. Thank you so very much. I can't imagine what I'd have done without you.

Susie Warren, superwoman! Thank you so much for jumping into the quagmire when I was sinking. You were an instrument of God that dark night. Thank you for brainstorming at the drop of a hat, praying, and shoving me forward. You are a blessing.

Colleen Coble, for being a friend and mentor. Thank you for being on the other end of the phone to encourage me. You are a gift from God to me and so many others.

Ellen Tarver, for reading this manuscript in its early stages and offering ideas.

My mom, grandma, sister, and Aunt Betty for praying and believing in me. I love you.

Tony, the best husband ever. Each book is fragrant with your heart for me and Jesus. Thank you for allowing me the freedom to pursue this calling and dream.

Anna Marie, Ted, Lin, Chelle, and the many others who listened and prayed. Your reward in heaven is great!

Jesus, my friend, Lord, Savior, inspiration. You are the core of me, thus the core of each story. I long to write about You in a way that is pleasing to all of heaven. Thank You for being with me even when I don't sense it. *You* are faithful. I love You.

Reading Group Guide

1. In the first chapters of the book, we discover how Caroline has fallen into a pattern of giving up her wants to help others. Discuss a time in your life when you gave up your goals and dreams to serve others. What was the outcome?

2. Raised with a troubled mother, Caroline fell into the role of caring for her Dad and brother, bearing an emotional burden. How can we bear one another's burdens while each one carrying their own weight? Do you carry burdens that are not yours?

3. Caroline's friend Hazel offers her an amazing opportunity. Did it come at the right time? Does Caroline make the right decision?

4. Country star Mitch O'Neal wrote a song about cruising over the "yellow line." What picture is he painting? What yellow lines have you crossed and how did you respond?

5. Caroline decides to give J. D. a chance. Discuss her motivation and hope in this.

6. What personal value did Caroline learn from her daddy? Discuss the importance of setting values early in our lives. Can it ever be too late?

7. The first time Caroline goes to church, God touches her. Discuss a time when you felt distant from God and He reached out to you in mercy and love.

8. Giving inspires giving. While Hazel is touting Caroline's virtue to her boss Carlos, what does Caroline discover about the café and the cook, Andy Castleton?

9. Caroline makes a gutsy decision to turn down Mitch's proposal. Why does she do this? How did you respond to her decision?

10. This story is about inheritance. Caroline inherits things from her Mama, Jones, and Jesus. Discuss her tangible and intangible inheritances.

11. Caroline muses about how her life changed the day a man died. Discuss the double-meaning of her insight.